Broken Angels

OTHER BOOKS BY GEMMA LIVIERO

Pastel Orphans

Lilah

Marek

Broken Angels

GEMMA LIVIERO

Published by Lake Union Publishing, Seattle

www.apub.com

Amazon, the Amazon logo, and Lake Union Publishing are trademarks of Amazon.com, Inc., or its affiliates.

ISBN-13: 9781503934863
ISBN-10: 1503934861

Cover design by Patrick Berry

Printed in the United States of America

What I really need is to get clear about what I must do, not what I must know, except insofar as knowledge must precede every act. What matters is to find a purpose, to see what it really is that God wills that I shall do; the crucial thing is to find a truth which is truth for me, to find the idea for which I am willing to live and die.

—*Søren Kierkegaard (1813–1855)*

PROLOGUE

1996

Mum rests in the mountain's sweetly perfumed, red-brown earth, under rows of plaques in battle formation, and beneath a field of fluorescent plastic flowers, painted ceramic vases, and laminated photographs. Seemingly token gestures, yet for some who place them—those of us who can't let go—they are bread-crumb trails for the dead: an irrational, grief-stricken hope of luring them back.

Above my mother people murmur their prayers and tributes and leave their imprints in the thick grass. A coffin of mahogany lined with white satin was chosen from a catalogue. Mine will be walnut, placed on top of hers. I jokingly promised that I would follow her into the afterlife this way, though I meant it when I said I wouldn't sell the house, to remain close by. She had brushed the words aside, frustrated by the fact that I felt I owed her something. *Find a partner; settle down; this place too isolated for someone your age.* But there is another reason to stay, and she understood this, also. Sometimes solitude offers the kindest company.

Her name is etched, then raised in gold, not on metal but on stone. I made sure of it. I have long seen the romance of majestic, crafted stone. What is the good of death if we can't respectfully yet unashamedly announce to the living who we were? If we can't demand a moment of recognition for life: for reaching an age that many dreamed about? While others died among strangers—cold, hungry, without a name, their ancestry buried or burned with them.

It was not the intimate service Mum would have wanted. Some had seen the death notice and driven far—those she had touched, not necessarily in a big way, but who had silently taken a piece of her to cope with their own private disquiet, once they had learned her story.

Our group stands in front of an audience of hundred-year-old rain-forest trees, at the back of the cemetery, with their strange, tumorous growths and their moss-covered roots that are raised into steps for the grandchildren to dance between. Bright-yellow guinea flowers and salmon-pink kurrajong are planted in circular gardens: an attempt to brighten the perspective of death, to mask the scent of grief.

The priest talks between the whistles and snaps of whipbirds. He is talking about my mother's strengths, her private battles, her ability to rise up and create a loving environment for her family. I stand there listening, but only partially because I know all this already. I have a sudden memory, distinct and crisp because it was not singular; it was the first of many . . .

No breeze, the curtains still, with windows wide-open. Half a moon above the ocean in the distance. We could see the water unimpeded when we first arrived, but then came more houses and Pacific-blue glimpses only if we stood on the roof. Damp came in through the window that night, on wings of heat. It was difficult to sleep without squirming. No fans yet. Noises from another part of the house. Lights on. Lights off. Shuffling feet. It was not uncommon. Often I would find her sitting outside on a patch of lawn, smoking a cigarette, watching the shapes in the blackness. This time she was on the floor in the kitchen, knees pulled up. I thought that perbaps she was dead. I was sixteen when the night terrors started for her—a delayed reaction to the sudden death of my stepfather, whom we had buried earlier that day. I knelt to search for her in the dark, following the sound of her whimpers, afraid of what I might see if I switched on the light. I touched her face, which was wet with tears, and her whimpers then turned to sobbing, interspersed with breathless apologies she didn't need to give. I lay down on the linoleum, my arms tightly around her, until daylight grazed the room.

It was frightening, this first attack. And then over time, one adjusts to the strangeness of those they love.

My brother, Zach, flew up for the funeral from Melbourne with his new wife, Leanne. His first wife passed away a decade earlier by her own hand, without the warning signs, without a note. It took my brother years to accept that he wasn't meant to make sense of it; that sometimes people choose to take their reasons with them. I have only met Leanne a couple of times. She is pleasant enough, louder than we are, laughing lots, but we will not have the years to bond, or possibly the inclination. Though, I have to admit, she is nothing if not efficient: sandwiches and tea on a lace tablecloth ready on our return to the house, cakes and caramel slices, too. I could not have done as well.

My sisters, Clara and Louisa, came, also, along with several of my nephews and nieces. Clara's children: quiet and mouselike, courteous but from a safe distance, remote, as if they belong to someone else. Louisa has had it hard on her own after a complicated, expensive divorce, raising two teenage boys who look as though they would rather be surfing. Skinny brown legs, eyes darting around the cemetery for distraction, their feelings evident: disinterest in a grandmother who, though kindly and loving, was someone foreign, someone they had not grown up with. The boys with their sun-bleached hair, long and stringy, swept annoyingly across their faces like Cousin Itt from *The Addams Family*, as if they prefer not to see where they're going. How to tell them to pull back their hair, look forward, don't take the quiet moments for granted? How to tell any of them, these new generations?

Each time my mother sank to the bottom of cold despair, she would always find a break in the ice above, to breathe new air, to find new purpose. She never indulged in self-pity, nor did she point the finger of blame for her misfortunes. Her heart was clear of bitterness. I believe that if a person's strength of character is measured at the end of his or her life, it is by these qualities—qualities that allow a life to be lived, free of those restraints we place upon ourselves.

But that doesn't mean we should forget.

1942

SEPTEMBER

CHAPTER ONE
ELSI

I kneel in a pool of my mother's blood. I found her crawling the short space from the bed to the kitchen.

It was her moaning that woke me from a restless sleep. I cannot say that I ever sleep soundly with the springs of my bed squealing pitifully at every turn and the occasional bursts of gunfire in the distance, but I am not the only one who suffers the affliction of disturbance. Blackness circles the eyes of most of the residents here: another badge, as well as the star, that unites us in common.

It was sometime after midnight and well after lights-out. I felt for the matches on the floor beneath my bed to light the last remaining candle, used for emergencies, fearful of what was about to be revealed within the dim apartment.

The sight of my mother remains terrifying. Beneath her skirt, blood spills between her legs. She is awake and shivering, eyes squeezed shut.

"What happened?"

She doesn't answer.

"We have to take you to a doctor."

"I'll be fine. Just some water . . . I need to sleep. I need to sleep," she mutters, her words mashed together, eyes half-lidded now, roaming. I have seen these signs in others who have died, signs I hadn't seen before this place of a thousand hells. The first thing I've noticed in people just before they fall dead in the street is their overwhelming desire to lie down, anywhere. The second thing is that they talk as if intoxicated.

She pushes my hands away weakly. "Go!" she says.

And the last thing I have noticed is the desire to be left alone.

My mother could be dying, an idea that is not so alien now to most in the ghetto. I want to cry, but this is one of those times when Papa would tell me to be strong.

I help her up. She weighs only slightly more than me. Leah, my sister, is asleep in my bed. She will be inconsolable if she sees Mama like this. I check that she is sleeping heavily—one of the few gifts she is somehow afforded here—and pray she dreams till morning, that she doesn't wake and search for us.

Mama walks hunched, one arm across her stomach, one holding on around my neck in a monkey grip. She leaves a trail of blood drops on the stairs, or what's left of them. At the base of the steps, I grip Mama tighter around the waist, and we enter the frigid darkness. There is always a chance that we will be shot. Sometimes no reasons are given before they fire. Again I think of Leah and pray for her sake that one of us will make it back safely.

Three weeks ago, thousands of children were deported from the ghetto. After the announcement that children must leave, several parents were shot in their attempts to escape the ghetto with their children so they would not be separated, and in the washroom I overheard a conversation about some parents who had poisoned their own children, and themselves, rather than see their little ones taken. Leah was somehow spared from the deportation list, even though she was within the age-group required to go. Since the deportation, Mama's nerves have worsened, and Leah has not been allowed to leave the apartment.

Mama says that many people—those whose children were taken—will be jealous that my sister was allowed to stay.

"She is safe," I whisper to Mama, but I am not sure she understands. *But you are dying.*

Mama is so weak I have to drag her along the pavement, across the cobbles, several blocks to the hospital. I avoid the circles of light from the sparse lamps, and we make it all the way without being stopped. I thank God for this small thing and wonder if it is perhaps of his doing. I hope that it is also his plan to save Mama tonight, and not take her away.

I knock softly at the door and wait for what seems too long. The building is in darkness, and I knock again a little harder, the sound cracking open the stillness of the thick, fetid air in the ghetto. I wonder briefly about the people beyond the gates: if they are somewhere listening to the occasional sounds that pierce the gloom, if they wonder about the poor souls confined within these walls, and whether there is any sympathy out there. Or if they feel relief, from the safety of the trams, when they view the pathetic human remnants now contained.

A light from inside is switched on, the gleam of which creeps dimly through the space at the bottom of the door. A young man opens the door partway, peering through the gap suspiciously. It is a familiar expression inside these barbed walls.

"What do you want?"

"My mother is bleeding badly. She needs to see a doctor."

"There is no doctor on duty. You'll have to come back in the morning."

"But she is dying . . . please . . ."

"There is nothing I can do." He shuts the door, and I knock again. He opens it wider, but this time I can see the anger that lies just beneath his skin, threatening to burst through.

"Do you want the guards to hear? I tell you that you *don't* want that. Now be gone!"

He shuts the door again, and the light inside is extinguished immediately.

Mama is getting heavier as she leans into me.

"Elsi, take me home," she whispers. But I ignore this. Tears well in my eyes. She cannot die here, not in the street like a beggar, not after all the sacrifice, the charity she has offered to others. She cannot. I attempt to push off the sudden weight of sadness. *What to do? Where to go?* I am racked with indecision, facing more empty streets that carry no answers.

"Lilli," she whispers.

Yes . . . Lilli.

But I am wary of Lilli because she is not like the rest of us. She has friends in the council and German friends who do her special favors. She has extra food coupons as well, and it is something that Mama refuses to speak of. She wants to protect me from the various activities that happen after curfew.

We slip down another street to begin walking the extra blocks. After a while, I put Mama down where she can lean against a wall, and I sit beside her, leaning my aching shoulders against the cold bricks, grateful for the cool air. I watch a guard cross the entranceway to the street and look our way. But he will be staring straight into darkness, and I stare back, invisible eyes from a moonless night. Once he is past, I stand again and carry Mama across my back along the final stretch of road, hunched and hobbling on unsteady legs.

Lilli lives in a small house with a front garden on the other side of the ghetto, where the fortunate Jews live: the ghetto administrators and the Jewish council, or *Judenrat*. There is a field behind her house. The only time I can smell flowers is when we come here. It always reminds me of my childhood: when the days did not have so many worries. Lilli and my mother knew each other years ago before the war, when they were children. Apart from the ghetto, they have little in common, yet they have somehow found friendship again. Mama says that it is fortunate we have her as a friend.

Lilli is the mistress of a senior German official, Hermann Manz. Her house has its own toilet, and she had coal to burn through last winter. The residents who live nearby do not talk to her. They see the strange visits by officers at night and are concerned that she is a spy. Mama thinks that Lilli is in danger from her detractors. They could turn on her if Hermann Manz is removed from his ghetto posting. Anonymously scrawled death threats have been slipped under her front door, but she shrugs fear aside. She is casual about most serious matters.

I worry that Lilli will turn us away.

"Elsi! Good God! Quickly . . . bring her in." She lifts Mama from my arms and puts her on the couch. Lilli is small and strong, with sultry, coal-black eyes and milky, smooth skin. She is a woman who has made the most of her looks, both before and during the war.

"Why is she not in the medical center?"

"They would not admit her."

"Bastards!"

She examines the blood and where it is coming from, then wraps a coat around Mama. Against the quiet, Lilli's silk nightgown makes a swishing sound as it brushes against itself, and Mama's teeth chatter.

"Hannah, my darling. I will get you help."

Mama doesn't speak, though I see the whites of her knuckles as she squeezes Lilli's hand. Several tears escape Mama's closed eyes.

"Stay here," Lilli says to me. She leaves the small house without her robe, unaware, if not caring, that her ample flesh is exposed. Twenty minutes have passed when I start to worry that she may be finding a guard to take Mama away; I wonder whether she wants to be rid of us, or whether even she—one of the favored—has been seized by guards for breaking curfew.

She returns with Herr Manz, who eyes me with disdain. I am to know my place. He does not step far into the house but views my mother from a distance, the lamp beside the couch illuminating her blood-drained complexion.

"Bring her out to the trolley!"

Lilli nods to me to help her lift Mama, but I hesitate. I have seen sick people disappear and never return. It is easier for the officials if they don't.

"It's all right. He knows someone who can help her. Hurry!"

Lilli and I carry Mama to the wooden trolley and lay her down. Lilli adjusts the bloodstained coat around Mama with gentle, soothing hands. This is a side of her I rarely see. Her hands are usually busy, gesturing around her face and body as she speaks.

"I will handle it from here," Manz says to Lilli. It is not said coldly, just directly; perhaps such a tone is for my benefit since their relationship is less than formal. "It is not safe for anyone after curfew."

"Except perhaps for you," says Lilli, her eyes locking on her lover's. "You will no doubt return safely."

"Yes," he says, and there is a faint lift at one corner of his mouth, suggesting something more in this exchange, something that I am excluded from.

She nods. "Thank you," says Lilli before turning to me. She grips my chin with her narrow, bony fingers.

"Now, Elsi, look after her and do everything that Herr Manz tells you to do, yes?"

Mama does not want me to know that she has lain with another man while my father has been gone in a labor camp for fifteen months. And though I pretend that I don't see, I know what is happening. She has been suffering from morning sickness. I didn't put the pieces together until recently: the conversations I overheard between Mama and Lilli, and the times she would disappear just before curfew, then come back in the morning, coupons in hand and the strain lines around her eyes deepened. It was not only for food that she sacrificed her dignity but to stop the loss of a daughter to deportation.

The crimes and misdemeanors that occur in the ghetto are piling one on top of the other, the layers becoming so high and thick that it is often difficult to see above them, to see forward. Theft and murder are commonplace and acceptable under the banner of oppression and war. Mama has said she will never resort to theft, and that we must be able to live with ourselves when the war is over. That was in the early days, before she sold herself for food and Leah's safety. I hope she can live with herself now.

Hope is something I still have. I wear it around me like a favorite shawl. I cannot—*I will not*—die. And I will not lie down for any man. Mama used to joke that I would tease the boys who came knocking at our door, that I could not make up my mind so I chose none. I chose myself, she said. She used to call me fanciful, a dreamer, but Papa saw something else. Papa said I was like a butterfly that did not know how to land, that flitted from one thing to the next. He said that I preferred to float in the air, but that one day, when I finally found my place to land, I would give the whole of myself to someone who was worthy.

At the time those words flew above me, not landing, perhaps because they could not catch me in the air. Now they are firmly planted in my heart because they are precious words spoken by my father— words that are worth even more now that he is gone.

"And, Elsi, it is not what the world will give to you—it is what you must give to the world that matters. If we all just give a little . . ."

That was years before we were sent to the ghetto, before he disappeared. Before we kept giving until we ran out of things to give.

I follow the officer and push the trolley that holds Mama. We pass a guard who salutes Herr Manz and lets us walk by. I have to walk very fast to keep up with him while also trying to keep the trolley steady. Mama moans as it rattles and bounces over the cobbles. We arrive at a small office door that he attempts to unlock with several different keys, cursing and fumbling in the darkness before finally the door swings free. There is no sign on the front of the building.

"Sit there," he says, pointing to some chairs in a waiting area. I lift Mama up and allow her head to rest against my shoulder. The officer walks to the desk and uses a telephone. He asks someone to come. I know this because Mama, Leah, and I have spoken fluent German among ourselves since we arrived in the ghetto, because the Polish language is considered offensive to Germans. The officer replaces the receiver and sits on another chair, to stare at a wall ahead of him.

It is quiet, and Mama has fallen asleep. I look around the room. It is neat, with a desk and papers and a phone and a door with frosted glass that leads into another room. There are paintings here, landscapes of places I know and some I don't, of large cities that I plan to visit one day, of cafés where I will sip lemonade with friends, of mountains I plan to climb.

Memories filter in through the gray less often now. It is my imaginings that I look to, which have become more real.

CHAPTER TWO
WILLEM

The women I see are referred to by some as Nazi whores. They are part of a new order under which some of the rules can be broken, some bent, but it is a system that is not by my design. And women are just one of the many groups who must conform to the new order, who must accept the control. Some might say they are best viewed peripherally, because they are easier to work with if we don't study their faces too deeply, if we don't know their stories—if we tell ourselves that these people, *these Jews*, do not feel like we do. This approach, perhaps, is something I have failed to master since I am interested in their stories, their backgrounds, and because I believe it is essential to learn much about patients before I can accurately treat their illnesses. But I am also able to distance myself from them. I am able to shut the door firmly behind me when I leave the surgery. Some would call me cold. Many would call me efficient.

A consequence of this war is presented to me daily in a form that very few prefer to see. Women who are forced to endure not just imprisonment but a type of Viking subjugation as well, though I am told that such arrangements are agreed upon by both parties. I deplore the whole idea of it, yet I profit from it, also.

My life is a juxtaposition. I break with one hand and fix with the other: it just depends on which line you stand behind as to which service I can offer you. The type that heals and offers hope, or the one that simply heals with inevitability. The first service for wives of ghetto administrators, the second for Jewish mistresses.

I was called in the night, broken from deep sleep. Lena, my wife, rolls over, her growing belly taking up part of the room—a third person in our bed.

"Do you have to go?"

"Do I have a choice?" I say.

She sighs. She knows my father. She knows that privilege comes with restrictions. I kiss her closed eyes and another for the belly. I could dive into her loveliness. Sleepy and warm, she is achingly alluring. She is mine.

"Don't wait up," I whisper.

She murmurs and nestles into the pillow, her face now turned away from the light in the hall.

Outside the bedroom is the sitting room where we hosted dinner for our party counterparts the night before, and beyond that, the gleaming pots in the kitchen lead me to the front entrance. The housekeeper left only two hours earlier and will let herself in again at six o'clock. She was handpicked by my father, as are all the staff we employ. A Polish woman who hates the Jews, who rarely converses, thankfully, though she did speak up once. She revealed to Lena that several months earlier she reported a family of Jewish fugitives living next door with fake identities. She perhaps thought that Lena would repeat this revelation of her competence, and I in turn might mention it to my father, who has the power to offer a letter of commendation, or more important, increase her pay. I do not know, nor do I care, how much she gets paid since that is organized from headquarters in Berlin.

I pass the windows at the front of the apartment, with views of a narrow, lethargic stream, and step quietly across the diamond-patterned tiles. The apartments in the building have spacious rooms and, by my father's account, were formerly owned by self-indulgent, bourgeois Jewish families. The extravagance of owning anything of quality is now reserved only for the German elite. I sometimes scoff quietly to Lena about this swap in fortune that likely portrays us as a nation of scavengers, but I am by no means ungrateful for our circumstances.

On the side table at the entrance stands a framed photograph of my father standing taller beside his friend Heinrich Himmler. I climb into my coat, then upon exiting, lay the photo facedown. Not because of who is in the picture, but because I feel restrictively obliged to place it there in case my father visits with unfair warning, sometimes with other dignitaries, as happened the previous evening. The photograph is proof that I belong to the order that can suppress the masses with a stroke of a pen and a finely tuned military. I know the significance of the photo, since our station is a topic of conversation that my father seizes upon at every opportunity. Behind my father and Himmler, the National Socialist flag flies proudly in the wind. It is a reminder of where I am from and where I am headed. Where all of Germany is headed. We will no doubt win this war, *but*—that niggling word I often have to force to the corners of my mind—at what human cost?

At dinner parties, the obliteration of selected humans and their rights is something that we discuss more in terms of ideology for future generations, of the potential for greatness because of it, rather than dwelling on the atrocities that are happening right now. That is not to say I do not view the ironies. As I pointed out to my father, ours is a system full of holes and contradictions. After sitting through a painfully dull film—*The Eternal Jew*—commissioned by Goebbels, I pointed out a certain fact to my father: if Hitler so abhors anything less than race perfection, as outlined in *Mein Kampf*, why is it that he has employed a cripple to act as party spokesman? Blunt and cold—and somewhat ashamed that such thoughts could be expressed by his son—my father, a devoted party member, reminded me that we were on the side of good, not evil, of greatness, not mediocrity. Through teeth that barely separated when he spoke, he told me to never again question the motives of our Führer.

I have continued to question, but only to Lena, who does not reproach, who considers everything with openness. We share opinions—secret discussions held in our dark sanctuary between the sheets—though neither of us complains about our enviable circumstances.

Lena will right the photo when she rises, as she always does.

There is a car waiting out front, along with a driver, and I slide into the backseat and check my watch. It is one o'clock in the morning. An autumn fog builds outside. The air is crisp.

At the checkpoint, the guards are quick to open the gates; the presence of an official Nazi vehicle is synonymous with fear and urgency. We drive northeast of the ghetto, along its lonely, wide streets and eerily vacant tram tracks lit only by our headlights and a few dim street lamps. The ghetto is a bleak, bland enclosure by day and a strangely alluring, ghostly town at night. Except, of course, for the wire fencing, the guards, and the smell of open sewerage. These give away the horror. These are what set it apart from other places. I am glad that Lena will never come here.

Inside the surgery is a rather detestable colleague whose arrogance steps over a threshold before he does. Hermann Manz was called upon for help by one of his own concubines, Lilli, whom I have treated more than once for an unwanted pregnancy. Lilli's case is not the worst I have seen. Self-inflicted fetal termination that has been left too late for treatment, anal damage caused by licentious Gestapo, and sexually transmitted diseases rate as the worst. The most common, though, are menstrual pain, mild infections, and a rarely welcomed pregnancy confirmation for the wives of administrators.

I am not always prepared for the sights I see. That is not to say I am in any part squeamish, but there is often a temporary adjustment of emotions that occurs in the first stage of diagnosis, and a rush of adrenaline before I begin treatment.

It is not my job to judge, to be motivated by sympathy or hastened by patient anguish. That being said, the sight that confronts me moves me slightly before I have time to calibrate my feelings—to tell myself not to feel. A woman in pain, a girl in fear.

The woman I am here to treat is dripping blood on the floor beneath the chair. This patient request comes from the imbecile, "the ghetto rabbit"—this term given by Lena, knowing of his many affairs—whose ego it is necessary to stroke for the sake of goodwill. I am disgusted that the bleeding woman has not been led to the treatment room at the back to lie down and has not been given a towel at least. Though I suppress the disgust by keeping my expression passive as always.

"Thank you, Herr Manz," I say. "I will take it from here."

"Do not write this in a report. This one is unofficial. She is a Jew, of course."

Of course. Most of them are. Lilli, for one.

I was told by my father not to question the directions of Herr Manz, as most of his orders come directly from the Reich Governor. But I doubt this is one of them.

Hermann Manz is a senior ghetto administrator whose power has gone to his head and who has deciphered how to administer it in his own way. He is loathed by many of his colleagues, but because he is feared he is also obeyed. Things rarely end well for the people who question his decisions. It is my intention to never be on first-name terms with him, to avoid a friendship. Our forced alliance *will not* contaminate my reputation outside the ghetto.

Despite the political side I am fated to take, I have yet to determine a patient's level of care based on his or her race or character. I am guided solely by the affliction.

"I will keep a guard outside in case you need some help," Manz croaks. "Some help" is code for "someone to be carted away"; should patients die in my care, their bodies are then dumped unceremoniously. The air becomes cleaner once he is gone from the room.

I feel the forehead of the woman who is slumped sideways in the chair, her knees pulled up, blood seeping through her woolen skirt and down her worn stockings, body shivering. Her hair, though unwashed, is pulled back and pinned. A woman who, I notice straight away, wishes to appear well groomed despite the fact that she has been given few tools to achieve this. A woman, I imagine, who was once of means.

I pay very little attention to the girl beside her as I help the woman up and lead her to the surgery. The girl helps me lift the patient on top of the bed.

"You must wait outside," I say to the girl.

"Will she live?" she asks.

Her tiny wrists made me consider her a child, but it is only when I focus on a face that wears experience beyond her years that I realize she is a woman.

"And you are?"

"Her daughter."

She is of medium height like her mother, similar in features yet with different coloring. The girl, lighter skin, fair-haired. The irises of her eyes are a flawless blue, sullied only by the flesh beneath, which is reddened and swollen from crying.

"I will do what I can," I say. "But you must wait outside."

She looks at her mother and opens her mouth to say something else, words that never come. She is reluctant to leave her mother's side, mistrust hanging between us. It is unlikely that she trusts anyone. I feel the first pang of self-reproach that I must again squash into the corners of my mind: shame over the luck of birthright that I should be the one on the side of victory.

These thoughts creep around the back of my mind, infiltrating the parts that are currently unfortified by Nazi expectations. It is not just her vulnerability that moves me, or the despair that lies beneath her delicate frame, threatening to surface should the person she loves most in the world die; it is the weight of her heritage that she carries on her narrow shoulders that bothers me most, and the question of how someone so delicate, so Aryan in appearance, could end up in such a dark, ugly place as the ghetto.

"I promise I will do what I can," I say. "Now, please leave."

The girl closes the surgery door behind her as she retreats to the waiting room.

I roll the woman on her back and place a small pillow under her head. She is reluctant to stretch out her legs, which I have to gently straighten. I put on gloves, then take a needle from the cupboard and inject her with enough pethidine to calm her. Manz has said that I must not "waste" so much on those who are unworthy, even though he knows I have the advantage of my father's power to keep up an endless supply.

As I pierce her arm, her eyes open, and I see they are olive-brown. She is watching me without sound, without complaint, trying desperately not to wear her suffering on her face. Her eyes roll back as the drug slowly takes its effect, her arms slackening beside her body. She is relaxed but conscious.

I ease her skirt off and lift her now-heavy legs into the stirrups so that I can examine her.

It is not good. I sigh and shake my head. This is not the first such occurrence I have seen.

"What did you use?"

"A metal pipe." She makes a small coughing sound.

There is damage there, of course—not just to the fetus, but a slight tearing of the lining. Her skin is hot to the touch.

"Twelve weeks?"

"Eleven. The sickness has always started at eleven."

"How many children do you have?"

"Two."

"And pregnancies?"

"Three . . . four. A daughter. One baby died straight after birth . . . the second one. The third terminated itself. Then another daughter."

"Just relax now. I have some work to do."

She has done half the job herself. Only remnants of her pregnancy remain, though there is some infection that might have killed her eventually. With the aid of a curette and medicine, she may recover in a few days. In my experience, the women in the ghetto are resilient.

"The man involved is a senior officer, I presume?" I can't think why else Manz would call me for this. I would think it extraordinary if he was doing a favor for Lilli only.

"I didn't have time to ask him his rank," she says wryly. She has not winced or flinched throughout the expulsion. When you become a doctor, you see the full character of a person in these testing times. You learn not just of their ailments but of their fortitude and their ability to function above the pain. The temperament of this woman reminds me of Lena's.

Once the procedure is complete, I help remove her feet from the stirrups and recline the bed to a sitting position.

"What is your name?"

"Hannah."

"Don't move, Hannah. Rest a moment."

The drug has made her sleepy, and her eyes close involuntarily.

I move behind my desk to make some notes in my report, then remember Manz's instructions. Instead, I write a prescription and then take a moment to look at my work schedule for the next day.

After a reasonable time period, I check her temperature then gently press the patient's shoulder to wake her. She sits up gingerly, clutching her lower abdomen. I help her to the edge of the bed, then steady her as she steps into the fresh underwear and sanitary towels I have handed her. She wraps her coat around her lower half, tying the sleeves together, and slips her feet back into shoes that have almost worn through.

"Try to rest for the next few days. Don't lift anything heavy. And next time, don't attempt this yourself."

I take two small bottles from the medicine cupboard and note the dispensary on a chart on the wall.

"Take these painkillers and the others for the infection. Make sure you rest to build up your strength. In a few days you will need to take this prescription to the hospital for more medicine."

She reaches for the bottles and piece of paper I hold out toward her, and our eyes meet briefly before she averts hers out of modesty.

"There is an easier way, you know. I can operate so that you never have to go through this again."

"You mean operate on the Gestapo so that I am never again forced to have sex?"

I must appear passive at this admission, though I am suddenly aware of a tremor within my chest. It is the same tremor I felt after arriving at the ghetto, when I first viewed the haunted expressions of the hopeless. This war is constantly throwing small grenades into my once-ordinary world. At every step, I've had to fight within, to accept the things I see and hear.

"Herr Manz said nothing about a rape." I lift the stethoscope diaphragm and proceed to listen to her heart.

"Perhaps because it is normal practice here. We just aren't allowed to talk about it. 'Companionship,' I discovered, means something else."

She is lucid now, the effects of the drug waning, and I interrupt my final examination to carefully study her countenance. This makes her uneasy, and she searches the walls of the room for something to distract her from my sudden scrutiny. Lena once accused me of distancing myself in difficult situations, of making people feel inferior, but this is far from the truth. I am simply unable to speak until I am sure of my own thoughts and analyses. This is also a way of protecting myself, of not giving anything away before I have to.

The woman breaks the stunned silence between us, perhaps regretting her outspokenness and attempting to make some kind of amends. "You mean sterilize . . . remove my ovaries?"

"A surgical sterilization method, yes."

She thinks about this, her eyes hard on the door to the waiting room.

"This is something you shouldn't have to go through again." It is all I can think of to say, though from the sounds of it there will be more women to suffer such treatment.

She nods her head in resignation.

I retrieve another syringe and poise a needle once again near her arm.

"This is for the prevention of tetanus. I recommend it."

She nods. I could give her anything right now and I don't think she would care.

"Does your daughter know the circumstances?"

She shakes her head.

"When you are healed, come back and see me, and I will schedule you in . . . perhaps your daughter, too, if she agrees."

At this, her expression becomes vivid, her eyes wide, moving side to side in fear at the mention of her daughter.

"No . . . please. Not yet. She is too young."

Ethics demand that all doctors, even in this war, should honor our patients' choices, even if we do not always agree with them. And yet I understand that hope can override rationale. A mother thinking that in the future, when the war is over, her daughter will find love, perhaps like she did, settle down, and have children of her own.

"Of course. As you wish."

She stands up gingerly, and I step around the desk to bear the weight of her. Her uterus would still be very tender, though with pain now dulled and her temperature reduced.

In the waiting area, the girl jumps up to greet her mother, to take her from me. She does not even look at me, so relieved is she that her mother is no longer bleeding.

I pass the daughter a paper bag that contains her mother's soiled skirt and stockings and open the door to the black, filthy streets of the ghetto.

"You must bring her back if her temperature is still higher than normal after three days of medicine."

"Thank you," the daughter says, but I ignore this. Gratitude in these instances always gnaws at my conscience. I do not need her thanks.

"Guard, escort these women back, and wheel the mother gently."

He looks at me, his expression bland and unreadable. He will do what I say whether he agrees or not about carrying a Jew. He knows who I am. I am one of Hitler's champions.

OCTOBER

CHAPTER THREE
MATILDA

Theo is holding a long stick in front of him for balance as he creeps along the log, one slow foot at a time. He lifts one leg from behind, swings it slowly to the front, and places his foot carefully onto the narrow log that forms a bridge across the flowing creek. This is his third attempt, and he is drenched from falling in the water twice. Even though it is agonizing to watch, my chest hurts from laughing. Dragos is goading him to reach us. He is going "cluck cluck" like a chicken. Dragos never falls in. He is surefooted and fast. He is like that in everything he does.

I have already had my turn. It took two attempts, but I made it all the way across. Ever since I could walk, my brothers have always included me in their games. Soon my menses will come and I won't want to play anymore, says Mama. Sometimes I wish that I were a boy.

Theo is a third of the way from the end. It is more dangerous there where the creek is shallow, and we have all, at some time, cut our feet on the fallen branches and sharp rocks that litter the gully.

I stop laughing because I really want Theo to make it all the way across this time. I tell Dragos to stop taunting him, but he doesn't.

"Come on, *chicken*," he calls to Theo. "Or perhaps you are a girl."

"Stop it, Dragos!" I say. "There is nothing wrong with girls."

Dragos turns to me, his green eyes shining like mirrors. He wears a grin that is often followed by trouble.

"You are right. There is nothing wrong with girls!"

There are seven years between us, but he has always treated me well, so I know there is nothing in what he says. I also know that he loves girls. He spends much time looking at them. And because of how he looks, they spend much time looking at him, too. Dragos is grown all the way up to Tata.

Theo is four years older than me, and I have more in common with him than with Dragos. We both love to learn things from books.

Theo makes it to the end of the log eventually, but he is dripping and sore. It was Dragos's idea, and Theo never wanted to do this. He is tired of our brother's games and tricks, and when he finally jumps off at the end, he ignores both of us and begins to walk home. He has "a face full of dung." That's what my father says when he makes fun of our bad tempers.

"Hey, what is wrong with you?" says Dragos to Theo. "You finally made it. You finally shed your feathers."

"Shut up!" yells Theo, who does not let up his stride.

"Perhaps if you did not have your nose in a book all the time, like a girl, you would be better at games."

Theo stops and turns. "Reading is not just for girls," he says, showing fangs like an angry cat.

Dragos is amused that Theo is so sensitive. My oldest brother is becoming too mischievous. He does not always know when to stop.

"Run along home to Mama, and don't forget your apron to help her with the cooking! You are good at that, too."

Theo pushes Dragos in the chest, and I know that this will not end well. Dragos is three inches taller and five inches wider than Theo. He is a soccer player and a long-distance runner, and powerful like a bear.

Their sparring is far from equal, and lately a lot more frequent. It is as if they have outgrown each other and our house. The cat will always lose to the bear.

"Why don't you just go to war, instead of always talking about it!" says Theo.

Dragos's smile shrinks to nothing. Theo has touched a sore point. Dragos has yet to sign up because he is wanted for the soccer team. Mama and Tata refused to sign the papers until he is old enough. Tata went to war in his place.

"In a few months I will go, stupid! But you already know that. You are just jealous."

Dragos shoves Theo hard, and he falls back on the ground. As he lies there, Theo shakes his wrist, which has taken most of the fall. He stands up and growls; his face is red with rage as he pounces on Dragos. I have never seen him this strong as he pushes Dragos back a few paces, but it does not knock him over. Dragos is built of oak, says Tata.

Dragos kicks Theo's legs out from under him and pins him on the ground, and Theo fights with all his might, clawing at Dragos's face and attempting to knee him in the thigh. They are rolling in the mud.

"Stop it!"

I grab at them and tell them to stop, but they cannot hear me because of the sound of rage in their ears. I attempt again to separate them, but Dragos is shoved back suddenly, and his elbow hits my mouth. I yelp loudly, and this time they stop.

"Matilda!" Theo says.

"See what you've done, you idiot!" says Dragos.

"It was *your* elbow."

I can taste blood, and Dragos turns my face gently toward him.

"Open your mouth, Little Sun."

I do.

"All teeth intact, but you might have a fat lip."

"Sorry," says Theo, stepping between us. "Are you hurt?"

"No, I'm all right." I'm not, really. My mouth is stinging, but I don't want them to think that I can't be part of their games. I don't want the attention.

Dragos holds out his hand to Theo.

"Shake hands . . . all forgotten?"

Theo goes to shake his hand, but Dragos pulls it away teasingly, then runs in the direction of home. Theo picks up a stick and chases after him, but at least he is smiling now.

I follow, as always, drenched and laughing once more. I love my brothers the same. It is always like this. One minute we can be fighting; the next we are friends again.

I am a long distance behind them as I step on their muddy tracks with my own. I like to follow the creek that travels between the hills, some parts so narrow I can jump from side to side. In other parts I have to wade through shallow water with long reeds up to my knees.

It has been raining, also. Mama will be mad that we are wet. She says that we are teasing the spirits who carry the dead when we play such games in this weather. She says they will come and collect our spirits early if we are not mindful of the damp.

Our house is the last one at the bottom of the hill. It is made from spruce logs and was built by my father. Up the mountain behind our property my mother and I harvest lavender that grows wild. We collect the buds and place them into bags made from gauze and tie them with ribbon. My mother, Catarina, sells them at the village each market day. The herbs are popular for women who suffer from nervous conditions, and also for women who suffer menses cramps. But since the war, people are not buying any longer, and the tourists who used to come to the markets have gone. We sell very little.

Mama says she is sick of coming back with most of her stock, and that I can take over all the work. She also complains about our house that Tata built. She is tired of filling the gaps between the logs with moss to keep in the warmth. She wishes we could live in a city and she could work as a dressmaker like her mother before her. But my tata says there is no other place on earth like our home. He says it is a small piece of heaven in the hills. Tata used to work as a supervisor in a factory near the city, and he loves the smell of the pine air that has replaced the smell of burning coal.

Tata fights on the side of the Germans, though it is not by choice. I miss him. I miss the way he dismisses Mama's complaining and makes fun of sour faces. The way he fixes a broken fence while whistling. But mostly I miss the trips with him on the cart to town to purchase supplies for our farm. We used to have pigs, chickens, and horses, but the war has seen them gone.

Dragos runs through the front door, slamming it back on its hinges. I watch Theo disappear inside after him.

I am nearly out of breath when I reach the house. I am surprised to find both my brothers standing still just inside the doorway, blocking my entrance. I push between them to see what they are looking at.

Mama is at the kitchen table. Beside her is a man in uniform. He wears a long, gray coat despite the fact the air is warm, a hat that has an eagle on the front, and his boots are made of soft, black leather. I know that Dragos would like these boots. He is envious whenever he sees a soldier in uniform.

I think at first that he is here to deliver some news about Tata, who is away at war. My next thought is that he is here to take my brothers away like they did Tata, because Tata is filled with German blood. That they, too, must fight for Germany in a war, says Tata, that means little to any of us.

But the German officer is not looking at my brothers; he is looking directly at me while he talks to Mama.

"Frau Steuben," he says. His voice is sharp and hard like nails; the kind of voice that makes loud and furious speeches in the town center. "This is your daughter."

It is not said like a question.

"Yes." Mama does not look at me but stares at the honey bowl that sits between them. They have shared some tea.

"Mama!" says Dragos. "What is going on?"

I look up at Dragos and see that he looks frightened, which is bad, because he is not afraid of anything. My heart beats faster. I don't want them to take him away.

Mama stands up and rubs her hands down the front of her apron. She looks away from Dragos and then steps toward me. She takes my hand and pulls me toward the table to sit down in her place. The officer's eyes follow me. He is watching everything I am doing. It is as if I am a light to which the insect is drawn, and suddenly I am so close to him I can smell the leather of his boots. The kitchen is too small for all of us, and I wonder if I should run out the door. But Mama will be so angry if I do. She might send me to bed without dinner.

"Would you excuse us, gentlemen?" says the officer to my brothers.

"No," says Dragos firmly. "I'm afraid that we cannot—not until we find out what you are doing here."

"Dragos!" says Mama. "Take Theo outside the house! This is not a matter for you. It is between the officer and me. We have important matters to discuss with Matilda."

"What important matters?"

Mama is staring at Dragos as if she is staring at someone she has never seen before, as if her eyes can't find what is in front of her. As if she has lost something and knows she can never get it back.

"Mama, what is this? What is wrong?" asks Theo.

Mama doesn't answer, and Dragos takes another chair at the table, as does Theo. We are squeezed in tightly together.

"It is clear you have no control over your children, Frau Steuben." The officer's voice has become a smooth, sharp blade now, carving pathways through the air. I do not want to be here in front of the blade.

Mama bites her lip.

"As you wish," he says to my brothers. "You may stay. But I must warn you—if there is any trouble, I have people waiting for me outside."

"Trouble?" says Theo. "You speak in riddles! I didn't see anyone outside."

The German looks at Theo, and I wonder if he will hurt him. Fury from the stranger's eyes burns holes into the eyes of my brother. I recognize this fury. I have seen this same look coming from Tata when Dragos has disappeared into the town and not come back till morning, and when he has not completed his tasks. I place my foot on top of Theo's under the table to warn him not to speak.

"Now, are we all calm?" says the stranger.

No one answers. No one has to, because he doesn't wait, but directs his speech toward Dragos.

"I have been talking to your mother, who has been most hospitable and very agreeable. We have decided that your sister is perfectly suited for our program in Germany."

"What sort of program?"

"One for young women with German backgrounds. I understand that your father and your grandparents hail from good German stock."

I do not like the way he talks about them as if he is referring to horses.

"So, what is so important about this program?" asks Dragos.

"It is conducted at a training center where young girls learn to be intelligent, accomplished women."

"My sister is already intelligent."

"Do you speak German, Matilda?" the officer asks me.

"*Natürlich,*" I say.

"What else can you say?"

I count to twelve in German before he puts up his hand to stop me.

He takes out a notebook and pen and passes them to me. "Can you write them?"

I write the numbers down, then examine my work before I pass it to him.

"Stand and read this, please." He passes me a piece of paper that has German words typed on it.

The application of force alone, without moral support based on a spiritual concept, can never bring about the destruction of an idea or arrest the propagation of it, unless one is ready and able ruthlessly to exterminate the last upholders of that idea even to a man, and also wipe out any tradition which it may tend to leave behind.

I have to sound out the syllables of the words I don't understand.

The officer is looking around the room at all the books that my grandfather sent from Germany before he died. Mama thinks we should sell them.

"Impressive," says the officer, who is also looking around at our moss-filled walls. He is speaking more softly now.

"I understand that you are quick to pick up other languages, too."

I look to Dragos, who shakes his head. I don't say anything further. I think that perhaps I have said too much. Mama might accuse me of showing off.

"No matter!" says the officer. "I have heard enough and can see that future opportunities for learning are limited here. At these centers, Matilda will be well educated and will participate in many activities . . . athletics, cooking, sewing. She will be given lovely clothes, and her prospects for marrying into a good family will improve." He opens his hands to show his palms, as if everything he says is written there for us to see. Dragos has done this, too, even when he is lying.

I suddenly think of Oles from school, whom I have loved for months. He does not know that I exist because he is always examining bugs from the ground. But if I have to marry anyone, it should be him, not a German stranger.

"How long would it take?" Dragos asks.

"Your sister will need to relocate to Germany."

"For how long?"

"As long as required."

"How long is that?"

"She won't be coming back."

Dragos stands up suddenly, knocking over the chair that he was sitting on. Mama, Theo, and the officer all stand then, too. I am the last to rise, and I step closer to Dragos.

"That is absurd!" says Dragos. "She is only a little girl. She is nine years old. She needs to be here, with her family."

The man with the eagle stares, unblinking, his hands as still as the table they rest upon. No one is talking except for the house, which creaks and groans.

"We cannot make such a decision until we discuss this with our father," says Dragos.

"The decision is effective immediately."

"No! Never!" yells Theo, and I am suddenly frightened for him. Mama appears to be frightened, too, and steps in front of him. Theo is always the one who gets injured when he speaks his mind. Always the one to be hurt in a fight. "She is staying here! She does not need your stupid German-speaking centers!"

"Stop it!" yells Mama.

I clench my fists against my chest. I feel the first prick of tears at the back of my eyes, and my breaths grow shorter. His words flood my ears, and their seriousness sinks into my head. I imagine that if I could reach a knife to cut myself, the blood might carry the words back out again.

"You have no choice." The officer has remained seated. He squeezes his fists, tightly, as if his temper is trapped in his hands and he must keep it from escaping. Even Dragos's height does not scare him into leaving, and I watch his hand move slowly to the gun at his side. "Your mother has read and signed the custody agreement. It cannot be revoked."

He pushes a piece of paper toward us. At the bottom of the page is Mama's scrawl. Her name is one of the few things she knows how to write. My father tried to teach her, but she complained, saying that a lavender farmer does not need to learn to write so many words. I wonder how my mother could have read the paper in front of her, even if the document wasn't typed in German. Theo picks up the document.

I need to find air again. There is no air with so many people in the room. I back one step away from the others, then turn, but Mama has read my thoughts and steps between me and the door.

"Mama! I can't go! This is my home. Who will look after the lavender?"

"You are going, Matilda. It is done."

Dragos walks past Mama to stand behind me, and he grips both my shoulders. If we were playing a game, I would try and wriggle free, but this time I do not want Dragos to let me go. Theo is staring at Mama as if she is the one who has caused all this anger, but I know he also does not like looking at the officer's eyes.

"No!" says Dragos. "Over my dead body."

The officer is clenching the end of his other sleeve, and his face is hard like stone.

"Stop it!" says Mama, sneaking a look at the officer. "Don't say such stupid things."

"You can't sign anything without Tata," says Theo, who is now reading the document. "He would not approve. Does he even know?"

"Your father is missing," says Mama. "Until he is found there is no pension."

The house is suddenly silent again. Her words are puzzling, and I cannot make sense of them while they jump around inside my head.

"Officer Lehmann, may I please have a moment with my children?" Mama says in a low voice, and I see that her hands are trembling, as if she is afraid of her own words.

The officer looks at each of us. "I will give you a moment. But do not keep me waiting long." He picks up his hat and takes two long strides to reach the door at the back of the house.

"What has happened to Tata?" Dragos asks Mama.

"Your father has been missing for two weeks."

"Is he dead?"

"No one can say for certain."

"That means he isn't," says Dragos, pacing the room. "And until he comes back, this decision should not be made."

"If you want to fight this and get yourself shot, then go outside and tell the officer that she isn't going. Go ahead!" She is making an idle threat. She knows that Dragos does not want to die.

Dragos says nothing.

"Where is Tata?" I ask, because I am not sure what they mean by *missing*.

"Mama, you cannot do this," says Theo. "She is your daughter."

"But what about Tata?" I say, louder this time, because it is as if they have forgotten I am here.

"What did he say, Mama?" says Theo. "What has he threatened?"

Mama sits back down and puts her hand against her forehead. No one wants to answer me.

I look at her dress, which I have never really looked at closely before. She made it last year. It is pale pink and has buttons down the front and a full skirt that stretches to her ankles. I suddenly want to touch the fabric because I may not see it again. I kneel down in front of her and place my head in her lap, feeling the smooth cotton against my cheek as I fight a war against my tears. "Mama," I whisper. "Please don't do this. Please wait for Tata to come back."

I can feel her warm, coarse hand on the side of my head. "It is too late. I have made a bargain with the devil so that all my children are safe."

"What do you mean?" says Theo.

"He said that he was within his rights to take both my boys to war if I do not consent to this . . . to Matilda going. He also said that I would not receive my husband's wages if I do not sign. We will starve. At least Matilda will go to a nice place, and when she is older, she can come back. It is a choice that I did not have, and an opportunity that the other girls in the village have not been given. He told me that. She has been selected."

"*Tch,*" says Dragos, which means he doesn't believe it. "How do you know it's a nice place?"

"No, Mama," says Theo. "Dragos and I will go to war if that's what it takes. We will send all our money back to you."

"No, that cannot happen. In any case, it is too late."

When I stand up, I look through the back door that the officer has left open. A car is parked behind our house, and several men in uniform stand beside it. They carry guns.

"Mama," I plead. "Don't let them . . ." Just for a moment she looks as if she will break apart—her mouth twisting, her eyes blinking fast, her head falling forward—and then she is back to normal. She pushes me away. She has given her daughter away with a scratch of ink. She cannot love me.

"Matilda, if you don't want your brothers killed in war, if you don't want to starve without your father's pay, then you must go with the officer."

Mama sounds angry, as if this is all my fault.

I rush to the room I share with Mama and throw myself on the bed, burying my face in the pillow. I draw in the scent of crushed lavender and freshly cut wood, the smells of my mother and brothers. How can we be apart? How will I cope without them? My tears bleed into the pillow.

Theo has come into the room. He touches my back so that I will look at him. His eyes are red, and he whispers into my hair, "Tilda, I'm so sorry."

We hold each other, and I do not let go until the knock at the door. The front of Theo's shirt is wet with my tears, and I squeeze my eyes shut. When I open my eyes, Mama is in the room.

"I will pack your things," she says with her back to me. I do not want to look at her, so I leave the room. I find Dragos smoking tobacco in the kitchen. His face and neck are red. Sadness has replaced his anger.

"This is wrong," he says to me. I hear no sign of the mischief that is usually in his voice. "Tata, Theo, and I will come for you one day. You will come home. We will make sure of that."

I throw myself into his arms, and he lifts me slightly off the floor.

"You are a good little sister," he says. "You always forgive me for my teasing. I cannot imagine the house without my Sun." This has always been his name for me. He says my head is covered with curling, golden rays.

"I am going to war anyway," he tells me. "There is nothing to keep me here. I must fight to help end it quickly, and after that, whether they allow it or not, we will bring you home."

Catarina, my mother, whom I no longer think of as "Mama," carries a leather suitcase from the bedroom. She has packed up my life.

"You cannot keep the officer waiting."

My eyes are dry when I take the case from her. She has always said that tears are a sign of weakness. She looks at me, waiting for something, but I turn away toward the door. There is nothing more to say.

"Be strong, Matilda," she says.

I do not feel anything for her, even when she puts her hand on my shoulder. It is as if someone has cut me open and taken out my heart.

Outside, the car is waiting silently, like a spider for its prey. As I get closer, the engine starts. The spider is getting ready to snatch me away. My legs are suddenly very weak, and I'm not sure if they will carry me these last few steps. Officer Lehmann holds the car door open, and I slide across the seat, which is smooth and firm like the side of a horse. The smells of burning fuel and new leather quickly block out the sweetness of the forests in the hills. He shuts the door that now separates me from my brothers.

I don't want to look back, but I do. Catarina has collapsed on the ground, one arm across her head, the other across her stomach. Dragos and Theo bend down to help her up. That is the last I see of them. I don't have time to wave because we are quickly on the dirt track that will take us out of the village and into the town.

Tata will be angry to find me gone. He once told me that when I was born, he cried with tears of love.

Outside it is getting dark, and the hills and the birds are disappearing into the sky to sleep. Tata said that fairy tales are like the wings of a bird. They set your mind free. I close my eyes where I can be free.

CHAPTER FOUR
ELSI

It is four o'clock in the afternoon. I am sitting in the waiting room of the doctor whose door has no name plaque. I am worried that the operation is dangerous and is taking too long. I am also worried that we will not be home by curfew, and worried, also, for Leah, who has been left alone in the apartment and may come searching for us if we are not there by nightfall. The guards have stepped up the patrols since too many people have been caught wandering at night. They perhaps will not be as lenient now as they have been. *Lenient* used to have a different meaning outside the gates. It used to mean that my father would not be angry with me for getting home late, that he would not stop me from seeing my friends. Now it means that we will not be shot or imprisoned.

It is silent behind the frosted door. Mama is having an operation that will stop her from becoming pregnant again. She says that it is a decision she might have discussed with Papa if he were here, but now there is no time to wait.

The doctor steps out from behind the door. He doesn't look at me straight away but remains focused on a paper in his hand. I remember him from several weeks earlier, when he treated Mama and saved her life. He is tall, with light-brown hair and a short forehead with brows that jut forward over deep-set eyes. Everything else on his face seems to fall into place evenly.

When he finally puts the paper down, he folds his hands together and examines me over the desk as if I am a specimen of some tiny, interesting species. Though his is not the smug look worn by some officials. It is more questioning. The scrutiny, however, becomes too intense, and I drop my eyes to look at my lap. He does not wear the Nazi uniform, though the guard who carried Mama home last time we were here had been pliant in the face of his commands. I am curious as to how a doctor can have such authority.

When he does speak, it is in a formal voice.

"Your mother is still a little dazed from the medication. She needs another half hour."

I look at the fading light coming in from beneath the front door.

"I will sign a form that says you can be out past curfew. Tell me . . . where is it that you live?"

I tell him the street.

"Do you have running water or toilets?"

I shake my head, and he looks away first this time. He scratches something on a piece of paper, puts down his pen, and leans back into his chair. He then checks his watch before his eyes find mine again.

I do not know where to look, so I stare at a painting of a raven on a spindly branch above a desolate land. It reminds me of Hitler looking upon the remnants of Poland. He follows my eyes.

"Do you like that one?"

"Yes." But I don't. It looks evil.

"Ravens are my favorite birds. They are very intelligent and learn from their mistakes. If only we all could."

I think this may be an attempt at humor; it is difficult to tell because the edge of his mouth, which almost formed a smile, has repositioned itself, expressionless as before.

He opens a drawer and pulls out a packet that he holds toward me. "Would you like some chocolate?"

Even from where I sit I can smell the cocoa and sugar, and my tongue becomes moist at the thought of it.

I stay seated, and my eyes drift between his face and the chocolate. "What is your name?"

"Elsi."

"It is all right, Elsi. I promise that I will not be poisoning you today." This time he does smile, though the expression is small and rehearsed. It is something that does not come naturally to him. He breaks the bar of chocolate into pieces. "Here!"

I stand up and cautiously take the small offerings, then place one inside my mouth quickly before it can vanish, as if part of some cruel magic trick. The chocolate melts, spreading across my tongue: so sweet and creamy that I want to cry with pleasure. I eat the rest slowly, letting each tiny piece melt so that it lasts. It has been more than a year since I have known this sensation. The doctor puts the rest of the chocolate back in the drawer.

"Can I ask what your family did before the war? Can you describe it for me?"

I am instantly suspicious. I want to ask him why he wants to know this, but that is not how it is done here. You do what is asked, you answer whatever question is asked, and you lie when you have to. Mama has told me so many times not to talk, not to trust, but there is something inconsistent about this man. He does not seem like the Gestapo. And he saved Mama from dying.

"Are you writing this down?"

"No," he says, and gives a short laugh this time. It is neither soft nor brittle, but somewhat genuine. It is not a laugh like those of the soldiers, ones that reach all the way to their boots when they kick a man or a woman who has fallen in the streets. I have memorized that sound. I know what amuses them.

"You can say whatever you like."

I say nothing.

"You are also welcome to sit there silently if you wish." He returns to write something else in his notes.

If he is a spy, then what I tell him will mean little. And since I do not think he will hurt the people he has also saved, I tell him—though not everything. Not the details about Papa, or the things Mama says about the soldiers, not the fact that Leah is often ill. Germans do not take kindly to sick children. And suddenly it feels good to talk. My parents always said I talked too much, but it was not until the ghetto that I stopped. It has been so long.

I was sixteen when the bombs first struck, and then seventeen years old when soldiers came to take us away. Next month I turn nineteen.

When the bombs were first being dropped, our family sheltered in Mr. Krolewski's apartment building. The bombs made a whistling sound while they were in the air, and the engines groaned across the skies. The basement was the size of a small apartment and choked with voices and pipe smoke and the smell of onions cooking on small gas burners. Despite the raging argument happening in the skies, the basement felt ordinary. It was a hub for people to gather, bringing with them blankets and bedding, small chairs and tables, cooking pots, needlework, packs of playing cards: mothers, grandparents, children, teachers, carpenters, shop owners, and others randomly thrown together to continue the domestic tasks they had started earlier that evening.

At the time I couldn't understand why Leah had to be dragged from the cupboard, trembling and whimpering at the first sound of warplanes. Everything was exciting in a way, because I had yet to experience fear. Perhaps because our parents had always shielded us from bad news.

At first the sounds of planes seemed to be coming from too far away to concern me. But mayhem arrived quickly, and the sky was covered with fire. In the streets, people were running in all directions to find a safe place to hide from the bombs. Some of my friends were in Mr. Krolewski's basement, too. We played Truth or Dare, told stories, and sang "Poland Is Not Yet Lost," and everyone in the basement joined in. Life had not yet changed, just shifted position ever so slightly.

Leah stayed on Mama's lap, frightened, her hand gripping Mama's blouse the whole time. Her eyes watched everyone walking past with their lanterns and matches and candles and blankets, calling to one another, their noise penetrating her sensitive ears. Leah doesn't like loud noises. Mama said it had something to do with an ear infection she had when she was a baby. Leah didn't like leaving the house at all. She was scared of going to school. She wanted routine, and she wanted silence. It was like dark clouds were always following her. We were nothing alike then. It is different now, of course. Today we share the same fears.

Mama was displeased with me for being too boisterous, for interrupting other people and chasing my friends around the basement. She accused me of not acting my age, of not listening. She told me constantly to calm down. I liked the sound of the bombs more than the sound of Mama's cross voice. But I didn't know the truth. I couldn't see what was ahead. How could anyone have foreseen that life would be altered to such a state that our time together in the basement would seem like a fond memory compared with the suffering that was to come?

When the skies eventually grew quiet, Papa went out to survey the streets. When he came back, he told us that there were no casualties or damage in the immediate streets, though other parts of the city had been destroyed, and he heard that some people had been killed. He said there was a crater the size of a creek in one part. Papa had not gone to the front to fight for Poland because he ran a successful furniture business.

We slept in the basement that night because we weren't sure if the planes would return. I remember Leah being restless and keeping me awake before she eventually burrowed into Papa like a badger to sleep. And at one point, in the dim artificial light, Papa looked across at me and reached out his hand, which didn't feel right. His hands, which were always so warm and firm, were cold and trembled slightly. But now I understand that he knew more than he told. Perhaps Mama did, too. They could see what was going to happen.

When we emerged from the basement the next morning, the city was ceilinged in smoke that smelled of burning metal. Papa said it was the smell of war.

Then when the German soldiers came, the city seemed to divide between German Poles and Jewish Poles. A month passed, and then the telephone services were canceled, followed by the mail service. Papa and Mama would listen to the radio broadcast from London to learn the truth, and that is when we heard that England had declared war on Germany and that France and Australia were also participating. Mama's face grew paler every day, and she stopped wearing makeup. I used to smile at the soldiers, and they would smile at me until Mama told me to stop. She said they were not our friends; they were burning pokers, prodding us into poverty. (At this part of my story, I look at the doctor. His eyes are fixed on a point above my shoulder, but I know he is listening. I can tell when someone has lost interest. Their eyes begin to roam.)

I was not frightened at first. Many of us in the city thought that perhaps things would go on the same as they had. But things changed drastically. We stopped attending school because teachers were not turning up, and there was no money for books anyway. And then came the shortage of food.

Mama and I began fighting more. She was becoming annoying. She did not want me out of her sight. I hated the sound of her voice. Like the buzzing insects in the reeds beside the lake, she did not ever stop. When she said I could no longer go out on my own, I ran away to my friend Marta's house. It was dark when my papa came to take me home. He was not angry, even though I was having pancakes with cream and sugar because Marta's papa was a German Pole, and he had not lost as many privileges. At the time, I didn't recognize that fact. I still did not fully understand the difference between Marta and me. I was immature. I refused to believe that anything could affect me. I liked the drama, in a way, and believed that eventually things would go back to normal.

With the schools closed, Marta and I received lessons from Marta's mother at her home. But after a while, Papa said that I should not spend so much time away.

Just before all this happened, I had auditioned for a play at a theater that had recently opened. I was to play the part of Rastilla, a fairy who transforms a poverty-stricken town into paradise. But after the bombings, the theater was abandoned, and that is when I first began to resent the changes: because I wanted the part of Rastilla so badly, and it had suddenly been taken away from me. I began to focus more on the circumstances surrounding me, the things that were causing me grief. And, perhaps because I grew up almost overnight, I began to see the effect all this was having not just on me but also on my family and others like us.

After this, the paper stopped being published, and we received only Nazi news . . . (I falter. We have heard that the term *Nazi* is considered disrespectful by some Germans who command the title of Socialist only, but he makes no gesture to suggest he finds this offensive.) . . . about how wonderful Germany was and how mighty was its army, how the Jews must not take over the country, that Germany must not let them. And that is when I first felt fear. Up until that moment when Papa read from the paper, it seemed that these things were happening to someone else.

Mama was a Jew, not Papa—but that didn't matter. He did not have to sew a yellow star on his shirt, but he did so in support of Mama.

Then one day Papa came home and did not remove his hat as he stepped through the doorway. I knew straight away that this was a bad sign, that something was wrong. He said that the shop had been seized. I asked lots of questions, and Mama told me to keep quiet, to not rush at Papa. He said that he was no longer allowed to buy supplies for the store. A Jew was not allowed to pay for things. He said that Poles would be placed there to run the store instead.

Mama said, "What do you mean, *Poles?*"

But there was no need for the question. We all knew. Mama only wanted to put the word out there, to highlight the impact it was having. To highlight the fact that Poles were now divided into two: Poles without Jewish blood, and Polish Jews who no longer had the right to call themselves anything but Jews.

From the days when the Germans first arrived in the city—several days after the night in the basement—German national pride had risen among non-Jews. They now saluted and mingled with the soldiers as if they, too, were "the chosen people." (I explain to the doctor that the phrase was borrowed from someone else, not something that I had come up with.)

We lost friends and neighbors because of this. Papa stormed out of our neighbor's house after he had the urge to hit Konrad, who'd suggested that the Germans would save the human race—would save the Aryan race—from extinction.

"We will never go back there. We will never again be friends," he said to Mama, Leah, and me. And I understood. You cannot go back once you learn the truth about people's feelings. Mama kept telling us that we had to be careful who we spoke to; our own countrymen could not be trusted. (I stop to see if I have said something wrong, but the doctor's gaze has only shifted to my other shoulder; his expression remains the same. Mama still thinks that I am too trusting. That I speak before I think sometimes. But I do not tell the doctor that Mama said, "It is criminal. Someone will get word to the British and perhaps the Americans that Germany has lost its mind, that they have employed a totalitarian, an anti-Semite, to undo the world.")

Papa boarded up the shop windows after someone threw a brick in through the glass. I begged him to remove the yellow star from his clothes. But he refused. Another night, Papa came home in a rage after he discovered that his shop had been smashed again and profanity scrawled across the windows in paint. He thought it was Polish anti-Semites, not the soldiers. He grew so angry. He got his gun and stormed off down the road. Mama ran after him, but she could not stop him. She came back crying and fearful.

When he did eventually return, we could smell alcohol on his breath, and he was accompanied by friends, some non-Jews who sympathized and had convinced him that finding the culprits would be impossible. There were too many suspects. This was the first time I had ever seen my father lose control, pushed beyond his usual high level of tolerance. He collapsed on the couch, and Mama soothed him with her soft voice. She had that effect on most people; she could calm them with her touch. Not that she was always like that. Sometimes Mama needed Papa as much as he needed her. Sometimes the nerves got the better of her, too. They looked after each other. (I hope that one day I will find someone, and we will be like my parents.)

Papa kept working in the shop for a while, stocking the shelves, while Hugo—whom my father had originally employed as a junior clerk—ran the store. (Hugo was Polish, with no bloodlines that said he couldn't be classed as "suitable for management.")

Mama put her hand on Papa's arm then, and suddenly I saw the whole thing as ridiculous. I was angry that Papa was wearing a yellow star when he didn't have to. That he had given up so much for Mama. I did not realize at the time that he had given it up for his children, also.

We did not observe all the Jewish customs, not like my grandmother, especially when it came to food. I had grown up in a household that celebrated yuletide from my father's side and Hanukkah from my mother's. Both these celebrations included candles, food, and gifts. We had twice the celebration. I used to think that we were the luckiest family, with so many celebrations. Those same people who now ignored us had often come to celebrate with us.

I said, "But Papa is not a Jew. It is because of you, Mama, that we have to live like this. That we are considered Jews. That we are all at the bottom of the human pile."

"Elsi! Don't ever say that!" said Papa, red with fury. He rushed forward and slapped me across the face. He had never hit me before. Mama stepped toward him to pull him away.

"Victor, stop it!" she yelled. He gripped my arm so hard that tears sprang to my eyes.

"Victor!" cried Mama again. For a brief moment my father became someone I didn't recognize. His hat had fallen, and his wavy, white hair stood up wildly around his head; his squinting eyes were bloodshot from too many sleepless nights. He hadn't changed clothes for many days, and he smelled of alcohol and sweat. He released me then with such force that I fell backward, and he walked from the room, his giant frame stooping slightly.

I held my sore face and tears came. Papa and I had been an unbreakable union. When I was little, I would sit on his shoulders and he would gallop like a horse while I squealed with laughter, and we would go to the lake to race each other while swimming. Leah was not yet born then. It took Mama two failed pregnancies before she produced a sibling for me, and I was sorry that my little sister had never experienced what Papa and I had together, and the feeling of freedom and carefree, sunny days.

Mama checked the side of my face. "You poor thing," she said. She wet a cloth and put it on my cheek and apologized for Papa. She then disappeared to search for him.

It should have been Mama who slapped me for the comment, but she has forgiven everything I have ever said and done.

When Papa came back, he said he was sorry for losing his temper, and we started talking again, and things went back to a new kind of normal, though I knew that war was now taking something else from us. It was taking away simple relationships and twisting them into something complicated. It was splitting our family apart. Leah was always frightened now, clinging to Mama and crying as if she could hear and sense things that none of us could. I started to miss the food that had once been plentiful on our table.

"What can we do about the shop?" I asked.

Mama suggested that we write to the British newspapers, that we somehow get a message to them. But Papa said that they have too many things to worry about than one family in Poland. (It is only when I suggested stealing some guns that Papa completely returned to normal. He said, "You are always so dramatic, Elsi; what a shame the theater is closed!")

And shortly after that we came here.

Mama moans from the back room. The doctor is leaning forward in the chair now, his eyes fixed on mine. He has moved only once since I began speaking, and that was to interrupt me to check on Mama. He is interested. I do not believe that he has missed anything I have said.

"Your father—where is he from?"

"From Denmark originally."

"And where is he now?"

"I don't know," I say. "He went to work and never came back."

CHAPTER FIVE
WILLEM

"Guess what I am about to tell you?"

"That we are leaving this dreadful place today?" says Lena.

We are strolling beside the river, the water murky, reflecting the sky. The city itself seems to pour dullness back into the air. The name Lodz—"boat"—suggests there is an abundance of moving water, yet this name is a contradiction in terms. There is an absence of life and movement here, except what is artificial: the steady flow of cars and trucks ferrying soldiers, prisoners, and laborers.

It is not a good day for walking. The wind has risen, but Lena doesn't care. She doesn't wish to be trapped indoors for too long: accustomed to the many walks we took in the Black Forest during our last German summer, before the war.

"Close!"

Lena turns to face me, gripping my hand with hers in anticipation. She looks both tense and hopeful.

"I have been promoted."

"Thank goodness!" she says, breathing out deeply and dropping her shoulders to amplify her relief. "Does that mean you will leave that horrible ghetto surgery?" She has never seen it, of course—I would never allow this. But I have described it to her many times.

"It will not happen for several months, but we are moving to Berlin."

"Oh," she says. "Very well then." She casts her eyes downward so that I cannot see them, and her voice no longer signals her earlier enthusiasm.

"What is wrong? You sound disappointed, not pleased."

"It was just that . . . I was hoping our situation would change *before* the birth."

"Yes," I say. "So was I. But you have to trust me. I will be at the hospital beside you. I will not let another doctor touch you, and nothing will happen without my approval, not—" I stop there. I do not want to frighten her.

"Not like your mother, you were going to say. It's perfectly fine, Willem. I am not fearful of the birth itself. It will not be the same as your mother. I was just hoping for the child to be born in Germany, not Poland . . . and close to my family."

When I learned at the age of thirteen that my mother had died of puerperal fever several days after my birth, the subject of women was suddenly seen in a new light. Until then, they were part of the human race, just like men but with different working functions. The physical makeup of a woman had never been a question. But this tragedy struck in me a sudden yearning to learn the differences in detail. Women began to fascinate me, not as objects of desire but something enigmatic. The boys who brought to school illicitly purchased photo cards of women draped provocatively across chairs, wearing nothing but a string of pearls and stockinged legs, certainly appealed to my primal nature, but overriding those feelings was more the desire to master the art and science of women. I deemed, by my own assumption and observations, that if they weren't nurtured on both an emotional and physical level—both states completing the whole—then the human race was potentially doomed.

And the more I learned about women through the course of my studies, the more I realized that my mother did not have to die.

My mother had a rather uneventful, quick birth, considering it was her first. My father—a doctor himself—wasn't there, hidden away at a laboratory, performing commissioned and highly secretive bacterial trials by a pharmaceutical company. It was a time when there was a race to find an antibacterial agent against infections, especially with the commencement of the first war and the amount of casualties that were expected because of it.

A midwife came and delivered me that night, then bathed my mother and left. My aunt, who had also been present, sent a telegram to my father to announce the good news of my birth. My mother then developed a fever, admitted herself to a hospital, and quickly died.

The irony was that my father did not tolerate unhygienic practices and, while working as a supervisor at a hospital, was known to dismiss people who failed to wash their hands, before or after caring for a patient. A further irony was that not only would he have ensured the sterilization of anything that came into contact with his wife and unborn son, which would have protected her from infection, but that the very antibacterial products he was testing at the time would likely have killed the infection and saved her life.

I have only photos to remember her by. Although people have noted we share similar characteristics, and said she was a woman with impeccable moral standards and humility, I do not feel that we are connected. Any feelings of guilt about her death—that I was somehow to blame—came and went early, perhaps from the persistent ideals my father instilled. That it was men who were the ones to be educated and relied upon, and who would pave the way for new life. He taught me not to dwell or attach myself to things from the past that were no longer useful, and that sentimentality was for people who did not want to move forward in this world. I embraced this preaching, as my father represented success and control, traits that were highly sought after for men with professional aspirations.

For much of my early years, I was cared for by my aunt, who was stern as well as fair, various nannies who were instructed to discipline rather than nurture, and a father devoid of emotion and rarely there. I had several friends even though my father did not allow visits outside school. This obviously had an effect, because even in my university years, although I made many good friends, enjoyed class discussions, and visited clubs usually by colleagues' insistence, socializing was not something I craved. And if it wasn't for Lena's temerity, I doubt I would yet be married.

As a boy I learned to play the violin, an instrument that was thrust into my hands by my aunt when I was six. The instrument was much loved by my mother, whose own father had played to some acclaim. I enjoyed it and played well, and many said I had a natural ear for music. One evening when I was around the age of eleven, I performed a solo at an event at my school. My father clapped at the end of the piece, though his face, as always, was unreadable.

That night after I had climbed between the clean, starched sheets of my bed, I heard music coming from downstairs. Apart from the violin, Father did not allow other music to be played in the house, and he rarely accepted invitations to concerts. I crept down the curved stairway, my hand sliding silently over the smooth, polished wood banister to feel my way. The door to the front sitting room where my father worked was ajar, and a light shone from within.

I peered into the room and noticed that the soft music was coming from a phonograph, and Father was facing the window, holding a photograph of my mother. In the reflection of the window glass, he saw me and angrily told me to return to bed or receive a caning. In the seconds before I was sent away, I had enough time to see his face in the reflection and to see that it was a different kind of face than I had seen before: one that was reflective and sorrowful. I disappeared from his sight quickly because my father always carried out his threatened punishments.

To this day, I can't touch a polished banister without thinking of my father's face in the window glass.

The morning after my concert, he called me into his study and announced that I was not to play the violin anymore, and that I must work harder in science and mathematics and prepare for a career in medicine.

This is the only time I can remember feeling disappointed for a prolonged period. The violin had been my only physical connection with my mother—something she would have once held and caressed, and ours to share. I cried for several nights because I had so enjoyed the applause I received at the end of the recital, and for the first time wondered what my mother would have thought—if she would have been pleased by my performance. I believe my father had seen this sentimentality developing and decided that a sharp separation from the instrument was the cure.

It was my aunt who came to my aid, telling me that when I was grown, I could do whatever I wanted, including play the violin, but for the time being I was to accomplish what my father had planned for me—that he knew best how to raise me. As an adult, I wonder whether she had believed her own words—since I am still often under his strict direction—or whether she had convinced me in the interest of maintaining household harmony. There are few people who have the courage to object to Father's decisions.

My father frequently traveled to other countries to talk about his research and to observe the work of others. When he personally attended to the medical needs of the families of Heinrich Himmler's inner circle in 1933, his competence was noticed and he quickly moved up through the ranks of the party. His own field of research was set aside. He was asked to consult on other issues, such as inexpensive chemicals needed for Hitler's euthanasia program. He began working in an exclusive sanatorium in Lychen, treating athletes and Hitler's protection squad, the *Schutzstaffel*, or SS. He was trusted. He put the Nazi Party before family, before me. I was groomed from birth to be loyal.

But the idea of women's intricate physiology continued to plague me into adulthood, hence I combined the study of general medicine at the University of Munich with the disciplines of gynecology and obstetrics also. War broke out three months before I was due to graduate, and my father summoned me to Berlin for urgent talks. He needed me packed and ready for transfer to Poland to be the personal physician to the SS. I would follow them around, repairing and sending them off for more brutality. We argued, as I wanted to return and finish the degree. It was the physiology of women that I had spent years attempting to understand. He knew that it was my intention to open a fertility clinic, and I could not have foreseen that voluntary abortions on Jewish girlfriends would be part of my work. (Meanwhile, abortions on Aryans were otherwise illegal.)

It had been a long time since I had stood up to him, and, as always, he won in the end. He dismissed my concerns. "It is just the paperwork." With a slash of his pen on party letterhead, a request was made, and a week later I held my medical and gynecological degree. I certainly knew all the material, and had achieved high results throughout my education, but I still cannot help feeling a fraud sometimes, having not completed the final exams that many of my colleagues were presented with, simply because I am who I am. The son of Anton Gerhardt, a respected member of the National Socialist German Workers' Party.

"So, what is the promotion?" Lena asks.

"I will be working for my father, unfortunately. He wants to send me to a women's camp just north of Berlin. It seems the number of patients per doctor is rising fast."

"How long have you known?" She sounds suspicious. She is always one step ahead of me.

"He told me at our last dinner gathering. I wanted to think about it before I told you. I needed to summon up the courage knowing how you feel about Father." I say this, half joking. Part of my delay was deciding whether to take the promotion or not. Though I hugely dislike my current placement, I have grown used to being secluded here with Lena, partly cut off from my father in Berlin. The gathering the other evening reminded me how much I detest the pomp and sycophants who follow him around.

"Do we have to be so close to Anton?"

My father tends to make people tense, especially Lena.

"You can't have it all your own way," I say playfully.

"If only that were true."

"At least we will be back in Germany with the family, yes? To celebrate his first birthday and every other event."

"How do you know it's a *him*?"

"I keep dreaming of a boy. A little boy with brown hair, like yours."

"Maybe it is your own childhood you're remembering."

"Thank you, *Herr Freud*."

She ignores my teasing dig. "Who is replacing you?"

"They haven't approached anyone yet. I suppose the medical centers will provide the services I do now, until a replacement is found."

I have tried not to imagine what will become of them. Pregnant women will most likely be turned away at the general medical facilities. But my wife does not need to know this.

"Lena," I say, "there is more to tell you. My father wants me to observe and participate in the research methods being conducted at Auschwitz. There are procedures being used there that he wants me to implement at the camp near Berlin, as well as at other camps. He believes that the work being done at Auschwitz is promising for women. I have to go to the camp soon, but it is not a place I can take you."

"*No!*" Lena has stopped to face me. "You have told me before it is an awful place. I don't want you to go there."

I take her arms gently. "It is only for a short time. A few weeks."

"And what of these women in the camps? What sort of procedures?"

"Sterilization methods that don't involve surgery. That allow women to recover twice as quickly."

"Do these women consent to it?"

It is a question I have asked myself. I know the conditions are even worse in the camps than in the ghetto. I have heard the guards joke about them, and my father refer to the women as "subjects."

"I didn't think so," she says, reading my vacant expression. "What a ridiculous idea! Suddenly a Jewish woman is also an animal that can be subjected to tests for research purposes? Who but Himmler would have thought of that?"

"I will make sure they agree before such procedures are performed."

Lena is independent and strong, yet fragile when it comes to the subject of women and babies—especially now, in her condition. Thankfully she has not had to witness the thinning limbs of the children within the ghetto.

"Did you know that her father had been a member of the Catholic Centre Party?" Father said several days after I had introduced him to Lena. We had already been seeing each other for months, but he did not know this.

"No," I said.

"Don't you think that it is strange she hasn't mentioned it to you?"

"No, Father. There are other topics more interesting than politics."
I remembered Lena's expression when I had boasted of my father. She
had been unimpressed, rather amused.

"Why would you search her records?" I asked him.

"You know why. I hold an important position."

My father had come to the Führer's notice for his work in research-
ing diseases, and more recently had been promoted to SS *Gruppenführer*.
Even I have to admit he is successful on so many levels.

"I have to do checks on everyone," he told me.

I mentioned this to Lena later that evening.

"What now?" she asked, challenging.

"What do you mean?"

"I suppose that it is over between us. I suppose you want to end it."

"No!" I said, shocked. "Why would I want that when I am in love
with you?" It was the first time I had declared my feelings for her.

She smiled, looked down, like she always did when she was thinking, and our relationship was sealed that day, thanks to my father.

"Trust you to declare your love as if it were there all along, as if I
should have known it!" she said, though it was clear from the redness
of her face that she was pleased.

The fact that her suitability had been questioned seemed to drive
us closer together, and I soon learned, and kept secret, that her father
had attempted to convince other members of the Centre Party to vote
against changes to the Constitution of the German Reich—changes
that were proposed by Hitler's government in 1933—allowing Hitler
to enact laws without parliamentary consent. Lena's father's attempts
at opposition failed, and his party supported the changes. This support
for a new parliamentary act would ultimately assist Hitler in obtaining
unlimited political power.

For reasons of self-preservation, and the threat of reprisals, Lena's
parents eventually felt forced to align themselves publicly with Hitler
and his party. My father had put my father-in-law's earlier alignment

to being disillusioned, and manipulated by church leaders. Though unbeknown to my father, Lena's parents have privately kept their Catholic faith.

Of course, that was not the end to differences. I have had to counsel Lena on what she says in front of my father.

At a dinner party held shortly after our engagement, Lena overheard my father and colleagues discussing the removal from their jobs of certain scientists and professors who had been too outspoken about certain Nazi practices. Lena then commented—perhaps it was the wine that brought out some truth—that "dumbing down the masses" was important for the party's success. To which there was an awkward pause.

"Until solutions can be implemented by the powers of the state, ignorance is sometimes a good thing," Father replied coolly before changing the subject.

After the dinner party, I chastised her and she stormed out, secluding herself at the house of a friend and refusing to meet me at the door, until I found myself writing her long letters of apology, begging for her to come back to me.

"All right," Lena said, finally agreeing to speak with me. "I will be a good Nazi wife if that means staying with you. Besides, I have learnt something about you. You are not so wooden after all. You have some passion hidden very deep down that your father has kept suppressed." She put her hand on my chest. "Perhaps I can bring more of that out of you."

We married not long after this. My father was unable to attend the wedding, having been called away at the last minute to travel to a secret location for political talks. The following year, war broke out, and after completing my first commission as a military physician, Lena gave up her teaching career to join me in Poland.

The sun breaks through the clouds, streaking color across a city that struggles to find reasons to meet the day. We pass the remains of a synagogue that has been gutted by fire.

It is a long way back to the apartment, but Lena says she doesn't mind. She believes our walks might halt the phantom pains she's been having. I explain to her that this is her body simulating the feelings of labor, giving her a glimpse of what is to come.

"Thank you, Doctor," she says. "Or should I call you something else now? Now that my important doctor husband has suddenly grown two inches taller."

"You may refer to me as SS *Hauptsturmführer* Gerhardt, no less," I say, making myself sound falsely pompous. Though, there is no denying, the promotion has given me the pleasure in knowing that life will be good for us.

CHAPTER SIX
MATILDA

The train ride to wherever is tedious, and the carriage bounces and jolts across the dark places of Romania as we head toward Germany. I shift and sigh loudly to show that I'm bored, looking out into the blackness through the glass in the rattling doors, and then rolling my eyes back from the window and into the dimly lit train instead. The lights above us on the ceiling make the faces of the other passengers appear ghostly white and cast large shadows into the corners of the booths. People stare at me as if I am something they haven't seen before. I stare back until they look away. I have been on a train before, to visit Tata's brother in Poland, though I do not know the name of the town. That time the journey was exciting, because my whole family was there. Dragos kept jumping onto the seat as Theo and I watched and laughed. Now I am on a train headed to a hotel somewhere in the north, traveling with a soldier in a colored uniform and a strange woman with a square face.

We arrive at a station late at night where another soldier is waiting for us. He is wearing a darker uniform and a hat, and he doesn't look at my face. It is as if I am invisible. The first officer will return on the train, and the new one will take the woman and me to a hotel. We climb into another car. It isn't as nice as the first one that carried me away from my home. This one smells of oiled hair, and the cold wind sneaks in around my feet. The soldier leaves us at the door of the hotel and says he will be back in the morning.

I have never stayed in a hotel before. A boy walks around from behind the front counter and stretches out his hand toward my case. I hold tight to the handle, and the boy pulls back his hand and looks at the square-faced lady.

"She can carry her own," says the woman and hands the boy her suitcase. We follow him upstairs to the first floor. Inside the room are two beds, a desk, a chair, and lamps on the walls. I am told there is a bath and a toilet at the end of the hall. The woman pays the boy after he sets down her luggage and gives him an order for food. She does this without looking at him. She is familiar with this place.

It has been many hours since I have eaten, and despite the fact that I am thinking of Mama's stew, which suddenly makes me sad and hungry, I am eager to try the food the lady has ordered. When it comes, I have to eat it at the desk.

The woman does not eat hers straight away. She opens her case and takes out several items of clothing and places them on the bed that I'll be sleeping in.

I wipe the last potato dumpling in the thick gravy. I have already eaten the slices of pork and now there is apple, wrapped in pastry and rolled in powdered sugar.

I don't finish my milk, which does not taste as fresh as the milk at home. My stomach is full, and I feel guilty that I have this food and my brothers don't. At home Dragos and Theo will not have eaten this much between them. But then they are at home in their beds, and I am here with a strange woman. They are the lucky ones.

"You must drink all the milk," the woman says in Romanian, although she does not speak it well.

"You can talk in German," I say. "Tata always spoke to us in both. Tata reads us stories in German."

"You are a growing girl, and you must drink this milk as well to make your bones healthy," she says in German. "Children should drink plenty of milk."

"How would you know?" I say, since I am doubtful she knows anything about us. I don't like this woman who tells me what to do. She is not my mother. The woman speaks without looking at me.

"I have a daughter your age."

This is a surprise to me.

"Where is she?"

"Back in Germany."

"Then why are you here?"

"You ask too many questions for a young girl."

"Theo says that I am the most curious person he knows."

"Who is Theo?"

"My brother."

She is shaking out a long nightgown, and this time she stops to look directly at me. It is the first time she has looked at me for this length of time. She pulls her lips together and returns to her task.

"I see. Then he is probably correct in what he says."

"Why are you here and not with your daughter?"

She stops at her task again, puts one hand on one hip, and watches me with large brown cow eyes. They are the only pretty things about her.

"I think you have to learn to stop being so nosy. Now, you must change into your nightwear. I have laid it on your bed."

I examine the piece of clothing. It is fine and white and gathered at the front. It is very pretty and not like the one I have in my suitcase, made of fabric that has yellowed in places, passed down from Catarina.

"I don't need it. I have my own."

"You are very willful. Unfortunately, such a temperament won't do. I suggest you change your attitude before you arrive at the Center. You will not find your new supervisor tolerant of such behavior . . . but that is not my concern. You are not my problem after tomorrow."

I suspect this woman does not care at all for her daughter—that she stays here all the time so she can be paid to watch the young girls they steal.

Later in bed, after I have changed into Catarina's old nightgown (I have left the other one at the bottom of the bed), I watch the woman as she writes at the desk.

"Why aren't you sleeping?"

"I will sleep later," she says.

"What is your name?"

"It doesn't matter what my name is."

She gets up to switch off the lamp above my bed and then walks back to her desk. She goes back to not looking at me.

I turn and face the wall beside my bed, tracing my finger along the floral pattern of the blue-and-gold wallpaper. I am feeling very sleepy since I was unable to sleep on the long train ride. With the tip of my finger I write words in German on the wall: *drache, hexe, dämon* . . . dragon, witch, demon. I think of Theo then. He would think of even better words.

"My daughter is nine, the same age as you." The woman's voice has pierced the silence, bursting through the yellow air. "I have not seen her in a year now. Not since I was hired by the Germans to care for other girls who aren't my daughter. She lives with my brother and his family."

I do not know how to respond. I cannot find any words that would be suitable. I don't know whether to feel sorry for her. But suddenly I am thinking of the daughter and wondering if she is missing her mother. Wondering if we are feeling the same. I wish the woman had brought her daughter with her so there was someone else for company.

"Will you see her when we get to Germany?"

"No. I have to return straight away."

We are on another train at daybreak and will soon be at my new home, says Square-Face. I ask her what it is like. She says she doesn't know, but that it is an excellent German center for Aryan children, and these "excellent centers" are being built across Europe. She tells me the place she used to take the children to was a nice house beside a lake, but that this center is somewhere else: just inside Germany, near a small town that does not have any creeks. Already it is sounding dull, but I think that it might not be so far away from my family, and they might bring me back sometimes. When I say this, she looks out the window and pretends not to hear me.

Now, in daylight, I can see that there are lots of houses, farms, and trucks outside. It is much busier here than in the town near my house. I hate the sound of the train.

It was dark for most of the first train journey and is raining for this one. It is not long before the train slows to a stop, but we are not at a station. Then it begins to go backward. And then it stops again. The soldier sitting across the aisle informs us that the driver has left the train to check something ahead on the tracks. He thinks there might be something blocking the train.

As the minutes pass, there are murmurings within the train. Someone is lying on the track up ahead, planning to kill themselves, though no one knows for certain.

Some small children stand beside the track below my window. They have appeared out of thin air, like fairies. They wave and I wave back. They are still in their nightgowns, and their feet are filthy from running through fresh mud. I wish I were outside running in mud, feeling it squeeze between my toes and feeling the rain on my face, away from the smells of strangers and their strange perfumes.

My watcher is no longer with me. She is at the end of the aisle, speaking to the ticket man to find out more information. "We can't be late," she tells him. The soldier is suddenly missing, also; perhaps he has gone to see what can be done. I open the window.

"Hello," I call down to the children.

"Hello," says the smallest one, the one with the dirtiest face. "Are you a princess?"

"Yes," I say. "I have had to leave my castle because an evil witch has stolen me." I run my hand down my new dress: a dirty-green pinafore with a bright-white shirt underneath. It is an alien fabric, stiff and uncomfortably tight.

The children look at one another, their mouths open. They were not expecting to meet a princess, much less one who had been stolen from a castle.

I turn to see if Square-Face is coming, but she is now out of view. I am alone. There is no one watching me, and I think this is a sign. It takes me only four steps to get to the door of the train carriage, and I jump from the doorway onto the track. The children beside me stare in awe. They were not expecting the princess to escape.

"Can you help me?" I ask. "Can you take me to your house so that your parents can return me to the castle?"

"Yes," says the oldest of the three, who is still younger than me. "This way."

I follow him away from the train. His younger siblings are behind me. Beyond them I can see what has stopped the train. A man lies in several pieces across the track. The small children have seen this, too, but they are not surprised.

"What has happened?"

"People come here to kill themselves. They have no food. Quickly! This way!"

We run from the train, through long grasses toward a clump of trees. "Our village is behind there."

"Stop!" yells a man from behind us, and I can hear Square-Face calling my name.

I do not slow down, but the older boy turns and stops, and I am then forced to do the same.

One of the train guards stands halfway in the space between the train and me. I cannot believe how far we got. In one arm he holds the smallest girl, who is no longer smiling. In his other hand he holds a gun.

My feet are suddenly frozen to the ground.

"Come here!"

It is several seconds before I find my voice.

"What if I don't?"

"I will kill her." I hear a click from the gun, and he puts the tip against her temple. The little girl has no expression on her face; her eyes are unblinking, fixed on mine.

Behind him stands Square-Face, her face the same color as the light-gray sky.

I walk slowly back toward the guard. When I reach him, he puts the girl down and grabs my arm, his fingers digging deep into my flesh as he drags me back to the train. I squeeze my lips together so as not to cry out. So that he doesn't know he is hurting me. I see that there are two men with shovels scraping the remains of the victim from the track. And before I realize what I am about to do, I vomit on the officer's shiny shoes. There is the taste of sugared apple in my mouth, but tarnished now with stomach juice.

"Get her away from me!" says the guard to my caretaker. "Take her back to the seat and keep your eye on her. I will report you for your carelessness."

Square-Face escorts me back to the same seat. I am thinking of the man who killed himself, wondering if he has any children or a wife or a mother. I look out the window. The small children, my would-be rescuers, are nowhere to be seen, but they are hiding somewhere, watching me. I sense this and wave at the empty field.

"You foolish girl," says Square-Face. This is not said in anger but in disbelief, with a shaking of the head.

"Will you get in trouble?"

"I might be killed," she says uncaringly, like Catarina, and I think of Square-Face's daughter. Another one, like me, without a mother. "But more than likely they will demote me temporarily and suspend my pay. You will have to learn to run faster if you want to escape."

I look at her, but she is not looking back. She is looking at something outside the window. Perhaps she can see the children hiding. Did she know that I might try to escape? I wonder. Could it be that she turned her back on purpose?

I think about the man on the tracks—or what's left of him, because he is no longer a man.

"Do they know who he is?"

"He was no one, like everyone else in this godforsaken place. It was his way to escape."

Later, during the journey, we pass foreign towns filled with beautiful buildings that look like castles. There are lots of steeples and archways.

When we finally leave the train, my caretaker and the soldier walk on either side of me to a car that is waiting. When I climb in, Square-Face shuts the door behind me. I am disappointed that I have to travel alone with the man.

"Good luck," says Square-Face, faintly, through the glass between us. She turns back toward the station in her dowdy gray skirt and jacket, her face full of dung.

CHAPTER SEVEN
WILLEM

The woman sitting in front of me asks for a drink of water. She is dying, slowly, of uterine cancer, and there is little I can do for her beyond what I have already done: injecting morphine to help with the pain.

Her children sit patiently and quietly beside her while she sips at the water I have brought. She hands back the glass, and I see that the simple act of holding up her arm is nearly too great. I offer the two small boys a piece of chocolate, which they eagerly take. I offer the woman some, also, but she shakes her head. She is too ill to care for her children anymore. Her husband died of diphtheria six months earlier. Without the influence of her husband, a former member of the Judenrat, she was forced to leave her house—which has utilities better than most—and live in a run-down apartment on the other side of the ghetto. After today, she will no longer have access to my services, as I make preparations to leave the ghetto. I have been treating her without Hermann Manz's knowledge. Not that this treatment would continue for much longer anyway. She has perhaps weeks left to live and now requires full-time care.

"Frau Markstein, as soon as you take your boys home, you will have to admit yourself to the medical center," I say. "I have written a note to the doctor there. I will make sure they give you a clean bed and something for the pain."

I hold out the piece of paper, but she does not lift her eyes or extend her hand to take it. I fold and place it in the top pocket of her coat. Her spirit is already dead.

"Do you have anyone you can leave the children with . . . while in the hospital?"

She shakes her head.

"The boys . . ." she says but doesn't finish. She doesn't need to.

It is a situation I have seen before. Twice I have made inquiries, on behalf of those single mothers who are no longer able to care for their children. But I have learned something about human nature here: survival outweighs charity. The boys will be left to their own devices. Though there are fewer children in the ghetto since the mass deportation, more keep arriving, many of them orphaned. These two boys were once protected from deportation by their father's position. As I have witnessed over the time here, deportation, for even those with station, is merely delayed.

I retrieve two boiled eggs from my medical bag and place these in the woman's hand, which rests as a deadweight on her knee. Lena often gives me extra food to bring in to work, though she knows that I am not the one in need. Anna Markstein surveys the eggs as if they are something foreign or unrecognizable. When she finally looks up with weary, vacant eyes, I see that the idea of food is little comfort.

"I will get you some food coupons for the children," I say. "I will have them sent down to you. The boys will have extra rations for several weeks. By that time someone will likely have taken them in to raise."

She is still looking at me. The gaze between us is heavy, weighed down by the false hope I have just offered. What I have said is unlikely.

The apartment will be given to someone else, and the boys evicted to live on the street.

"Doctor, I want you to know that everything I had before . . . it is as if it didn't exist. And when I am gone it will be as if I didn't exist either. But the strange thing is that I no longer care. The pain is all I think about now, and to have it gone means more than anything."

It is a curious thing that chronic and acute pain can produce one of life's greatest anomalies. The sufferer comes to appreciate death.

"The pain can be addressed. I have made sure that enough medicine is available to you."

Her eyes wander around the office before resting on a photograph on my desk, of Lena and me, our closeness and contentment evident in our smiles. I usually keep it in a drawer, and I silently scold myself for this mistake. It does not help to remind patients that life is normal for some.

"Will you be all right to walk home from here?" I ask, to distract her quickly. "I can call a guard to help you."

She smiles weakly and shakes her head.

"If I fall in the street, he will probably leave me there anyway."

I start to say that I will make sure this doesn't happen, but she interjects.

"I am fine to walk home. The pain is dulled. I am weary only."

She stands to leave, and I hurry ahead to open the door for her.

"Good day, Anna."

She stops and turns to stretch out her hand, which I hold on to longer than normal, before something inside me tells me that this is not what I should do. To not show the kind of compassion that offers even the faintest hope.

"While I see nothing good in most of the people here, there is something I see in you. Perhaps it is goodness. I am not sure . . ." She touches her forehead and closes her eyes briefly. I step back to end our meeting, but even in her feeble state she seems determined to continue.

"But it is something else that the others don't have. Perhaps it is that you somehow don't fit in a place like this, that you remind me of what people were like before I came here."

I nod. There is little to say at this point that might console her. Often patients feel gratitude, and I am forced to hear words that I do not want to hear. I am what I am, and the words of my patients must be left behind in the surgery where they belong.

I watch her leave, and her boys—with their yellow eyes and swollen bellies—follow. It is doubtful I will ever see any of them again.

CHAPTER EIGHT
MATILDA

It is a short, jiggling drive along cobbled streets, and then we are out of the city. I want to go back to the city where there are lots of interesting people and cars and trams. It is disappointing that we are heading through places that have only cattle and barns and a factory and fields, and the houses become too few the farther we drive until there is nothing but a small town with houses built way up hills, and lonely lanes and trucks that sit empty on the side of the road.

The car turns toward a tall, lonely white house with a roof that points toward the dark sky, at the end of a long driveway. I wonder if we are the only living things. There are no voices, no cyclists, no people walking on the roads. My chest begins to jump through the front of my dress, which is stained after the reappearance of my dinner from the night before. The car stops at iron gates at the front that are guarded, and there is barbed wire on top of the fences that trap the house.

We are let through because the driver has waved at the guard, and then the car stops only yards from the front door. I suddenly don't want to leave the car. I don't like it here. The driver, who also wears a guard's uniform, opens the car door.

"Out!" says the driver. But I don't move. The guard who is standing at the front door to the house comes over to the car.

"Out!" he says, too. But I look the other way. I feel a hand close around my wrist, and then I am being dragged from the car. I kick the arm of the driver, who lets go with a shout. He moves to hit me, but the guard from the doorway says to stop. He leans his head into the car.

"If you don't get out, we will feed you to the lions at the zoo."

"What zoo?"

The guard says, "She is a brazen one, yes?" He laughs, but the driver I kicked is not laughing.

"Now, don't be a naughty little girl," says the guard. "You *do not* want to get on Frau Haus's bad side."

The lions didn't scare me, but the mention of an unknown person does.

I think about this. Something tells me he is making this up, but I am suddenly hungry since I have emptied out my dinner and had nothing more on the train.

"Is there food here?"

"Of course."

I slide out and stand up as tall as I can, but the guard is twice my height.

No one offers to carry my case here. The doorway guard, whom I follow, does not hold the door open for me. The driver leaves in the car without saying good-bye.

The officer who spoke to Catarina said the house was in a delightful location, but there is nothing nice about it. There is more dirt than grass; the forests behind it look straggly and barren. There is no lavender growing wild on the hills. The ground is patterned with car wheels, and it feels colder here than at home. Catarina said that the new winter would freeze hell.

The long hallway to the back of the house leads off to several rooms until we are at the last room, beside a kitchen. The guard knocks on the door.

"Enter," says a woman from inside.

We do, and I see a woman sitting at a desk littered with files and papers. A draft from the open door swirls the papers on the desk, and the woman has to catch them, but she can still write with one hand while she does this. She looks up briefly and then back down at her paperwork.

"Sit down," she says to the paperwork. "I will be with you in a minute."

The guard leaves, shutting the door as he goes. There is a soft couch and a wooden chair in the room. I am not sure which one to sit on, so I choose the soft couch, which is farthest from the desk.

"On that one," she says in German, pointing without raising her eyes. I move to the wooden chair in front of the desk.

It is so silent that my breathing sounds very loud. I hold my breath until I can't do it anymore.

"Stand up!" says the woman harshly, and this makes me jump. She is watching me now, peering at my face, her eyes rolling down my plaits and then to my legs. I lean from one foot to the next, the watching making my body twitch.

"I have been told that you tried to escape. If you attempt it here, the guards will not catch you. They will simply shoot."

Shoot. It is simply a threat that adults make. No one will shoot me, I do not think, otherwise they will be put in prison. Otherwise, why bring me here? The smell from the kitchen is making my mouth water. If I am good and quiet, then perhaps I will be given food soon.

A woman in a nurse's uniform has entered the room. She is carrying a writing pad and a pencil. A sewing measure hangs around her neck. "Is this the one from the east?"

"Yes."

"Any good?"

"Better than the last one we sent away. But not by much. Can you take the measurements?"

"Matilda . . . is that your name?"

I nod.

"What do you think, Nurse? Should she keep it?"

"It is German enough."

What do they mean, "keep it"? Who would they give it away to?

"Your parents both spoke German—is that correct?"

"Yes."

"Yes, Frau Haus," says Nurse.

"Your father was from Germany, yes?"

"Yes, Frau Haus."

"And your mother? Gypsy?"

Nurse is smiling at her pencil.

"No, Frau Haus. She is Romanian."

I don't know about my mother. Tata used to call her a gypsy as a joke, and sometimes she liked it and other times she didn't.

"Never mind. Apparently she has some German blood, too."

From on top of Frau Haus's desk, Nurse picks up a long metal ruler with a bar at the end and a bar across the middle that slides up and down. She moves the bar up and down as she measures the distance from the top of my forehead to my nose and then to my chin, then the distance between my eyes. She takes the sewing measure from around her neck to measure the width of my head. I want to laugh at this. Dragos would find this very funny. But this is not a room for laughs. I keep my face still because theirs are so severe.

Then the distance from shoulder to elbow, and knee to ankle. Then across my shoulder, then from the top of my spine to my tailbone.

Frau Haus writes down all the measurements. The nurse makes some observations that are quite strange, and again Frau Haus writes these down.

"Fine white hairs on limbs."

"Skin is unflawed, pale olive."

"Hair, yellow blonde."

"Eyes are . . . blue . . . pale aqua . . . detect a slight blemish near the centers."

"Hips very narrow."

"Hmm," says the older lady, but the nurse continues.

"Small for age, sinewy."

"She passes," says Frau, "but not by much."

"What have I passed?" I ask.

"A special test to see how big your meals will be," says Frau.

The other one laughs into her hand. It is a private joke, like the ones I sometimes share with my brothers.

"I understand that you can speak German—is this correct?" Frau turns to the other woman. "Extraordinary for a Gypsy. That will be helpful at least."

"I'm not a Gypsy," I say.

Gypsies get burned to death.

"Do you speak German, Gypsy?" asks Frau, and Nurse laughs behind her hand again.

"Not very well," I say in a mixture of German and Romanian.

"Not very well, Frau Haus," corrects the nurse.

"So what German do you speak?"

I pretend that I don't understand the question she has asked in German. In Romanian, I ask her to repeat it. When she asks again, I say some words in German, mispronounced on purpose.

"That's odd. You answered several questions I asked in German, and now you can't answer anything. I've heard that you speak it very well." She looks at a piece of paper in front of her.

I do not say anything. Again I pretend that I don't understand.

Frau stares at me silently. She has hatred in her bones like the German child thief, Herr Lehmann.

"Take her to the shower; then show her to a room."

I am led up some stairs that creak and grind. I am already looking at possible escape routes and decide the stairs could be a problem, that people will hear me. We enter a room with a bath and a shower and small basin and toilet. There is just enough room for two.

"Take your clothes off," says Nurse, pulling at my clothes. She has a tight bun pulled to the back of her neck, a long narrow nose, and a chin that juts too far forward. There are deep lines down the sides of her cheeks. Her eyes are blue with patches of brown, like bird droppings.

"You will need to leave first," I say in German, forgetting that I am pretending I don't speak German.

"What did you say?"

"I'm not getting undressed in front of you." This time louder, in Romanian.

I do not see the slap coming. It is done with such force that it jolts my head sideways and steals from me a loud breath. I touch the side of my face. I am deciding whether to slap her back, but her eyes are inflamed and her hand is raised to strike again.

"You want to do that again? Do you, really? How dare you, you little hellcat! You have no idea who you're dealing with."

"Hure," I say. It is a hateful German word toward women, but I do not know exactly what it means.

She grabs my shoulders and shakes me hard, and I scratch her neck with jagged nails.

She slaps me again, and I fall back into the bath. This time it hurts.

"You have a lot to learn."

She puts out her hand to help me up, but I ignore it.

I get up slowly by myself. My side hurts from where I hit the edge of the bath. Frau Haus stands in the doorway.

"What is going on?"

"She did this to me!"

Frau looks at the marks on Nurse's neck, then bends over me. "Get up!" she shouts in my face. She turns to Nurse. "You may have bruised her. Always the back or the skull, where the marks can't be seen. I have told you before!"

"What was I to do? She came at me like a wild animal!"

"Don't ever do that to a superior again—do you understand?" Frau says to me. She does not raise her hand, but there is something in her tone that suggests there are worse things to be concerned with than a slap from Nurse. Then I remember what the guard said, and I believe that Frau could be my enemy here.

"Look in the mirror!" She turns my head forcibly toward my reflection.

There are finger marks on my cheek. Nurse has left the bathroom.

"Hopefully that will not have to occur again, because the new commander will not like to see anyone marked. Marked ones are sent elsewhere. If you value your life, you will not do anything to incite punishment. Now, clothes off and get in the shower." But she is already pulling at my clothes.

"I need to use the toilet."

"After the shower."

I don't think I can wait that long, but she is pulling my dress over my head and pushing me toward the shower.

Catarina said that I am not to let anyone look at my naked body. I try to cover my nakedness with my hands. Lukewarm water drizzles down on some but not all of me, and my teeth chatter. I cannot hold my bladder any longer, and urine runs down my leg and into the water hole. I think perhaps Frau hasn't seen, but she has and she tells me that it is disgusting what I have done. I feel ashamed that she has seen and angry that I am being watched.

I have never had a shower before, and I hate that water falls on my face. Next time I will ask if I can use the bath instead. Once I am finished, I wrap a towel around me and follow Frau to a room at the end of the hall.

"Now get changed into your nightwear," she says, pointing to my suitcase.

When I open the suitcase, I discover that none of my old clothes are there. Square-Face must have taken them when I was in the bathroom at the hotel. I no longer have the nightwear that carries the smells from home.

"Where are my clothes?" I ask in Romanian.

The woman leaves the room, and I hear her turn the key in the lock on the outside of the door. I check the distance from the window to the ground. There are no window ledges to climb onto, but perhaps I can tie sheets and clothes together. Outside there is a barbed fence and the woods beyond it. There is nothing in the room except a bed.

It is dark by the time the door is unlocked by a girl who looks the same age as Theo. She is beautiful. She has long, muscled legs, and her hair is fair and pulled back from her face with a silver-colored tie.

"Follow me," she says. Her tone is rude.

I follow her toward the smells of cooking. My stomach rumbles.

"What is your name?" I ask her in German.

"None of your business," she says.

In the kitchen there is a dining table laden with bread and bowls of soup, beans, and potatoes. Several children sit around the table. I am about to take a seat when the girl pushes me toward a door at the other side of the kitchen.

"Not there! Follow me!"

She opens the door into darkness, and the wind is so strong it pushes us back toward the house. Once we are outside, the door slams in the wind. The girl carries a torch to light our way across the back garden. The ground is cold on my bare feet. Wind whips under my nightgown, which becomes full of air like a balloon, and I fear that I might float up into the sky. I want to hold on to the girl in case this happens, but she is walking fast ahead. I follow her farther away from the house. I follow the light from the torch until we reach a small unpainted house.

The girl opens the door, but she does not step in.

"Inside," she orders.

"No," I say.

"If you don't, Frau Haus will beat you to death with a shovel."

I am shocked by the viciousness of the words coming from such a pretty face. But I still don't move. Half her face is illuminated by the lights from the house. The other half is in complete darkness. She looks like a monster now, no longer beautiful.

"Inside is a plate of food and a warm bed. There is a light beside the bed. You can turn it on when you get in."

"Why am I here?"

"It is where all the new children spend their first night. It is a very special room in which to think about your new life ahead."

The wind tears a hole through my back, and I imagine a warm bed with covers, soft with duck feathers.

"Hurry up. It's cold out here." She is wearing a short coat. I have only my nightgown. I don't move inside the doorway, a black opening into nothing.

"I was only kidding about Frau Haus. It was just a joke. In the morning I will come and get you, and you can play with the other children in the sun. Would you like that?" Her voice has become softer, kinder.

"Yes," I say, though there has not been any sun for days.

"Very well," she says in her kind voice. "Be a good girl. Here, I will shine the flashlight in so you can see where you are going."

"Do you mean it? Will you come back?"

"Of course! What am I? A liar?"

The light shows a piece of floor just inside the door. I imagine the bed and the food and the light are on the far side of the house.

She shines the torch on her face briefly to show that she is smiling. She is beautiful again. Then she shines it back through the doorway.

I step into the house and stop. I cannot smell any food. It is very dark, and I cannot see where I am walking. I am about to turn around again, but her hand shoves me in the back, so hard that I fall forward onto the floor.

She slams the door behind me, and I hear the bolt in the lock. I hit at the door and shout at her and call her names, but she is gone and I am alone. There is no sound except the howling wind. I am afraid to walk because I don't know what I am walking into. There is no light and no windows. I listen to sounds like heavy breathing, perhaps coming from inside this house, but it is just the wind. I crouch down and crawl around slowly, feeling my way across the floor. My hands find only scratchy, loose dirt on a rough, hard floor, until I reach a corner where they touch a mattress and a blanket. The house, I think, is the size of a small room.

I crawl under the blanket and pull it over my face. It is not big enough to keep my feet warm, which might fall off during the night. This upsets me because I need my feet to escape.

The wind is too noisy for sleeping. My brothers would say that it is not the wind; it is the moaning of spirits searching for Gypsy souls to burn. I pray that there is no Gypsy blood inside me, and then I weep into the darkness, where no one can see my tears, and hope the death spirits don't come to take my soul.

NOVEMBER

CHAPTER NINE
ELSI

"Mama," I plead. "Please . . . no." She is about to cut off all my hair.

"You have to trust me."

"Why? Because someone referred to me?"

"Elsi," she says quietly, crouching beside my chair. "There are men here who are not like ordinary men. They do not think like your father and the people you grew up with. They use power to hang our basic necessities in front of our faces and use them as bribes." She stands again and starts cutting my hair, and I wonder what she had to endure so that Leah survived the deportations. Mama has given up so much since she came to the ghetto—not just possessions but also a sense of pride.

She grew distant in the weeks of her pregnancy and worse after the night of the surgery. There have been times when she is so distant, it seems she is barely in the room with us. I think that this place can strip a person of human traits. It can make one desire nothing and hope for even less. I believe it has changed my mother this way, so much so that she finds it hard to live within her own skin. Sometimes I believe that she survives only in order to function for Leah and me. When I try to hold her, or talk, she pulls away as if she is not worthy of holding. Leah has noticed this, too, and I have had to spend more time with my sister to compensate for Mama's distance.

Before the ghetto, we used to have nice things. Mama used to wear fine dresses and hats and new shoes when we strolled into town, hand in hand, to buy ice creams—before I became too old to hold Mama's hand. She walked proudly, head high—not arrogantly, more that she was in control of a life she had planned, was still planning at that time. Before she was no longer allowed to plan.

Marta once said it was jealousy that had driven people to hate the Jews. She said that some of my friends thought our house was much better than everyone else's, and that we had too much money and too many fine things, and that we were greedy. We had a fight, Marta and I, because I believed she thought that, too. But she had cried and apologized and promised me that she did not. I didn't believe Marta, and I left her feeling resentful.

If they could see our apartment now, Marta and my other friends would no longer know jealousy. If they could see what we live in. If they could see the change in Mama. If they could stand in our shoes, imprisoned behind tall barbed-wire fences.

It was early in the morning when fists pounded on the front door of our house outside the ghetto. Papa was not home at the time. The knocking was a familiar sound. We had heard it before, during the raids by German police and by those Jews who helped the Germans. We had already endured two of these raids, and they took any precious items they could find. I knew the boy who assisted the police. We had been at school together. He smiled at me like he had at school, as if nothing had changed. Mama said later that she was curious how quickly these Jewish recruits had coated themselves with German pride to betray their former friends.

As we were squashing our pasts into suitcases, Papa arrived and argued with the men to give us more time. But to no avail. The men in their dull-green uniforms did not want to listen; their ears were blocked with indifference.

I helped pack food and bedding into a crate, and Papa brought a cart from the furniture store so we could carry our chairs as well. Then the men returned. They had knocked on several other doors in the meantime. They told us to hurry.

So rushed was she, Mama did not think to turn off the gas in the kitchen. One night after we had been in the ghetto for several weeks, she woke me in the night. She was panicking. Had someone heard the whistling and turned the gas off? Had the kettle burned down? She eventually calmed down, and I hoped that the house had burned to the ground so that Germans couldn't live in it.

Then after we were forced from our house, there was a line of Jews as we were herded like farm animals, toward the poorer end of the city. The poorest Poles living there were told to leave their homes, to vacate for the Jews. I do not know where they went to live. We followed a long stream of yellow stars along the roads. People carried as much as they could. Mothers cradled babies and held hands with the older children, while fathers carried small children under one arm, and bedding or furniture under the other. The elderly hobbled along; some were helped, some not.

"Will there be a piano there?" I asked. "Will there be a school? Will I have my own room?"

"I don't know," Mama said just once to all my questions.

As we walked down the street, many non-Jews watched from the footpaths: some stony-faced, some waving—including Marta. She called to me, and I rushed to hug her and found that she was crying.

"I'm so sorry we fought," she said.

"It doesn't matter," I said. "We will always be friends."

Marta's mother was there. She handed Mama a large dish of stew.

"Thank you, Petra," said Mama.

"Maybe when the war is over, everything will go back to normal," said Petra, "and we will share many more dinners again."

Once we had parted, I heard Papa say to Mama, "I wonder how much she knew. I wonder how much our friends have kept from us."

I have since thought about that comment, after the reality of our circumstances finally set in. The idea that friendships are so fickle, so fragile, makes me angry, and I think that if I am ever freed from here, I will not live in Lodz. I will live far away and never see Marta and my other friends again.

Arriving at the ghetto, we were ushered by guards past apartment buildings that were gray and blackened with soot and sadness, and lanes buried beneath a thick spread of mud. Despair seemed to choke these buildings. Leah grew weary, and I carried her piggyback the rest of the way.

There was no key for the door to our new apartment on the second floor. Papa had to shove the door hard, which had swollen in its frame. In the room were three single beds without any bedding, and the smell of mold and damp.

In one corner there was a wood heater that had no wood, and in the kitchen a gas stove that still has no gas.

"Do we have to stay here?" I asked. "Are there any other places?"

Papa's silence gave me my answer. We had no choice in where we lived. We had been assigned this place.

"Where is the toilet?" asked Leah.

But Mama and Papa had lost the will to speak. Leah looked at Mama, waiting. She is like that. She will not ask something twice but will stay close to that person until they can bear it no longer, until they eventually give her an answer. But Mama refused to reply, and Leah began to cry. It was perhaps because of the strange smells in the apartment and the pained look on Mama's face.

"What is wrong?" Papa asked Leah finally, failing in his attempt to sound good-humored. "This is all right for now. It is only for a short time until the governments can work matters out." Then, leaning in to speak a bit softer, "Until the rest of the world puts Germany in a corner where it belongs."

Mama went straight to the window to watch the streets below, crowded with people waiting to be assigned apartments by Jewish officials. One of the officials followed us in shortly afterward. Mama was the only one who didn't face him. She refused to turn around. The man handed Papa some coupons and explained that they were to be used to acquire food, but if we wanted more than the amounts allowed, my parents would need to find suitable employment within the ghetto. He said that Papa should report to the Judenrat in the next couple of days if he wished to work at the labor camps, from which he would be able to send home money to his family in exchange for ghetto currency.

After the official left, Mama told Papa that he was not to go.

"I may have no choice."

"This place is disgusting," I said, only fueling the anguish that we felt. "Why are we here, and why can't we live back at our other house? What is the point of this move?"

"Because the Germans don't know where to put us while they are fighting their war, since they think we are the cause of their problems."

"Will they send us to another country?" The thing that worried me at the time—before I had worked it all out—was that I might never see my friends again.

"We can hope."

"Don't say that, Mama! This is only temporary. You said that. Papa said that!"

"Then we lied!" said Mama.

"We will be all right," said Papa. "We didn't lie. I will find a job, and we will find somewhere else to live."

"Oh, stop it, Victor!" said my mother, unnaturally shrill, in a voice that I had not heard her use before. "Why can't you see that this is where it ends for us? Why don't you just face it . . . we have lost everything! We will never get our life back."

"Hannah . . ." said Papa.

Her veneer of reserve had cracked, and Papa couldn't find the words to change her line of thinking. He knew her too well. He also knew the truth, deep down. He had known, ever since that time in the Krolewskis' basement, that life was only going to get harder.

Leah continued to cry, and Mama could not move herself away from the window. She was scanning the faces of the people. I found out later that she was deciding who she thought was hopeful and who was not.

I rushed to Leah's side. "Don't worry," I said, picking her up. "Mama is just having a spell." This was Papa's expression when someone changed their mood.

Mama later said that she was ashamed of her outburst, and that it was something she had needed to release. Something she had been holding on to for weeks.

"So you think my hair will make me too ugly for the ghetto men . . ."

"It is because of the lice, as well as the men," says Mama. "The rashes on your head from scratching are getting worse."

We had left Leah in the apartment while we went to collect our coupons, but I was not prepared for the ambush by Mama and Lilli's scissors.

"You could never be ugly," says Lilli, who is sitting on her couch, watching us. Her house is much nicer than ours, and she always has more food. "You have your mother's bones and your father's coloring."

"But I want *my* hair."

"I want to get out of here," she says, gesticulating, her voice smoky and rough. "We can't always have what we want." She draws back on a cigarette: a present from Hermann Manz.

I watch with disappointment as the long, fair curls fall on the floor. My father used to ask me where I kept my horse, saying my hair was like Lady Godiva's, and I often acted out the famous story using a broomstick for a horse, galloping around the dinner table. This always made Papa laugh.

"I wish I was still acting," I say.

"You acted?" says Lilli. "I didn't know that about you."

"Yes," I say modestly. "Though not like your famous stage years in Germany." Lilli told us that she worked as an actress once and was paid very well.

Lilli possesses several glamorous photos of herself that she displays on her shelves, in which she poses in beautiful clothes. In one she is looking backward over her bare shoulder, directly into the camera lens, like a film star. She was very popular with German men, which makes it all the more strange that they placed her in the ghetto. I used to believe that she was a spy. Now I think she is just unlucky, like the rest of us, to come from a family of Jews.

"Oh yes," says Mama. "You should have seen my daughter. I was there at a school performance when she stood proudly facing her audience, her long hair trailing behind her, large dangling earrings, lace-up top, bright-red scarf around her head, and sword in one hand. Her class was reenacting a historical piece, and Elsi was Agustina de Aragón standing behind a paper canon defending Spain against the French. She was magnificent!"

"Yes. I imagine she was," says Lilli, eyeing me carefully.

"I enjoyed playing Agustina because she was so brave," I say, trying not to sound too boastful; meekness had been pounded into us behind the barbed wire. "Agustina lost everything, including her son, who died in prison after fighting for her cause."

"It is an image I can never forget," says Mama. "One could almost see the original heroine standing there. Sometimes I love her spirit so much it hurts," she says to Lilli. She is referring to me, not Agustina. And Lilli is watching me still, attentive, aware of things that I am perhaps not.

"Maybe after the war I will take you to Germany, yes?" says Lilli to me.

"Oh no, she is never going to Germany," says Mama.

It is quiet then, except for the clacking of the scissors.

CHAPTER TEN
MATILDA

I have been kept locked in the small house behind the big house. Catarina would not complain about our house in Romania if she lived in here. There is no fire, and the floor is too cold to walk on in the mornings. There is no moss here to fill up the gaps in the wood that let in the night air. I throw the blanket across the space between my mattress and the toilet pot each morning so that my feet don't touch the floor. I do not have a window, but I can see a few things through the narrow gaps of wood. Each morning a boy walks to the small house and takes my pot, which I must pass through a flap he opens from the outside. He empties this, then returns it and bolts the flap again. When I said hello, he replied in badly spoken German that he is not allowed to speak with me.

I was counting the days in my head at first, but now with the end of my spoon, I scratch a line into the wood for every day that I am here. I must stay here as long as I can. I am hoping that Papa has come home and found me gone, and that he is on his way to take me back. I want him to see where they have kept me. I want him to be very cross with Catarina for signing a paper that says I am the property of Germany.

In the mornings a girl—a different one from the one who brought me here—brings a bowl of oats and water, and these are passed through the flap, also. Another of the smaller children comes to collect the empty bowl in the afternoon. She does not talk either.

It is so dark at night. One time I heard something howling; another time I heard something scratching at the wood. I think there are rats that are trying to get in.

Nurse came with a piece of paper and a pencil on the first day. She said that I must write something in German, and each day she comes with a new sheet of paper and takes back the last one. The first time, I returned it blank. But now I draw pictures. The first one was of a dog with a really long tongue, and the next was of a goose laying an egg. Then the next one was a picture of the dog standing upright on his hind legs and cooking the goose on a frying pan. I know they want me to write in German. I will not give them what they want.

"You are your own enemy," says Nurse. "You are making this harder than it needs to be."

I can tell that Nurse hates the task of visiting me here. She does not like to step too far in from the doorway, and she is always in a hurry to leave. Perhaps she is afraid that the small house might trap her, too.

I do not know the person in the reflection of my spoon. It is a girl with wild hair and a very pale face. I would love a bath. Better still, I would love to swim in the creek where my brothers and I used to play, or lie on the grass and let the warm rain wash my face. There is never enough to eat. I wipe up every trace of the thick oat porridge with a piece of bread.

"I'm still hungry," I say to Nurse next time she comes. She leaves and returns with Frau.

"Nurse tells me you are still hungry."

"Yes."

"Yes, Frau Haus."

I do not see it coming: the baton to the side of my head above my ear. I believe that Frau likes to have reasons to punish. The sudden pain is like a burn, and I rush to the other side of the room. When I turn back, the door is already shutting behind her.

If I should die in here, what will Mama say? She will first be angry with me for not speaking German.

The only links I have to the world outside this house are the women who punish me and the children who open the flap in the wall. I put my eye against the gaps I find around the walls. The small children come to play on the swings outside, and several older girls sometimes sit in a circle and talk or jog in a paddock next to the house. Sometimes the older girls sing while they march in the fields. I put my ear against the wall to be close to the sound. They are happy when they sing. The two groups—the small children and the older girls—do not mix together.

Sometimes the children from the swings look toward my house. I have waved at them, but they cannot see me. Nurse is always there and tells them things I cannot hear. I wonder what she has told them about me. One time one of the older girls opened the flap to look at me. I tried to talk to her, but she just pointed at me and whispered to one of the other girls nearby, then broke into laughter. I wonder what it is they find so funny.

Early in the mornings the little children carry buckets with their urine and turds to empty in the outdoor toilet. I cannot see where they live, but I do not think it is in the big house because they walk from a different direction. There is also another small house on the other side of the swings, and I sometimes watch another woman walk in that direction from the kitchen and return from there with bowls of fruit and small sacks that I think carry food. Frau rarely goes outside, except to punish me for something I said.

I am given a German book to read, about the Führer of Germany, but the book remains shut on the floor beside the mattress. I do not want to know about him. I have heard Tata say hateful things against him, and my father is a learned man, says Theo. The next day I put the book in my toilet pot and push it through the flap when the boy comes to open it. I am wondering when I will start my schooling. I am wondering what I am doing here. When I was home, I went to a school. Tata used to say that the school was not smart enough for me, that one day I will go to a university. Mama used to tell him to stop telling me things like that. She did not want me to get silly ideas. Sometimes I tell myself stories out loud, like the ones Tata told me, so that inside my head I am free. Sometimes I make up my own stories.

I do not like to be alone, thinking about my brothers somewhere, in another place where I can no longer go. The freedom to run, pushing each other into the long grass where we would roll on our backs and squint to see the sun through the tall leaves. Our last horse, before it was taken—stolen like I was—how it felt to rub my cheek against its smooth, warm flank, to stroke my hand across its long neck, its stringy mane. These are things I think about, with so much time to think.

Will Dragos go to war, or will he stay to play soccer? Is Theo lying on his bed, his head "stuck in a book," as Mama used to say? Since Tata went to war, no new books have come into the house. Theo will read all the same books over and over again until new books come from Opa. Mama will be last to bed, turning off the lamps, checking the windows.

It is becoming unbearable not to hear others breathe in the night. Sometimes I imagine my brothers breathing nearby. Theo would always play a game before sleep. He would say a word, and I had to find another word that had the same meaning as the first. Then we would play the game in German. Tata used to say that the more words we can think of, the smarter we will become. Tata loves words as much as I do.

The sun is shining on the other side of the world, and I feel the blackness closing in on me again. The room, a hole, too deep to climb out of. My eyes start to flood, and I blink away the tears.

One morning after Tata left to fight, I saw my mother's sad face and puffed-up eyes. When she saw me, she looked away, ashamed.

"It is fine sometimes to show your sad face," I said.

"We are never alone, Tilda," she said. "If the night spirits hear you crying, they will sit at the bottom of your bed and laugh. They follow the ones who are weak. Their souls are the easiest to steal."

I wish someone would tell me what I am doing here. Perhaps the children outside don't know either. Perhaps they are waiting for the commander to come and tell them.

*

I cannot stand it anymore. With the spoon I hit at the wood at the bottom of the flap to split it from the lock so that I can crawl out through the small opening. After several hours, the wood has chipped in places, but it is not enough for it to break. Before Nurse comes with her piece of paper, I put the blanket near the wood I have marked. But Nurse is quick to notice everything, and she removes the blanket and sees the damage. She goes to find Frau.

"You stupid girl!" And Frau is once again raising her baton.

Afterward I lie on the bed, sore—and hateful of everyone, especially Frau, and even my mother. But not my brothers or Tata. Not them. They would hate Frau, too.

Catarina once said that my mouth would get me into trouble. If she were here, she would tell me that I am foolish, that I need to control my temper, to speak to them in German. But my brothers would not tell me that. They would tell me to stab Frau with the end of the spoon. But then my brothers did not get taken.

Later I unbutton my nightgown, and with the reflection of my spoon, I try and see if there are bruises on the backs of my shoulders. I cannot see much, but it hurts when I wrap my arms around my back and press on the skin. Frau is breaking her own rules. I hope the bruises are still there when the commander comes so that I can be sent elsewhere. Anyplace else would not be as bad as this prison.

When Nurse comes in next, she does not look at me. Her eyes stay fixed on the floor as if I am someone who must not be looked at. I feel like an animal that has been trapped in the forest. I know how they must feel, to suddenly have their freedom taken, to no longer have the trees and the air and the space.

My shoulders ache from the bruising.

The nights are even colder. I have one blanket, but it is not enough. A draft comes through the bottom of the walls. My skin feels gritty with dirt. The mattress is stained with filth.

Each time Nurse comes, I ask for something. I want the beatings now. It is contact, at least.

"Can I have more blankets?"

"Can I have something more to eat?"

"Can I see the children?"

"Can I come out?"

But Nurse has stopped telling Frau.

The last time she replies, "You have shown nothing but insolence. Only when you can conform to the rules can you come out. However, Frau Haus is losing patience. Matilda, help yourself. Do what Frau wants. She is thinking of getting rid of you even before the new commander arrives. He will never even know you were here."

I do not think this is a bad thing. It is what I want. To go elsewhere. She seems to know that this is what I am thinking.

"I can tell you that the alternative will be worse. The rooms there are even smaller than this one, and they will chain your legs to the floor."

That night a storm erupts from my face. Under the blanket, I cry and cry until my eyes are stinging. I don't care if the night spirits are watching from the end of my bed. By the time I stop crying in the middle of the night, I have made a plan.

It is the next day when Nurse enters my room again. Sometimes she does not even look at me, like today. In perfect German, I say, "I am sorry that I have not been honest with you, that I have been difficult. Please, may I see the other children? Please, can I help with chores?"

Nurse crosses her arms. There is no expression on her face, but I know that she is pleased she has broken me. I would be pleased if I were in her shoes.

She returns with Frau, who wears glasses and a warm coat with fur at the collar.

"So, you are speaking German. Let us hope that you are remorseful, too."

Remorse is the last thing I feel.

I then decide to do something else. I break into the German song I sometimes hear the older girls sing in the field, about German loyalty, and German women, and noble deeds. It is a hideous tune, and I stretch the vowels as I sing, to make the language and the song sound even worse than they are. This will show them that they do not have complete control, and they cannot tell me how to think. Though, even as I am singing, I am aware that Frau still carries her baton.

When I finish, Frau is staring out from tiny eyes, and her lips are pinched into a straight line.

"We need someone to teach the other children how to speak and write German," she says at last. "Unfortunately, since Berlin will not be sending any new teachers until our dormitory is full, for now you will have to do."

"I am too young to be a teacher." I do not want to teach. I want to play.

Behind her, Nurse shakes her head—a warning, perhaps.

"But I will do what is required." I try to sound contrite, but even to me the words sound false. I should stop there, but I can't help myself—I have to know. "Why don't the older girls teach them?"

"They have their own lessons to learn. They have their own teacher."

"Will I be having that? I was told that I would have special instructions."

"Some girls are designed for greatness, and others designed for purpose."

These words are confusing to me, but I don't ask, in case I sound stupid.

"I would like to learn how to be great," I say, though I have no idea what that means.

"We shall see. I am hoping that you have learnt your lesson. From now on we only converse in German. If you didn't speak it, you would have been on a truck to a place full of dysentery long ago," she says, smiling like a cat. *Any more smug,* Dragos would say, *and she might start to lick her own genitals.*

Nurse nods in agreement. "You should count yourself very lucky."

"Frau Haus," I ask in my soft voice, "I was wondering if I might pen a letter to my family to let them know that I am well and happy." I will of course tell them that this place is run by morons and monsters.

"We do not allow letters; however, we do send progress reports to your mother." I imagine the letter:

Dear Frau Steuben, your daughter is in need of food, locked in a cold room without a warm blanket, and beaten regularly for asking questions. But she has learnt her lesson and is very happy to be here. Frau Haus

Catarina would perhaps be pleased. Perhaps she would think this outcome just.

Nurse returns with another blanket and the Führer's book again, called *Mein Kampf.*

"It is an important book to read from. Every morning you must recite to me a paragraph by heart."

She tells me that the children I will be instructing must learn it, also.

"You must spend several more nights in here while you read the book, and then you can join the others."

More nights! *Hure.* I squeeze my lips together so that the word cannot escape.

CHAPTER ELEVEN
ELSI

I have seen the stranger before. He is tall and long-legged, with straw-berry-fair hair, and always seems in a hurry, but today he waits at the front of the building where I have recently started work. I have a job sewing badges onto shirts. For that I will receive coupons for goods. Mama is back working in the laundry—to replace someone who has died.

When I begin to walk home, the tall man falls into step with me. I button my coat as I go, cold nipping at my fingers.

"Hello," he says. "I know you."

"Do you?" I say shyly, surprised. I wear a hat not to protect me from the cold winds but because of my hair, which is barely an inch long all over. I begged Mama to leave some. Mama borrowed Lilli's scissors and cut my sister's hair, too. Leah did not fare so well, though she did not complain as much.

"Yes. You are Elsi."

"How did you know?"

He shrugs. "I know things."

I am going through the list of people I have met in the ghetto. I have not made too many friends because of how quickly circumstances change.

I made friends with a girl who lived here once, and we might have become close. We used to sit in the stairwell and talk. She told me that her father was a teacher, and when they first came here he would teach her the things she otherwise would have learned at school. When I went to her apartment a few weeks ago, there was no one there. The neighbors said that after her young brother was deported, the family disappeared. It is like that in the ghetto. People come and go, move to other places, vanish. Sometimes one or two relatives, sometimes whole families.

"I'm Simon," the man says. He holds out his hand, and I take it formally in mine; his skin is cool and smooth, and his grip is firm.

We stop walking. I look around to see if he is alone, or if we are being watched or followed. It is habit now.

"Where do you live?" I say, and then wonder if I should be asking this.

"Around there," he says, pointing in a direction I can't discern, his finger moving too fast in the air. "I remember watching you at the theater group. My brother was also part of it. I would come in and watch you rehearse sometimes."

I redden, knowing he has seen a different side of me. Several groups came to watch from time to time, but I took little notice, too self-absorbed.

"You were wonderful. Do you think you will act again, when you are out?"

"I hope so." The way he says "when you are out" means that he is an optimist. Such people are getting harder to find. "Who is your brother?"

"Was," he says. "Gustav died shortly after we arrived here."

"Oh, I'm sorry. I remember a boy with that name."

He shrugs.

There is silence, and I can see that people are rushing home around us.

"I should be going," I say.

"Yes, you should. If ever you are looking for something else to do, you should come and visit our group. My friends and I meet every week to talk about the ghetto and improvements we would like to make."

I look up the street and see that several soldiers are stopping people randomly to ask questions. I turn back to Simon, relieved that he has slowed me down. This has given me an opportunity to take a detour. Sometimes the soldiers find reasons to punish even if there aren't any.

"Where does the group meet?"

"Somewhere secret."

I am relieved that it is behind closed doors because the Gestapo does not like meetings.

"Once you have permission from your father, no?" he says.

"My father isn't here."

"The camps?"

I nod.

"I see."

"And yours?"

"I haven't seen any of my family for months. I don't know where they are. I don't think they are coming back." He says this casually, as if he is already resigned. "That doesn't mean they won't or that your papa won't. I'm just not going to wait. There are too many things to do."

I am about to ask *what* things, but remember that Papa always said I often speak before I think, and I should learn restraint. I will perhaps ask later because he is interesting, and I am keen to know what he does to fill his days.

I look again toward the guards, who are not far away now. They have not yet noticed us.

"We shouldn't be talking, not in the street. I should go."

"Yes, Elsi, you should. Maybe one day after work you can walk with me to where our group meets."

I think about this.

"Perhaps." I decide not to tell Mama, who will tell me to stay away from him.

"Good-bye, Elsi! May God and good watch over you."

I watch him go. He wears a flat cap and a black coat and walks briskly, disappearing quickly from the main street.

I walk fast down Brzezinska Street. There has been talk of roundups being made to stop the dissent that has been rising among the Jews. I suspect this is why people are being stopped in the street this evening. Those "troublemakers," as they are known, are taken from their homes at any time of day or night, from workplaces, from the soup line, or the community washroom. They are told to gather all their possessions. Sometimes they are taken with just the clothes on their backs. Sometimes the Jewish police deport them immediately. Sometimes the Gestapo arrives: senior officials dressed in fine tailored jackets and polished boots and badges that mean nothing to any of us. They stuff their pockets with stolen money and jewelry first, before taking their victims to places unknown.

Searches have happened in our apartment building. They are happening everywhere. Mama cannot take the door knocking. Any sound makes her jump. Mama and I always walk fast along the street. You must never stop in the street and talk for too long to people you know. Idle people are more noticeable. Conversation is best made behind closed doors. Conspiracy is a punishable offense.

When Mama passes people she knows, salutations are brief and questions remain trivial and nonpolitical, as anyone could be listening. Eyes wander over one another warily. *Are they on our side?* This is what we have become: suspicious of our own people. It is what the Nazis want.

Last week a fire started at the back of a plastics factory that, along with a second building, almost burned to the ground. The Gestapo says that the fire was deliberately set. They are thinking of changing the curfew to five o'clock. The guards have become more alert, and they patrol the streets more frequently. Lilli says they have been told to look at us closely. To see if they can see the word *spy* written across our faces.

As I near our building, I see a family on the footpath. They hold some saucepans that they want to sell. I have seen them before. They move around to various locations. They are always told to leave. Last time they were here was weeks ago. Their faces are emaciated, their eyes fixed; they have the look of the starved. I notice that the youngest child is missing. There was frost on the window this morning, and I wonder how they coped with the night. I shivered for most of it. Mama was visiting Lilli today to see if she had any spare coal, as the nights become colder.

There are more homeless on the street. It is a worrying sight. It means the ghetto buildings will burst at the seams. We surely cannot fit in any more.

A thick cloud of smoke hangs above the city. Someone yells that there is another fire. There are whistles in the distance. A fire truck speeds down the center of the road, narrowly missing an elderly man who is crossing. One more life gone would not make a difference.

"Move!" says the officer. "Away from here!" The officer is speaking from behind me to the beggars on the street. Begging looks untidy to the Gestapo. The family is near the main street that visiting officials drive on.

When we first arrived in the ghetto, Leah and I would play board games on the stairs and on the footpath with other children from the building. We were hungry and cold, but we kept our hope. Papa, Mama, Leah, and I would spend a lot of time together in the apartment. The toilets did not work in the building, and we had to line up for the public amenities. Even this I didn't mind at first, because it was an opportunity to see people we knew. The guards scared me, but I did not think that they would harm us, not if we kept to ourselves.

Leah and I would play skipping games with string, also, even though I was too old for such things, and sometimes we would sing at nighttime, but we don't do that anymore. We are too tired to play and too hungry to talk for long.

Papa left the second month we were here. He was large and strong, exactly what the Germans wanted. We have not seen or heard from him in well over a year. I miss him and the scent of timber on his clothes. I imagine him coming in, brushing sleet from his shoulders as he takes off his hat and shakes out his hair.

Mama doesn't talk of him much anymore. After he had gone, she sat by the window for days watching for his return. They'd had nineteen years of glances and touches, something that belonged only to them. I am hoping that one day I will share the same with someone I love.

We have stopped asking the Judenrat if Papa is coming back. At first we were checking every few days, and they would tell us that he was not on their list to return, though they couldn't be sure of anything. They know as little as we do, but they like to pretend that they are more important, that they are privy to much more information. Mama went to the Gestapo, also, thinking they would know more, but they sent her away and told her not to come back.

There are no curtains to close. It takes five long steps to get from the kitchen to the three beds. Mama and Leah share a bed now. Leah can't stand to be alone. Sometimes when Mama is too tired or not feeling well, Leah will sleep with me. Leah doesn't talk about our old house anymore. For her, those memories are disappearing. But I remember the freedom clearly—the walks to the park, the shops, the little theater, Marta's place, and my other friends. How Leah and I each had a bedroom, and how there were thick rugs on the floor and a garden out back. How we had lace curtains and so much food. Small things that I never really noticed. Until now.

It was so cold during our first winter in the ghetto that we would join our mattresses on the floor and lie together with all the blankets over us. One of us on either side of Mama, snuggling up to take some of her warmth, when she had so little herself.

In the mornings Mama would light a fire in the wood heater to boil some water and hand out slices of bread. Sometimes there was tea, but it eventually ran out. Mama would buy honey, which did not taste like honey, and biscuits with real money on the black market, and we would dip the biscuits in hot water and honey. Such biscuits, dry and hard, would have been considered flavorless before the war. Now they are much sought after.

After that, Mama tried looking for work. She worked for a short time at the laundry before someone else was given her job, and then eventually back there again. That was where she met Lilli, whose clothes she was employed to wash.

Then when the cold eased and the heat came, it was nearly as bad. The smell of sewerage was so strong we sometimes had to shut our window even on very hot days.

I saw my first dead body just after Papa left. I knew there had been public executions in a courtyard nearby, but we avoided that area as much as possible.

On the way back from the soup line, we discovered an old man lying on the cobbles, still wearing his thick coat in the midday sun. Mama said he was homeless. I did not know that there were those without apartments, and the horror of realizing that we were some of the luckier ones was even more abhorrent, even more soul destroying.

"Don't look," said Mama. But it was too late. His face was gaunt, his skin gray and mottled.

"Mama, why?"

"Shh! Wait till we get home. Don't draw attention." I tried not to cry, but the tears were about to flood my cheeks, and Mama made us walk faster to try and beat my tears. Mama told us later that it is likely the man had died of starvation.

Leah didn't cry, but she put her hands over her ears so that she couldn't hear Mama talking. Sometimes it is better not to hear.

I quickly stopped thinking of the ghetto as a place for temporary adventure and rather as a place of barbarity that I must sustain indefinitely. Mama says that the ghetto chips away at our souls, at the life within, and she is sorry that this is happening. It is true what people say: fatigue and hunger can turn people inward to shut out the world around them. Even Mama doesn't watch us anymore, does not ponder our futures; now she thinks too much about the horrors that surround us, wondering how we will survive the rest of that day.

Darkness creeps into the ghetto long before dusk, and the cold creeps in between the cracks. On the floor surrounding the heater are splinters of wood and a trail from where Mama has carried some wood to light a fire. I watch the fire die down to an orange glow. Mama is more distracted than usual and does not seem to hear when I ask her questions. She is feeling restless about something tonight, and her hands are shaking.

She says she does not want to talk in front of Leah. I sing to Leah until she falls asleep.

Mama then tells me what she saw from our window. It was an execution—another one—this time over a piece of bread. She saw someone put the victim on a trolley and wheel him to the front gate.

The man who was executed had a loaf of bread wrapped in paper, which he must have bought on the black market. He did not hide it well. He was stopped by the Gestapo, and his answers seemed to infuriate the interrogators. They accused him of stealing it.

The man then handed the bread to the Gestapo and walked off. "Take it!" he shouted, shaking his head in frustration. He began to walk away, and one of the policemen called for him to stop. But he didn't. The policeman then raised his rifle and shot him through the back. The shooter walked over and kicked the man hard, but he didn't flinch, which could only mean that he was dead.

"And then do you know what they did?" said Mama. "The murderers ate the bread. It made me so sick, I clutched my stomach as if my breath had suddenly been stolen from me, as if I could feel the bullet myself."

She is trembling, and I put my arm around her. I am wondering if the ghetto has finally broken her, whether her nerves will ever recover.

"Mama, it is not the first time. You have seen this before. You must not get so upset. We have not done anything wrong. No one will kill us for doing nothing."

"The young man was Imran, from the apartment below us."

I am shocked. I have seen him many times. He is a little older than I am and always running errands for his parents, who live in the apartment with him. Mama has often commented that he leaves the apartment most nights to make deliveries. It is perhaps more shocking that this has happened because they are people we speak to every day. The ghetto suddenly seems much smaller.

"I can't take it anymore," she says. "All this death. Your father gone."

I am thinking of Simon, and I say, "We will be out of here one day, Mama, and we will be free to live as before. You'll see."

"Oh, Elsi, what would I do without you? You are a shining light."

I look into Mama's eyes. Once a vibrant hazel, they have grown duller in the past few months to reflect the colors of the ghetto buildings.

Mama knocks on Imran's apartment, but there is no one there. We open the door to find that the place is in darkness, chairs overturned, Imran's parents missing. When we tell Lilli, she says that the bread was probably just an excuse to kill him. They were probably watching him, though for what reason she couldn't say. There are too many reasons. We have stopped trying to understand.

CHAPTER TWELVE
WILLEM

In less than a fortnight I will be leaving for Auschwitz. In our bed Lena radiates heat from her condition, and the sheets are tangled around us. I do not want to sleep tonight. I want to stay awake beside her body. I want to feel my child kick in the night. Should I fall asleep, I want Lena to wake me whenever he does. I will spend four weeks at the camp to learn some important work. To study the achievements of other brilliant doctors. Part of me is excited, the part that wishes to become the best at what I do. Three weeks after my return from the assignment, our baby is due.

Sometimes my thoughts rest uncomfortably on the ghetto, and my mind recalls the face of the young girl I met in the surgery. She is the face of discord when it comes to this cause: the fact that someone so intelligent—uncontaminated, if you will—could fall on the wrong side of acceptance. Most of the patients are closed, their emotions bricked in, unforgiving, whereas Elsi had let me in, innocently, to her life, which deserved to continue as it had been. I had not expected to experience such trust, for that is the first thing people discard when they enter the ghetto. She deepened the stain on that doubt-filled corner of my mind that is not yet conditioned to believe that *we*—the Aryans, the Nazis, the Germans—are the chosen ones.

"I would like to talk to you about something that happened recently," I say to Lena. "Something I have been reluctant to talk about." It has been nearly a month since I last treated the mother who attempted to abort her fetus. The mother's forced pregnancy and the very personal account given by her daughter, on their second visit to the surgery, has not strayed far from my thoughts—the memory like a faint, nearly indiscernible, yet persistent noise in my subconscious. And I have been reluctant to release the information to Lena, given her present sensitive state.

"Why?"

"The nature of it is something I have not encountered before. It is perhaps something that you may find distressing." I have discussed with her some of the conditions I treat. Lena knows why I was appointed, and we have always been honest with each other.

"You know you can tell me everything. I carry a child, not a heart condition."

Perhaps it is for selfish reasons that I reveal this now. To speak of this—to release it—might eradicate the noise inside my mind.

"A mother came in to see me. She was hemorrhaging badly from a self-inflicted wound to remove a baby."

"That's terrible!" says Lena. "But you have treated such cases before, yes?"

"Yes, yes. Of course."

"Can she not be more careful in future?"

"I have ligated her fallopian tubes so that it doesn't happen again."

"It is a pity that such actions have to take place. If she had been more careful, she would not have put herself in such danger."

"It is something that she had no control of."

"What are you saying?"

"There are certain men who do not possess restraint."

"You mean she was raped?"

"Yes."

"Why can't you just say it? Why do you have to always talk in circles to protect me? By whom?"

"German officers."

"That is truly horrible! Despicable! Can't you stop it? Does Manz know about this?"

"He is part of the problem."

She nods as if she is not surprised. "You have to tell your father. You have to send a report."

"What can he do? We are not to interfere with the running of the ghettos. I am a doctor, and I have a job to do. Besides, they probably already know in Berlin. "

"Animals!" she says, and I notice that her eyes are watery. "I believe that you can do something. You can put a bullet between his eyes."

She is referring to Manz, but I wonder if she also pictures my father when she says this.

"Oh, Lena," I say. "How thoughtless of me! I should not have said anything."

"It's important that you always be honest with me." She considers for a moment. "I think I will tell your father or someone higher if you don't."

"Lena, my dearest, please don't say anything! We must keep going. Eventually things will stop."

"When the whole race of Jewish women is eliminated!" she says cynically. "I was at college with a Jewish girl for a while, and we became good friends, and then she was told she couldn't study. I was shocked at first, and then after a couple of years I accepted it. I thought that *yes*, this is Germany, *our* Germany. I didn't want things to change. I didn't want our principles, our culture, to change. Now I don't know if I can accept this anymore. I did not think it would get any worse. As if they are not downtrodden enough, they are now the playthings of idle German idiots, who break and fix at their will."

I know that nothing I say will change anything. She is sensitive about everything at the moment, with a heightened sense of protectiveness surrounding the future of our unborn child. I have always felt that keeping things from her was the same as betraying her, but perhaps my father is right. A certain amount of ignorance is not such a bad thing. From now on, the subject of terminations has to be carefully arranged around her, using words and phrases such as *necessary* or *lifesaving*, when in fact such procedures are enforced upon Jewish women whose married German sponsors do not want Jewish bastards.

"We must accept this. We must go on, Lena. For our child. For our life. Eventually we will be back in Germany. I will have my new posting, and one day the war will be over. Perhaps the Jews will be given their own cities to run as they please, and perhaps Germany will once again return to normality, after this madness is over. Let us not try to think too much. Please . . . Lena? Will you promise?"

"Then why tell me about this horrible incident?"

"I don't know. I thought you needed to know it. You have always accused me of being too closed, of keeping things from you."

We have rarely argued, but when we have, it is usually due to her accusing me of indifference. She has often said that when I recount something terrible—especially those things I have witnessed more recently in the ghetto—that I report it with detachment, removing myself from any connection with it. She says that I refuse to consider, in any depth, the wrongdoings of my peers and countrymen, historically as well as now; through absence or indirect involvement, I absolve myself by partial ignorance.

Though she is more or less right, I have had to defend myself in this. It is perhaps that I do not prefer to analyze what might have been, or what should have been, but rather to concentrate on what *I* must do. It is about continuation. Reflection of wrongs, past or present, is for those who want to blame or torment themselves with regret. This is a point of difference between us, for Lena believes that we are responsible as a whole, that what one does beside us must be carried by us all.

I love Lena as much as I could ever do. She is emotional and affectionate—traits that I had always considered a weakness until I met her. But she has drawn something from me, and that is to appreciate the good in people. She has caused me to break some of my own rules: to reflect on certain events in the past and apply myself better because of them. And I oblige her. I discuss my past because this makes her happy. My greatest fear is that I will disappoint her.

I first saw Lena in the front playground of the school where she was teaching science. She was bent over a small child, glasses on, hair out of place, no makeup. She was interested, curious, and the child so focused on her teacher it was as if there were no one else in front of her. Lena has that effect on many; she draws one in with her attentiveness. She is not perhaps someone that you might notice above everyone else in a crowd. But once her eyes have found you, they can hold you to her longer than is necessary.

Ours was not an easy beginning. I had taken girls out before, but my studies always came first. Some I did not take to meet Father, knowing straight away that he would be horrified. Some of the female students at university, though brilliant, were not the kind of women that the party promoted. They were freethinking, strong, and independent, and they talked openly about such subjects as philosophy, sociology, theology, and psychology. Some women voiced their support of Marxism, and others praised or debated the writings of Franz Rosenzweig and Karl Barth.

I myself dallied, although only briefly, with various theories, taking a special interest in the therapies and analyses conducted by the Jew Sigmund Freud, and even participating in secret forums on subjects that did not side with Nazism. But back at home with my father, Nazi ideology was first and foremost. It was to pay for my career after all. And Lena was now my passenger. She had given up everything for me.

I wipe away the tears that have pooled at the corners of her eyes, wishing to take back what I have just said. She wouldn't probably believe me, but sometimes I, too, wish I didn't see the things I see or know the things I know.

For Lena I will have to carry much in the future, for her own protection. I will not look so closely upon the faces I see, the ones we have broken. Yet even as I think this, there is a tightening of my chest as I picture the young girl, Elsi: the face of human conquest. I broke a rule and learned her past—not her medical records or birth date but how she felt and how much she had lost. This is something I cannot afford to do again.

"Let's dance!" says Lena, her mood fluctuating suddenly, as it often does in her current state.

"Now? At midnight? No, of course not."

"Oh, come on. Don't be so staid. If I didn't know you, I would think that you were a machine."

"Why on earth did you ever agree to have dinner with me then?"

"I could see inside you. I could see that behind the glass shield that was your gaze, you were interesting, far deeper than anyone knew."

She kisses me.

"And I had to release you from that terrible prison."

I follow her into the sitting room. In her nightgown she switches on the phonograph and places a needle on the record, to hear Bizet's Nocturne no. 1. It is her favorite. With her belly separating us, I sweep her cautiously around the floor. It was Lena who broke something in me, opening a doorway that had been locked against my own history. It was Lena who pulled out old photos, asked my aunt about my mother, and brought her back to life.

I learned that my mother had lost two children prior to having me, something my father hadn't told me. My older sister, Lizbet, died at age two, and my second sister was a stillbirth. I came a year after her.

When Lena first found out she was pregnant, she wept for my mother, and I suddenly felt connected to a past I'd never before considered. My past had been sealed and my future planted in conformity for the sake of my father's aims. Lena transported me to a history rich in detail. My mother had been born in France and was vivacious and kind. She liked to ride horses in the fields with her brothers and sisters and fell deeply in love with my father. Her parents had found work in Germany, where she met my father and swept him off his feet. Knowing him as I do, this is impossible to imagine. The losses of their children eventually put distance between them—this according to my aunt, who had passed this knowledge on to Lena.

For the first time I felt connected to, not restricted from, knowledge about my mother. It wasn't that I had changed outwardly, but now there was something else within, something that didn't involve secrecy. There were other things to consider: small things, other people, a past, a story. *Her* story. Life was suddenly not so straightforward. I was no longer just the son of a well-connected doctor. I was the son of two people who had fallen in love and desperately wanted a child.

"After the baby is born, we will hike to the mountains like we used to."

"You will not feel like hiking," I say.

"Who says? Of course I will."

Lena loves to walk. Anywhere: along city streets, in the mountains, through ancient towns. I could barely keep up with her stride up steep inclines.

"And I suppose I will be carrying the baby then," I say.

"Of course. It will be your turn."

CHAPTER THIRTEEN
MATILDA

Nurse does not come and get me until late afternoon. I am to be allowed a shower in the main house, but it will be my last one there. After that I must wash at the outdoor tubs with the other children. Once a month the children get a hot bath.

When I go to the bathroom in the main house, there are doors left open. I pass a large dining room. It is decorated finely, different from the rest of the house, with a chandelier, high-backed padded chairs, and a shiny dining table with curved legs.

I am given a light-gray dress with white stripes, which has sleeves down to the elbow, a long pleated skirt, and buttons at the front. I have seen other children wear this dress, too, but the older girls wear dresses of white. The dress is too big for me, and I can twist the front of it at the waist all the way to the back. I am also given a dark-gray cardigan to wear over this, and socks and shoes that have been used by someone else.

In the kitchen I am allowed fresh bread with butter and some tea. The bread is better than any bread I have ever had. Afterward I am shown to the laundry, where I must go each day to wash clothes. In the washing room I roll the clothes through the drying rods and then hang them on a line inside. There is no sign of Nurse, but I have discovered that there is one guard at the back of the house. Often he stands over to one side, close to the fence near the paddocks, where the older girls practice athletics. There is another guard at the front gate. Two others come and go at different times—sometimes patrolling at the front, and other times wandering around the back to inspect the woodlands behind it.

A few words in German and an apology, and now I am free to walk outside and smell the pine, to walk the several meters between the buildings. It is not a great distance, but this is a small piece of freedom that I didn't have before. If I had known it was so easy . . .

Nurse hands me a folded nightgown.

"You will be living in the dormitory with the other children your age. In the mornings you will teach them to read and write in German. They are from Poland. One of them speaks German but can't write it, and the others speak a few words only. I understand you can count in German, also."

I debate whether to answer the truth. My first thought is that I should lie, but then I remember the painful beatings and the cold, drafty room.

"Yes . . . some."

"All right, take her to the hut then," says Frau, who has been standing behind her, looking bored.

Nurse leads me between the buildings, across broken pieces of pathway sunk in mud. The world has less color on the other side of the pathway. From this short crossing, I can see the road at the front of the property and several houses far in the distance.

The dormitory, also known as the hut, looks like a barn on legs. Inside there are eight beds but only four children. Nurse says that she is expecting more children over the coming months. There is no fireplace.

Four faces full of dung greet me when I walk through the door. They each wear the same dress that I am wearing, except for the boy, who has long, dark-gray shorts, long socks, and a shirt with the same stripe. Nurse tells the children that I will be teaching them to read and write German words. She tells the boy that until the younger children learn some German words, he is to translate from German to Polish. He can only speak German. He has not yet learned to write it.

I sit on the bed and wait for Nurse to leave before I speak.

"Hello, I am Matilda," I announce to the children.

"You look too young to be a teacher," says the boy.

"They are not my rules," I say.

"How old are you?" asks the boy.

"Nine years."

"Ha! I'm ten. I should be teaching you."

I will try not to dislike this boy.

The boy is called Ernest. Adele and Luise are seven and they are twins, and the toddler does not have a name. I ask why this is the case. The boy shrugs. He says they just call her Baby. She climbs up on the bed to hide her face in the blanket.

"They just haven't given her a new name yet," the boy tells me.

"New name?"

"Yes, I was given a new name when I came here."

"Why?"

"Because they didn't like mine."

I am relieved that I have my name.

"What was your name?"

"Jacek."

I think that Jacek is a nice name.

"Would you like to still be called that name?"

He shrugs.

"I can call you that if you want."

He shrugs again.

"Where did you used to live?"

"Poland."

"Did you like it there?"

"I can't remember."

"What do you mean, you can't remember? How can you not remember?"

This boy is very stupid.

"It is has been a while since I left."

"So you cannot remember if you liked your country, but you can remember your age?"

"Of course," he says, crossing his arms.

I don't believe him at all now. I think he is probably a lot younger than he says.

"What will you teach us?" says Jacek, arms still crossed.

"Things, I guess." I scan the books on the shelves, none of which I recognize. Adele and Luise begin to speak their foreign language between themselves. I do not want them to be bored with my company. I want them all to like me since I have to share a room with them. "Do you want to hear a story?" I repeat the word *story* in Polish. I know some Polish words from when I visited Tata's brother.

"Yes!" they all say eagerly.

I tell them a story about the Gypsies of Romania who got burned in the forest by the Germans. How the children were on fire, running for their parents. It was a story told by my brothers. The storytelling is terribly slow because Jacek has to repeat everything I say into Polish, and sometimes I have to repeat the sentences slowly for him to understand the German words.

"That is a terrible story," says Jacek. "I don't think you will make a good teacher." Jacek turns to the twins to repeat what he said in Polish.

I am offended by this and look to Adele and Luise for support, but they have moved closer to each other and do not say anything. They are thinking about the story. They have small frowns on their foreheads.

"I have better ones," I say, hoping to get their attention again. The baby begins to whine, and she turns away to face the wall.

"What is wrong with her?"

"She is frightened of you."

"Why?"

"Because you are new. Because you might hurt her. Because of your story."

I look around at the faces. I do not know yet if they will like me.

Nurse comes in and tells us that we must go to sleep. When she leaves again, she locks the door from the outside. I lie down on a narrow bed that is as hard as the floor. The others fall asleep, and I listen to their breathing. At least I have that. At least I have other sounds in the night to listen to.

It is morning and Baby stinks. Jacek says that teachers change nappies, also.

"Frau will be angry if she comes in here and finds that Baby's nappy is unchanged."

This boy is very annoying. I do not know how to look after babies. I have seen them in their mother's arms, but I have never taken much notice of them.

I remove the small girl's nappy and wipe her bottom partially clean. She lies very still, watching me. I try to hold my nose while I do this. Adele has watched Nurse change nappies and shows me what to do. When we are finished, we throw the soiled nappy in a tin bucket by the door.

Nurse unlocks the dormitory, and the children get their bowls and plates from under their beds. We cross to the main house. In the kitchen I am given my own bowl, too.

Cook adds a pinch of salt to the oats and water in a saucepan, and then she beats the oats very hard with the back of a spoon while she boils them. She spoons the creamy porridge into our bowls. She then pours in some milk and a spoonful of honey. It tastes delicious. Even better than the porridge at home, which is made from grain. When I tell Cook this, she says the secret is in the beating of the oats. When I go back home, I will pass on this secret to Catarina.

After breakfast, Nurse takes us back to the hut. She says that I am to use the books inside to teach the children, and that after one week, Frau will give the children a test to make sure they are learning. If they are not learning, I will be punished. She locks the door when she leaves.

I pick up the books that lie on a shelf. There are books in German and English and storybooks that look uninteresting.

"Shall we start with one of the storybooks?"

"We always start with the pronunciation of the German alphabet," says Jacek.

"Says who?"

"Says Frau Haus."

"Has she been teaching you?"

"No. There was another girl."

"Where is she now?"

"They took her away when she got too big. They say she might be back one day."

"How big?"

Jacek holds a pillow across his stomach. "This big."

"Because she was eating much more than us," says Adele. "She was given special foods."

"I see," I say. But I don't. It is probably another lie. "Well, we should start with this story. I know this story. It is a good story." I am lying. I have never read the story before.

The book contains many different stories and has a picture of a dog on the front, which is why I have picked it up. I begin to read. The first story is about worker bees and drones, and about how the worker bees gathered up in force and fought the lazy drones, but the story doesn't stop there. I continue reading and Jacek repeats what I say in Polish, but I don't believe he knows some of the words because he seems to stumble over his sentences.

"Every nation has millions of workers, farmers, officials, and so on. They work hard, like the bees. The worker goes to the factory every day. The work is hard. But he does it gladly. He knows that his labor is necessary if his people are to live. There are drones not only among the bees but also among people. They, the drones, are the Jews . . ."

This is no story! I slam the book shut.

"Oh, keep reading!" whines Adele.

"No, that is the worst book I have ever read. I can find better stories than that."

"It was very boring," says Jacek.

I pick up another book, but it looks very dull, also.

"We like that one," says Adele.

"I hate that one," I say. "How about this one? About a farmer who falls in a hole and gets stuck, then loses weight and climbs out again."

"I didn't see it," says Jacek. "There is no book like that."

"Yes, there is." I pick up a book that has a German title but no picture on the front. I pretend that I am reading from the book while I make up a story about a farmer who gets stuck in the mud, and his farm animals come to rescue him but end up falling in the hole as well. I act out the parts of some animals so that Jacek doesn't have to translate everything.

Tiny smiles creep in from the corners of their mouths, even Jacek's. Luise wants me to read it again.

"Next time," I say. Jacek sits quietly with his hands in his lap. He is waiting for something else to happen.

I finally get the German-language book and have them spell and repeat some words and sentences after me. Baby falls asleep.

There is a knock at the door. It is Nurse, to say that dinner is ready. We follow her to the main house.

Cook has made some stew and ladles it into our bowls.

"That's enough," says Nurse to Cook. "Too much and they will become plump and lazy, and no one will want them."

Nurse laughs at her own words, but Cook doesn't laugh.

When we have finished our milk, we wash up our plates and return to the hut.

Back in the hut, Jacek asks me, "Are you staying with us for long?"

I am confused by the question.

"Yes, I think so."

"Sometimes they don't. Sometimes they go away with a new name straight away."

"Who?"

"Children who come to the hut."

"Were there more of you here?"

He nods. "Months ago they took all the good ones."

"Good ones?"

"The ones who are the closest to German. We were the ones that were left."

"Who took them?"

"People who want children. They take the ones they want."

I feel my chest fill with fear.

"Are they coming back?"

"I don't know. No one has come since last spring, since the last commander left. Then after that the teacher stopped coming, too. Frau says that once the new commander arrives, there will be more children. They might be keeping you longer because you are the teacher."

That night I lie in bed picturing the people who come. I cannot get Jacek's words out of my head. I have a bad dream that Frau steals me in the night and puts me on another train with strangers. When I arrive at the other end, there is a giant bee waiting for me.

DECEMBER

CHAPTER FOURTEEN
ELSI

The heavy rain has turned the soil into thick, glutinous mud. It pours all day and night. It beats my back and thunders on my head. My shoes are sodden, and my skirt muddied at the hem. I am trying to save some of my food coupons in the hope of exchanging them for a new pair of shoes: ones that fit.

Underneath the bridge, there is a tram full of Aryans and *Volksdeutsche*, who travel the road that cuts through the ghetto. This road is for Germans and Poles and protected from the ghetto by fences on either side and guards stationed at either end of the bridge. Some people on the tram watch us curiously, as if we are animals in a zoo, before turning away, perhaps because the walls, and the people within them, are objects of distaste. But some purposefully face forward the entire time, absolving themselves with ignorance. They cannot be responsible if they do not witness firsthand what is happening to their own Polish people beneath their very noses.

I carry the full buckets from the water pump. The muscles in my arms ache, but I must not slow down, not while the guards watch me from the end of the bridge. I have already seen them make fun of two prisoners by pointing guns at their faces as they walked past, making them run with fear, tripping over themselves in their haste to hurry on.

Once on the other side of the bridge, I do not look at the faces of the guards in their ugly gray uniforms and their beetle-shaped helmets. They stand underneath the shelter of a makeshift tin awning that protects them from the rain. Mama said we must always look away or down, to not encourage interaction with the men who patrol the streets.

"Take a break from the rain," calls one of them when I reach the bottom of the stairs. "Put down your buckets."

If I say no, I will appear rude and ungrateful, so I comply. My heart is beating fast as I step underneath the awning to share their dry space. The air around them is heavy with mischief. Rain falls around the shelter in sheets as thick as walls, and suddenly I feel vulnerable and trapped.

"Why do you go to the water pump?" asks the younger guard, who has a scar that runs along his jawline. He talks loudly above the noise of the rain. "You could just leave your buckets outside and catch some water there."

"If I leave the buckets outside, they will be stolen within seconds."

They laugh at this, then repeat to each other what I have told them, then laugh some more.

"What is a girl like you doing in this place?" says the same guard.

I do not know where to look or how to respond. It is a question, like many from the Germans, that might be filled with traps and hidden meanings, designed to elicit a response they want to hear—one that will cause them to act irrationally, cruelly. So I say nothing and pray that this silence doesn't offend.

The guard who is doing all the talking says to his older colleague, "She looks a bit like my sister."

"You haven't seen your sister in two years. You have stood too close to the front line; it has obviously affected your memory," says the second in a more derisive tone. "Did someone take to your sister's hair with a carving knife, too?"

This question is another source of amusement for them.

My knees tremble as my gaze rests upon the rifles that are slung across their middles, their fingers dangerously touching the triggers. I have witnessed how these weapons can end a heartbeat in seconds, maim someone for life. I have seen much in the time I have been here. Things that no one should see, that only a year ago seemed unimaginable. I have seen another kind of human condition that makes men turn into creatures unrecognizable—creatures whose sole motivation is to destroy the human spirit.

"Look at the eyes. They are not Jewish eyes," says the younger guard.

They like to play games with the passersby. They have their own rules out here on the streets.

"Are you from Germany?" says the same guard.

"No," I say.

"What about your parents, grandparents?"

"My father and grandparents are from the north . . . Denmark originally."

"I see. Pity, don't you think?" he asks his colleague. "The eyes say to me *Mischling*."

"Doesn't matter about the eyes," says the older.

"Yes, but she is an Aryan Jew."

"A Jew is a Jew." They are self-indulgent; they are bored, though the second guard is not as attentive as the first. Interaction with the prisoners appears beneath him. He walks a few meters outside the shelter for a better view of the streets, leaving me alone with the young guard.

"Your shoes are worn. Do you not have any others?"

I shake my head. "I am saving my food coupons to exchange for another pair." This is more a wish on my part, since not using food coupons is harder than I thought when there is so little food to begin with.

"There are other ways that you can get new shoes. Quicker ways."

I do not want to hear them. I have seen what has happened to Mama. I will die before that happens to me.

"I have heard that spying can bring a certain amount of privileges. I am sure that if you agree to spy on those Jews in your building, the chairman will give you a new pair."

"I don't think so. There is nothing that is worth spying on. They work and sleep. It is all they do."

"Are you sure they don't plan something? And they are not thinking up ways to escape, or to hurt a hardworking German guard?"

"Yes, I'm very sure."

The soldier looks around, his hand still on his gun.

"Still, you should consider it. Your feet must hurt. That is hardly a way to live—in shoes that are falling apart . . . your poor feet on the cold bitumen."

The other soldier returns to stand near his companion, cursing the rain that has dampened his coat.

"What are you saying to her?"

"I am suggesting that she keep an eye on things inside the buildings, to report if anything unusual is taking place. In return we will find her new shoes. What do you think?"

"Perhaps that is not the only thing she can bargain with?" says the second one, whom I trust the least.

The first guard views me carefully, then shrugs. "Perhaps. Though it is a little late for that. She is very skinny. Move along then, Fraulein Aryan Jew."

My chest heaves as I walk briskly to the corner so that I can disappear from view. The water is not as heavy as the fear I carry in my chest. I walk past the market where people trade their clothes for money. Some of the new arrivals from Germany and northern Poland—looking well fed and overdressed, as if they are here on holiday—are keen to swap their warm coats for extra bowls of soup. By the coming winter, they will regret it.

I will not tell Mama about the conversation with the guards. If I do, she will try and stop me from going anywhere. She will carry the load herself, and she is too thin, the weight falling off her before my eyes.

Lilli has told me of a job with the youth police to round up the homeless to make sure they are not causing trouble. It would mean an extra portion of soup. But it would also mean working for the Germans, and that is not what I want. I have come upon another group at the ghetto: ghetto youth whose purpose sounds more in tune with my own aspirations.

They are Jews, all hungry to fight the order, although that is all I know. Their activities are run by Simon, but I don't know yet what they are. It is enough for me to know that they are eager to make changes in the ghetto. Simon will not say more until I commit.

I once went to a meeting. There were a dozen other young people there in an apartment. We had to enter the building at separate times so that no one knew we were part of a group. Simon talked about the persecution of the Jews and about our history. He talked about the killing of Jews that is done out of jealousy and greed.

His speech was mesmerizing. When he speaks, everyone listens. What he said made sense. Since I arrived in the ghetto, very little has been said about the strength of the Jews. Everyone talks about the failures; we are constantly feeling sorry for ourselves. I have learned that Simon had a sister in the ghetto, also. She and his parents were taken one night by guards and are yet to return. I know that Simon doesn't have an apartment. He moves around, living with different group members.

He carries within him the same restlessness I do, and the same desire to fight against our forced containment and the harshness of conditions here. He does not offer the promise of extra food coupons or extra soup like the youth police does. But he offers something else. He offers a chance to help free us, not just physically but in thought. To unite and become part of a group that instills pride among us, who applauds our forebears and works to stop the Germans from weeding our heritage and accomplishments into extinction.

I reach inside the neck of my blouse and feel, hanging from a piece of string, the small band of silver that Simon has given me. We have grown close, though I feel I am yet to know him deeply.

He is thin, like everyone here, yet the hunger has not reached his face. It is still full of color and life, his light-brown eyes still bright with hope. He is one of the rare ones who holds fast to passion, and he has recognized the same in me.

Still, it is a lot to think about. I will not commit to the group until I am sure of its motives. Their plans—the ones they talk about in secret—are likely dangerous. I believe he had something to do with the recent fire because he confided in me that during this diversion, several Jews on a list for deportation managed to escape.

I walk up the stairs to our apartment, feeling a wave of resentment that Leah—even if Mama did allow her to leave the apartment—is too weak to help with the buckets. Not that it is her fault. Neither do I blame her personally. It is just that it *is* the case. More of the stairwell is missing. Someone has stolen the wood for their fires.

The door of our apartment is ajar, and I am instantly alarmed. There are foreign voices coming from within. A man and woman stand inside talking to Mama. Leah sits on the chair, watching me, expressionless as always. She is often able to hide her feelings, unlike me.

The older woman wears a fur coat, her hands at her throat as if she is strangling the animal she wears. Mama looks warily toward me.

"This is my other daughter . . . Elsi," she says.

The woman does not seem interested in my arrival. She is too busy looking disgusted at her surroundings. The man, however, steps forward to shake my hand. He wears a small beard and a hat.

"This is Yuri and Rada. They have been billeted in this apartment . . . just until your father comes back."

Papa isn't coming back, I want to say, but I know that such words will shatter my mother, who is already emotionally fragile. Simon has finally admitted that he thinks many have been killed in the camps. But I can never say this in front of Mama. Once when Leah asked her if Papa was still alive, she fell to pieces.

"They will share a bed—won't they?" I ask.

"Yes, they will have to. The Judenrat has said that the apartment is too big for only a mother with two children. Which is absurd. It is barely big enough for one."

I am disappointed that any precious time we have alone now has to be shared with strangers.

"Do you have any items to trade for food and bedding?" asks Mama.

Rada complains about the fleas that are biting her through her stockings, while Mama explains the ghetto system. Yuri sits staring at his hands for long periods of time, then at the window, then at the stove. He is in shock. They have come from northern Poland from their large country home. I know what they are feeling.

Rada grows pale and gray as Mama explains where they must attend to their toilet and how they must get their own water. She explains that they will receive rations for food, one loaf of bread to last five days, and that they must stand in line each day for their bowl of soup. And sometimes they must line up for hours to receive other rations.

"We have coin," says Yuri, "sewn into the hems of our clothes."

"You can't tell them that," hisses Rada.

"We aren't thieves," I say testily. "Besides, there are more important things to steal than money. You will find out soon enough."

"You will need to find the profiteers who will accept real money for items. They are getting harder to find, and check with me before you offer anything. They might also be spies. And you must not speak about this openly," cautions Mama. "The people who are selling items you might need—paper, blankets, coal, extra food—will be killed and you will be punished. And your coin will not buy you a lot. You will go through it fast. Everything is expensive. Everyone demands high prices for the items they sell. Work in the ghetto is paid in coupons for washing, for wood, and for food. Zloty is only for the black market. You could pick up another mattress from the markets."

When relatives die, some people are quick to sell their spare bedding for coupons. But Mama does not mention this. It is not yet the time. They are still coming to terms with the small, hopeless space they must call home, just as Mama first did. She knows what Rada is going through.

"Gracious God, what sort of place is this?" says Rada.

She looks upon us with disdain. Our clothes have stains, though Mama has always stressed the importance of keeping our faces and hands clean.

"You have to watch yourself," Mama says. "There are desperate, hungry people in the ghetto. It would do no good to wear your jewelry. You must hide it."

"Hungry people are often troublemakers," Rada says to her husband, pretending to refer to others, but I feel the inference directed at us. "We must sleep with all our possessions."

"Heating is scarce, so hang on to your coat," Mama continues. "Do not let anyone convince you to trade it just because you feel hungry. We have blankets you can share until you buy some for yourself. While I am out, I will see what your money can get for you."

It is a shock in the beginning. They will adjust in time. We stand and watch them, but none of us feels the desire to comfort them. It is enough that we are giving up space.

Mama turns to attend to something else.

"Thank you," says Yuri. His appreciation is genuine. Life here is cruel for everyone.

Mama nods and leaves the room, while Leah moves closer to me.

"What is wrong with your sister?" asks Rada. "Why does she walk like that?"

I look at Leah, who appears not to hear the question.

"One leg is shorter than the other," I say, surprised that Rada has noticed. It is only a minor impairment. "She can't run as fast as most children. That's all."

"Did she have an accident?"

"No, she was born that way."

"Not to worry," says Yuri. "Who said you need two the same length?"

"Hitler says," says Rada quickly. She is still pale and angry. "He does not want those who are different or damaged."

I want to cover Leah's ears to shield her from this information. Until that day, I had never viewed my sister with pity before. Now I am wondering if it bothers her—whether she feels the difference. Before the ghetto, Leah had tried many times to keep up with me, to not be left behind or left out of games, but I have never really considered how hard she must work to hide her condition. *It isn't her fault,* I remind myself, *that she can't help with the water.* As Mama said, it is not safe for her outside.

I sit by the window to think of Simon and consider the choices I have to make, but my thoughts are interrupted by Rada, who has begun to complain about the unwashed sheets.

I look at my shoes. How much longer? Like this? *How much longer?*

A terrible thing has happened to Rada. She was lining up for bread even though I had warned her not to go out alone, when a group of young men grabbed her and took her fur coat. People know when you are new because you are not always looking over your shoulder—you have not yet mastered 360-degree vision. I felt very sorry for her because she and

Yuri have brought so few possessions with them—only a few items to fit in a suitcase. Yuri went to the Gestapo to report the theft, but they beat him.

Rada keeps feeling faint, especially when she sees people falling dead in the street from disease or starvation. She has not yet grown used to tragedy like we have: she does not yet have an immunity to the way things are, or the acceptance that comes before you are consciously aware of it.

She and Yuri were driven by truck away from their home and straight into hell. Both had engineering degrees and professional careers but are now unlikely to get a job in a factory. Rada complains about the smells from the rubbish and about the toilets and the fleas and the lice and the heat and the cold and the old vegetables that the rest of us have grown to crave.

After Rada's coat was stolen, I shared some of my coffee with her, and she cried with appreciation. It is a way to gain her trust, since she is becoming more paranoid and fearful than everyone else here. It is difficult to know who is working for the Germans, perhaps snitching, telling them what the ghetto residents are saying. I know of another person who was recently taken by force at gunpoint and never came back. He talked often about how the Russians would crush the Germans to pieces. He said how stupid the German soldiers were. He was vocal about many issues, and it ultimately led to his incarceration elsewhere— or perhaps his death. This has stopped many of us from talking. It was perhaps someone from this very building who whispered into the ear of a Judenrat informant the day that Imran was shot.

Yuri has a miniature backgammon game that he could not bear to leave behind, since it belonged to his son. We play in the evenings just before the lights go out. We blow on our hands in between the rolls of the dice. Leah and Mama take turns playing the game, also, but Rada prefers to watch. She does not have the spirit for games, she says.

Rada talks, though. She says they had a large house. Yuri worked for a building company, and Rada taught engineering at the university. They have two grown children who live in America, and one who was studying in Paris when war broke out. They wrote to all of the children and heard back from the ones in America, but they did not hear from their youngest son in Paris. Rada dabs her eyes whenever she speaks of him.

In just days Leah has grown attached to Yuri. She sits on his knee, and he tells her stories before she goes to bed. I am so grateful for this because I have not had the mind or heart to tell her stories anymore. They seem too removed now from this life, as if the gap between reality and fantasy is now too wide for me to bridge. The only story in my head is the one that sees us leaving the ghetto. Some might call such a story a fantasy, but that is all I care to imagine.

Lilli says that I must hurry up and join the youth police before the positions are filled. Mama says that the extra rations will make up for the fact that I am working for Germans. Prices are getting higher. Bread is expensive and in short supply. Wood even more so. What will happen tomorrow? Nobody knows. Day to day. That's what life is.

Tonight Mama has brought home beets, cabbage, rutabagas, and a tiny piece of sausage. It is more than our usual fare: potatoes and cabbage. Food is spread thinly since Mama does not allow Leah to stand in line for soup. Lilli has also given us honey and coffee that isn't really coffee, and we have been using these sparingly. The honey was a present for Lilli from Hermann Manz. One day Mama came home with an egg, and we boiled it, then shared it between the three of us, before Yuri and Rada arrived home from the washrooms. Sometimes it is like that. Sometimes there is not enough to share. It has been so long since we have had any milk. I dream about fresh milk.

Mama keeps commenting on how distracted I have become lately. Even sleep does not shut out thoughts of Simon. Spending time with him feels a little like my life before the ghetto, before the hunger. I have something to look forward to.

Rada is constantly whining. Once I caught her stealing a piece of bread from us, and Yuri was very ashamed of her. He has apologized for her, but she does not seem to care. She moans constantly. She is selfish with food portions. She complains that I have more blankets than I need. Once she took one of our blankets during the night. It is sometimes difficult to feel sorry for her. Leah told Rada to stop complaining, and I caught Yuri smiling at this. It saved him from doing it that time. It is good that they are there for each other. It is good for Leah to have someone like Yuri.

Yuri shakes his head. "Rada has changed," he says. "She has lost a small part of her soul."

I believe that I am close to making up my mind. It has been almost a week since I have seen Simon, and the wait has been unbearable. He has organized his next meeting for tomorrow night. I received a message from someone who passed me this information discreetly in the street.

The more time I spend away from him, the more I am missing him. I touch the ring that rests against my chest.

CHAPTER FIFTEEN
WILLEM

I stumble on the hard soil, deeply grooved from hundreds of boot heels trampling before me. Above a set of gates is an odd message of hope weaved into curved cast-iron lettering. *Work makes you free.* I repeat the words silently while examining the razor wire and the armed tower guards who surround the prison. An official arrives to lead me through the camp that is structured in uncluttered formation with exacting right angles and enduring solid housing—architectural symbols of German order. I squint at the sun that has been released from its own gloomy prison today, and my armpits sweat beneath my heavy coat. The rattle of rail trolleys disturbs the stillness.

I have been told little about my assignment; Father was afraid to put anything in writing in case the information should fall into British hands.

The chief physician here—Eduard Wirths—is a man of great distinction. A hard worker, someone who I have heard possesses the same ethics and discipline as myself. I was told by my father that Dr. Wirths has plans to extend the medical facilities here, with particular focus on research in the area of women's health. But though such plans are inspiring, the truth is, I am apprehensive about my true purpose here, and this weighs heavily upon me.

I would be foolish to think that the people who have volunteered for treatment are anyone but Jewish inmates. However, I also have been told that the experimentation will not only benefit the future of women's alternative medicines but will aid the prisoners, also.

After Lena's reaction to the story from the ghetto, I will be careful of what I tell her about the camp. Before, she was strong and opinionated but objective. Now with the pregnancy, she is sensitive and reactive. The information she receives must be filtered.

There is a sharp acidic smell in the air combined with the odor of sewage, combined with the stench of moist earth. When I comment on this to the guard who is escorting me to my sleeping quarters, he says that he doesn't notice any smell. He is used to it.

I am taken first to see the commander, and I raise my right arm proudly. This act binds us to the people we salute, and although Lena might scoff, I admit it makes me feel closer to Germany. Despite some of the distasteful things I have heard and seen, there is something beyond my misgivings that still keeps me immersed in national pride. It is Germany's fortitude, her resoluteness, and her preparedness. Even forced commitment cannot negate admiration.

In the absence of Dr. Wirths, who is otherwise occupied for the rest of the day, I question the camp commander on the medical undertakings ahead, but he claims ignorance. He is not a man of medicine, he says, and is ill equipped to explain the research. We then make the expected small talk about the success of the war before I am led to my quarters.

My quarters are comfortable and private. The bed is soft, with clean linen. I unpack my suitcase and place a photo of Lena on the table beside the bed. It does not take long before I am interrupted.

A woman delivers a plate of ham, boiled potatoes, and coffee to my room. It is too late for the main dining area, since other workers have already eaten and dispersed for the evening.

After my meal I fall into a deep sleep that is all too brief; I am suddenly woken by the sound of whistles and shots. Heavy running steps sound past my room. I quickly get dressed to learn what is happening and follow the running soldiers toward the building entrance. A young man yells, "Escapees!" as he passes me. Outside I enter sheets of heavy rain that fall from the blackness.

I follow the pack through the buildings, the white steam from our breaths disappearing in the bright strobes that have brought daylight to the camp. A siren blares across the bustling camp and into the frosty stillness beyond the wire. There is no sign of any prisoners—buildings black and still.

Ahead, several shots tap at the night air, followed by several more. The group fans out near the front of the compound, the men forming a circle to view something that I cannot yet see. As if participating in some kind of ritual, I step forward to form part of the circle. Several fresh corpses, blood marking their striped garb, are the objects of study. The bodies are slightly sunken in thick mud, some twisted grotesquely from their midrun fall. Some appear to be curled in sleep. One of the soldiers steps forward and shoots one of the corpses in the head. The sound, up close, seems personal, offensive, and leaves a ringing in my ears. He walks to the next and does the same, then the next.

Several other prisoners in pajamas appear from the night behind us to carry the bodies past me, and I turn away before I can meet their eyes. A numbness spreads through my head, a feeling that this is happening to someone else.

"Is this normal?" I ask the officer beside me.

"It is expected."

I am not sure whether he means the shooting of the fleeing prisoners or the frequency of escapes.

I return to my room and pat myself dry with a hand towel. My blood pumps hard through my veins, unable to find an even flow, and images of the dead inmates flash through my mind, preventing me from falling asleep. I picture one of the faces of the men, his mouth and eyes partially open. Did he have a family here? Does he have any children, a mother, father, siblings? I shake my head and stand to pace the room, the ringing still in my ears. I turn on a lamp and write a letter to Lena to distract myself and to tell her I can't wait to be with her again, then lie on the bed and wait for daylight to come to my window. The view from my room is the brick wall of another building. But before daylight another siren sounds, and I hear the shouts from guards as they call out numbers. It occurs to me that sleep in this place might be a luxury.

On the way to breakfast, and slightly on edge, I pass several people in the hallway. I introduce myself to one of the doctors, and I'm relieved when he shakes my hand warmly. I follow him to a table where a prisoner brings me a boiled egg and some bread. The prisoner then returns to pour me some coffee.

To the other doctor I have just met, I comment on the events of the previous night, but he says that he slept through any disturbance, that he didn't hear anything. This lifts my spirits a little, the knowledge that normality continues in the light of day, and I remind myself that my function here has nothing to do with what happened the night before. We touch on the subjects of our families back home, his interest in the health of children, and the successes of the German campaign until we have finished our meal.

Dr. Marquering is pleasant enough, even jocular at times, but he becomes somewhat preoccupied and nonconversational when I question him on the treatment of prisoners within the camp. The overall pensive mood of other diners suggests an absence of camaraderie here and a lack of cohesiveness among its workers, or perhaps what I sense is merely the usual fear of speaking freely on certain matters. When I inquire, Dr. Marquering directs me to where I should report for work.

But later, before I attempt to leave my room after having returned briefly to attend to my personal needs, a guard knocks on my door to escort me to a medical facility that accommodates mostly women.

Arriving at my destination, I see that the brick building looks slightly pink, even amiable, in the gray, filtered light. I am beginning to feel some measure of enthusiasm and confidence. Memories of the previous night are slowly being overridden by the events of the day at hand, and I remind myself that what I observed is part of war: one of the ripples between many other unsavory events that precede an ultimate calm.

Inside I am taken to an office first for briefing on schedules and paperwork where several doctors have assembled to meet me. Dr. Wirths is there, warm and welcoming, though I am disappointed to learn that he will not be directly assisting in this research, and that I will be instructed by Dr. Kohler. The necessary introductions are made before Dr. Wirths makes his retreat, and Dr. Kohler then takes me on a tour of the facility.

I am led past several women who lie in hospital beds. Kohler points to one of them and advises me that she is scheduled for a procedure later that morning. I am told that I will be sterilizing several of the women from this ward.

"How are they screened?" I ask.

"Screened?"

"Do they have a history of illness, mental or physical? Have they agreed to this? Standard questions prior to surgery."

The doctor looks at me over his glasses.

"They are prisoners." He waits for my reaction, of which I show none, then turns away, expecting me to follow. I feel unclear about this response and offended by such an offhand explanation, yet I remain convinced that more information will come to hand once I am assigned a patient.

He takes me to a surgery and leaves me to familiarize myself with the items I find there. Inside are shelves filled with tools and instruments. There are variously labeled chemicals but only a few bottles of morphine and sulfonamide. There is a bed covered by a linen sheet that looks used: crumpled, with light and dark stains of undeterminable origin. At the end of the bed sits a colposcope to photograph the womb—another tool to understand the science of women, to diagnose diseases, and to capture the effects of medicines and treatment.

Moans come from a room nearby. The hallways are strangely empty of doctors, and some of the windows are boarded up. I trace the sound to a woman strapped to a narrow bed in another surgery. She is unsupervised, naked under the light sheet that covers her. Her body is so thin I can see the outline of her bones beneath the sheet. The women in the ghetto were thin, their rations small, but the size of her is confronting. When I ask her what is wrong, she replies in what I perceive as Hungarian. Judging by the arm she clutches across her stomach, I can see she is in much pain. I check her chart, which says that she was given a small amount of pain medicine the previous day and a solution identified only by a number—which I do not recognize—an hour prior to that. She is shivering, and her head is hot with fever. I look in the adjoining rooms but do not find any doctor, so I return to my allotted surgery to retrieve some medicine for pain and find more blankets to cover her. Back with the patient, I pass her a cup of water along with the tablets.

"What are you doing?" says Dr. Kohler, who enters the room.

"This woman is very sick."

He walks over and takes the aspirin from her hands.

"You cannot interfere with the testing!"

"But she is clearly in some discomfort."

"These subjects must not be touched," he says impatiently. "We are measuring their responses to certain chemicals."

"Exactly what chemicals? Dr. Kohler, you have yet to explain the procedures here."

He ushers me from the room. I look back at the woman, whose eyes are partially open, watching us. I wonder if she understands any of our conversation.

"You must come with me, and we will have a little talk, yes?"

We walk down the hall to a communal room where we interrupt several doctors who appear to be taking a break.

"Please . . ." he says, his arm held out to direct me to sit at a table with the others.

Another female prisoner, Aryan in appearance, serves us each some coffee.

Kohler tells me that the prisoners brought to these rooms are available exclusively for our trials, but that pain medicines, anesthetic, and sulfonamides must be used conservatively, if at all. I am told that these drugs are used mostly for SS and general German military patients, and with the war not progressing as fast as had been hoped—it is the first time I have heard someone say this out loud—we need to be careful with the use of medicines.

"But pain relief is a large part of the healing process," I say. "If they are not coping mentally, then how will they help their own bodies recover? I would have thought that this would help achieve positive results for your trials."

"The way in which they cope with pain is not the issue we are testing. These particular tests are purely from an anatomical aspect, not a holistic one."

The irritations and doubts that surfaced briefly in the ghetto loiter once more in the corners of my mind. I picture Lena beside me, asking questions. *This is work? Advancement? This is personal . . .* Yes. Yes. No, I answer her. The quality of treatments conducted under someone like Dr. Wirths must not be questioned.

The other doctors return to conversing about their patients. It seems that they require more "subjects" to test, and it seems there is a shortage of pregnant women. All the participants—I have yet to learn if they are willing or not—receive extra food.

I am then taken on a tour of other rooms, on a different floor. Two prisoners almost naked, a man and a woman, appear burned, the skin on their stomachs blistered and raw. I learn that this type of sterilization is radiation therapy. I can hear whimpering in the distance, and when I question Kohler, he says, too casually, that he doesn't know the particular source; there are several other tests being performed at present, and I will no doubt come across these at a later stage.

Tomorrow I will begin my own work. I will be assigned a female for sterilization. Kohler has given me a list of chemicals to use in the trial: silver nitrate and new compounds that shrink the size of the ovaries, until they eventually dry up. This is meant as an alternative to surgery, which has sometimes led to complications. I tell the doctor in charge that I have not heard of this particular practice being effective, that I have only heard of its success in theory. *Niggles. Doubts. Lena. Elsi.*

"Silver nitrate is not yet qualified, and there is little evidence to suggest that this and other chemicals like it are safe for the woman during these procedures," I say.

"It is why we are here, Dr. Gerhardt," says Dr. Kohler. "Silver nitrate is only one compound, and there are several others that you have seen on the list. We are developing a solution that could alter the practices of sterilization and pregnancy termination. It is now a matter of eliminating options until we find the most effective solution, the most effective method."

"And the effectiveness so far?" I ask.

He pauses, his lips forming a straight line for a smile. I cannot tell if he is pleased or irritated by the question.

"You should be aware that our work here has barely begun, and the procedures in need of refinement. Our intravenous method has led to some complications, but I am confident that intrauterine will prove the fastest once we have completed our trials."

"It sounds very promising," I say, though I am not sure if I sound sincere. *Primitive* is perhaps the word I want to use for a procedure that I once read had been abandoned decades ago.

"One day, Dr. Gerhardt, we will be able to perform hundreds, perhaps thousands, of sterilizations a day."

He has called out to another doctor he has seen in the hallway and ended our conversation before I have a chance to ask him in what circumstances such numbers would be necessary. A guard collects me then to escort me back to the block where I am being housed.

Tonight I dine with several other SS men and women. We are fed roast beef with onions and beans. I am offered some rum, but I decline. Then we are served small cheesecakes with cream and oranges. There is so much to eat that I do not finish it all.

That night I sleep well. There is some commotion during the night that disturbs and rouses me briefly, but I am too exhausted to investigate the sounds.

I wake early the next morning with renewed vigor. I am looking forward to meeting my patients. First, I wish to discuss with them their genetic histories and learn of their previous environments. They may be prisoners, but it is important to understand their mental states and hereditary factors before we perform the testing, to enable us to determine their suitability for such and apply certain methods accordingly. The psychology of what we do is equally important as the physical methods applied. I will have to disagree with Kohler on that point. I am in charge of my patients. My work will make a difference to women's choices. Anatomical methods are only half a treatment.

Dr. Kohler greets me coolly. He says that we must go immediately to our first patient. I cannot say he is an amiable man, not warm like Dr. Marquering, who accompanied me in the dining area on my second day. Dr. Kohler has a face that is too small for his large, balding, misshapen head, coned at the top back of his skull and wide and fleshy near his chin. *Disorganized*, I would say if I had to describe his looks: his features and body parts not arranged in any considered order.

A woman is waiting in the surgery I have been assigned, brought here in the early hours. A nurse and a female guard—who I am told has no medical qualifications—stand nearby. The new patient lies on her back on the surgical bed, her legs apart in stirrups.

"What is this woman here for?" I ask Dr. Kohler.

"She is pregnant, and we will be applying a solution to abort the fetus."

"She does not want the baby?"

"She wanted larger portions of food."

The woman is emaciated. Her hospital gown lies flat across her middle, as if there is no body beneath it but rather something shapeless—something that does not suggest the presence of a woman here. Her legs and bony knees protrude like some garish, skeletal display, and I think of a butterfly that has been pinned onto a board.

I struggle for words at first. This is not the procedure I would follow. There are a number of steps that must be taken before placing a woman in such a vulnerable position.

"Has the patient been explained the procedure?" I ask.

"Of course not!" snaps Kohler. "That is completely unnecessary."

"Dr. Kohler," I say, which comes out in a stutter, confused. I am rarely flustered. Many will attest to this.

"Call me Karl."

"Can I speak to you?"

"Yes."

"Outside."

"We can talk here. It doesn't matter."

I lower my voice and see that the patient is watching me, though I cannot tell whether she is fearful or in pain.

"I must talk to my patient before any procedure. It is a matter of course."

"Willem," he says, squeezing my shoulder, condescending in this effusive familiarity. "This is Auschwitz."

He is suggesting that this name alone gives the treatment legitimacy. That he is free to instruct me as he wishes. I wonder then if I should use my father's name to remind him that I have certain influence here, that I am best to decide how the procedures will take place. To someone older, and as experienced as Karl Kohler, I will perhaps come across as a spoiled child.

"You must learn and watch," says Kohler. "This is a prison camp."

I turn to the patient, who watches our conversation intently, although it is doubtful she has understood any of it.

"Can you please tell me your full name?"

She stares at me blankly.

"What is your name?" says the guard aggressively in what sounds like Polish.

"Wira," she says.

"Wira, my name is Dr. Gerhardt. Are you aware what is happening to you?"

She does not answer. She does not understand the German language.

"Dr. Gerhardt." Kohler's warm familiarity is suddenly gone. "It is unnecessary to question her. Her name and other details are written on the chart here."

I ignore him. "Wira, do you agree to have your baby aborted?"

She averts her eyes perhaps because of my tone. Her eyes dart toward Kohler—for support or out of fear or in the hope of interpretation.

"I believe you are frightening her," Kohler says, and for some reason the female attendant finds this amusing.

"I would like some time alone with her, please, and could you find an interpreter, another prisoner?" I want the guard gone.

Kohler ignores me, and the nurse passes him some fluid in a bottle.

"A woman must be absolutely certain she doesn't want the baby," I say.

Kohler abruptly puts down the bottle, leans into me, and hisses in my ear. "Come with me, please."

He leads me into an office down the hall and shuts the door behind us. On the desk is a picture of a woman and two grown boys that I presume are his family. In the background is a large gabled house.

"I'm afraid that you have been misled into thinking this a private practice," he says. "Here, we do not treat our prisoners as well as our officers. All prisoners here have forfeited certain rights. Yet we are generous and offer food. That woman will likely end up dead from her pregnancy. The baby will steal valuable nutrients that she needs for herself. As for the baby, if it ever did see the light of day, it might only be for a matter of minutes while it is transported to the gas chamber."

I stand there as if fixed to the floor. These are things that I have listened to in group conversations, things that may or may not have been rumors, that I assumed had been exaggerated by the speakers, the boasters, the mockers. To hear this firsthand—to be here, to know for certain—stabs sharply at something deep inside me, some place vulnerable, where regret and shame reside, that until this moment had been protected by an impenetrable cordon.

"All she cares about is food," Kohler tells me. "Do you understand? For now, she will be living in this block and receiving extra food. If you take that away, she will go back to the block where she will live on half a bowl of watery soup and a small piece of bread. What would you have me do? Send her back to more uncertain misery? Or can we continue with our work and make progress for women in the future?"

He looks around the room as he speaks, shifting from foot to foot several times, and I am reminded of an organism beneath a microscope that is so concerned with its own survival it is unaware it is being observed.

"Although you will be mainly focusing on sterilization methods, there are other things done here, like tests to check for cancerous growths. Make the most of the opportunities we have."

His redeeming quality is that he is calm in nature, but he fails to see the truth of what he does. I nod to agree, not because I do, but because my concerns seem unsalvageable. *I must endure.*

"Today you are merely here to observe."

I follow him back to the surgery, my head hung slightly lower: a student after caning or, Lena might say, a dog with his tail between his legs.

Two guards are now in the room and stand on either side of the woman. Kohler retrieves a large syringe from a medical tray, and the nurse passes him a vial of liquid.

"Which solution are you using here?" I ask.

"You can read the breakdown of the compound on the patient's chart," he says, as the nurse passes it to me. "We hope not only that the dose kills the fetus but that she finds it difficult to get pregnant again."

"How many weeks pregnant is she?"

No one answers me. The woman's eyes are wide. There is heightened fear there that wasn't there before.

"She was pregnant when she arrived several weeks ago."

"Does her husband know?" I ask.

"He is dead."

I am being led to believe that she does not care what she is doing. That the hunger has taken much of her rational thought. I think, sadly, that it is a blessing her husband is dead. That he is not aware she did not fight harder for the life of their child. Yet the fear in her eyes gives way to doubt.

"You are certain she knows the consequences of this testing?"

Kohler ignores my question.

The two guards put pressure on the woman's shoulders. She has not moved, and I think perhaps such force is unnecessary.

A narrow tube is inserted between the legs of the woman and through to her uterus, and Kohler begins to inject a brown-colored liquid. The woman eyes the intrusion suspiciously and then moves in discomfort. To stop her from wriggling, one of the guards and the nurse hold her down firmly on the table. The patient is now completely immobile and too weak to resist. I step toward her, but the way is blocked. There are too many people in the room.

Kohler withdraws the tube, but the guard and nurse do not release their patient.

"Please," she says in broken German. "Not my baby."

I take a step back, aware suddenly that I am part of a deception. This woman was not aware of the consequences, or perhaps any protest she previously made was ignored.

She begins screaming in pain, and Kohler shoves a cloth in her mouth. After several seconds, the guards and nurse step away from the surgery table, and the woman draws her knees up toward her chest to alleviate the pain. Outrage consumes me.

"This is inhumane! We have to give her something for the pain."

I take a vial of Novocain from my own medical bag and draw up the contents into a syringe, then thrust my way past a guard and inject it into the patient's arm before Kohler realizes what I have done. The sheets below her are suddenly thick with blood.

Kohler's face is as dark as mine, but I do not care. I push roughly past him and storm from the surgery and the medical barracks to head back toward my accommodations. My breakfast is burning a hole in my esophagus. In my shock, I do not at first notice a group of prisoners being led in a straight line between two of the buildings. This world inside the camp is suddenly so far removed from the outside. I do not look up; my fury threatens to rupture every cell within my body. I was told that I would be in charge of my own procedures, yet here I am reduced to follow, like sheep, into practices I find hard to accept.

"Willem!"

I turn to see the group of men in their pajamas, shoeless, trouser bottoms torn and filthy. They look identical: thin, long-faced, shaven heads. I cannot distinguish one from the next, nor the person who has called to me. A man steps forward.

"Remember me?"

I don't at first, but then comes a faint memory.

"From school!" says the man.

A boy—a runner, an academic, a mathematician. Someone who beat my own marks.

"Omar?" I say.

Omar is a man driven to something beyond impoverishment, but joy illuminates his ashen face. Recognition is perhaps a rare experience here, and for someone to remember him as he was before—to acknowledge the man within the frail shell—gives him this moment of pleasure.

"Yes," he says, and I step toward him, eager to shake his hand.

Suddenly, he falls forward, facedown into the dirt, and a German guard now stands in his place. It takes several seconds to understand that the blow from the heavy butt of a rifle has made an indentation in Omar's head.

I look at the guard who has done this. He looks back at me, stony-faced.

"What for?" I yell, rushing to Omar's side.

"He was out of the line."

I roll him over to check his breathing. There isn't any. His heart has stopped, also. It did not need much to give up so quickly.

"I will have you imprisoned for such actions!"

But the guard isn't listening. He is marching the others toward a wall.

I look down at the wretched form: a person, a man reduced to rubble.

Someone steps beside me.

"He was as good as dead anyway." I turn to look at the speaker, another guard, who nods toward the wall at the end, between the two blocks.

The prisoners are being lined up. I stand up, back away, then turn and walk briskly to my room, legs trembling, heart racing. Breathing is difficult. The sun burns through the clouds to uncomfortably rest on the back of my neck. I feel a cold sweat break out over me.

This is not a world I belong to. It can't be.

Nothing can be the same.

Behind me are the sounds of gunshots.

CHAPTER SIXTEEN
MATILDA

I am instructed by Cook to take some bacon and rolls to Nurse and Frau, then return to the kitchen to clean up. When I return, I find another girl sitting at the table. I have seen her outside the house but never this close. She is older than me and lives in the big house but must spend much time in her room. She has pretty cloud hair, white and fluffy, but she reminds me of an owl with her angry, watchful eyes that look over me suspiciously. She wears a white dress like the older girls.

"Hello," I say. "My name is Matilda."

"I know who you are."

"Are you going to tell me your name?"

"No."

"Alice!" says Cook, frowning at her.

"There! You have it now," she says, without looking at me.

"Do you know the story about Alice and the looking glass?"

"No."

"It is a storybook about a girl who climbs through the mirror into a strange place."

"How would a stupid peasant girl know any stories?" she says.

"I'm not a peasant. I'm a lavender farmer."

"That means you're a peasant."

"We read lots of books. I can read lots of things."

"I doubt that. You're a liar."

"How come you don't go outside with the older girls?" I say. "Do they hate you? Do you smell?" I am angry that she has called me a liar.

"How come you don't shut your mouth," she whispers while Cook is emptying rubbish in a bin outside the back door. But her words don't deter me.

"How long have you been here?"

"Long enough for it to be annoying," she replies.

I smile at that. I like her attitude. When she sees my smile, her eyes linger a little longer on me. I see that she is slightly curious and wondering if perhaps I am more interesting than she thought.

Cook returns.

"Alice has been sick, but she is feeling better now. Aren't you, Alice?"

"Yes, Cook," she says. I believe that Cook may have overheard my question after all.

"What do you do here?" I persist.

"More important things than you do."

"What are they?"

"Learning to be a German woman."

A laugh escapes me. I am surprised at the sound that I haven't used in a while.

"What is so funny?"

"I don't know. It just sounded silly. The fact that anyone has to learn to be a German woman."

"Saying those things will get you into trouble," says Alice.

Cook has turned her back to us. She doesn't interfere this time.

"You don't sound very busy. Surely you must be doing something else?" I say.

"Are you always so rude?"

"Frau says that some girls are for greatness and others for purpose. Which one are you?"

Cook finally participates. She looks in my direction and shakes her head. It is a warning. Alice has gone very still, staring out from her very white face.

"That is enough questions," says Cook.

"Matilda," says Nurse. She has appeared at the door suddenly, hair like wire, a wicked troll. "Have you practiced the first paragraph from our Führer's book?"

I recite the first three paragraphs from memory and then begin the fourth until Nurse says, "Enough." I think I hear Cook say *remarkable* under her breath, but I can't be sure. Perhaps it was something else.

Alice is looking at me from under her large eyelids as Nurse leads me to Frau's office to recite the passage again.

There is no toilet inside our hut. We each have buckets that we must empty, ourselves, into an outdoor toilet in the backyard. Then we must wash out our buckets in the sink outside the building. I can see the room where I was locked in like an animal in a trap, and suddenly I feel I might vomit. I never want to go back to where it is dark and lonely. It is better in the hut, where I can sleep near others, though the mattress is thin and hard, on wooden slats. We must also clean our sheets when they are soiled, and it is my job to clean the baby's, too. I wonder why Jacek is not given such tasks. It seems I am given everything to do. Perhaps I am still being punished. Perhaps because I am a girl.

Nurse is like a ghost who haunts the house, appearing around corners suddenly. When we are in the kitchen, she appears silently behind us. Then when we are at the swings, she is there, watching us. Once she told us to keep the noise down when we were laughing. It seems there are rules even for laughing. One day she was called inside the house by Frau, and while she was gone, we chased one another around the yard and laughed very loudly. The best time is at night, inside the hut.

It seems we can do anything in there, and if we are quiet, we can even stay up late.

"Do you ever get frightened?" I ask the twins, who sometimes now respond in German when they can. We do two hours of German each day.

"We used to, but not anymore. Not with you and Jacek."

Jacek adds, "We used to play games in the dark. We used to jump across the beds like cats." He is smiling when he tells me this.

"Ah, I see. So you were being naughty then and not sleeping."

The smiles disappear into stormy faces. "No it was not . . ." One of the twins screws up her eyes as if she might cry.

"It is quite all right with me. I would have done exactly the same thing if I were you. I won't say anything."

"One time we were told on. One time they sent in one of the older girls to spy. Are you a spy?" says Jacek suddenly.

"Of course not," I say angrily. I know that the older girls will report anything they see. But they keep their distance, as if they will catch an infection from us if they get too close.

"In fact," I say, to ensure their trust, "let's all be like cats now."

The three oldest ones exchange guilty smiles. They can't quite believe it.

I saunter on all fours and pretend to lick my hand, then I skulk around the beds crying, "Meeooooow."

The others do it, too, though the baby just crawls, without the cat actions.

When we are finished acting like cats, I teach them some more words in German. It is enough for now. I open up a book with another German title. I pretend to read from it a story called *Rumpelstilzchen*, but they do not know I am pretending. They cannot read the front of the book. And I tell them another story that I remember from home.

"She's coming," says Jacek.

"Who?"

"Nurse. I heard the door squeak from the house."

Nurse turns the key in the door to enter. I begin to read a passage from the book. It is very boring, and I don't think about the words; my mind is on Nurse, who is standing and listening. I stop and turn to her.

"Carry on," says Nurse.

"More story," says Baby.

"Story?"

"She thinks it's a story," I say.

"How is the children's instruction of *Mein Kampf* progressing?" she asks. "They must learn a paragraph a day. They must be able to speak it from memory."

"Yes, I am teaching them every day. Is that not right?"

Jacek nods, as does Baby when she sees Jacek do this.

"Good! It is a very special book, and this would please the officials when they visit."

It is not a special book at all. It makes no sense.

CHAPTER SEVENTEEN
WILLEM

I have been to the commander to explain that I want to be moved. He has politely refused my request, citing a letter from Himmler's office that ensures I continue in these duties for several weeks yet. Again he talks of opportunity.

Here, there are no rules in medicine. We can make our own. But I do not want the opportunity. I do not want to *see*.

My body has been trembling over the past few days. I try not to look at the faces of the prisoners, out of fear that I will see someone else I know. I do not think recovery for patients is possible at this terrible place.

Yesterday a shipment of Hungarian Jews arrived. All the children and elderly were sent to special rooms to be killed by poisonous gas. I could hear a pounding, a stampede of animals, while they were locked in the room, slowly dying. And then the loud thumping slowed, then softer, until nothing.

How can I face Lena again after everything I have seen? She will see it in my face. I must not let her. She must never know this.

A guard comes to my door to advise me that I have a phone call from my father. I am instructed to go to the administration office.

"I have heard what you're doing," he shouts through the receiver. "Refusing to work."

"You hear everything, Father," I say flatly, forcing down the tremor at the back of my throat.

"You have made a spectacle of yourself. Get back to work. Be a man!"

And then he disconnects the call. He is ashamed of me, for my outspokenness. I have never felt so helpless. I have never had reason to, as I have never known anything but structure. Here in the surgeries there is none. This is a cold, brutal facility, and my father knew this before I came here. He is just as cold. My aunt once said that he changed after my mother died, but I don't believe that people change that much. My father was born cold; he was just able to hide it for a while.

Several days have passed. I have written several short letters to Lena, describing my room, the doctors, and the food, but nothing else. Dr. Wirths visits me in my quarters and says that I am to take my time. As soon as I feel better, I can return to my duties. He reminds me that our work here is pioneering, but he understands that for some, there is a period of adjustment. It is from these words that my trembles begin to disappear, that I begin to accept this is my prison, also, with no escape. When the walls begin to close in on me, I return to the medical barracks.

I will be handling my first case alone today. I have spoken to Kohler, who says that I am to have full access to the facilities to complete my tasks. He says that Dr. Wirths has said that I am to apply the experiments, but in the way I see fit. Kohler calls me aside to remind me of the state of the women.

"These women have no future. You must remember that."

I do, but while they live, there is always hope. I must not consider their fates as terminal. It is the only way I can treat them.

The woman I observed undergoing treatment the previous week is dead. She bled out that same night. I put her face out of my mind and focus on the one now in her place. She speaks some German, and I question her on her family background, though she does not say much. I tell her what is happening, and she has agreed to sterilization. She is thirty-four and hungry. She has children, but she does not know where they are. They were separated at the beginning of the war.

I hand the patient a fresh hospital gown and send her to be showered. When she returns, I help her up onto the bed and cover the top of her body with a soft blanket, not the coarse kind she is used to in the prison blocks. Such small attempts to give comfort are not common practice here, but the nurse does not question me. I suspect that she has been warned about me.

To calm my nerves, I begin to hum Lena's favorite tune while I work. I squeeze my patient's hands at times and think of Lena, imagining her at home by the large front window.

There are no guards to hold this woman down, as I requested, although the nurse does rest her hands on either side of the woman's shoulders in case she should move while I inject pain relief and apply the syrup. This time, though, I halve the dose that Kohler has written on the chart. There is some bleeding, but not like the last time. She moans slightly and clutches her lower abdomen. I give her more pain medicine that I have brought in my own medicine bag.

There is the sound of some gunshots between the buildings. Inside I flinch, though outwardly my hands are steady.

Kohler enters and reads the chart. "We have already experimented with this dose. This is too low. It doesn't work."

"As high as you did, and they die," I challenge him.

He says nothing and leaves.

I increase the dose in an hour, and the woman starts to writhe and sit up. I call the guards to hold her down while I strap her to the table. It is something I reluctantly have to do.

At lunch, the other doctors and I discuss our patients. I must remain objective as I listen to their various accounts of treatment. I hear horrid tales of people vomiting from radiation, of people too sick to stand and return to their blocks, and bodies in stacks to be cremated. A prisoner walks past the doorway of the lunch area wheeling away a patient who died earlier today from treatment that I am not involved in. His body lay on a hallway table for several hours.

A telegram is placed on the table in front of me. This communication is not from my father this time—he has sent several blunt reminders of my commitment—but from one of Lena's relatives. I read the message, fold it, and place it in my pocket.

In the evening I return to my quarters. Dr. Marquering passes me with several children. I was told at the meeting that medical trials will soon begin on children, also. The doctor between them holds their hands and tells them a funny story. Their eyes wander over the doctor, curiously, some rapturously clutching sweets in their little hands as if they will be their last.

I see a naked woman carry her dead child through the camp. The child lies stiffly in her arms, having been dead for perhaps longer than a day. The woman walks in the direction of the gas chambers willingly, as if there is no more to lose except her life—a life that she no longer wants.

I have seen some terrible sights in the ghetto: people dying from disease, starvation, and executions, and families separated. I have seen soldiers killed in the street. I have seen people mourn over their loved ones, wailing, the sound penetrating the souls of those around them.

But there is something about this place and the things that occur here that make me feel accountable. A feeling I have never had before. Perhaps it is the separation from Lena and the idea of fatherhood that deeply affects me on a personal level. I want to be imprisoned. I have carried out the most heinous experiments on women. I want to pay for what I have been a part of.

My father does not believe in God. Nazism is his chosen religion. But Lena does. If there is a God, I wonder if at that moment he is looking directly at me, waiting for me to act. Waiting for me to throw myself at his mercy.

I drag myself on heavy legs back to my room. I carry the weight of the atrocities and feel Lena's eyes upon me.

I walk with my eyes looking ahead, for fear they might fall on the eyes of the prisoners and someone I know. When I get to my room, I sit down on the bed and stare at the floor. I begin to shake violently, sweat on my forehead and in my armpits. The room is dissolving, fading, and stretching into one ghastly blurred and bloated shape, as if the objects around me are no longer solid.

I open the telegram again and read the first line.

"Lena has died."

1943

JANUARY–MARCH

CHAPTER EIGHTEEN
MATILDA

Cook made a cake on Christmas Day while Frau was away visiting family for two days. Christmas is different in here. At home, Mama used to make pies and cakes, and Tata would bring us home each a gift, and we would invite other people from the village, and people would sing. But we are not allowed to sing our songs from home. The older girls went home for several days, except for Alice, who stayed in her room.

Nurse has left a bag of washing at the back door. I do not feel like washing today. I say to Jacek, "Why don't you do the washing?"

"Because I am not a girl."

"Well, you act like a girl."

"That's mean."

"You're mean."

I storm off to the washroom, and Jacek comes in a little while later. He stands in the doorway and rubs his shoe back and forth on the ground noisily. I ignore him.

"I can help with some," he says. "We can do it together."

It takes longer than normal because we talk the whole time and stop more for breaks. He says he has a sister back in Poland somewhere. She was a few years older than him, and he remembers that his parents both worked and did not come home till late sometimes. His sister did a lot of the cooking.

I tell him stories about my brothers fighting, and we laugh all the rest of the day.

At breakfast Alice is there. She has porridge with apple, nuts, honey, ham, bread, and butter. The rest of us are to have only porridge now. I wonder why we are not to eat what she eats. She sits at the other end of the table and does not want to talk to us. With my hand I scoop up a handful of porridge and put it in my pocket.

"Cook," I ask, when Nurse has left the room, "why don't we have a proper teacher?"

Alice turns her head sharply toward Cook, who does not interrupt her cooking tasks; neither does she seem to want to answer.

"It is because they don't want to spend the money," says Alice. "They don't want to waste it. Until they see whether you are worth keeping, perhaps for the officers." There is bitterness in her words.

"Alice!" says Cook in a firm voice. She turns to me. "It is because they do not have enough good teachers."

I look at Alice, who stares at her breakfast.

"I was told I would have a good education here," I say.

"You just need to wait and not ask questions," says Cook.

• • •

If I am to be the teacher, I might as well do things my way. While the children sleep that night, I write down several stories of my own on blank sheets of paper. Then, using the sticky porridge from my pocket, I glue them onto the pages of *Mein Kampf.*

In the morning I say to the others in the hut that I have an announcement and a surprise.

I pause.

"I have decided to name the baby."

"But you can't do that," says Luise. "You aren't allowed."

"Who says?"

"Frau Haus says," says Jacek.

"No, she didn't," says Adele.

"Yes, she did," says Jacek sheepishly. He is lying, I can tell.

"Teachers can give names. I am sure," says Adele.

"What name? I'll have to approve it," says Jacek, who likes to think that he is in charge because he is a boy.

"I have decided to name the baby Sarah."

"That is a fine name," says Adele. Luise says nothing. She has an angry face most days.

I look to Jacek, who shrugs.

"It is better than *Baby.* Sarah is my cousin's name," I lie. I chose Sarah because I like it.

Luise fiddles with her fingers and looks at Jacek, who is finally nodding his head. "It will do."

"That's good. As long as we are all in agreement," I say before there is any further objection. "Now, here is the next surprise."

I pull out the book *Mein Kampf* and hold it up. Jacek's chin drops to his chest.

Adele is waiting for something more. She is a lot like me. She has a spark in her eye. I think she knows there is more to come.

"It looks like a boring book," says Jacek. "This is no surprise."

"Then you don't know that I have found some new stories inside."

They crowd around me, even Sarah, to look at my written pages.

"What are they?"

"They are my stories."

"Can you tell us one now before we do our spelling?" says Adele.

"All right, but it is our little secret. You must never tell that I have written them."

I read one of the stories. It is about a boy who does not lose hope that he will one day find his missing parents. He travels the world—across mountains, swimming through lakes, riding horses, battling soldiers—trying to find them, and one day he does. I have deliberately made my hero a boy to impress Jacek, since he is the one I must impress the most, and the others look up to him. When I have finished, Jacek has tears in his eyes, and the twins ask for more.

I write more stories that night and the next. The pages of *Mein Kampf* are filling up with my writings.

One morning we are woken very early, when there is still fog.

"We have a very special visitor," says Nurse. She has brought us clean uniforms and socks. And we must wash our faces, and the girls must tie back their hair. Nurse has also brought scissors that she uses to trim Jacek's hair. Adele dresses Sarah, and then holds her hand to follow Nurse. Luise is trembling.

I hope it is not the people who take children away.

We are led along the hall, toward the front of the house. I have not seen this part since I first arrived. In the front room there are couches and chairs, but Nurse says we are not to sit down. Four older girls are already there, sitting on wooden chairs, but we must stand in a line. One of the girls finds this amusing, and another points at my shoes with their laces undone. Frau Haus reminds them to behave like young women. She tells us all that we must not say anything until we are spoken to, and we must stand very straight and still. Alice is nowhere in sight.

On a tray there are plates with pieces of cake with cream. I can smell the vanilla that Cook uses in many of Frau's desserts. If I were to take two steps forward and stretch out my arm, I would be able to take one of the cakes. The older girls are not interested in the cake. They are too busy giggling and talking among themselves.

Sarah does not want to stand and crouches beside Jacek. When Nurse tells her to stand up, she ignores the command. It is too late for Frau to punish her, because there is a man climbing out of a vehicle parked near the front window. He wears a uniform like Herr Lehmann's and carries a shiny wooden cane.

"Who is he?" I whisper to Jacek.

"Shh," says Frau, to all of us.

Jacek shakes his head and puts his finger to his lips to tell me not to ask any more questions.

The cane man walks into the room and greets Frau Haus. His name is Major Sievers. They talk about his travel and the weather and the war, and then the major is led to a couch. He takes off his hat and places it on the seat beside him. He has a large stomach, and I can see that all the cakes will not be enough to fill it. Cook enters with a teapot.

Sarah wants to lie down now, and Nurse is looking at her with evil, narrow eyes. I pick Sarah up and hold her.

Herr suddenly shows an interest in the older girls as he bites into a piece of cake. He is looking them up and down as if he wants to eat them, too.

"What a lovely bunch of girls you are."

He asks them some questions, and they tell him that they have joined an athletics group and they have all won ribbons. One of them recites something in German, some kind of poem about loyalty that I have not heard before. His eyes keep dropping to her knees, and I see that there are crumbs left on his face. The girls speak very well and sweetly. But I have heard them talk in the backyard. They are not that sweet.

"And these are the younger ones . . . the orphan program," he says. He does not look us up and down, nor does he smile. With his mouth closed, his jowls sag halfway down his neck. "How is their conversion going? How are the adoptions going?"

I am confused why he has called us the orphan program, and where Frau has been to see these adoptions.

"We are further along than we hoped, Herr Sievers. They will soon be Germanized to such a high standard that our center will be ready to receive their replacements."

"And they all passed the testing?"

Frau pauses before she answers, and Herr's eyes, which had wandered back to the girls, dart back to Frau again. "Yes, Herr Major."

"Very well. I would like to hear some of them speak."

"Matilda," says Frau Haus, "I would like you to say a paragraph."

I repeat several of the paragraphs before the officer gets bored with me.

"That is all," he says, swatting at the air. "Who is next?"

"Ernest," says Frau Haus, "I want you to recite the first few lines of *Mein Kampf* for me."

Jacek is looking at the floor.

"Jacek!"

He says three random German sentences, but that is all.

"Jacek," urges Nurse, "a paragraph from the book!"

Jacek begins to tell my story, in German, about the boy who fights soldiers before finding his true home.

"What's this nonsense?" says the officer.

"Ernest!" says Frau Haus, with her lips together. "Speak a paragraph from *Mein Kampf*!"

He shuffles his feet nervously back and forth. This is to stop his legs from collapsing.

"I don't know it, Frau Haus," he says, his eyes on the floor.

The major sits forward. "What did you say, boy?"

"I cannot say the words," says Jacek, louder, as he sneaks a look at me.

"Adele, can you say a paragraph?"

"No, Frau Haus."

Frau is looking at me. Everyone is looking at me.

"I thought you said these children were being Germanized!" says the major.

"Yes, Herr Sievers, however with the teachers very busy with the older girls . . . we do not have the resources . . ."

"There is a list of people waiting for children. If these are not the ones, then they must be disposed of."

"Herr Major, we have been waiting for more children . . ."

"I see that this place needs better supervision, and the sooner we can recruit a commander for this place, the better."

He stands, his large body filling up the center of the room.

Frau assures him that she will rectify the problem and instructs Nurse to take us to the dormitory.

It is my fault. I am the cause of this.

"What is going to happen?" asks Luise.

She has sensed the mood. She has sensed that Frau Haus is close to exploding.

Back in the hut, I pick Sarah up and put her on my lap. "I will teach you German, and we will be all right."

Jacek is not looking at me.

We hear the squeak of the door at the other side of the crossing, and more than one pair of steps. Nurse is coming, as well as Frau.

They stand in the room and survey us. Nurse holds a leather strap this time.

"Stand up," says Nurse to Jacek. "Turn around and pull down your trousers."

Adele and Luise begin to cry.

She whips him once, and the sound cracks the air like thunder. I feel Sarah jump in my arms. I can see that tears are dribbling from Jacek's eyes, which are closed, his mouth twisted and trembling. Nurse raises the leather again.

"It was my fault!" I shout.

Frau lowers the weapon and takes two steps toward me. I take the book of *Mein Kampf* and pass it to her to show her my misdeed. She opens the book and views the sheets with my writing inside. She looks at me, and I can see the devil inside her before she slams the book shut again.

"Stand up!"

I do not resist when Nurse grabs me and rips apart the buttons of my dress, which then falls to the floor. Nor do I resist when she tears my underpants down to my knees. I cannot look at the faces of the others. I cannot look at the open mouths of the twins, or listen to the muffled cries of Sarah in her pillow, but I catch a glimpse of Jacek, who has squeezed his eyes shut, who is fighting back more tears. I am spun around and made to face the wall. The whipping makes the sound of a broomstick smacking the dust from the blankets on the washing line, although the sound of the strap is muffled slightly when it hits my hip bone. Then it is more like a thud.

"I doubt anyone will want to adopt you now," says Frau.

Even with the leather that eats into the backs of my legs, these words give me some hope. Perhaps now they will return me to my family.

We are up to five strikes. I do not know how many times more because I am sending my mind first to the hills behind my house where I can see my brothers waiting, and then next to the stories inside my head.

When the beating is done and the pain is burning through me, I am again sent to the small bolted house at the back of the property, where I curse the night spirits who have come to listen to me wail.

CHAPTER NINETEEN
ELSI

It is dangerous, what we are about to do past curfew, but I trust Simon and his friends, Andre and Paulus.

"I want you to know how brave you are, Elsi."

My heart beats a little faster every time Simon holds my hand.

We sneak along the alleyways until we stop at the end of one and sit still and quiet for several minutes, watching in the direction we have come. At the other end of the alley is a tall lamp, and the rain flickers in its yellow glow. There are no sounds of guards, only a slight pattering of rain on some rubbish near where we crouch.

Andre shines a flashlight onto a grate while Paulus unscrews bolts and removes it from the wall, sliding the metal to one side. Andre and Paulus crawl into the dark hole first, and Simon whispers for me to follow them. Inside the opening, which I presume is a vent of some kind, I can smell damp earth before my hands touch the floor's cool surface, and there is roughened concrete just above me. In the pitch black, I feel a hand on my back steering me farther into the space. Against the dim light behind me, I can just make out the shape of Simon as he climbs through the gap. He then slides the grate across the opening so that we are concealed from outside.

"Light the lamp," says Simon.

There is a strike of a match, a hissing, and light erupts around us. The space is only tall enough to allow a child to stand. I survey the new faces around me in the light. There are six others with us. They are on a list to be deported, so Simon and his friends have arranged to hide them. There is a woman with a baby sleeping in her arms, a boy around six, and an elderly man, all from the same family. There are also two ghetto orphans. They have been living inside this small space with stolen food from a truck that stops behind the kitchens. While the drivers make their deliveries, Simon takes some of the fruit and sausages, earmarked for the administrators, and delivers them to the boys.

He does not keep any for himself, or so Andre tells me.

Mama doesn't trust Simon. One day I invited him into our apartment and asked Mama if he could sleep on the floor. Simon was courteous, but Mama wasn't warm like she normally is with my friends. She was horrified when he called me *Angel*. "These terms are too familiar," said Mama. "He does not know you so well." She believes that such names are too personal, and that such intimacies should be built up over time between family and close friends. She is very old-fashioned that way, but she doesn't know that Simon and I are connected now. That we are very close.

It is after curfew, and this means it will be difficult to get home. I know that Mama will be worried sick if I stay out all night at someone else's place, but that is better than being caught and taken to the camp prison. It is not the first time I have done this—stayed out all night. Last time I went with Simon to Andre's apartment, which is closer to the group's secret meetings. When I came home the next day, Mama was so angry. Yuri just looked at me with those eyes that know things. He says things not out loud but in other ways: a touch on the back of my hand or shoulder. I have grown so fond of Yuri.

"We have to be very careful tonight," says Simon. After the fire in the washrooms, it has become more dangerous in the ghetto. People have been questioned. The Gestapo hates to appear careless. The Judenrat chairman has told his members to be more vigilant, to do more inspections more frequently. He wants to stay on the good side of the Gestapo. Simon hates the chairman as much as he hates the Germans.

These people inside this hole in the wall are designated to be shipped to the camps. From Simon's contacts outside, we are hearing that terrible things happen in the camps, even worse than in the ghetto. Some people are being executed in the camps to reduce the number of prisoners, and there is even less food there than in the ghetto.

Tomorrow night we are to meet behind the uniform factory with one of these contacts from outside the ghetto. Simon has been passing messages back and forth with him. Someone once told me that Simon never sleeps, and at Andre's I saw that this is true. He lies down and then gets up, paces, goes to the window, writes some notes. He is always thinking, always planning something.

He has already passed a dozen people through the fence, including a pregnant woman. He is sorry that he didn't save his sister, who was pregnant, also.

Tonight we stay in an apartment that has a window frame with no glass. We cannot stay in the hole in the wall because there is not enough room for the people to stretch out to sleep. They have a long journey ahead of them.

This apartment is infested with fleas, worse than ours, and I itch during the night and stay awake, also. Simon reaches for me in the dark, and I wriggle close to him.

"Thank you," he says, "for trusting me."

• • •

In the morning when I come home, Mama is so angry she can barely speak. Leah plaits the hair of her doll in the corner. She always looks frightened when anyone is upset.

"Where were you?"

"Safe. With friends."

"With that boy?"

I nod.

"No more!"

"Mama, I'm sorry I worried you. But there were several of us, and we were talking so long I didn't realize the time. I thought it was safer for me to stay there."

"What happens if you are caught out after curfew? What do you think will happen then? What?"

Mama is pacing, looking from me to the view from the window, as if the street and I are somehow connected, as if the answers are there if they are not with me.

"If you do it again—"

"What will you do? Punish me?"

She can't think of what to say. There is nothing she can do that could be worse than the punishment of being in the ghetto.

"As long as you are out of harm's way," says Yuri, bringing balance to the argument. Rada sits reading old letters. She does not want to be part of this conversation. Though occasionally she looks up over her glasses at Mama to check her expression. Leah stands up to put her arms around me, and we stand there in silence for several moments, until Mama finds it too hard to think. Her shoulders drop.

She nods her head. "All right, Elsi, you are an adult now. But perhaps you can let me know next time. At least that."

"Tonight, Mama, we are playing cards at Andre's."

It is partially true. I write down the address and hand it to her to make her feel better.

Leah says, "Do you have to go?"

"Only tonight, because I've promised. But then I will be home for many nights." I pick up her doll and straighten its soiled dress.

"Let's go and give her a bath today at the washrooms?"

She brightens slightly and nods.

Mama looks at me, frowning.

"She can't go," Mama says. "You know that. Only when necessary. Nothing that draws attention."

Leah has come with us in recent days to line up for soup and to go to the washrooms, though she can only go outside for these reasons, and she must link arms with one of us to better disguise her impairment. With so many more arriving in the ghetto each day, she is one of many young children now. Mama keeps her hair very short, paranoid that others, whose children were deported, will recognize her and try and hurt her for being allowed to stay. For me, it is a relief that Mama and I no longer have to share our soup with Leah, and we no longer have to dispose of her waste. Rada has not coped well with that situation either.

"Then I will get some water and we will do it here," I say, and Mama looks between us both, helplessly, as if there is so little she can offer either of us.

I wish I didn't cause Mama more worry and pain. She has been through so much. I will talk to Simon. I will tell him that my family needs me and that, after tonight, I must spend more time at home. He will understand.

We meet at Andre's and wait in the dark till midnight. It is drizzling with rain, and my legs are covered by stockings that do not keep out the cold. I pull my scarf tightly around my neck.

Simon touches my gloved hand. He has seen my worry. "Don't be scared," he says, steam gushing from his mouth. "All you have to do is keep watch for any guards while the others cut the fence and then repair it again once we have successfully smuggled them from the ghetto. Have you brought the medicine?"

I pull out the bottle from my pocket.

"Good!" he says.

"Just a spoonful . . . my sister needs it, also."

"Yes, of course. But it would be good if you could bring some more next time."

Simon says that the medicine will help save the life of one of the orphans. Lilli has been supplying medicine for Leah, who is prone to catching a chill. I feel certain that Lilli can get more.

We are planning to smuggle the people out of the ghetto through a fence behind the uniform factory where I work. I have seen the access to the world outside that can be reached from the loading dock at the back of the building. Simon had asked me to describe the rear of the property near the fence and describe any lighting. During a toilet break, I had managed to exit the rear door to view the area to study. I drew him a map, and he has been examining it for days. The loading dock is in a private courtyard. He has told his contacts on the outside to meet us at this point, where we will cut the wire fence behind an outhouse and pass the people through.

We walk along the street, blending into the dark. There is no moon, which is why Simon has chosen tonight for this mission. In the street across from the factory, we watch and wait until the guards have walked past the area; then we cross and reach up to the factory window, the one I unlatched before I left work earlier in the day. We climb through, passing the children in one by one, including the baby. Once we are all inside, we scurry toward the back of the room, which is filled with sewing machines.

Paulus opens the rear door, and we step out into a small enclosure that leads to the perimeter of the ghetto. We cannot be seen. We are totally hidden from the eyes of the guards. I show Simon the area of fence that is never seen, behind the outhouse.

We sit and wait in silence for many minutes for our cohorts on the outside to arrive.

"Where are they?" asks Simon. "They said twelve thirty."

Andre checks his pocket watch. "It is just after," he says. "They can't be far now."

"Maybe they have been and gone," says Paulus.

"No. They would wait in the shadows. I know them," says Andre.

"Are you sure they got the message?" says Simon to Andre.

"I gave it to Suri to give to them. She has never let me down. Elsi, go through the building. See if it is still safe—that we haven't been followed."

I enter the building and head toward the front of the building. There is some lamplight filtering through the front windows of the building, but I know this place well. I can find my way in the dark. As I reach the large sewing room, a flashlight is shone in my face.

"Stop! What are you doing there?"

I turn, squinting and blinded, to face the light. I resist looking behind me to check that the others are out of sight, which could give them away and destroy the operation.

"It is you!"

I put my hand up to block out some of the light. I cannot see the speaker's face, but it is someone who has recognized me. When he is closer, I realize that he is the soldier with the scar along his jawline, the same one who said I resembled his sister. The guards must have keys to the buildings.

"What are you doing here?"

He checks behind me to see if there are others, then points the flashlight upward; the light bounces off the ceiling, making it easier for us to see each other. My hands are in my pockets. I can feel the medicine bottle.

"I work here."

"It is an offense to be out at night."

He looks very young in this light, and his voice is a lot softer now that he does not have other soldiers around.

"Why are you here after curfew?"

I pull the medicine from my pocket. He shines the flashlight on it, then points it back at my face.

"Earlier today I collected my sister's medicine from the medical center, but it wasn't until I was at home this evening that I remembered I had left it here beside my sewing machine. I couldn't wait till morning. My sister needs it tonight."

"How did you get in?"

"Through a window with a broken latch."

My legs are shaking again, but I maintain control. I know that Simon and the others will hear us talking.

"Where is your card?"

I pull out my identity card from my other pocket.

"Elsi," he reads, then studies my picture on the card.

"All right then," he says, inspecting me in person now. "Your hair has grown a little but not much. It still looks odd."

"Yes," I say. "It's terrible."

He laughs softly. "It's not so bad. I will escort you back to your apartment. Other soldiers may not be so tolerant. You are lucky it was me who came. Come, Elsi! I will take you home before your sister starts to worry."

He points the light toward the front of the building, and I breathe a sigh of relief. At least the others are safe now. Even safer than before, now that one of the guards will be distracted.

There is a thud beside me, a groan and gush of air, and the soldier falls on the ground, his flashlight rolling across the floor. Then there is another thud, and another. I rush forward to pick up the flashlight to see what is happening. Simon and Andre each have pieces of steel, and they are beating the soldier with them. His helmet has rolled off, and his head has become a pulped and bloody mess.

"Stop!" I yell.

"Shut up!" says Simon. "You will alert more guards."

I back away slightly. I turn the flashlight away until Paulus grabs it from me. I cannot look.

"I could have taken him away," I say. "You would have been safe."

"He may have checked the window and seen that the latch isn't broken, that you lied," says Andre. "He may have seen that it was deliberately unlocked."

Or else that is just an excuse to kill him.

Simon tears the watch from the dead man's wrist. The fugitives are still waiting outside. They have not had to see this.

"We can bargain with this on the black market," says Simon. "Look and see if he has money."

The others scrounge through the soldier's coat, and I feel suddenly sick. Simon shines a flashlight on my face.

"What is wrong, Elsi? You look like you have seen a ghost. This is what happens in war. It is either them or us! Do you not want to save your own?"

"I have never murdered anyone."

"Your conscience is clear. This is survival, not murder. Here there are no rules of crime. Your German soldier would know all about that."

The men wrap his body in his coat and use his trousers to mop up the blood on the floor. They carry his body outside and bury him in the earth. Simon puts the watch on his own wrist. It is nearly one o'clock. His contact didn't come.

"We must go," says Simon, and we all climb back out the window. The family and children will be taken back to the hole in the side of the building.

"Be careful," says Paulus to me. Simon is out of sight. "Stay close against the wall."

• • •

I let myself into the apartment and ease myself quietly into bed. Mama doesn't move to question me, so I believe she is asleep with Leah beside her. From her loud snores, Rada is also asleep, but Yuri is awake.

He lights a small oil lamp that he bought at the market with one of his gold cuff links.

"Are you all right, Elsi?"

"Yes."

"You don't look well."

He gets up and passes me a bowl. "We saved it for you."

I take a sip of the broth, but I can't swallow. I am thinking of the soldier.

"Get some sleep," he says. "It looks like you need it."

He has kind eyes, and his gentle concern makes me start to cry. He sits on the bed and holds me, rocking me slightly. I have wanted Mama to do that for so long, but she has been too tense, too distracted.

"Yuri," I whisper tearfully, "I do not believe that anything I try to do amounts to any good."

"Elsi, everything I have seen you do is done with good intentions. But in these hard times, good intentions can only go so far and are rarely carried forward by the next person. Whatever it is that has caused you to doubt yourself tonight will be judged by God only. Remember that always. These are impossible circumstances we live in."

That is what I am worried about. That God might see this differently.

It is morning, and Mama comes to my bed. I am shivering, and my head aches. One blanket is not enough, and Mama says she will find some more wood to burn, that I must not go to work today.

"Oh, my poor darling." She wraps me in blankets and tries to feed me the rest of the cold broth. I push her hand away, and she kisses my forehead. Her lips feel cold against my skin.

"I will see if I can get something for your fever."

Simon comes to our apartment the next day. Yuri is pretending not to watch us, while Rada watches us closely.

"I'm sorry that you're not feeling well," says Simon, and then he leans his head in to whisper. It seems that Suri, another group member, did pass on the message, but they have since learned that one of their contacts on the other side of the wire had to leave the city suddenly. Suri thinks they may have to delay the operation for a while, that perhaps their contacts on the outside are now being watched. They don't know for certain.

"We will get another message to our friends outside, and try again in a few days."

He says that the family will hide in someone else's apartment for now. The orphans must go back to the streets and fend for themselves because Simon doesn't think he has enough food for all the fugitives.

"What will happen to them?"

"They must go back to begging and risk being caught and placed in the new children's prison, where they will eventually die of hard work or disease. Or they will be scooped up by the Gestapo and taken out of the ghetto to the camps. That is why we must continue with this cause. That is why we cannot stop the fight against this cruelty."

He whispers that he is sorry for what happened and tells me that I am very pale. I smile weakly. It is good to see him, even though he is a reminder that we have done something wrong: we have committed a murder.

"I know that you feel bad about the soldier. But remember what they have done to so many of us."

"I know," I say. "But it is a life we have stolen from someone else's family. I do not think the soldier was as bad as some . . ."

Simon sits up suddenly and releases my hand. His expression suggests that he is offended by this comment. "You will change. I am surprised you haven't already. You have been here even longer than me."

Mama is home before Simon leaves. He is suddenly in a rush to go.

"He is afraid to look me in the eyes," says Mama after he leaves. "What is he hiding?" She has had a good day at work and has brought home more food coupons and wood and an aspirin for my head that her supervisor has given her.

Mama reports that she has heard of a break-in at the factory where I work. She said blood was found on the floor, and the owner's dog has found a body of a soldier that went missing on guard duty the night before.

"He was beaten viciously to death, his money stolen. It looks like someone broke in to try and rob the place and was caught in the act. Guards are knocking on everyone's doors."

I feel a stabbing in my chest, and my temples throb.

"Are you all right, Elsi?" asks Mama. "You look very ill."

She gets me some water, and I swallow the aspirin.

"We might have to take you to the hospital."

"No," I say. "I will be fine." I force a smile so she will move away, so she will stop examining me, in case she can see my guilt. She returns to the kitchen.

"What has happened to the medicine I had in the cupboard? It is gone."

I remember that it is still in my coat.

"You mean this?" says Leah, holding the bottle.

"Where was it?"

"On the floor under Elsi's bed."

Mama looks at Rada, who has not been feeling well lately. Suspicion always falls on Rada whenever something goes missing.

The knock at the door comes after curfew. It is a member of the Judenrat, asking if anyone left the apartment the night before and if we have any information on what took place at the uniform factory. They are questioning everyone in the ghetto. Before Mama can lie for me, Yuri says that we were all there together. He sits on my bed, protectively. Perhaps he has sensed that I am shaking.

The official is a boy I used to know before the war. He was a few grades ahead of me at school. He asks about Papa and says that he is sorry my father isn't here.

"Did you know that Germany has nearly taken Stalingrad, and Russia will be wiped off the map in a matter of months? Russians are lining up now to join the German Army."

I cannot tell him that I have heard otherwise. Simon has heard that the war is not going well for Germany. The Germans had expected to have taken Russia by now, but the word is that Stalingrad refuses to fall, and its people will fight to the end, taking all the Germans they can with them. Russians are streaming through any cracks in battle, and they come back in greater numbers after each one. The British are steadfast. The Americans have an endless supply of weapons.

Simon also told me, "Though Mussolini is a sycophant, and has sworn allegiance to Hitler, he is not as keen as some on the idea of giving up his Jews as quickly as Hitler wants. Mussolini has also taken a beating from the Allies."

The boy from the Judenrat says that more deportations are imminent because too many people are coming to the ghetto.

"They have heard how good it is," says Yuri under his breath so only I can hear. I sneak a look at the old man, whose gaze does not waver against the official's. Yuri breathes fresh air into our suffocating apartment. Rada is watching me suspiciously as always, with those black eyes that are recessed deeply into her forehead.

When they are gone, Mama comes to my side.

"Elsi, do you know anything about the break-in? Did you see anything last night?"

I look at her while I think of how to answer, pausing perhaps a little too long.

She looks away, nodding her head. It is not a time for us to talk, though I long to tell her everything. To release the crime from inside my head. To say how sorry I am that this has happened. But I cannot burden her.

The next day Rada is out, and Mama is not scheduled for work.

"Do you remember your grandmother's house by the river?" says Mama. "I dream of that place. I dream that we are sipping coffee on the grass near the river reeds. I dream of the simple things, like helping my mama bake bread, feeding the horses and the hens, mending socks in the sunlight, and smelling the fresh scent of spruce from the hills. Sometimes I close my eyes and picture my mama's smile and the knowing look in her eyes as I tell her something, as if she already knows what I am about to say."

Mama turns to me, and her expression is more serene than I have seen in weeks. Memories are the places many seek to live. It is where people, like Mama, are happiest.

"You are so like your grandmother, Elsi," Mama continues. "You have her spirit. I remember when you were small, you swam out across the river, and when you got to the middle, you ran out of strokes and your father had to come and rescue you. You cried and stamped your feet once you were dragged from the water and said that Papa should have left you alone—that you would have made it all the way across. The next day you swam out again, and you made it all the way across, just as you said you would. Don't lose your ability to fight, Elsi. Even if it is for just one more day, it is worth it. I wish I had the fire that you have within you. But I can see it dimming. Don't ever let the fire go out, my darling."

She looks at me, her narrow face thinner than ever. I cannot let her down. I have to be strong.

"Mama, I will be fine. *We* will be fine. Don't worry so much."

She squeezes my hand, and I lean forward to hug her tightly.

Later that day I am feeling better, and by nightfall, I have made a decision to keep helping Simon.

CHAPTER TWENTY
MATILDA

My buttocks and the backs of my legs are still sore, and it is difficult to sit down. I lie on my stomach for most of the day. My underwear sticks to my skin. Sometimes when I twist, I can feel the scabs tear from the wounds. All I want to do is sleep, where I do not feel. Sometimes when the older girls walk past my window, they look in through the flap, and I expect them to say something mean. I imagine they will say things like "Grimy little Gypsy" or "How is your kennel today?" but they don't. They don't say anything. All is quiet most days, except for the sleet that patters on the roof.

On the second day, Alice came with a bowl of warm water, antiseptic, and bandages. She helped me take off my underwear, which tore the scabs that had formed, but she was very gentle.

"These aren't too deep. You will heal."

She helped me into a fresh uniform, a knitted cardigan, and new socks.

I did not say anything, nor did I wish to look at her.

"Matilda . . ."

When I finally turned to look at her, I saw that her face had become very blotchy, and there were dark circles around her eyes.

"Don't let this change you," she said.

After she had gone, I wondered which parts of me I shouldn't change.

I have not heard the other children out at the swings. Perhaps it is the weather, or perhaps they are being punished, also. I carry much guilt. If I had taught them the Führer's words . . . I decide that if I get out, I will be a good girl. I will teach the others how to speak German better than Germans do. We will speak it day and night. We will memorize the words from the book.

Or I will find a way for us all to escape.

I have not yet decided what we will do.

My meals are smaller, but I am not very hungry anyway. Sometimes Nurse takes almost a whole bowl of oat porridge away. She does not talk to me. I remember seeing her look away when Frau was hitting me. I do not think she has ever seen someone punished like that before.

I do not care that there is scurrying in the night. I am too sore to care.

One day, I think it is the fifth, I hear Jacek outside the hut. He has come to take my toilet bowl and empty it.

"Are you all right?" he whispers.

I crawl from my mattress to peer at his face through the hole. His face lights up when he sees me. I did not realize until then how much I missed him.

"Yes."

"Does it hurt?"

"Not so much now. But I'm very cold. Are you cold in the hut?"

"Yes. When are you coming out?"

"I don't know."

"I have to go. I will see you later. But we can't wait till you come back. We want to hear more stories."

Just the sight of Jacek's face has made things look brighter.

"I can't, Jacek."

"You can," he says. "We will just have to learn our German as well."

Finally Nurse comes to take me back to the hut. The snow clouds have come out to laugh, then curse at me. I am taken to the washrooms and then to the hut. Nurse says that Frau has made a new rule: no more Polish words are to be spoken at all. If Frau hears any of the "orphans" do so, they will be sent to the bolted room.

The others are still in their nightgowns. I want to run to the children and hug them, but they are solemn. It is then I notice that something is different. Luise's face is red, her eyes puffed out like they have been stung by bees.

I don't say anything until Nurse is gone.

"Where is Adele?"

"She's been taken."

"Where to?"

"To her new family," says Jacek. "Nurse said they were desperate for a child." He has known this would come. He has seen this all before.

Luise is lying on her bed sucking her thumb. I have never seen her do this before.

"Why wouldn't they take Luise, also?"

"They don't take children together. Frau says it is better if they're separated," says Jacek. He is picking a scab off his knee. He is not looking at any of us.

This is such terrible news. I thought we would stay together until our parents came to rescue us. I have grown used to them.

"Soon we will all be gone," says Jacek.

"I have parents. They wouldn't do that," I say.

"I have parents, too, but that doesn't make any difference," says Jacek.

"Luise, do you have parents?"

She nods.

"But why do they call us orphans?"

"Because that's what they want to call us."

"They can't take us away," I say. "That is wrong. My parents would not agree to it."

"Your parents will not even know," says Jacek.

I cannot sleep that night. Luise has been crying for much of it, until she climbed into bed with me. Sarah is at the bottom of my bed, also.

"Jacek," I whisper.

"Yes," he says.

I am relieved he is awake.

"Are you scared?" I say.

"Yes."

"I think we should run away."

He sits up on the edge of his bed. I ease myself off mine and move to his so I do not wake the others. I can just make out his eyes and nose, which look smudged in the dark.

"How? Where will we go?"

"Back to our parents," I say. "We can ask someone on the outside to take us there. We can give them the names of our towns. We can make up a story about who we are. We can say we were accidentally separated from our parents and lost our way."

"But Luise does not even remember her real name—how is she going to remember the town?"

I am remembering the files in Frau's office that have our names on them, which may also have our addresses. I also saw that there were keys in her top drawer. Perhaps one of those will open the hut. Perhaps they are spares. Perhaps she won't notice they are gone.

It is snowing today, a heavy fall. The snow is heavier up here in the north, though I saw a little wildflower the other day between patches of snow, fighting to stay alive.

I am teaching the children to write in German. Jacek is very good, Luise is not trying very hard, and Sarah is too distracted. The *Mein Kampf* that had my stories in it was taken, and a new one has appeared. I read passages aloud, and the others recite after me.

It is not the same without Adele. Luise lies on her bed. She is always looking at things inside her head now. She does not want to talk at all. She does not like the German language. Sometimes she even snaps at me when I tell her that it is time for washing.

"Luise," I say, "you should learn German so you don't get punished. The fat-faced officer might be back, and he might swear at you. Or worse, he might beat you."

But she still says nothing.

"Story," says Sarah. Sarah is not learning any words, German *or* Polish.

"Yes, story!" says Luise, suddenly alert. "The one about the boy who finds his parents across the sea."

Jacek nods his head in encouragement.

"I'm sorry, Luise. I am not allowed to tell any more stories."

She lies back down. Even Jacek has turned to face away from me.

Don't let this change you.

"Maybe just one then . . ."

• • •

While I am in the laundry washing our clothes, Jacek rushes in. It is Sarah. They have taken her. I run back to the hut and find only Luise there.

"Who took her?"

"Nurse."

"No parent?"

"Just Nurse. There was a van at the front of the house."

"Why?"

"Nurse says that she is going somewhere else where they can teach her better."

I have to see for myself. I have to stop the truck. There is a guard standing outside, so I run through the kitchen door and into the hallway that will lead to the front of the house. Halfway down, Cook grabs hold of my arm. She is very strong.

"Stop!" says Cook. "You will get yourself in more trouble."

"But Sarah—"

"Is about to leave."

"Where to?"

"To another shelter."

I don't know whether to believe her, my eyes scanning the vehicle at the front of the house. There is no sign of Sarah.

"Matilda," she says, "there is nothing you can do. If you go out there, they will put you on the truck, too."

"Then Sarah won't be alone."

"You don't want to go there. There is no chance, once you are on that truck, that you will ever see the others again."

I do not fight her. I want to cry, but people are here. The older girls have come to see the commotion. When they realize what has happened, they roll their eyes and leave again. They do not care. There is nowhere to cry in private, so I swallow my tears and follow Cook back to the kitchen. Alice is there with a lump on her stomach that I have not noticed before. She now wears the same dress as me but hers fits much more snugly, with the buttons straining to stay fastened across her chest.

"She was not good enough to be adopted," says Alice.

"What do you mean?"

"The baby isn't smart enough to be a German."

"Alice!" says Cook in a raspy, loud whisper.

"What?" says Alice. "Why can't they know?"

I don't understand what that means or where Sarah has been taken. When I am back in the hut, I tear pages out of *Mein Kampf* into little pieces in my anger. Jacek and Luise watch, but they don't say anything. Later I hide the torn pages in my toilet pot.

The plan is that when we come to breakfast, Jacek will tell Nurse that he saw people watching us from the woods. Then Nurse will alert Frau, who will walk out the back. While they are outside, I will go into her office and retrieve the keys.

The plan works, at first, though it is Cook who goes to find Frau because Nurse is busy. In the office the drawer is locked. I look around the shelves but can't find a key to the drawer. I return to the kitchen before Cook and Frau come in from outside. The plan has failed. We must think of another one.

I have asked Nurse if I can have more duties, if I can be of more help. In the month since I was released from the small locked house, I have been very good, always saying, "Yes, Nurse" and "Yes, Frau Haus." I have offered to take on extra washing. I sweep out the hut and wash the steps at the entrance. All these things I do without being asked. Sometimes when the older girls come into the kitchen, which isn't very often because they have their own dining room, I tell them how pretty they are and how I like their hair.

Frau has called Jacek and Luise into her office to recite some German. She asked them to answer questions in German and read some passages they have never seen before. Later they told me that she said they had done very well, and she was pleased. She said that perhaps they can be Germanized after all, and perhaps they will also be adopted. They didn't want to hear this, but they pretended they did. They acted like they were keen to leave and go to new homes once they had learned all the German.

But it isn't because I like it here that I am working so hard to impress. It's because I have a plan. If I can have more chores, then I may have access to more of the house. Then I can find the key to unlock our hut at night. One corner of the property is not patrolled, and I know the guards are lazy at night. I have heard them talking and laughing.

We plan to leave next month because the weather is still bad now and the ground is frozen. Luise is very keen to go, as is Jacek.

In Frau's office, I ask her if I can help Cook with the cooking since I was very good in the kitchen at home. I say I will also help Cook clean up afterward. While I am asking this, I am looking around the room to see where the key to the top drawer might be hidden. I know that Frau has a set of keys that she doesn't wear, and Nurse has a set of keys that she does.

Frau has granted me permission to do as I suggested, though I must be in Cook's view all the time, and I am allowed only in the kitchen, not farther into the house.

"You have shown great progress, Matilda. I hope that you will continue to do so well."

I want to ask her what happened to the good food and the teacher we were promised, but I bite my tongue.

"Thank you, Frau Haus," I say crisply in German. "I feel honored to be here."

When Cook finds out I will be helping her, she does not look surprised. Once Nurse is out of the room, she says, "What are you up to?"

"I want to help you," I say.

"Tch," she says.

I don't think she believes me.

A new child has arrived. She was brought in before dawn. She is frightened. She has fair, curly hair and bright-pink cheeks, and she clutches a small blanket that is covered with pictures of rabbits.

She is introduced as Juliane. Nurse opens the door to the hut and shows her to one of the spare beds. When the door is shut and she sees our foreign faces, she bursts into tears. Jacek and I rush to her and tell her that everything is good here, even though it is not. We tell her that we will look after her.

In the kitchen I help Cook and keep an eye out for Frau and Nurse. I know that Nurse occasionally spends time with the older girls in the paddock next door. I know that sometimes during the day Frau leaves the house. I am studying to know when it is a good time to go into her office. I also have to be careful of Alice. Sometimes she is in her room, sometimes in the kitchen, and sometimes she sits outside in the cold and writes something in a notebook.

Cook has given me the key to the storeroom at the back of the house. She has asked me to get some flour. Alice is sitting outside on the cold ground, and I stop to talk to her. She does not like to talk to anyone.

"Why is your stomach getting bigger?"

"That is a very rude thing to say. Go away, little Gypsy!"

I laugh because I like the sound of "little Gypsy."

"Why are you laughing?" she asks crossly.

"Because it does not sound so bad when you say it. Your voice is too sweet."

Something in these words takes the frown from her face, and the line of her mouth widens to nearly a smile.

"Well, you *are* still one," she says and goes back to her notebook.

"Are you having a baby?" I say.

"Yes," she says, and looks away toward the field where the other girls are in their winter-white uniforms, marching in the snow. I heard them complaining about the task as they left the house today.

I shift from foot to foot while I think up more questions.

"Why are you still standing there?" says Alice. "Haven't you got washing to do? I have a ton of it. You can do mine next."

"Are you married?"

"You are too nosy."

She stands up to walk inside.

In the storeroom there are sacks of food. It smells like lemons, wheat, and herbs. I love the smell. Some shiny red apples are visible through a gap in the top of one of the sacks. I take one and squeeze it into my underclothes. There is a bag of dried dates, and I take a handful and squeeze them in as well.

Back in the kitchen I have to walk very carefully so that nothing falls out from my underpants. Cook lets me roll some dough. She says that because I am such a good helper, she will make some extra pastries for us—which the older girls, Frau, and Nurse usually have—but that we cannot tell anyone.

I like Cook. She is not like Nurse, who watches everyone with roving eyes, and not like Frau, who carries a baton and is always looking for reasons to punish.

Once when Cook raised her hand to point somewhere, I flinched and she put her arm down.

"I won't hit you," she said. "You have nothing to fear from me."

At night I bring the apple out, and we all take a bite, and I share the dates. Juliane is keen for these, though she is still sobbing.

"I want Mama," she says.

"Your mama will come back for you one day, but for now we will look after you," I say. Because there is nothing else to say.

I sing songs quietly into her ear until she falls asleep. Little children are not as annoying to me as they used to be. I like that they follow me and listen to everything I say. And suddenly I am wondering whether it is a good idea to run away because Juliane is only four and a half and too young to run away. I am wondering what will happen to her if we leave. Who will look after her?

When she is asleep, I put this question to Jacek and Luise.

"She will have to live on her own for a while, like I did," says Jacek, as if he is throwing these words casually over his shoulder. "She is new. We shouldn't care so much."

"It doesn't matter about Juliane," says Luise, but with more desperate urgency, shaking her head. She is still not the same. She has not smiled once since Adele was taken.

"It doesn't matter," agrees Jacek.

"No, it doesn't matter," says Luise again.

But it does to me. A little.

It is afternoon, and we are having bread and soup in the kitchen. One of the older girls runs into the room. She says that a girl is injured from a fall in the field and for Nurse to come quickly, that the girl is bleeding from the nose. Nurse rushes through the back door with her medical bag, and Frau follows, leaving her office door wide-open. When Cook leaves to go to the storeroom, Jacek nods.

This time the drawer sits open. Frau has not had time to lock it. I search through the keys in the drawer. I take two of the largest keys that look like the ones Nurse carries and hope that one of them unlocks the hut. The cabinet where our files are kept is locked.

When the lights are out and Juliane is asleep, we put the key in the lock and turn it. We have success.

"We can go now," says Luise, who is coughing. She has had a fever this week. "We can go tomorrow!"

"No," I say. "Not yet. You have to get better first, otherwise you won't be able to run far, and it is not warm enough. We leave next month, like we said. Besides, we still have to find out where you have come from. We need to find the documents that your parents signed."

Jacek agrees with me. "It will be too hard to dig under the fence. We need time for the ground to thaw. But we don't need the documents. We just have to get to Poland. Luise might remember where she came from once we are there."

Luise looks confused, and Jacek explains again our plans to her in Polish.

"Yes, I can find my way home from there," she says, but I know this isn't true. Not even Jacek and I know how to find our way home.

I hope that more children come by the time we go so that Juliane is not left alone.

But worse is the thought that we will be caught and I will be put permanently in the tiny, cold, bolted house, away from everyone and alone with the spirits who whisper to me through the gaps in the walls.

CHAPTER TWENTY-ONE

ELSI

There are heavy footsteps on the creaking stairs. Then come the knocks on the door. They are not the same knocks that we have heard before: they are more urgent and angry. Before we have had a chance to get out of bed, the door is kicked and swings back violently. Two members of the Gestapo burst in, and the room explodes with light.

"Get up!" The voice that speaks is harsh and screechy, and it jolts us all to a standing position, except for Rada, who is slow to sit up, as if she is sleepwalking. She stands, turning her eyes downward and then to the wall. She is looking for something to hold, something that will support her. She looks sideways at her husband, avoiding the eyes of the police.

"What is it?" asks Mama, wrapping a shawl around her shoulders modestly to cover the top of her nightdress.

One of the Gestapo steps toward me and pulls me by the arm toward the door. Mama tries to push him away, her shawl dropping to the floor, but she is grabbed around the throat by the other.

"Mama!" I say, fearing that she is about to be killed.

"Elsi," says Leah. Whimpering, she rushes forward to throw her arms around my waist. We are quickly torn apart.

The policeman releases Mama, who then reaches for Leah to pull her close. I am suddenly unreachable behind the guns and the uniforms and the badges.

"What are you doing?" says Mama.

Behind the Gestapo members, an officer appears. He wears a badge of seniority. We are becoming more familiar with badges.

The officer pulls up a chair, and Mama looks close to collapse. There are red marks on her face and neck.

The officer looks around the apartment. It is dingy, one of the bad ones but certainly not the worst. It is tidy, things put away or folded, but there is also an odor of mold and something rotting that the neatness cannot mask. He probably smelled it as he came up the stairs. The look on his face says that this is the most disgusting part of his job, having to mix with Jews, having to smell their apartments, having to step over bodies in the street, having to wipe the thick soot off his boots. There is no coal burning, and the room is cold.

"I will make this quick," he says to no one in particular. "To be honest, I have had enough of hunting and killing and interrogating the last couple of days. I am tired. This should be the last one, and then we can go home." Then he speaks to Mama directly. "Do you know what your daughter has been doing, Frau Skovsgaard?"

Mama shakes her head and raises her eyes briefly to catch the fear in mine, the acknowledgment that what I have done might be beyond resurrection.

"Your daughter has committed the worst of crimes in the ghetto. She has been helping people escape, even though she clearly knew the rules. Your daughter will be executed, and you will also be punished."

"My mother knew nothing!"

Mama looks at me with eyes that are as lifeless as fields of dry earth. She opens her mouth to say something, but no sound emerges. Her mouth works hard to find her voice before stammering out the words, "I'm sure she did not mean to disrespect the rules. Perhaps she doesn't fully understand them . . . she tends to act spontaneously."

The officer twists his mouth into a small smile. He appears to enjoy Mama's distress.

"Frau Skovsgaard, as true as that might be, if we made such generalizations and moved the rules left and right, up and down, side to side, there wouldn't be any point in having them. Do you understand?"

Mama does not acknowledge his words.

"Did you hear me? Do you understand?" he says.

"I understand the rules, but I think that she probably didn't understand what she was doing, that she can learn from this . . . and perhaps any others—"

"Oh, it is far too late for the others. Most of them have been shot. However, we believe that your daughter and her young lover should be hung, to make an example of them."

My knees weaken, and I start to shake. Mama convulses slightly as if she has been charged with electricity; her shoulders drop by inches, and a small whine escapes. The officer watches her change and reshape into something stricken, ugly. Leah is shaking uncontrollably, her eyes wide and bulging.

"Can you please give her one more chance?" Mama beseeches. "We can work harder in the ghetto. Please give her another chance . . . I will work for you for free."

"You already do. That's like asking for something you already have."

"Please . . . she has learnt. I can see it in her face!"

The officer takes his hat off and scratches his head.

"You had better not give me lice. I have a young son, you know. I only hope that the smells and infestations of this apartment don't follow me home."

No doubt his son has a bed that is unsoiled, with hair shining and smelling like clean mountain air.

The officer sighs deeply before addressing Mama again.

"You have shown rebellious behavior, after we have fed you and given you a place to sleep. For spitting in the faces of ordinary Germans, you and your younger daughter will be deported to the camps." On cue, one of the policemen steps forward and stamps the back of Mama's hand and then Leah's.

"No! Please!" says Mama.

"Shut up, or I will hit your young daughter. Is that what you want? You want to hurt your children?"

I screw up my eyes so I cannot see his hateful face. I am pushed to one side by one of the Gestapo and collapse against the other. This one pushes me roughly upright again before commencing to drag me out of the apartment. I reach out for my mother.

"Please don't hurt them," I beg the officer.

"Elsi," pleads Mama.

The policeman and I are nearly beyond the door.

"Wait!" says Mama. "I know someone. He is a friend of mine. He will not like to learn that I am leaving. He would not like to hear what is happening here."

"There is no one who can help you, Frau Skovsgaard."

"Herr Manz!"

The officer laughs. "I doubt that. He couldn't care less about you. I have seen him strangle a Jew to death with his bare hands."

"He will speak for us," says Mama.

"He would toss you in a ditch himself if he could. So why would he have anything to do with you?"

"He knows me," says Mama. "I have done his colleagues many favors. My friend Lilli will tell you this, also. Perhaps you know her."

The officer wears a scowl as he looks across at me, then back at Mama. But he is thinking about this, and perhaps wondering if he has missed something about us.

"How well do you know Lilli?" he asks my mother.

"We are very close."

The officer curls one hand into a fist while he thinks. He was expecting this night to be over with by now.

"Stay by the door," he says tersely to one of his men, and turns to Mama. "If you are lying, Herr Manz will be angrier than he was before. He wants this night finished. He was the one who ordered the execution of anyone implicated."

He leaves with one of the Gestapo.

Mama and Leah sit on one bed, Rada and Yuri on another. I am told by the remaining policeman to stand by him near the door, to not say anything.

"It was you, wasn't it?" Mama says to Rada. "You have been watching her, and you sold her out for a few measly coupons."

Rada looks shocked. "Never!"

"Hannah," says Yuri, "I know my wife. For all her complaints, she is not so heartless."

"I would say you know nothing about her," says Mama in a vicious tone.

"Hannah," says Yuri, "please . . ."

He looks at me, and I do not know what to believe. Rada has been trouble from the start. She is selfish. She would do anything for food.

It seems well over an hour before Herr Manz arrives. His face is red with anger.

"I have been woken for matters, Hannah, that I should not be attending to personally. What special treatment are you asking for, that you believe you deserve, that should interrupt my sleep?"

"I'm sorry . . . it's just . . ."

He waves for her to be quiet. "It matters not what you think," he says, and turns to look around the room, his expression of distaste at his surrounds as evident as with the first officer. "I know all about the arrest, and I know why I'm here now. Normally I wouldn't bother, but I think that you still offer some value to the ghetto. You please several of my men. However, your daughter is troubled, Frau Skovsgaard. There is very little I can do for her."

Mama opens her mouth to protest.

"Shh! No more groveling! I understand that she has not been a member of this group for long, and I have to admit I was quite surprised when I learnt of her involvement. Just before I came here, I stopped to question the ringleader to discover that your daughter has blindly and stupidly followed her heart for a boy who had no interest in her, other than to use her in his designs for trouble."

I wonder what has been done to Simon to make him say this.

"You were used, dear Fraulein Jew," he says, spitefully. "He said he saw you at the factory and knew he could convince you to help him break in. He has freely admitted it. And now, unfortunately for you, stupidity cannot go unpunished."

He turns to Mama.

"She will be taken to the ghetto prison, where she will remain indefinitely. First, though, she will stay in a different cell tonight and watch her boyfriend endure the consequences of his actions before she watches his execution tomorrow."

Leah is crying uncontrollably.

"As for you and your other daughter, you will not be deported. I will see to that! But you must have no contact with your oldest daughter from this point on. If you do, you will be executed."

"But my daughter is innocent—"

Herr Manz strikes Mama across the face, and the blow twists her head to one side. Yuri stands up to protest, but the other senior officer points a gun at his head.

"I think a simple thank-you would have been more appropriate," says Herr Manz to Mama. Then he turns to lead the others through the door. The policeman pushes me to follow.

"Officer," I hear Yuri say to the senior official who first broke into our apartment, "perhaps you can take the smells with you when you go this time. A present for your son."

I am already on the stairs, so I do not see Yuri being punched repeatedly, only hear his groans and Rada screaming over and over again as I am dragged down the stairs.

I am taken to a small cell manned by the Gestapo. There is no bed, just a blanket on the floor. I wrap this around me, rest my back to the wall, and look out through the bars into a dimly lit prison.

Simon is strapped to a chair across from me in another cell. Blood streams down his face. I do not believe he is aware that I am in here. I do not dare run to the bars to talk to him for fear that any contact will make matters worse for him. Despite our shared history, we are suddenly strangers, and the short distance between us is an ocean too wide to cross.

They beat him over several hours. I close my eyes, but I am unable to shut out the sounds of the beating, of his cries.

At dawn, as light comes in through the window, I drift into sleep.

I am shaken roughly awake and led to a cart wheeled by other Jews. Simon and another boy I don't know are propped up in the back of the cart. My arms are burning, and my wrists sting from being bound tightly behind my back. I am lifted into the cart and left lying on my side.

Blood has dried and caked in places on Simon's torn and battered face. In other parts, his wounds are fresh, the skin split apart, and thick red blood oozes through. One eye is swollen, unseeing, and his arm hangs limply at his side, perhaps broken.

"Simon," I whisper, but he does not attempt to look at me. The other younger boy hangs his head, half-asleep, his body half-destroyed.

We stop at a public square where many public executions have been held. Only a handful of people are nearby to watch—others recognizing that such proximity to the Gestapo is unsafe. Any one of the residents might be taken next. But Mama is there in the small crowd. She sees me restrained, and carted like livestock, and fights the urge to run to me.

Simon and the boy are dragged so roughly off the cart that they fall hard to the ground. They are kicked until they stand and then walk to the scaffold erected in the center of the courtyard. They drag their weary legs up a set of stairs.

I sit up to watch Simon stand to face his accusers, not buckling like me but strong. He turns to look at me, finally, but the wounds and blood hide his expression. I know that he is sorry that he has led me here, that he involved me. I am nearly blinded by my tears. Simon turns to the other boy who is also to be executed. The other boy is visibly trembling and muttering something that could be a prayer.

The boy is executed first, and Simon does not watch. The boy does not die straight away, kicking at the air, and then he stops, body swinging. The rope is lowered and the body removed and carried back to the cart I am sitting on. Then it is Simon's turn to die. I want to look away, but I feel I must be with him to the end so that he is not alone.

I watch life leave his body, the body I once held on a cold night. And when the swinging stops, I close my eyes and pray that his spirit will live on peacefully.

The cart begins to move again, and Mama suddenly appears out of the crowd, rushing after me. Our hands meet briefly, and then we are parted. *I love you*, she mouths, and then I lie back on the cart and stare at the sky full of souls. It is a bright and clear day, something I would not usually pause to notice.

CHAPTER TWENTY-TWO

WILLEM

Lena was buried in Munich at the beginning of the year in the same graveyard as her grandparents. Friends and colleagues came, but not my father. I asked him that no officials from Berlin be there, and he gladly saw that this request was honored. For obvious reasons, my father did not want to be there either. Lena's parents wanted a Catholic service and burial, presided over by a priest who is on the Nazi dissident watch list. After he had personally seen to the transportation of Lena's body from Poland, my father sent condolences to Lena's parents along with his regrets, citing war commitments as his reason for not attending.

At the funeral, many tears were shed for Lena by family, past friends, and colleagues. I held Lena's mother briefly, though the embrace did not feel sincere. Although we had met several times before, we were never able to form a close bond. Lena's parents had seemed fearful of me, even though Lena's words about me were always kind. But it was mostly my father who had been an invisible barrier between us. Their fear of him and his high connections was far greater than their fear of me.

I had felt disconnected from everyone who was there, perhaps because at that moment—and from the moment I had learned the news of Lena's death—I had felt disconnected even from myself. I was numb. I was someone I didn't want to know.

"I know you loved her and she loved you," said Lena's mother. "I hope you will remember her compassion and tender ways, and these memories bring you comfort in the years ahead."

"Thank you," I said, then moved away, not wanting to be reminded that Lena loved me. This made our separation more painful.

"You will move on in time," said Mary Anne, my aunt. She made the trip from Berlin even though her brother couldn't. She has remained loyal and kind to both my father and me.

"Yes, I will."

"I know you loved her. Your mother would have loved her, too."

"I don't want to talk about my mother."

I did not want her to be brought up at this time. It was Lena who brought her to life for me. My mother was something sacred between us—something that I believe no one else should share. Mary Anne studied my face.

"I know that words are futile oftentimes. But you must know that I was very close to your mother, also."

"I'm sorry, Aunt Mary," I said. "I did not mean to sound so callous." I took her hand, fearing that I had offended someone who had cared for me unconditionally—who never once failed to acknowledge my birthday, my achievements, and other significant events and milestones in my life. How inconsiderate I had been toward her at the time.

"I understand that you are hurting," she said. "Your mother was decent and kind, Willem, and I saw early that you carried those same traits. I know that you adored Lena, and she resurrected that sweet, thoughtful boy I will forever hold dear to my heart. Your father did his best, as he saw it, but he cannot change the person you were born to be. He saw the same things in you that I did, and perhaps he was fearful that your mother's soft heart would not serve you well, and he sought to change it. Go with your instincts and your heart now, Willem. Raise yourself above those barriers that were imposed on you from an early age."

I held her close to me, touched by the selflessness she had shown me over time.

"Thank you, Aunt Mary," I said, wishing I had noticed her kindness long before now.

After Munich, I stayed in my apartment in Berlin to settle some property and financial affairs before my return to Lodz to pack up my belongings. But before leaving Germany, my father asked me to visit a private sanatorium in Lychen, where the SS are treated after battle and where Father conducts his wound bacterial experiments on women incarcerated in a prison nearby. The sanatorium is located in a beautiful area, away from large towns and cities, and surrounded by pines and acres of green lawns, housing prestigious offices and the best medical equipment and facilities. It is where the elite sporting stars were once cared for, and it looks more like a chalet resort than a treatment center.

Sitting opposite my father in his office at this private facility, I thank him for helping to arrange the transport of Lena's body back to Munich. He then offers some words about Lena. Dry-eyed, the both of us, we speak briefly of her strength of character. He says that she was a woman of considerable worth. Despite a lack of sincerity at times, especially with regard to words of condolence, I do know that my father will rise above certain preconceptions to recognize intelligence and strength of character in others, even those he considers enemies. While admitting that they were not close, he says that he regrets not spending more time with Lena, and we discuss her cause of death, as we would with any other patient who has passed on.

Lena died from an embolism. The coroner discovered a piece of our baby daughter's hair in her lung. "These things are not to be expected. These things are so rare," says my father, as if speaking from a distance. The logical side of me found the explanation thorough, though the part of me that had boxed in the grief could find no justification for why she was gone.

It was no one's fault—a premature birth, a medical anomaly—and yet I remember the promise I made to be with her at the hospital. Perhaps I would have noticed her fever before it was too late.

"Do not embark on the unhealthy obsession of self-blame," my father warns me. "I do not believe there is anything you could have done."

There is something festering beneath my skin: an itch that I cannot reach. It is grief I feel on a subconscious level, held at bay until such a time that I can shape it into something that makes sense, if I ever can.

"Do you think you and I are being punished, Father? First Mother and now Lena."

"That is ridiculous, Willem! Do not speculate on God and punishment! That is for philosophers, priests, troublemakers—those who encourage others to wallow in idle thoughts and self-doubt, who have plenty of time to waste."

He does not say that it is Lena's influence that makes me talk this way, even though he knows this.

"Mother was a Catholic," I say.

"Briefly, in her childhood. You must stop this talk. You must move on."

His dismissiveness makes me agitated. "You are probably relieved that Lena is gone. That you can release some of the baggage that might cause damage to our name."

"What you say is wrong. Lena was a fine woman of good breeding." But these words are a description only and not spoken with any depth of feeling.

"Return to Poland and pack up your life there," says my father. "You will not work there again. I will see to it. But you need to start thinking of Germany. You need to think about the future, not the past. You are a good doctor, but fortitude is something you will have to develop if you are to survive. I can't carry you forever. I can't make excuses—"

"I never asked you to."

"After you've had a rest . . . you do not have to go back to Auschwitz. You can come straight to the sanatorium to help with research here."

"I do not want to work here."

Father pauses briefly, letting my words dissolve between us.

"We have to talk about Auschwitz. I want to discuss the treatments. I want you to work here with me. If you want to help women, this is where you should be."

"I cannot do it," I tell my father. "I cannot do any further testing on prisoners."

"War isn't supposed to be nice," he says.

"War isn't supposed to be cruel either. Does the Red Cross know what we are doing?"

"It is what we have to do. There is nothing immoral taking place here." He has ignored the question. He has swept the idea of ethics under the carpet. It is how he deals with everything he chooses to avoid.

"I am not interested in research, Father. I am interested in treatment."

"It is not beneficial to look away. Never again will we have this opportunity. You can research the causes and management of conditions like the one Lena died from. You can find ways to stop our German women from dying. Isn't that what you have talked about, what you have worked for?"

Just hearing her name on his lips again makes me angry.

"I will not come here."

He is quiet for several moments, his thoughts lost in the lush woodland outside his window, before rubbing his hand across his forehead tiredly. I wonder what he sees before he sleeps at night. Whether he is tormented by those faces of victims he has used for testing, and the work he performs. When he turns toward me once more, there is nothing reflective in his gaze; rather, I recognize in his expression a dogged disappointment that he did not have a son made in his own image.

"Very well! You have heard about the Lebensborn centers?"

"Yes, Father. Used to house Nazi bastards, or as work farms for disenfranchised children, from what I gather."

"Your conclusions on administrative matters are sometimes baseless, Willem, as is your choice to remain ignorant . . ."

He pauses, holding back any further reproach, perhaps deeming his timing to be inappropriate or insensitive—or, more likely, just a waste of words at this point.

"Always be careful what you say out loud, Willem," he then says in a more even tone. "It would be unwise to make such statements outside this room."

"As you say, Father."

"I want you to visit one particular center before you return to Poland. A commander's posting has become available there. The facilities are good, with a surgery already installed. It is the first of many centers that will combine several different facilities and ages. This center was once a school for young women from various foreign backgrounds to make them suitable for German marriages and other occupations that will assist the war effort. Some of the girls have been sponsored by their families and sent to the centers willingly, to remind them of their responsibilities to Germany."

I am thinking it is likely that some coercion was used here on the families. Some people, it seems, will give up anything, including their children, to appease the party.

"Early last year," continues my father, "the center was expanded to include foreign orphans—babies and children of both sexes—placed there in a safe environment and reeducated in the German way before being adopted by German families. We are planning to build more of these centers in the future and expand the training facilities. This is the first of many. The center I wish to send you to is now also providing a temporary refuge for pregnant single women who will give their babies up for adoption."

"I am a doctor, Father. This sounds like a post best suited to someone else. I'm not sure that I am qualified to take on such a responsibility."

"Currently, the supervision there is limited. This center needs both a doctor and a commander to ensure that practices are followed there. You are far more qualified to do both those tasks than the woman in charge. I believe this is well suited to you, Willem, though I will not give up the idea that eventually you will turn to research."

It is not the time to tell him that I have nightmares about Auschwitz and the treatment of prisoners. That I would rather die than experiment on innocent Jews. The return of such thoughts causes me to tremble inside. At these moments I have the feeling of falling, as if the earth below me has become fragile and unable to withstand my weight.

"Are you listening to me, Willem?" asks Father, drawing me back from the fall.

I nod.

"Please continue to pay attention." He pauses before continuing. "You would monitor the health of these young women and children and fertility issues, an area that I know remains of great interest to you. But you would also ensure that the women and children who are admitted all have Aryan traits. I know that you have seen this testing done at the ghetto. You know what is expected. If you take this posting, you will screen the ones who are brought in."

I had assisted with some of the orphans brought to the ghetto, taking their head and body measurements. Some farmed off to Germany, others to the camps. This testing was a task I avoided whenever possible.

"So I am to nursemaid spoilt little Aryan children then."

My father's smile extends suddenly to his startling pale-green eyes, which have always stunned me into submission. As a boy, they could freeze me to the floor.

"Yes, I suppose that is the job I ask of you."

Our smiles meet briefly in the middle of our conversation, and just for a moment I remember a different father: gentle, something faded now, a memory torn at the edges and buried beneath others.

"You should visit there before you return to Poland to collect your effects. I think you will be pleasantly surprised. You will find it very different from the camp."

My father thinks me soft, but this does not worry me. I no longer care how I appear to him. This posting is a cushion, an excuse to be rid of me. To place me somewhere where I will no longer embarrass him. I should perhaps be grateful.

I travel in the new uniform my father has given me. It is gray with two insignias on the dark-green collar. It is the first thing that people look at, before the eyes. Mine says that I am a loyal and ranked Nazi member. That I will do whatever it takes. That those I instruct must do what I say.

My father has given me a typed report on the Center that offers little more than what he has just told me. The older girls there are all German; the younger children come from the east, the occupied territories. These children have been given up by their parents or orphaned.

As I drive near the entrance, I see that there are several girls standing in a line, presented to me like a row of horses to be examined. They wear white dresses with collars, socks and shiny black shoes. Their hair is either short or tied back. They are German virgins ready for reaping, I think, somewhat callously, here to be groomed for marriage and to provide more Aryan specimens for the future of Germany. It is hard to observe without cynicism.

I greet the girls formally, nodding, a shake of their poised hands. They titter among themselves once I walk past.

Frau Miriam Haus, the program supervisor, ushers me through the line.

"I must say that we were only just told of your visit this morning."

"Please accept my apology. My father directed me yesterday to see the facilities. It seems that you are waiting on a commander here."

"Yes. Perhaps it will be you, Herr Gerhardt."

"Perhaps."

It is peaceful here. The only sounds are birds—a startling contrast to the guns, heavy boots, trucks, and cries to which I have become accustomed. I imagine that this is what life would be like without war. I have often imagined a life in a house such as this with Lena, though each time that memory surfaces I push it out again. It is certainly a place far from the ghettos and camps. Perhaps worth considering.

I am given a tour of the ground floor, walking through the house to a kitchen where a woman is cooking. I am not introduced to her. She is not considered important enough for introductions.

At the back of the house it is different, as if a facade has been lifted. Apart from patches of snow, the Center grounds are barren. Another guard sits lazily at his post. I wonder if the guards are keeping people in or out. Behind the property I see winter trees in a stretch of wooded forest. From the kitchen door, broken pavers lead to an old army-style hut at the side of the house. Miriam attempts to steer me back to the room where I was first received.

"What is that building used for?" I ask, pointing to the hut.

"It is where the younger children are housed and Germanized."

"The reeducation program."

"Exactly, Herr Gerhardt. Some are orphaned, and others have been given up by their own foreign parents so they can specifically learn to be loyal to our Führer, loyal to Germany."

A nurse walks into the house from that direction, muttering. She wears a frown, and her lips are pressed tightly together like washing rollers. She appears startled when she sees me, her gaze shyly dropping somewhere below my chin, before she looks to Frau Haus to offer an explanation.

"Oh, it is a pleasure to meet you, Herr Captain," says Nurse Claudia, morphing into something else, the skin on her face lifting, with some effort, into a smile.

More pleasantries again, though I will not be deterred. The cook bangs a pot down hard on the sink, her plump, round back refusing to acknowledge any of us.

"And you look after the younger children?"

"Yes," Nurse Claudia says. "They are just having their afternoon sleep."

There is a shout and a thudding on wooden floorboards, the sound stretching across the sink of mud between the buildings.

"I would very much like to see them."

I sense hesitation on the part of Frau Haus.

"Certainly, Herr Gerhardt."

From the back door, I briskly cross the mud that has replaced a broken pathway, as the nurse and Miriam nip at my heels, attempting to keep up with me. At the other end I try the door to the long, hall-shaped building, but it is locked.

"Afternoons the dormitory is locked . . . for their safety," says Nurse, who has stepped quickly beside me to turn the key in the lock.

Inside the room is dark with only a few small, high windows. It reeks of urine here, and that of old vomit left to fester for too long—smells that have leeched into the wood grain.

Several children jump up to stand beside their narrow wooden beds. They appear shocked to see me: eyes wide and still. All four wear the Nazi symbol; they are fair.

I smile, but they sense it is not sincere, for there is nothing here to smile about, and they do not smile back. They do not recognize it as a smile.

"They come here somewhat damaged and out of control," says Miriam. "It takes some time."

"How long does it take to obtain control?"

"It can be months. Two have been here for nearly a year. They are sometimes difficult to tame."

"They are children, not mountain lions, Frau Haus."

"Pardon me?"

"I am just curious about the degree of difficulty."

She is temporarily shocked into speechlessness. I suspect she has had the run of the place too long, and I gather from her querulous expression that she does not like to answer to anyone.

"They come with certain baggage from their foreign homes. It is different from most of the older girls who are already German, who come here because they want to."

I turn toward the other faces in the room.

"Hello," I say.

There is no response at first, and then a greeting is spoken from somewhere in the room. I scan the four pale faces awash with hope and fear to find the source.

A girl, around eight at a guess, appears to be the one with the voice.

I walk between the beds to reach hers at the end, my boots making a scuffing sound on the untreated, moldering pine. There are eight beds and several shelves of books. I scan the titles: *Mein Kampf, The Poisonous Mushroom, Trust No Fox on His Green Heath and No Jew on His Oath*. I doubt they understand anything from the first, and much more from the others.

As I pass the last girl, I see that she is hiding something behind her back, some paper. She sees that I have seen, and her expression is frozen, I suspect, with fear. Something inside me sinks. These are the places I have sent the little Aryan orphans: locked, drafty, dark rooms. From one prison to another.

"What is your name?" I attempt to sound soft, but the words are terse even to my ears.

"Matilda."

I think it is a sweet name, though it suits a strong nature, something I believe she might have. I am not good with children, but I am good at summing up a person in the briefest possible time. She stands very straight. She is the only one to look me in the eyes. I think that her mother has named her with foresight.

She scrunches the papers behind her in an attempt to make them disappear. I cannot put her through any more suffering. I turn to leave, and the two women fall in line behind me.

"What will happen to those children?" I ask once the door is closed and locked again.

Miriam tells me some of the wives of the SS like to adopt, and that these children will soon go to good German families to be raised. "The younger ones anyway. But children like Matilda . . . well, she is a difficult one, though her German is exceptionally good, and she is particularly bright and useful in some ways.

"These children barely passed the Aryan testing," continues Frau Haus. "And so, unfortunately, they are not so easily disposed of. However, if you are assigned here, Herr Gerhardt, you can sign the paperwork that will order all those unlikely to be Germanized sent to the camps. It is difficult and time-consuming sending the paperwork to Berlin and then waiting for the response and collection."

"Do some not return to their parents if they fail the testing?"

"Most parents sign them away, Herr Gerhardt. I hardly think they would want them back again. We will perhaps be doing them a favor."

I do not fail to see the glance exchanged between Frau Haus and the nurse. They are guilty of things, too. But possibly no more guilty than I.

I nod politely and tell myself that children left in cold rooms is no worse than other things I have already seen. We return to the reception area, where the older girls still hover.

I sit on a sofa in the sitting room where guests are entertained. This is, I realize, where the older girls learn to speak to visitors to learn manners and etiquette, in order to serve distinguished gentleman. I have been given tea in a fine china cup and served cakes.

"I understand that you still have work to complete in Poland," says Miriam. "Will you be there long?"

"I will be returning to Germany very soon."

"Your wife must be looking forward to it."

Wife. They would not know of her death. It occurs to me that this is one place where she can remain alive.

"Yes," I say. "Could I trouble you for some coffee instead of tea?" There is a thickening at the back of my throat.

"Of course," says Miriam.

Of course I can. I am a Nazi official. My father is a close friend of Himmler. I am also an abortionist and a sterilizer of women. Do they know that? *Throw out the memories. Make new ones.* My forehead and neck feel uncomfortably hot.

I am shown some photos of the girls in training at the Center, and Frau Haus relays some uninteresting facts about their affluent backgrounds. Hanging above the fireplace is our party insignia and a photo of the Führer. In the corner on the bookshelf is another copy of *Mein Kampf* and books on food preparation and dressmaking. Everything is perfectly arranged: everything in good, working Nazi order at the front; everything to be forgotten placed at the back. My coffee arrives.

"Herr Gerhardt, I hear that you have worked as a doctor in the ghetto, and you have done much research on pregnant women."

I take a sip of coffee before I respond to Miriam. I can take all day if I choose. The insignias on my collar say so. But the question itself strips me of power, and I drag my eyes upward to meet hers.

"Yes," I say, and squeeze out a small smile from the corners of my mouth. Sweat drips beneath my collar.

"That will be most helpful here. Especially with the pregnant girls. We have one here now."

"How is she?"

"She is . . . how should I put it?" Miriam looks across at the nurse. "Sour, at times, would you say, Nurse? Less than resilient?"

Nurse nods her agreement. "At times, yes."

"She has some concerns about the impending birth, as she is only fifteen," continues Miriam. "And, of course, naturally hopeful that her baby shows Aryan traits and can then be adopted out."

"Of course," I say. "Who looks after the babies?" I do not ask my other question: What happens to the baby if it does not show Aryan traits?

Did my father know about this? Is this a test?

"Nurse takes care of all the children, and we expect more pregnant women to be sent to us very soon."

"Why is that?"

"Because our men must do what they have to."

One of the girls giggles too loudly and is reprimanded by the nurse.

"As you know, our girls here are groomed to be good Nazi wives. But we are so short of marriageable men because so many are out in the field. If we can marry them off, that's a good outcome. But if not, some of the girls will continue on here until a suitable service or pairing can be found."

Nurse throws a glance my way before avoiding my gaze altogether and shifting around in her seat. The girls stare at Haus as if they are expecting more to come. There is something I am not being told.

"And they are all here by choice?"

"Yes," says Miriam. "Their parents have helped fund the Center by donating large sums of money to make sure their daughters get a placement. We rely on those donations, since only a small amount of funding comes from Berlin."

It occurs to me that the older girls to be reeducated here are chosen not only because their parents must have had some alliance that did not initially include Nazism, perhaps something that offended the party that must be recompensed, but also because of their wealth.

"Our full-time nurse here, Claudia, looks after the girls, making sure they are cared for; however, with the first of our births a few months away, we have been assured by headquarters that a doctor—hopefully yourself—will be here soon."

"And the orphans? Who currently takes care of their health?"

Frau Haus smiles; she looks as though she is not sure if she should. Her false benevolence is tiresome.

"Nurse, of course. She treats them all as if they were her own. Very recently we hosted our first dinner party and invited some of the party officials in for an inspection. They were suitably impressed." Under my intense scrutiny, she appears suddenly uncomfortable and pauses to clear her throat. "I am sure that you will host your own gatherings should you take the position. All those children under the age of twelve are to be made available for adoption, provided they can be easily Germanized. Once the girls reach adolescence, they are then groomed until they are old enough."

"Old enough for what?" I believe I know the answer, but I do not intend to make this comfortable for her.

"As I said, for marriage. Or some may choose to join the Hitler Youth."

"Or for breeding, perhaps," I say, hoping to unsettle her with my conjecture.

"If that is required, yes," says Haus, unsettling me instead.

More giggles on the other side of the room. The sound is irritating, like the buzzing of a trapped fly. I want to shout and tell them this. I stare into the black liquid of my cup until the sound of their giggling becomes drowned in my own thoughts.

This place is little more than a breeding farm for the Schutzstaffel, and another opportunity to discard children who are racially impure! Perhaps it is my father who is ignorant after all. Or perhaps he knew this and chose not to tell me. His weak-minded son unable to deal with another Nazi reality.

"You'll have to excuse my girls," says Miriam, sisterly. "They find you very attractive, and it makes them quite silly."

I force a smile and look at the girls. One looks away, her cheeks reddening. Another does not: eyes lingering too long. I sense that some might not be as innocent as they appear. They have everything they need, while the little ones, the ones who won't be paraded for German men, wait for something else: a strange new home with people they don't know, or a trip to a camp that offers no future, no life at all.

"It must be wonderful here," I force myself to say.

I think of the women in the ghetto and wonder if any of them have died since I left. I think of the women who are undergoing surgery at the private facility at the hands of my father. My hand starts to shake, and a bead of sweat from my forehead lands on my trousers.

"Are you feeling unwell, Herr Gerhardt?" says Miriam.

"It's all the travel," I say, dismissively.

I raise my cup to take another sip of coffee, but it never reaches my lips.

"I think you will like it here," says Miriam.

The world fades in and out. I put the cup back on the table, carefully, slowly, afraid that it will slip from my hands. I wonder about the women who will never have children.

I close my eyes and the cup rattles in its saucer, my hand shaking violently. I feel liquid pooling underneath my eyelids.

The grieving for Lena has begun.

Miriam does not know what to say to me.

I get up and leave the room and walk to the car that waits for me. Haus and the girls are calling good-bye, but I do not turn around.

CHAPTER TWENTY-THREE
MATILDA

I am having second thoughts about running away. Juliane follows me around everywhere. She has become used to us, though she is still calling for her mother. Sometimes she starts before daybreak.

I have spoken to Jacek about taking her with us, but he doesn't like this idea. It is perhaps best to leave her since she will slow us down, he says. She will make an escape impossible. But I think she could be put on the truck like Sarah if I am not here to teach her German.

No one has noticed that the keys from Frau's office are gone.

Jacek now thinks that we should leave before the month is ended, because there is a break in the weather. He speaks to me when Luise is not there.

"I am worried that we will be taken if we don't hurry. I think we should leave soon."

I have thought of that, too. Every time we hear a motor vehicle, we fear that one of us will be taken by strangers or placed on a truck. Last week an officer arrived to inspect the hut. Normally we have to go to the front room of the house for any kind of inspections.

He was tall and frightening and spoke with a deep voice. I think he might have seen one of my stories that I had hidden behind my back. I thought he was about to ask what it was. Perhaps he didn't see. When he was gone, Luise started throwing books around the hut, and I had to hold her down until the tantrum passed. She is so fearful of being taken. That was also when I learned her fever had worsened, and went to get Nurse to give her some medicine. Her chest rattles and squeaks in the night.

Each day I take some food from the storage house to hide in my pocket. We have a stash of food for when we run away. I still tell the children stories, but Luise lies down facing the other way. I tell them about the time a little girl, who was made to sweep floors by her stepsisters, met a prince and married him. Juliane loves that one. When I am finished, she acts it out. Jacek and I roll around on the floor laughing. It feels good to laugh. Luise watches, but she doesn't join in. She frowns at our laughter.

Juliane is talking more. She tells us that on the way here, she was on a train with lots of German soldiers, and that most had bandages on their heads and some were missing limbs and eyes.

CHAPTER TWENTY-FOUR

ELSI

We sit against the inside of a fence heavily strung with razor wire. There is little cover from the elements. Inside the building there are rows of bunk beds and a wooden floor. A blanket and a bowl rest beside each cot—our only possessions. I wear a prison dress so soiled it is impossible to tell its original color.

The communal grounds are brown and barren, and there are few living things here, except for the guards and the angry dogs that bark in the night and the prisoners who are just barely living. On the first day here, I witnessed the mauling of a prisoner who had tried to escape and heard her shrieking as flesh was torn from her calves. It is the noises here that set my teeth to grind. I have had little sleep. The ground is sodden from the last of the melting ice; the sun still barely finds gaps to shine through. During the day, even when we are not working, we must sit outside. We have to walk far in order to plow fields. Some of us—when we are not digging up the soil to plant vegetables—huddle under blankets, sheltering from the rain. I am luckier than some, those who are put to work at the cemetery with the task of disposing of corpses, or what the guards refer to as "human waste."

At night we line up for soup before bed, and then I sleep alongside several others. Some are in prison for crimes of stealing, some just for vagrancy after curfew.

Today I see a figure at the fence in a coat I recognize. Mama stands there waiting. I have seen her here before, but I don't dare go down to talk to her. We will both be in trouble if I do. She just watches me.

The next day she comes again, but this time she doesn't leave. I wait for the guards to go inside, then sidle along the fence until I reach her.

"Oh, my sweet angel," she says, her fingers trembling. She looks aged beyond her years. She begins to cry. I put my fingers through the fence, and she kisses them.

"You can't be here," I tell her. "They will send you away to the camp."

"I can't bear not to see you . . . I have lost too much already . . ." She breaks down; she is inconsolable. I look around to see if the guards have seen. They are changing their posts, their dogs nowhere in sight.

"What are they doing to you?" she asks.

I tell her about the work. That we are so tired at night. But that it could be worse.

She says that Leah is crying constantly and has bedsores and a fever and an ache in her bad leg.

"Yuri was banned from ever having employment after his comment to the Gestapo about his son. He and Rada were living on the streets last time I saw them. I told them to get out of the apartment, and they did, though Rada keeps coming back to say she is innocent. But I don't believe it. She has been difficult from the beginning, and she has done this to you. It was Yuri who had to convince her to leave and stay away because I threatened to hurt her. I have no job now. I am not sure what I will do."

She holds out a piece of bread. "This is from Lilli."

Gemma Liviero

I look around again. The guards are on the move.

"Mama, you are not to bring me food. You must stay away."

"I will come back every day."

"Mama, this is all my doing. I was a fool to do what I did. I was a fool to follow Simon."

Mama's tears have stopped, and her tone is suddenly fierce. "Do not believe a word of what Manz said! I believe that Simon was gallant in those final hours. I believe he said what he said to try and save you. I did not like him at first, but I believe now that what you and the others tried to do was brave. It is what I would have expected you to do. I am so proud of you."

Her eyes are watery, though they remind me of how they used to be—full of passion and life and love for her child that cannot be measured in words. I feel sick with shame that I led her to this by following a boy I believed in. I release her fingers.

"Mama, you need to get back to Leah. Do not come back here. You must let me go. You must save yourself."

I get up and walk away so that she will go. I feel that somehow my punishment is deserved.

CHAPTER TWENTY-FIVE

MATILDA

I feel a cold breeze on my face and wake to see that the door of the hut is open. I rush to the door and look outside. I wonder if Nurse has not locked the door properly and the wind has blown it open. The wind had been howling through the night. Tiny pieces of snow float to the ground. It is beautiful, I think, despite the wind that blows through my long nightgown and the cold that seeps through the cracks of the floorboards and into my feet. I close the door, and in the light that is just spreading across the hut, I see there are two other bodies inside, not three.

I shake Jacek awake. "Luise is gone!" I say. He rubs his eyes and slowly climbs out of bed. Spiders have crawled across his eyes and webbed across his eyeballs. He rubs them clear. Juliane is making a small bubbling noise as she breathes.

I put my hand under my mattress to find that the key is gone. The food is also gone.

We run to the door and down the steps and search under and around the hut. There is no guard near the woods. He is probably patrolling elsewhere or having breakfast with the other one who guards the front. The door to the kitchen is still locked. Cook has not yet arrived.

Back in the hut, we discuss the ways that Luise might have escaped. Perhaps she is halfway home by now.

"But how will she know where to go?"

"Perhaps she doesn't care, just as long as she is away from here," I say.

We wait until Nurse comes. She cannot hide her surprise when she sees that the door to the hut is already open. We explain that Luise has left.

"Where is she?"

"We don't know," I say.

"But you must have heard."

"No," says Jacek.

"We think she had a key," I say, and then regret it. Jacek doesn't look at me. I suddenly feel ashamed that this could get Luise into worse trouble if she is caught.

We are called to assemble in the backyard. The snow has lifted after a heavy fall the night before. The guards and the older girls are called, also. Frau has not yet arrived at the house. Nurse questions us again, but this time we tell her that we do not think she had a key and we know nothing more.

Several of the older girls have been searching the property. One of the girls says that the fence is undamaged. It is curious that she could have gotten out, says Nurse.

After breakfast, Nurse locks us into the hut again, but we are too worried to work. Juliane keeps crying. She is very much missing her mother today.

Jacek thinks that Luise is far away now and on her way home.

"She doesn't know which way to go," I remind him.

Nurse lets us out later that day so that we can play on the swings. We are relieved to be out because we thought she would lock us in all day. But we are too sad to play on the swings, so we sit on the ground instead and stare at the woods, wondering if Luise is hiding there watching us, and we look for signs of any movement in the trees. We are only out there for a short time when one of the older girls runs past us from the back of the property. She is calling loudly for Nurse. We follow her to the kitchen, but I do not hear what she says, and when we get there, Frau is shouting orders at the guards from the doorway.

"What is happening?" I whisper to Jacek.

"I think Luise has been found."

I feel my heart beat rapidly. I should be relieved, but I know for certain that Luise will be punished, probably locked in the small house.

A guard arrives at the back door to lead Frau to Luise. Jacek and I follow.

"No! Wait!" says Alice, but we do not listen. I follow Frau, expecting her to send me back, but she doesn't. At the back of the hut near the fence is a huge pile of wood. On the side that does not face the house, several pieces have been pulled away, making a gap that leads to within the pile. Frau peers through the pieces of wood.

"Yes, that is her. Take her out!"

Luise has pulled away pieces of wood from outside the pile; then, once inside, she must have pulled some of them back in around her. A bird within her nest. It was a clever place to hide, but it is a pity she could not get through the fence instead.

The guards drag out a blanket that is frosted with ice. Several strands of white-gold hair hang through the opening at the top of the blanket, and tiny blue feet are exposed at the other end.

"She climbed in and perhaps fell asleep," says the guard, cradling her like a baby.

"She was ill and possibly felt too cold to move," says Nurse, who does not sound angry or happy. "She probably just went to sleep." Each word seems to drop down further than the one before, as if her sentence has rolled down a hill.

"Wake her up!" I say. In my heart I know there is something wrong, but I cannot yet see what it is.

Frau turns to look at me.

I begin to rush forward to touch Luise, to see her face, but one of the guards grips me by the arm.

"She died here in the night from the cold and fever. You see where your meddling leads!"

Frau, I realize, is talking to me. It is only when I look at Jacek, who has begun to bawl, that the horror dawns on me, and I am caught between the sadness of Luise's death and the horror of Frau's words clawing at my throat.

"Someone must have stolen a key, and I cannot see Luise having the skill to perform such a task." Her eyes are boring into me. They send shivers and sickness into me, and my knees are suddenly not strong enough to hold my legs straight.

Frau directs the guard to take Luise's body to the back of the house. She will be buried near the forest.

As the guard passes me, my shoulder catches the blanket, and it falls back from Luise's face, which is blue, and her eyes are closed peacefully. She is wearing her nightgown, and several shards of wood are stuck to it. One arm is positioned slightly forward, stiffened, her hand bent as if she is waving good-bye to me. She looks even smaller in death.

Why couldn't she wait? Could she tell that I was changing my mind?

Nurse marches after Frau and the guard.

"Did you know she was hiding there?" Nurse whispers to me.

"No."

"Did you take the key?"

I think of Jacek.

"Yes."

Nurse nods her head as if she knew this answer was coming. She does not look pleased. She blinks her eyes several times as if she is blinking away my crime, as if she wishes I hadn't told her this.

"I'm sorry," I say.

But she does not want to look at me.

They lay the body near the door to the kitchen. Cook is told to bring some burlap from the storeroom, and as they wrap her up, I see that Alice is staring from the window, crying, and Juliane is watching from the door of the hut. There is no sign of Jacek. He cannot look anymore.

"Go to the hut!" says Frau, but I cannot leave Luise. I put my hand on her small chest. As soon as I touch her, tears slip out from the corners of my eyes before I can catch them.

"Did you hear what I said?"

I fall to my knees now because everything has failed; this can't be fixed. This is an evil place where only bad things happen. Children here die.

"Get into the hut!"

I stand up and punch Frau in the stomach, and both guards grab at me and drag me away. I know where they are taking me. I am screaming and kicking, and they open the door so hard that it bounces back on the wall. They push me in. I turn and rush back out and kick one of them in the shins, but I am pushed back in even harder this time—so hard that I hit the other side of the wall.

They slam and bolt the door before I can try and escape again. I hear the click of the lock.

I scream and hit the door.

"Luise! Luise! Jacek!"

I scream and hit the door until I am so tired I can no longer stand, and my ears are buzzing and my throat burns.

CHAPTER TWENTY-SIX

ELSI

I dig for coal beneath the slush and mud in one of their fields. I find nothing. I wonder if the guards have made up this task today so they can watch with amusement. My arms are covered in brown earth. At the end of the day, I come back exhausted and with my sack empty.

Back at the prison yard, Mama is waiting for me again. I fall out of the line to meet her at the fence when the guards move up ahead. The dogs prance proudly alongside their masters, often growling at prisoners and things in the distance that I can't see. Mama's face is desperate, fearful, downtrodden—it says that nothing good will come.

Through the holes in the fence, she squeezes some bread, then breaks apart a biscuit. I catch every crumb that falls on my filthy dress. She has an orange, too. I am so hungry, I can think of nothing right now but the food she hands me.

"I will get more food from Lilli. Don't give up, Elsi. Stay strong. Don't walk too quickly. Conserve your energy."

It is not that easy. We have to plow the fields with our hands and carry heavy sacks from the fields that we reap. If we are caught eating the vegetables, we are beaten and then sent to dig for coal instead.

"You don't look well," I say, noting that my mother is paler than I have ever seen her.

"I have been bleeding occasionally since the operation, and some days are worse. But do not concern yourself. It is you that is the worry here. You are too thin, my darling. You must demand more food."

The guards have split up as usual to patrol the various borders. One of them has seen us.

"Mama, please go."

"I will come—"

There is a cracking sound, and something passes by my ear. Then Mama is sideways in the mud, her head turned slightly, a tiny hole in her temple and blood trickling from the circle. Her eyes are open, her mouth, also, as if she is about to tell me something.

"Mama!"

I crouch low, crushing my face against the fence as I stretch my arm through the wire to touch her face, but she is inches out of reach.

"Mama," I whimper. "Don't die." But I know in my heart she is gone.

The dogs behind me are getting closer, but I do not turn. I cannot lose sight of my mother. I cannot let her die alone.

"If you can hear me, I love you," I whisper, the words broken with grief. "I will not forget . . ."

The earth moves beneath me from the stomping of guards who are nearly upon me. I can feel the warm breath of the dogs as they smother me, their fur against my skin, the growls deafening. Someone grabs the back of my collar, and I see a blinding light that fades to nothing.

CHAPTER TWENTY-SEVEN

WILLEM

"You cannot do this. I have given you everything!"

My father is shouting at me through the phone. He has received my letter telling him that I plan to remain in Poland, in our apartment: Lena's and mine.

"Do you know that I put you above someone far more worthy for the Lebensborn job? That I personally vouched for you? Did you know that I risked my reputation to get you that job because you were too weak to deal with research, too weak to do your duty?"

"I will work again in the ghetto until I find something else."

"The surgery has been closed. There is to be no *women's* practice in the ghetto any longer. It was a ridiculous idea in the first place."

"Where will they go . . . these women?" I am wondering if this was my father's decision and whether anyone else has been informed.

"What does it matter?"

"Then I will find work in a hospital or open my own practice."

"With what? You don't have a real medical degree. I have covered for you. It wouldn't take long for people to learn you didn't complete it. But as your father, in employment that I assign you, no one will dare check."

He is right, of course. I have been given work in the field of women's health only because of my father.

He ends the conversation abruptly and hangs up the phone.

It is good that he is gone. It is good that I can be alone to listen to the sound of silence, to remember my life before the war.

I sit at the front window, staring out at the empty stream, at the mist snaking around the straggly trees along its banks. I haunt the halls and rooms, imagining Lena. One night I wake to hear a noise in the kitchen. I creep toward the sound, hoping it is her. But she isn't there, of course. Only in my mind. She is gone and has taken our child with her.

It is difficult to put into any words, or any type of order, the pattern of grief. It rises and falls unevenly like waves. In those moments when I catch myself thinking of something else apart from Lena, guilt descends like heavy rain, and I turn again to rely on time to ease this pain. I have seen people grieve and wonder why it is they do. It is not until something happens, until someone leaves one alone in this world, that one truly understands the magnitude of loss.

The housekeeper comes and goes silently. She is aware that I am not myself and does not engage in trivial conversation. At least she understands grief, even if she has her flaws. I wonder how much of a raise my father has given her to watch me, to report back.

"Helena!" I call to her one day. I have decided that I don't want her here, and I dismiss her. I suspect that she is reporting to my father.

"But what am I to do?"

I take out several banknotes from the safe, part of a bottomless well of funds to which I have access, thanks to wealthy, dead Jews who prop up my father's finances. It is a ridiculously large sum that I give her.

She looks at it, masks any surprise she may feel, nods her head, and leaves. Money is like that. It can make people disappear, though it cannot always make them return.

Christmas came and went while I traveled from Auschwitz. Last year, before the assignment, Lena and I had planned to have a tree.

Several years before I completed my schooling, my father banned Christmas trees in our home and ordered my aunt to organize a Christmas dinner only, and not to buy gifts. Celebrations became bland and uneventful: a time to meet with family and my father's associates, and always with the topic of politics. The symbolic tree did not reappear in my life until my first Christmas with Lena's family. Nazi ideology could not strip them of all their traditions.

There is a piece of paper on Lena's writing desk. I have left it exactly how I found it. It is significant somehow. In the top-left corner she has written *Dear Willem*, and the rest of the page is blank. I often sit to muse over the paper, trying to imagine what she was thinking or doing when she stepped away from the desk. Was she about to tell me that her pains had started, or perhaps the name she wished for our child? Or perhaps how lonely she was without me? Guilt again rises to the same height as my grief when I imagine how frightened she must have been, unable to contact me, far from her family. To then have to phone another doctor at the hospital.

As the week passes, dirty dishes begin to pile on the table. My apartment has become my shield. If I stay indoors, I do not have to hear gunfire or witness the misery on the streets. I do not see the war. No one knows yet that I am here. My father is unlikely to reveal where I am, since he is so ashamed.

Some of my dreams seem more real. One night, out of habit, I put my arm across the space beside me on the bed. It was so cold that I drew my hand away. The shock of the emptiness hit me, and I began to sob. When I look in the mirror, I see that my hair has grown and there is growth about my chin. I have not changed clothes in days. I have the look of a vagabond: a crushed shirt that I wear both day and night, pants that are now too loose around my hips, shoeless feet.

I have begun to wall up the memories of my time at the camp. Brick by brick, I am building up a defense against the things I have seen, while Lena stands beside me, guiding me.

I choose a blustery day to finally leave the apartment to walk to the store. Around me other people also walk, their heads down as they battle the whipping winds and the rain that flies sideways. They are not proud people, but they are living, and that is all they can ask for here. I do not feel so alone. We share a feeling of entrapment and isolation, though mine is self-imposed.

But the air outside is moving, changing, shouting at me to do something, to move on. I rush to return to the apartment where the air inside has not changed. Trapped in a time that I shared with Lena.

I do not want to move on. I do not want the air to change.

There is a knock at the door. I do not answer it at first, hoping that whoever it is will go away.

Knocks come again, this time more determined.

I open the door a fraction and spy two small boys wearing caps and socks that have lost their stretch.

"Yes?"

"Excuse me, sir," says the older one, in rehearsed German. "We were just wondering if you had any work for us to do."

They have seen the nice apartments. They know that Germans with money live here.

"No, I do not." I am about to shut the door when I have an idea. "Wait here!" I say. I do not want them to see, fully, my disheveled appearance.

I return with money and place it in their hands. Their eyes widen in disbelief.

"That is so you don't come back," I say, and shut the door softly.

I hear them scurry down the stairs, perhaps afraid I will change my mind.

From the front window, I watch them run across the street, coins jingling in their pockets. Their legs busy, faces eager and innocent, and I envy the autonomy that is felt only by the young in these times. I sift through memories of my youth. Did I ever have those feelings?

I stay by the window for hours, hoping to catch a glimpse of the boys again, to perhaps share what I have never known.

I am the one who has never been free.

The air has grown stale. The warm, perfumed aromas of the apartment have been replaced with stale air: the stench of rotting food.

I fall asleep in the chair and dream of Lena. She is telling me, as she always did, that we must live the one life as if it is our last. When I wake up, I am suddenly ashamed. My grief has turned me into someone else, someone I don't recognize.

Life is something I still have. It is time to move forward.

I put on my uniform and call for a car to take me to the ghetto. Perhaps it is inherent, this will to continue on as before.

CHAPTER TWENTY-EIGHT

ELSI

I am taken to a courtyard, where I must await a truck that will take me away from the ghetto. A guard shouts at me to wait in a line.

I hear a familiar voice calling to me from somewhere, but it sounds far away. My head hurts, and I am shivering. The view around me is foggy, perhaps imagined. I have on a dress but no coat. I do not know what happened to my shoes.

Then I hear the voice again. It fades in and out. The ground feels aqueous, as if pulling me downward to where I can sink away, unseen—a place where I will be safe and warm, where I can dream.

"Elsi," the voice calls.

My vision clears, briefly. Yuri is standing on the footpath on the other side of the road.

"Elsi, I have Leah! I will look after her. I'm sorry I can't do any more for you."

I close my eyes.

CHAPTER
TWENTY-NINE
WILLEM

The sight of the ghetto instills in me a sense of failure. That I should heal people only so that they will die of starvation or disease or, worse, at the camps. Oddly, though, perhaps desensitized, the sight of women and men, very thin, in threadbare clothing, does not touch me so much now. As if there is nothing more within me to touch. It is a process perhaps that every German serviceman must go through—some quicker than others—the peeling back of every ethical layer that must happen before one can perform to the Führer's expectations.

I call into Administration, dreading the possibility that I will have to speak to Hermann Manz and hoping that I can avoid it. He is there, however, and greets me with superficial Nazi nationalism—*Heil Hitler*. I respond with feigned enthusiasm, aware that these two spoken words are meant to stifle original thought until there is no more.

Manz says that I am missed, and that many of the women have had to be examined elsewhere. *Elsewhere* is something I don't want to know about. But I don't doubt that he misses me. It is in his best interests that I am there to take care of his victims.

"I have put in a request for you to return. I have yet to hear," he says.

I shrug. I could tell him the answer now if I wanted to. I no longer care that I won't be returning, though I express the opposite out of politeness. It is a veneer that I slip into too easily. I will need to wear it more if I am to return to Berlin to carry on the good name of my father. Where I must carve out some existence: but only that.

I stop by the ghetto surgery to retrieve some personal items I had left in a drawer. The patient files are still there, but it is likely that Manz will destroy them before he leaves.

The car arrives to take me back to my apartment. Its wheels jolt uncomfortably over tram tracks, and ghetto dust swirls outside my window. Near the entrance to the ghetto is a line, of sorts, of dozens of Jews, waiting to be taken to the camps. They were there when I first came in, but then I had looked the other way. Now I scan the faces, my soul impervious to their despair and loss of hope. A girl, a familiar face, comes fleetingly into view at my side window before disappearing into the colorless haze behind us.

I am curious.

I have the time.

"Stop!" I say to the driver. "Wait here!"

I cross the street and patrol the line of people until I find her. The girl, Elsi, does not look up. She sits, knees against her chest, arms crossed, staring at the footpath. Even my shadow across her does not stir her curiosity.

"Elsi?"

She turns her head to look at my boots and raises her head slowly. I recognize in the color of her eyes, ringed in black, the infection within her. Her hair has barely grown to cover her ears. Hers is a small elfin face and a dangerously thin body. She is even smaller than I remembered, a tiny yellow flower wedged between others who appear similarly devoid of comprehension—too sick to care. The stamp on the back of her hand tells me she is to be deported.

"Stay away," says a guard. He holds a handkerchief over his face.

"Where are your mother and sister?"

"My mother is dead."

I feel some odd feelings surface again, a tingling of compassion that I always felt around Lena when she spoke—something I thought I had left behind me at the camp. My chest opens slightly, and, just briefly, a delicate hand reaches in to squeeze my heart.

In those seconds a thought, a plan, has come to light. A touch of madness, a touch of sun.

A butterfly with broken wings.

I turn to the guard. "What is your name?"

"Baimgarten," he replies carelessly.

"Bring this girl to my car!"

"She is to go on the truck of the dead. She is contaminated."

She will never arrive anywhere. The trucks will be filled with gas. I look up the line. It is also full of sickness. I have learned many things in Auschwitz in the short time I was there. Most never reach the camps. It is doubtful that these people would last the drive anyway.

The truck of the dead is a term used among some of the guards, even some of the Judenrat.

"There appears to be a mistake," I say. "This girl passed Aryan testing. She was meant for one of the Lebensborn centers in the west. She is not to go east."

"Lebensborn?" he says, unfamiliar with the name. "She is too sick to go anywhere. You will not want to touch this one."

"Check your orders," I say, ignoring the comment.

The guard looks at my collar, then flicks through his pages on his clipboard.

"What is your name?" he asks Elsi.

I answer for her.

"No, there is no mistake," says the man confidently. I believe he likes his job. He likes the power of sending people to their deaths.

"Then the request has been lost. I witnessed the testing myself," I lie.

"It is too late."

"Do you know the position I hold, Herr Baimgarten?"

"Yes, Herr Captain."

"Do you know my father?"

Baimgarten shakes his head, eyes narrowing. He can see where this is heading.

"My father is Major General Gerhardt, and a personal friend of Herr Himmler. I have full authority to do with the prisoners as I wish. And I will report you if you do not comply with my command."

The guard looks uneasily at his feet before he answers. "What are your orders, Herr Captain?"

"Strike her name from the list and bring her to the car."

"Her history says that she is more Jew than Aryan," he says to me. He can't help himself. Perhaps he has seen the madness in me. Perhaps he is still unsure I am who I appear to be.

"Sometimes history is wrong," I say.

It is only one person he will lose from his manifest. At the end of the day he will no longer care.

"Get up," he barks at Elsi.

The guard drags her from the line roughly.

"I will take her from here," I say.

She looks at me suddenly, warily, pulling nervously at her own wrist. I can sense her reluctance.

"Don't be afraid."

I help her into the car. She is very frail.

"What are you going to do with me?"

I slide in from the other side.

Her eyes wander around inside the car as if she is expecting some-one else. The filth of her dress against a pristine pale canvas of leather. Mud on the backs of her calves, dirt caked under jagged fingernails, lips white.

"I am not someone's whore. I won't be yours."

"You are not anyone's whore. You have passed the Aryan testing. It is my job to recruit for Aryan centers."

I say the last bit for the benefit of the driver. Drivers are sup-posed to look the other way. It is why they are carefully screened and employed. But it depends who they are employed by. One can never be too cautious.

"I am not Aryan," she whispers. It is the typhoid fever. It does strange things to the brain. It causes one to lose complete and utter hope and reduces the will to survive.

I tell the driver to leave the car running as I let myself into the surgery once more. I take supplies of sulfonamide for her infection along with other medicines. The cupboards, I notice, have already been raided of much.

Back in the car, we follow the streets once more that lead us out of the ghetto. The girl's head is resting on the back of the seat. She stares out of the window through a cloud of fever. Her legs move restlessly.

As we pass the checkpoints, I wonder briefly at what I have done, at the spontaneity that I have never had before, whether I will get away with it. How proud it would make Lena to see me do something that goes against convention. To do something truly righteous rather than what looks right. And I feel a weight lifted. For the first time I feel free.

I smile at the risk I have taken.

"You are Aryan enough," I whisper back, but she doesn't acknowl-edge this. It is unlikely she even understands the full weight of its mean-ing. It means, of course, that she will not die.

APRIL

CHAPTER THIRTY
WILLEM

In the past month I have received several calls from my father, asking when I am coming. I need some more time, I said. I am not yet through my grief. On the other end of the phone line, his silence confirmed his bitter disappointment in a son who continues not to deliver.

In the kitchen, Elsi is preparing dinner. I have never asked her to do this, but it became her role this last week. It is what she says she enjoys most: to have a kitchen and a stove that works. To have a choice of foods to cook with. Color is returning to her face, fullness to her cheeks. I have trimmed her short hair, neatening it slightly.

When I brought her to the apartment, she could walk but only just, so weak was she, her temperature high. She was too ill to fight me when I helped her undress to place her in a cool bath. The rash across her abdomen was another symptom of the disease. After she was cleaned and dressed in a nightgown of Lena's, I led her to one of the spare bedrooms, where she collapsed. There was torn skin and a lump the width of three inches on the back of her skull where she had been struck with an object, most likely by a guard.

The typhoid fever had not yet reached critical stages—I judged she had been ill for between one and two weeks. Another two weeks and she may have died; however, an even quicker death had been planned for her by way of the trucks for the dead. She stayed in a room of the apartment, speaking vaguely at times but mostly coherent, her large, round eyes watching me as I treated her with medicine to kill the bacterial infection and painkillers to reduce the fever.

The fever broke after several days of treatment. She had been saved, unlike most who were admitted to the ghetto hospitals long after their fevers had progressed too far to be helped.

I gave her several dresses of Lena's and have been helping her improve her German speech. She had not taken to the language in her early years, she confessed, but she was a fast learner and had picked up much of it in the ghetto. It was in the third week that she bombarded me with questions after I suggested we destroy her identity card.

Why did you help me? What will become of me? Do you know of my sister? These are questions I am still unable to answer. Though she is grateful, I can tell that she often thinks I have more devious reasons for helping her. In time she will see that I do not.

I have told her briefly about Lena, though it is often in the middle of other things I am talking about, her name so connected with much of my past: the activities we shared and the places we went. I do not discuss my work at Auschwitz, only of the work ahead, and that I will return again to Germany eventually. That is usually where our conversation stops, since I have not yet thought of ways to protect her when it comes to that time.

Her sister is still in the ghetto, which is a constant concern for her, and I have promised to learn what I can. Her mother is dead, shot by the Gestapo for visiting the ghetto prison. I could not look at Elsi when she told me this for fear that I would give something away. She has yet to know what kind of man I descend from. It is only from the photo at the front of the apartment that she knows I am someone with connections to the Führer and his plan to rid his empire of Jews.

In recent days it is as if she has come alive. That is not to say that she is unbroken. Sometimes I hear her cries and whimpers on the nights there are no whistling winds. It is a curious thing that we live like this. The question of our future does not come up as often as I thought; both of us will it to remain the way it is now—uncomplicated.

It is easy to see what type of person she was before the war. She is colorful at times, talkative, a girl with dreams that were suddenly interrupted. But sometimes she is the color gray: withdrawn into memories of her imprisonment. This is to be expected. Grief is neither black nor white.

Light rain accompanies a howling wind from the north. The streets are almost bare, and those who are out by necessity hold fast to their hats. The blanket of snow has disappeared to reveal broken pavements and water-filled craters streaked with oil. I pay someone to bring food from the markets to limit my contact with the outside world; to stay hidden within this apartment, now a sanctuary for the disaffected—although I know that such places are only ever temporary. I recently sent a letter to my father telling him that I am progressing well, that it won't be long now before I can work—words and promises that can hopefully give me more time to come up with a plan.

Elsi has seen the nursery that Lena had been working on while I was away. Lena had not been as keen to finish the decorating once she had learned we were returning to Germany. Part of the room has been painted, the other half not. It is as unfinished as Lena's and my time together. I have been inside the room once, to see the lace-covered cradle in the corner. I cannot look inside again. Elsi is sorry for my loss. Her regret is genuine.

She talks of a boy in the ghetto who nearly sent her to her death, but she stops the conversation suddenly, her eyes sad and fearful; perhaps she is thinking she has said too much.

"Go on," I say. "I am not going back to that place. I don't care to sell your secrets. I am in just as deep."

She starts to cry then, and I wonder about the boy.

"Did you love him?"

"No," she says. "Maybe . . . I don't know." She puts her head in her hands. The dimming light outside paints the front living room in colors of sorrow. Elsi's heart is as heavy as mine. I wonder if we can ever heal.

I reach out to touch her shoulder, then draw my hand back. I cannot contaminate her further. She has been handled enough.

She raises her head and rubs at her eyes.

I hesitate to turn on the lamp beside me in case she does not want me to see her face.

"The nights will soon be warm," I say, to break the silence. "I do not miss the winter."

"Yes," she says. "I know what it is like to experience a winter in the ghetto. Those unfortunate souls must be grateful for spring."

Silence.

"Thank you," she whispers.

I look not at her but out the window to the mauve-and-orange clouds on the horizon. Such beauty found even here, near the abode of the damned.

"Elsi," I say, "do you fear me?"

"Sometimes."

"Why?"

"Because you are a Nazi. Because you are a man. I have seen what they do to Jewish women."

"Elsi, please understand that I am not like those other men. If I could, I would not have any of you live in the way I have seen. And I will not treat you like other men."

"What would you do if you were in charge of the ghetto?"

"First, I would condemn Hermann Manz to be hanged."

She nods.

"They didn't need to kill my mother. She did nothing to them."

She leaves the room then. We are from opposite sides of the universe. This apartment, a neutral haven where we can meld our pain.

Morning and rain falls heavily. A knock at the door startles me. There is no sign of Elsi. I open it to find Hermann Manz. Coldness spreads down my spine.

"So it *is* true! You are still here."

"Yes." There is a moment of panic. Perhaps he knows what I have done: I have taken a girl from the ghetto.

"Are you going to leave me out here?"

"Come in!" I say with feigned courtesy.

He shakes the raindrops from his coat before hanging it on a hook near the door. The floor of the entranceway is now wet and muddy. He has not bothered to wipe his feet.

I usher him toward the sitting room near the front viewing window, and I notice with some concern that Lena's cardigan lies across one of the chairs: evidence of Elsi's presence. We sit here often to watch the stream slowly filling with rainwater, to sit in silence. Manz does not appear to notice. I look toward the hall. There is no sign of Elsi.

Manz looks around the room. "Ah yes . . . as nice as I remember. Much nicer than mine." He turns, his large body blocking out the light, his face in shadow. "Someone in the town saw you. I had to check. To make sure."

I clear my throat, which has thickened. "It is taking some time to adjust to her death."

Manz thinks a moment. "Oh yes, yes. Your wife. Such a shame." Forced sympathy, something I have used myself.

"But I will return to Berlin in due course."

"Fortunate for some," he says. He knows I have more rights than most. Then in a lighter tone, "But everyone should have a break from such a hellhole."

Manz walks to the window. "A better view than most, yes?" he says. This is followed by a short, gruff laugh. "You are lucky you are not facing the ghetto."

"Would you like some tea?"

"No, I'd prefer a whiskey."

He was warned by the Reich Governor to stop drinking while on duty. He is always breaking some rule.

"I'm sorry. I don't have any left. It was the first thing that went upon my return."

"Never mind. This is business. And I can't help but be relieved that you are here. The hospitals have limited staff now. I need your help . . . it is a sensitive issue."

Some of the tension leaves my back.

"Please . . ." I gesture toward the lounge, where he takes a seat. "What is this business?"

"There is a particular woman . . ."

There is always a woman.

"And she is in a delicate way."

"Lilli again?"

"Yes, unfortunately, but nothing to do with me this time. You would be helping out a friend."

He finds it hard to meet my eyes when he says this.

"I see."

"Can you come and see her? I have been transferred elsewhere in Poland and will be finished at the ghetto in several weeks. I owe her this favor, and who knows what will happen to her after that."

"Of course," I say. I need to get him out of here. "That is very considerate of you." He is an egotistical tyrant who always has an ulterior motive. "I can come straight away."

"No. I will send a car to collect you later tonight. It is more discreet. One last favor . . . for comradeship, for the purity of Germany."

He laughs, a sound from deep inside his large torso. I laugh, too, a rehearsed response.

We make small talk. He says that the ghetto is overcrowded. They have had to deport many of the children and elderly, evacuate the hospitals, get rid of the sick. Too much disease. *Deport* is another name for eradicate. I suspect that Elsi is behind a corner close by, listening intently to this conversation.

"And you wouldn't know about the unfortunate incident involving the killing of one of our men. Of course you wouldn't—you had already left. Apart from her regrettable racial background, she has served us well."

"I don't understand. *Who* has served us well?"

"Lilli! She works for us, Willem. I thought you knew that! It was Lilli who revealed the names of the people who were setting fire to buildings. It turns out the woman she had befriended—you treated her once—had a daughter who was part of the group. Lilli is excellent at knowing the right questions to ask, at getting people to trust her."

"Forgive me for my ignorance. I had no idea she was a spy."

"Oh yes, one of our best," he says. "I don't normally believe in gratitude, especially toward Jews, but she is always coming to us with new information, and with your help—"

There is a sudden, loud clanging noise in the kitchen. Manz stands up.

"Please, stay seated . . . it is just my housekeeper. Excuse me while I check to see if anything is broken."

In the kitchen, Elsi sits in the corner, one hand over her mouth. I rush to her and whisper in her ear.

"You have to trust me. Don't make a noise," I say. "I will find out the truth."

Her eyes are wide. She is holding back a scream.

"Wait!" I put my hand on her shoulder and scan behind me to check if he has followed me in. Elsi takes her hand away from her mouth. I am not sure what she will do if I leave her, but I must return to Manz and hope she stays hidden.

"My apologies for the interruption. Everything is fine," I say, returning to my unwelcome guest. "Just a pot that has fallen on the floor."

Manz eyes the doorway to the kitchen.

"Please. You were saying . . ."

"Simply that gleaning information is never too difficult. You know those Jews and Poles . . . They always protect themselves first. Friendships crumble for the sake of a nice coat and fresh milk and coal."

"Yes, I imagine so," I say. "If you send around the car, I will come and do as you asked, Hermann." The time for familiarity in this instance only, since I, too, am about to request a favor. "I must ask that you tell no one I am here," I say. "I prefer the solitude for a while."

"Of course."

"And another thing. Tonight, if you could, make sure there is a guard outside the door as is usual. I would feel more secure, in light of the fact that one of our own was *murdered*." I use the word only to dramatize, to highlight my supposed concern.

"Yes, anything you need. Do you require more medicine?"

"Has anyone had access to the surgery and taken items I might need?"

"Absolutely not." He is lying; perhaps the missing medicine was taken for himself.

"Then I believe there should still be enough."

I walk him to the door, the negotiations of our arrangement nothing short of civil, even in times of genocide. Then he is gone, but the scent of his cologne still lingers.

Elsi rushes toward me. Her eyes are wide, frantic.

"I want to kill her!"

"Calm yourself," I say. "Lilli will be left alone in the ghetto without the support of Manz. She will suffer there—I am certain."

"It is not enough," she says, eyes dry, hatred burning a hole inside her fragile heart.

"I will speak to her tonight," I say. "I will find out the truth. Who knows what lies Manz will say to protect himself, to make himself look heroic?" This to appease her, but I am already treating this as truth. It is unlikely that Manz would make this up since I had already agreed to help him prior to this knowledge.

"You will definitely go?"

"Yes. I must play the part of one who is supporting the cause. It might stop any further inquiries."

"You can't trust them."

"I am one of them," I say.

"No," she says. "You are not. I believe you now, that you are not like other men."

I am at the ghetto for the last time. I shall never return. After this, I will make plans to return to Germany and find a safe place for Elsi.

I wait in the surgery for the woman I am about to treat.

She arrives in a silk dress with a fur collar, lipstick on, as if she is not part of the ghetto, as if she is part of the German elite. Though her eyes are dark, her face is pale with fever.

"We meet again," Lilli says huskily.

She holds a cigarette between her fingers and draws from it greedily. Normally this would offend me: her arrogance and the smoke filling up the small space. But there are more disagreeable vices by this woman that I must contend with today, making the lesser irritations bearable.

"We might as well get this over with," she says, believing foolishly that she is the one in control.

She heads to the back room and sits on the surgery bed, then stubs out the cigarette in a surgical dish. She unbuttons her dress, drops it on the floor, and takes off her underwear. This is nothing new to her. These surgeries are commonplace.

"Fraulein Pedersen," I say gently, "you must look at a more permanent surgery. These abortions will take their toll."

She shrugs. "Someday I might marry a rich German who will beg me for children. One can never know what is ahead."

One can never know. However, I do know that she will not be marrying any German officer in the near or far future.

I drape a sheet over her body, but she is not concerned with modesty. She is watching me carefully. She is used to watching. I put on gloves and take out some instruments that have accumulated dust. I am missing some vital medicines—ones that I took home. *No matter.*

I hum a tune, in my head, the one that Lena and I danced to at midnight, while I conduct an internal examination.

"Why would a doctor choose to work here?" she asks. "You are too handsome for this line of work, let alone working in such a hole as the ghetto."

"Ah, well, there is much satisfaction in taking care of women. There are so many variables. It is challenging work . . . I hear that Herr Manz is leaving soon."

"Yes," she says, and just for a moment I see a flicker of the eyelids: a touch of fear. I wonder what the new supervisor will think. Whether he will employ similar tactics. For Lilli's sake, she must be hoping that he is just as debauched.

"How are you feeling?" I say with faked concern, temporarily withdrawing my hand.

"A little tired. It has been a stressful couple of months."

"Tell me—what has happened? I'm a good listener."

"You're probably a spy."

I laugh softly. "There is no motivation for me to spy. I have everything I need. My father is a good friend of Himmler."

Her eyes widen.

"Well, then, what am I doing with Hermann Manz?"

I ignore the flirtatious comment and turn to put on a gown in preparation for an abnormally large quantity of blood.

From inside my bag I retrieve some morphine and silver nitrate taken from Auschwitz. I cannot say why I have this: perhaps as proof to show my father, which it seems now would have been a waste of time, since he is immune to injustice. I inject some morphine into her arm, and she sinks back slightly, the drug taking instant effect.

"So, Lilli, I'm concerned about you. Because you are far along, this will be difficult. Will you be able to rest afterward?"

"For a short while," she says, words now unhurried, her body slackening.

"Do you live with someone? Someone who can take care of you?"

"No. I live on my own."

"Has this always been so?"

"I did have a young girl with me, the daughter of a dead friend. An old man who had been taking care of her was about to be deported, so he brought her to me."

"The young girl must owe you a great deal for your kindness."

"Yes," she says distantly, eyes closed.

She is clever. Even under the influence of drugs, it is difficult to induce information from her.

"Perhaps you are relieved that you are once again living alone. Of course, there is little future for orphan children, is there not?"

"Exactly! What was I going to do with her? Such a burden. After a week I asked Hermann to arrange some transport for her."

I fight the urge to search her expression, to know immediately, afraid I will show a break in my reserve. She is used to studying people and their reactions and may see through my charade.

"To the camps?" I ask casually, still without looking at her, pretending to examine the surgical tools on the trolley beside us. I have to hope that the drugs will impair some of her inherent mistrust, that the brazen question will not end further inquiry.

"She was so ill after all. What was I to do? The Germans are planning to take them anyway, I heard. I have a very busy life. Hermann did not like a child around."

"Of course not." Even with heat rising to my neck, I remain calm. I was raised to stay in control. "Lilli, I have heard good things about you. I heard that you brought to the attention of Hermann Manz an operation smuggling people out of the ghetto."

"Hermann told you this?"

"Yes, of course. We are very good friends."

"A group of vigilantes, murderers, they were. In fact, the friend I mentioned earlier, Hannah, had another daughter who was involved with the group. That stupid girl got her mother killed."

"How did you glean such intelligence?"

"You seem very interested in this."

For several moments I ignore the comment while I clamp the cervix in preparation for the procedure. She winces.

"Does that hurt?"

"I'm fine."

I turn away to retrieve an instrument.

"It is my job to be interested, and this moment is all about you and your future," I say. "Talking about things keeps your mind away from the task at hand. I had no idea of the important role you have. You are quite artful to obtain such important information. Perhaps you will receive an award for such service."

This time I meet her clouded gaze. She is perhaps thinking of something beyond the surgery for us.

"Hermann recommended you highly," she says.

"I must thank him later. Please . . . talk about whatever you want to. Continue, but only if you wish. You can trust me."

She is lost again to the drugs and my hypnotic words of reassurance, and she closes her eyes.

"Hannah told me that she suspected her daughter and friends were involved in something and showed me an address where she thought they were meeting. Naturally I don't like misfortune for people that I am close to, but Hermann needed to know everything. I had no choice but to reveal the names of those attempting to destroy order in the ghetto."

"Of course," I say. "You must have felt cornered, but you were only doing your job."

"Exactly."

"And this troublemaker, this friend's daughter. . . also on the trucks?"

"Elsi? Oh yes, thankfully."

"Now, if you can keep very still . . . that's it. Just a pinprick."

"What is that?"

"Painkiller."

I have given her a double dose of the narcotic I have brought with me. Lilli's eyes roll back, and her head falls to the side. Her speech now slurred, almost unintelligible, she asks for some water, a request I ignore as I proceed with my work to remove the fetus from the womb. My task is difficult, and incisions are made in the uterine walls that are not part of normal procedure. I then take another bottle—silver nitrate—and, through a tube, syringe the contents into her bleeding, now-empty uterus.

Lilli moans slightly and shifts in discomfort, but it is doubtful that she can articulate the pain now, eyes shutting involuntarily. I stop what I am doing to watch her face: a pretty mask for something false and worthless.

"How are you feeling?"

Her eyes open briefly.

"I feel quite cold," she murmurs.

I watch her for several moments before injecting more morphine. Then I retrieve two straps that I keep in the surgery to ensure my own safety, if necessary. She is unaware that her wrists are now fixed to the side of the bed. Not that this step is perhaps necessary. She is so close now to losing complete consciousness.

Then I whisper, close to her ear.

"How do you think Elsi felt in the prison while she watched her mother die?"

Her eyes open suddenly. She has just enough cognizance of my meaning.

"Elsi . . ." she whispers back.

"She is safe and free," I say lightly.

Her eyes move from side to side. She blinks to recollect, to find sense in her now-addled brain. Her head rises slightly from the table, but her will is no match for the weight of the drug. Saliva bubbles at the corners of her mouth.

"Relax," I say, patting her limp hand. "Elsi will not die alone. You, however, will be buried with the decaying bodies of the people you sold out—your name thrown into a pile of irrelevance."

Words fail her completely now. She emits a series of low, garbled cat cries, her fingers weakly clawing at the bed. I shove a small towel into her mouth to soak up the sounds.

I watch the blood pool on the table between her legs, occasionally mopping it up with towels. An hour later she sleeps, her skin becoming translucent in the bright light. So much blood, some of it transferring to my coat, as I predicted.

I check on the guard outside and tell him that the patient is not faring well, and I must remain until morning.

Sunlight. I must have dozed in the chair opposite the surgical bed. I touch her cold, lifeless body, pen a note, then to the front of the surgery.

"Guard, the patient didn't last the night. Please arrange for her to go to the crematorium immediately, and when Hermann Manz arrives, give him this note." The guard leaves at once to get help to move the body.

A debt for the lives of Elsi's loved ones has been paid, in the only way I can, since the true perpetrators behind Lilli's crime are, for now, unreachable. And in a brief moment on the previous evening when I questioned my own action, *justification* was the clear answer given. But I also believe a worse fate lay ahead for Lilli in the coming months; it is doubtful she would have lasted the ghetto without Manz. Despised by her own people and, though she believed otherwise, despised by mine, also.

You did what you had to.

As I commence to leave the room, I stop to study her face one final time. She does not look so different from when she first walked into the surgery, the changes between the two states too subtle, as if the leap between life and death is insignificant.

I am numbly detached from the final outcome: an oddly weightless sensation. But yet there is enlightenment, also, something attuned to hope. A premise perhaps from where a greater cause can build.

In the front room of the surgery, I phone for a car to take me home. While I wait, my thoughts turn to Elsi and what she must never know.

Dear Hermann,

I regret to inform you that the patient I was looking after at your request has died. Unfortunately the pregnancy was too far gone; however, she was persistent in her request for termination, despite my recommendations. She mentioned that a child would interfere with her work, not to mention the inconveniences to those she worked alongside. I believe that she had begun termination herself, which contributed to a rupture. Had I had access to a larger medical facility, there would have been only a slim chance of survival at this point in time.

But rest assured, she did not feel pain and was made very comfortable toward the end.

I wish you the best and trust that the service she provided will not be forgotten.

Yours sincerely,

Willem

CHAPTER
THIRTY-ONE
ELSI

Willem has said that we are leaving for Berlin and that he has accepted a posting as commander at a center for young Aryan women and children.

After Willem finished at the ghetto for the last time, he contacted several camps and pretended that he was looking for a missing Jew whose daughter Leah may have been sent to one of the camps. This Jew, he said, might possess useful intelligence about other Jews. But he found no one by the name of Leah Skovsgaard.

He has told me that it is unlikely she has survived. He says things in a way that makes me think he doesn't care, but the fact that he has taken care of me, has bothered to look for Leah, tells me otherwise. He is a good man, though complicated and emotionally controlled. But I should not be one to judge. I am complicated, if not damaged, also. Sometimes I shake in the night when I relive the shot that killed Mama or the sounds of the dogs as they bore down on me. Sometimes I feel my heart rise up high into my chest, my lungs feeling so crushed it is hard to take a breath.

After Willem informed me that Leah had been sent away, I wandered the apartment, bent on revenge that I could never take. Then came the surge of loss and grief and rivers of tears. My time in the ghetto stretched further and further away, my time growing up with Leah dissolving into a handful of memories. Sometimes I dream that I am still in the ghetto and Leah and Mama are with me, only to waken and have to begin the grieving process again.

It feels like hollow justice that Lilli died from a uterine rupture and blood loss due to pregnancy complications, as I wanted to confront her, to ask her how she could be so cold when my mother trusted her. I feel she got away with her crimes too lightly, that she didn't suffer like the rest of us. She used us all to give herself a more comfortable life.

Willem has suffered, too. He has lost someone he loves. I sometimes examine the photo of Lena in the sitting room. She is tall and thin, her hair dark. It is strange that with Willem's background he would marry someone so unlike Aryan. She is neither beautiful nor plain, and ordinary in her glasses and her pressed white blouse and tailored trousers. They were good together, which is obvious from the way they smile at each other in the photo. She has died before her time, but at least she died knowing that she was loved.

Willem has not spoken much of Lena other than the places they went to, the food they ate. He is remote but not cold. Kind but not loving. I have caught him many times staring at the photo of his wife. He understands my grief and has kept his distance. He is considerate. He does not want to interfere.

He says that he will look after me, but it is difficult to know what is expected from me. That someone could rescue me from death and ask for nothing in return is a concept I struggle to accept. I am used to begging for more and receiving even less.

I nearly gave my heart to Simon, but I do not believe that he loved me, not in the way I was hoping. I believed in his cause, but I have to admit that he felt no love for me. In Simon's life there was no room.

When Willem first posed the idea to me about leaving for Berlin, I was reluctant and said that I should stay in Poland, to try to learn news of my father and Leah.

"How will you find this news? Where will you live?"

"I will search for members of the resistance to help me, and move from Lodz where no one will recognize me." I have not left the apartment for this reason. I have been inside these walls for weeks.

"It is your choice," he said. "But without me you will not be safe. I can give you some money and put you on a train if that is what you want."

I thought about this, tossed all night wondering, and by the morning I had come up with the obvious question: How can I be apart from Willem? In a short time I have grown attached to this man who sleeps in the next bedroom yet is so far away.

"Let me check your heart?"

Willem places a stethoscope against the bare skin at the top edge of my blouse. Every few days he checks that there are no secondary infections from my serious disease and from my time in the ghetto. He is thorough, gentle, and firm in his treatment. He listens intently to the noises inside my chest, as if I am not connected to them, as if I am not in the room.

He has been leaving the apartment lately, especially at night. He does not say where he goes, and it is not my place to ask.

"Very good," he says, turning away. I can still feel his warm touch on my chest.

"Why me?"

Willem studies me, not answering at first.

"Why didn't you rescue someone else that day?"

"You know why. You are easier to hide."

He retrieves something from his medical bag and passes it to me.

"Here," he says. "This is yours."

He hands me a card. It is my face that peers out from the photo. The card says that I am a German Pole. It says that I am Aryan. I look at the name, which is not mine.

"How did you get this?" I ask.

"Forgery here is a thriving business. It did not take long to walk around in civilian clothes and learn of someone willing to make such a document. And an envelope full of money to the forger means that you don't even have to give your name."

"Elsi Gerhardt," I read aloud.

"Yes. I thought it safest if people thought we were married."

I smile.

"Is that funny?"

"Yes . . . no. I don't know. Just strange, that's all."

He looks away, perhaps with embarrassment. It is hard to tell.

"When we are traveling it will keep you safe."

"What if we see someone we know?"

"I am an officer, and you are my wife. And there is no reason for you to speak unless you are asked a question directly."

He has been helping me with German. Because of my strange accent, I am a German who has been living abroad for some time with my parents who opened businesses in Warsaw, and now I look forward to returning home. Willem believes that it is safer to live in the heart of Germany, under the very noses of those who might despise me. The streets of Germany are cleared of Jews.

"And what of your father? What if he comes to visit?"

"I have thought of that, too. It is all arranged."

We arrive in Berlin at midnight. I can hear sweet piano music coming from somewhere. We walk along the streets, and my body trembles beneath the Nazi banners that Willem does not appear to notice. I feel as if I am shrinking into something small and insignificant here. I do not belong, and yet I want that: to feel part of a community that is free. And I wonder if Papa could see me, if he would feel ashamed that I want this, that I am living with Germans.

We walk up a flight of stairs to an apartment. It has a kitchen and dining area and two bedrooms and windows overlooking the street, blacked out with heavy curtains. There are two sitting rooms, also, and a small room where a housekeeper might stay, behind the kitchen. The apartment is not large, but extravagant in design and well furnished.

"Is this your apartment?" I ask.

"One of them," he says. "Though it will only be temporary. There are other places we will move to. The Center I will be working at is too far to travel to every day. I will find a place not far from there . . . for you, also, of course."

Inside the kitchen there is a refrigerator filled with meat, and fresh bread waits for us on the dining table. He has organized for food to be here ahead of us.

I don't know what to say. I do not know how to thank him anymore.

He makes some tea and cuts some bread while I unpack my case. We sit together, and he raises his teacup.

"To our new life!"

I raise mine.

"Willem, I don't know what to say. I still don't know why—"

"This is about righting some things," he says, interrupting me. He does not like sentimentality or gratitude.

But in a rare moment of affection, he reaches across the table and touches my fingers. I look at the taut skin on the back of his hands, my heart racing.

"It is something I can do. Lena would have wanted this for you."

Of course. His wife. She had seen the wrongs. This is all for her. I feel a little disappointed, though I can't yet find the heart of this, perhaps because I don't want to admit anything.

"What is wrong?" He has read the disappointment in my face.

"Does it make you feel powerful?"

He frowns.

"What do you mean?"

"I'm sorry. It's nothing," I say, and regret the shift in tone. I am thinking too hard, and weary from travel. Willem drove his own car. We were stopped several times along the way to show identification and were warned of resistance fighters who may show no mercy to German women. I was not afraid of the resistance fighters but of the German soldiers who told us about them.

"Elsi, you are still so young and have suffered much. This is hard on you—I know it is. And you have lost so much. You should be with your family, but if Lena were here, she would tell you to stay with me, to give you every possible chance."

You are still so young. He thinks of me as a lost child. Perhaps because I know too little of the world, whereas his wife was scholarly, interesting, and well traveled.

"Go to bed and rest, and tomorrow we will talk again. We will talk about a future for you. Eventually I may get you some work, if that's what you prefer."

I nod, but I'm feeling angry. *Why am I so angry? Why can't I just accept things as they are?*

We have talked about many subjects, though it is more from his side. He knows much of the world. He has taught me many things about other countries. We have shared meals together, listened to music.

· · ·

During the day I watch couples walk arm in arm beneath my window. I have caught glimpses of parkland from our small balcony in Tiergarten. I see children with their parents. I wonder if they know of the suffering elsewhere.

I have named this my weeping window because when I sit here I think of Mama. In another time she would have loved it here.

It is still light by the time Willem arrives home. I have cooked him some sausages and sauerkraut.

"Why don't we go out?" he says.

"But I have cooked all this food."

"It will not go to waste. We can eat it tomorrow."

I am feeling excitement. I have watched the streets from the window. It looks as if there is no war here at all. I long to walk where no one will recognize me.

"Yes," I say.

I unpack one of Lena's dresses, which is striped mauve and white with a black-velvet collar and belt. Her shoes are slightly too big, so I put paper in the toes to make them fit. There is no makeup or lipstick. I pull my hair up with pins.

When I come out of my room, Willem is watching me. His eyes do not roam like the eyes of other men. I wonder what he is thinking, and I am feeling suddenly self-conscious that I wear the dress of his dead wife. It is then I see the uniform and feel a stab of terror. He is one of the men who run the camps. He is one of the men who fire a pistol at the heads of innocent people. I feel slightly dizzy, and he catches me around the waist.

"What is wrong?"

"It's the uniform. Just a thought . . . ," I stammer. "Please forgive me."

He looks down at the clothes he wears. He is too intuitive to not see what it is that bothers me.

"I'm sorry, Elsi. This is who I am. Or rather, who they think I am. This uniform will keep you safer than anything. I promise you that."

We walk along the streets as the late sun sinks behind the city. People look at us, but their eyes linger more on Willem. He has station. He is someone to respect.

"Remember! You are my wife. You have nothing to fear."

Fearlessness is easier said than done, and as we walk along the beautiful tree-lined streets, I find myself looking down. I am afraid to meet anyone's eyes.

He takes me to a restaurant with high arched windows that overlook a wide footpath with large trees planted among the pavers. Inside are chandeliers, high-backed upholstered chairs, and white tablecloths. A man plays the piano in one corner of the room. They are tunes I don't recognize, soft and melodic. I have never sat anywhere so fancy, and I remember a painting in Willem's office at the ghetto that had a similar setting. It is as if I have walked into someone else's dream by mistake.

Willem orders us roast chicken and wine. He talks to me again of places he has been. He tells me of a time that he and Lena went walking across the Alps, how they nearly got lost. How Lena led the charge to find their way back to their hotel. How they were soaking wet and cold, and several nights later they were back in Berlin and ate here at this restaurant. They ordered so much from the menu; the walking had given them large appetites. Lena appreciated good food. He smiles when he tells me this. He becomes more animated with memories of her.

The smell of food is wonderful, but I am distracted by the people in the room. Men and women, even children, are served large portions of food, while people in the ghetto are starving. Their laughter hurts my ears. It sounds foreign and harsh and spiteful. These people know nothing about life, about the horrors several hours away by train.

Another man in a uniform similar to Willem's stops by with his wife, and introductions are made. He has seen the rank on Willem's collar. I raise my eyes and smile politely, though I cannot control the shaking of my hand when I put it forward in greeting. Willem has seen this and distracts us all by commenting on the state of war while my eyes remain fixed on the woman's earrings that dazzle beneath the light of the chandelier. It seems an eternity before they leave.

"You did well," says Willem. "It will get easier."

A piece of chicken is caught in the back of my throat, and I force myself to swallow. The pain in my head is worsening, pounding for release, and I rest my head between my hands. The room is swallowing me up. These people are killers. They are no better than the officers in the ghetto.

"Willem . . ."

"What is it?" he says, putting down his knife and fork to reach forward to take my arms.

"Please take me home." I close my eyes so I do not have to look at these people. Willem pays the bill, and we walk back to the apartment. Once inside I rush to the bathroom to empty the contents of my stomach before heading to my room to be alone.

"I'm sorry," says Willem, following me in. "I should have not suggested that, with so many officers around. Tomorrow we will go someplace where we can blend in with civilians. It will get easier. I promise.

"Your false maiden name, Winthur, also on your new identity card, belonged to a family killed in a bombing at the beginning of the war. In the months before the ghetto clinic began, I was sent to look after the SS and military, following them into the heart of war, waiting on the sidelines to patch them up. Many Volksdeutsche Poles were killed, whole families, their remains and a few personal belongings left behind in the bombing rubble—spectacles, a clock, shoes, a door plaque, so many items. The name of one family I saw on one of these items has stayed with me.

"No one can prove you are not one of them. There is no one left to expose you. No one to say you died or lived. They cannot prove you are anyone other than who it says on the card. You are safe, but it is up to you.

"You must be brave if you want to live."

● ● ●

Black motorcars chug past us on four short legs. Willem and I follow several other families on a wide-paved footpath toward the central gardens, alongside streets lined with square table-topped buildings that have a patchwork of arched and square windows. There is an overload of architectural shapes everywhere I look: elegant street lamps, steeples, dome-shaped roofs, columns, cross-windows, and small gabled shops with colored awnings. Red, black, and white flags hang off a wine bar, murmurings inside like the hum of bees, the tinkling of glasses, laughter spilling outside onto the pavement. Willem says the bar used to be a jazz dance hall when public dancing was allowed. Now dancing is only permitted for the private functions of those with rank.

In the park, children run about in light woolen dresses and shorts, waving a rainbow of balloons and streamers, their coats discarded in the newly risen sun. Meandering through the gardens is a lake in shades of green, and the grassy spaces around it are filled with tanned sunbathers and soldiers on leave. There is a celebration of some kind. A band of musicians starts up nearby, their instruments glinting, their music blending with loud conversation.

Willem is not dressed in uniform today: white shirt rolled up, golden forearms, pants pleated, baggy, and belted. My heart beats a little faster. I must not forget myself. He is a German. My rescuer, but that is all. *Then why can't I believe it? Why must I have these feelings that are getting in the way of others more practical?*

He carries a basket, and I follow him to a small patch of grass. He lays down a blanket, and we sit close. From inside the basket he pulls out bread, ham, mustard, and wine in tiny flasks. He has said it is doubtful we will see any senior officers here, not in uniform anyway.

A cool breeze blows across my back, and I can hear my mother in some distant part of my brain, telling me to put my coat back on.

"It is beautiful," I say of the day, a little too loudly so that I can drown out my mother's voice, which will only make me sad and guilty that I am here and she is not. For one moment, maybe more, I want to feel guiltless.

I feel a little giddy from the wine and raise my face to the sun to draw it closer, to caress my skin with its warm hands. To be touched. People walk by in front of us, taking little notice of the couple they pass, each from opposite sides of the battle, who have witnessed atrocities unimaginable.

I must blend in. I am no one of particular mention. I like that. If only it was easy to forget where I'm from and where I'm also meant to be.

"It is pleasant here, yes?" says Willem. "I used to come here a lot."

I am strangely relieved there is no mention of Lena.

A woman wheels her baby carriage up a short rise toward a group of older children waiting patiently for the food package she has under her arm, and like eager birds they crowd around her, pecking impatiently. A girl in a bathing suit catches the eyes of shirtless male sunbathers— soldiers on leave, says Willem—as she brazenly walks close to them.

Willem looks across at me several times, and I wonder what he sees. I look away, afraid that he sees only the Jewish refugee from the ghetto clinic. I want him to see more.

"You are a good person, Elsi. You need some time to adjust, but you will. You must move on."

Can I?

As if to clarify, he reaches over and takes my hand. It is friendship, I'm sure, this rare gesture of affection.

He releases my hand just as quickly, something perhaps he would do for his patients, to give them courage, like he is giving me.

We have been here for an hour, and I notice his restlessness. He is thinking of something else, something I presume that doesn't include me. I want to be part of his life. He perhaps believes friendship is what I want. But it isn't. I want him to throw his arms around me. I want to cry into his shirt. I want to feel loved.

With Mama and Papa gone, and Leah, too, I have forgotten what it is to be loved.

CHAPTER
THIRTY-TWO

WILLEM

She has waited up. She has cooked some beef and fried it with cabbage.

"I thought you might be hungry. You didn't eat much before you left yesterday."

Today I have been to see Father, who lectured me. I have said all the right things to him. I have told him that I see the error of my ways. That I behaved irrationally. That I cannot change things, and I will not look to the past for any answers to the future. I am not sure if I have convinced him—he is far too intelligent to be fooled—though he looks somewhat appeased. If there is any truth that he can glean from my words, it is that I will honor the commitment I made to work at the Center. He says that he has pulled many strings to stop another officer from taking the post, and has allowed for my time to grieve. But he insists I must start within days. There are several new children who will be arriving, and two more pregnant girls who require care. The woman currently in charge is not equipped with the number, nor is she suitable. Father has said again that the party needs someone with rank and expertise in health. I have agreed to everything.

Elsi has set the dinner table. She has poured a glass of wine for me. I see there is an empty glass on her side of the table.

"Have you been all right here alone?"

"Yes," she says, though there is distance in her tone. "Today I left the building and purchased new shoes with the money you gave me for emergencies. The color matches the dress beautifully, don't you think?" She talks slowly, clumsily, perhaps from the wine. I notice another bottle lies empty in the kitchen and wonder if she has been drinking during the day. I am somewhat alarmed, not just about the wine but about whether she has made the shopkeeper suspicious.

"Elsi, you should not go out alone."

"The sales lady was very polite to me, especially when I told her the rank of my husband." She smiles, leans forward to pour some more wine. I catch the bottle first.

She watches me with sapphire eyes that are round and shining with alcohol. The food is suddenly dry in my mouth. She is wearing one of Lena's dresses: one of my favorites. It is red and belted tightly at the waist. She has a tiny waist, narrow hips, and small breasts. These are things I have not appreciated. Not until now. Not until the dress. Her short, light ash-blonde hair now long enough to frame her face.

"What day do we leave?"

"Wednesday, most likely."

She nods and looks away.

"I have been thinking a lot of home and wondering if you should not have left me at the ghetto. I have no right to be here."

"You have every right. Stop punishing yourself. You were lucky. Some people haven't been. It is as simple as that."

"That is too easy an explanation. Nothing is that simple unless you strip away all the emotion. Is that perhaps what you are? Emotionless?"

"Sometimes it is the only way," I say.

I can see she is minutes away from breaking, her words fracturing. I choose something that I think Lena would say.

"You are the only person with the power to control your thoughts and attitudes. No one can touch you in here," I say, pointing to my head. "You don't have to change who you are because of what has happened to you."

"Mama changed. Some of us don't have a choice."

She pauses, looks at the bottle of wine out of reach, where her eyes stay fixed.

"I was not a good daughter. I was flighty, irrational, and argumentative."

"You don't seem that way . . ."

"I've had to change, too," she says in a tone that is forceful and alien. It is a tone that does not suit her gentle nature. Her eyes lock onto mine, and I find I cannot look away.

"I remember the day Leah was born. Mama didn't have time to call for Papa or a doctor. I had to run next door to find a neighbor to help. She gave me instructions. Told me to find plenty of linen to clean up the blood, to talk to Mama, to squeeze her hand for comfort. Leah came quickly and quietly into the world but took some time to open her eyes. I remember the moment she did, lying in Mama's arms, and the look in my mother's eyes, as if something so great had happened there were no words to describe her feelings. Then Mama had noticed me there, speechless, perhaps for the first time in my short life. I was still shocked from all the blood, from this slippery, ghostly purple mass that had come from inside my mother.

"She said, 'Elsi, come hold your sister's hand.'

"I looked into Mama's eyes. I had never seen that look before. I had never seen so much love in them. And looking at Leah, I did not understand this love that had caused my mother so much pain.

"But now I understand things. I know that to know love, you have to feel pain first. That is when you can truly understand what it is and how to appreciate it. I have felt pain and I know love, yet the people I should have loved more are all gone. Before the ghetto, I should have spent more time at home. I should have appreciated the people in my life. Everything I wanted was in front of me, around me."

I study her wistful expression, and she turns to stare at me. My appetite is gone, my throat suddenly tight. New feelings arise for this girl, as if I, too, can finally understand her. I drain a second glass of wine. My mind is foggy, the room too warm. Voices from the streets fuse a mass of undulating sound that travels through the open, heavily curtained windows.

Tears well in my own eyes before I realize it, and Elsi stands up to walk slowly to my end of the table and steps close. I look up at her, both confused and mesmerized by this action. She leans against me and strokes my head, which then rests against her stomach. Something tells me that I must stop this contact, but her touch is so soft, and the scent of her, Lena's dress, makes me disappear into her. I reach up and put my hand against her thigh. Then she gently turns my face upward and bends to kiss my lips.

I am unprepared for this and push the chair backward to distance myself.

"I can't," I say, shocked more for her sake than mine.

She looks bereft, then suddenly ashamed, disappearing down the hall to close herself behind her bedroom door.

It is my fault this has happened. I have encouraged such action. We have spent so much time together.

Or is she doing this out of fear, perhaps to reward me?

I take my coat and leave the apartment to walk. I pass several soldiers and show them my identity card when they step toward me. My head is not clear. I did not foresee these feelings from Elsi, distracted by my return to work and a desire to keep her safe. Yet, strangely, I am not disappointed. I should tell her that *we* can never be, yet I don't believe it myself.

Can I take something else from her?

She's in love with you.

She has no one else. And neither do I.

Two irreparable souls.

I return to the apartment. Elsi's door is shut, and there are no sounds within.

Forgive me, Lena!

I open her door.

CHAPTER
THIRTY-THREE
ELSI

Late afternoon. I have slept heavily and wake to feel Willem's lips on my bare shoulder.

"I'm sorry to wake you," he says. "I have to go shortly."

I roll over to face him and put out my arms. He climbs between them again.

Last night Willem became someone else, and I saw the core of him beneath the layers of gray and black and formality. His mask discarded, he was passionate and considerate. I have only known intimate physical love with Simon, which was a fleeting, distant, urgent love, against a backdrop of fear—necessary, almost. Such love in the ghetto was another mode of survival, to hold and touch, to feel human, and something that we may not have shared outside.

When I heard Willem leave the apartment after my disastrous display, I thought perhaps I had ruined everything we had together. I despised myself, tearfully vowing to leave in the night, to give myself up to the soldiers on patrol in the city that once rejected me—the city that may reject me still. Hours I lay there, thinking that Willem might not return.

And then he came through the door with soft steps and whispered apologies when he saw my distress. He drew me to him near the window, took away the cloth that separated us, and wrapped me tightly in his arms. With my head resting against his warm chest, for the first time I was able to forget our titles, our blood.

He dresses now, gray pants and jacket. Despite what we have been through, the uniform makes me anxious. It is something that represents death, yet something that has also kept me alive.

"Don't make me anything. I have a dinner meeting with Father and his associates. I could be quite late."

He is formal again, polite, as if the night didn't happen. But I know him better now. I know at least that he is capable of love. I wrap the sheets around me and sense a new beginning.

I have been knocked to the ground, waking me violently from sleep. I blink and see lights in the sky from our window, the sound of sirens in the street. The brick wall separating our apartment from the next is shattered, pieces landing only inches from where I lie. I crawl under the bed and cover my ears. The noise is deafening. Then a lull in the storm. It takes me a moment to adjust to the new world, to the gaping hole in the wall behind my bed, to the stillness in my ears. Then gunfire retaliates from the ground from somewhere near. I have to get out. The building is falling down around me.

I crawl out from under the bed wearing only a slip that is covered in white dust.

I examine my hands through a thick haze of smoke, then reach down to feel my feet. I am relieved to find they are still attached. When I stand, the weight of me is almost too great for my trembling legs. Nothing broken, though I am bruised, and something stings my leg. I press my hand against my strangely hollowed thigh, as if the flesh has been scooped. Alarm for this injury is brief when a whistling sound that barely reaches my deafened eardrums reminds me that I am still in the middle of danger.

There is just enough time to reach the stairs before another blast sends me into the wall and nearly tumbling down the stairs that have been showered in glass from the tall foyer windows. Several other people crowd behind me, stomping impatiently like bulls, huddling, each creature slowly released through the gateway at the top of the stairwell and funneled into the void below, now blackened with dust.

I think of Willem then: wondering where he is, hoping he is safe, that he has found a shelter.

Someone lies at the bottom of the stairs. I bend down to check on the man. He stares at me blankly at first, takes my hand as I help him to his feet; both of us then rush into the street.

The sound of war is above us. We are too close to the battle. Some people run, screaming, into the clouds of dust that disguise the night. Fires burn on roofs nearby. Outside a man is yelling, describing yellow-and-green flashes smoldering and spreading across the rooftops.

"You have to cover that quickly," calls a woman to me as she rushes by. It is the first time I have seen the gaping wound on my leg that burns as it meets the air.

I cross the road, following the group, hoping they are leading me to shelters. I look back at the building, once majestic, made from red brick and imported stone, according to Willem, its facade now torn away. My heart sinks at the sight of it, not from the damage but that Willem cannot find me there.

A truck pulls up beside me, and several men jump from its bed, bravely running toward another large pile of ruins. Several floors still hang, bizarrely, from the sides of the apartment block: it is a giant, abstract sculpture, a broken dollhouse.

I follow the men from the trucks. The streets are lit up from fires. Several men carry the elderly through doorways, their faces unrecognizable under blankets of ash and dust. Someone pushes an elderly man out of a doorway. He can barely stand. I catch him and lead him to where people are laying down the dead beside the living. One man is burned, one eye burned closed; the other stares out at me as if he knows me. At first I think I know him and then am selfishly relieved that I don't. I hold his hand and tell him that a doctor will be with him soon.

Some people are pulled from the rubble, while ambulances tear around corners. Someone is yelling that he has found a woman still alive and buried in the debris. I step across broken bricks, the soles of my feet tearing, as several of us begin to clear the area, pulling away the shattered pieces of buildings. We work furiously. It is a race for life. As the woman is pulled from the debris, I see that we have lost the race.

Someone is screaming that the zoo has been hit.

The bombing has ceased, but a siren still wails somewhere in the distance. Another person announces that the raid is over for now. Tall floodlights are erected along the footpath, and ambulances arrive to collect the dying.

"Sheets!" someone yells. They have already started to wrap the dead.

I have come to the restaurant where Willem and I had dinner, where I could not look upon the faces of those considered superior. The glass is smashed, the ceiling now on the floor. The men from the trucks are yelling that there are no survivors inside.

I stop and crouch down on the footpath. Blood has streaked my leg. I am too tired to move, my ears and eyes filled with dust.

Then out of the haze he comes, streaked with artificial light: the man with golden skin.

I rush to him and he to me.

He enfolds me protectively in his arms and kisses my temple.

"I thought I had lost you! I went first to the apartment. You weren't there. I can't lose you. Not you. You are all I have."

We are the same, I am thinking. *We are meant to be.*

"Who were they?" I ask, while he bends down to check the wound on my leg.

"British," he says, though it is not with hostility. "It is time to leave Berlin. This city will not fare well in this war. I can sense it."

Not even Germany is free from death.

MAY

CHAPTER THIRTY-FOUR

MATILDA

"The new commander is coming," says Jacek from underneath the flap. "He will be here tomorrow."

This news makes no difference to me here in the small house. I have nothing to say on the matter. Every time I hear a truck, I think it is time to go. Nurse has told me that I am to be sent away on the next one that arrives, that Berlin has given permission. I do not know what Berlin has to do with it. I do not want to know.

"Why don't you talk?" says Jacek.

I don't answer. I lie on my mattress and carve words into the wood. I have become quite skilled with the end of my spoon. There is dirt under my fingernails. I pick it out. Mama used to say that it is a sign of the poor.

I have been here for weeks. While I am in here I turn the age of ten. Sometimes they let me out during the day, but I am tied to a rope attached to a stake in the ground so I cannot go far. I can sit in the sun and watch the other children play on the swings but they are not allowed to speak to me. Juliane has been missing from the group. Jacek has whispered through the gaps in the walls that it was Cook's idea to let me out, and Nurse finally agreed. Though it is only when Frau is not there. At these times, Cook gives me some fruit and milk. When playtime is over for the children, I am locked back in the small house.

I am kept separate so that I do not influence the new children who have arrived.

I am not allowed any paper to write on.

The door of the hut is open, and the sun is glaring down at me.

"Out! Now!" says one of two older girls. She steps back slightly when I emerge into the air. She does not want to be too close.

"She smells," says the other girl, who holds her nose. She looks just as disgusted, though her eyes linger on the scratches and bites on my legs. Then she looks away.

I follow the tall girls in the direction of the hut where I used to sleep. I notice that the door is closed. They probably don't yet know that I have been released.

I have been in the room for weeks.

The girls walk past the hut, and I tell them they have gone too far. That they have missed the doorway to the hut for the orphans.

"You are not going there."

I am suddenly worried that I will not see Jacek again.

"Please . . . can I see the others?"

The first girl comes up close to me this time. "You are not in a position to ask for anything, little Gypsy. Frau doesn't want you here."

"Frida," says the other. "Stop! That is enough."

My legs feel wobbly—I have not been able to use them much—and Frau is standing at the front of the house with her baton.

"Go!" says Frau.

I walk toward her and see the truck with its large doors at the back, waiting like a monster, mouth open. The monster grumbles and hisses, angry and impatient; smoke is shooting from its back.

"Come on," says the one who is not called Frida, coaxing me. Her voice is neither kind nor horrible. It is just a voice that says this must be done and finished with, perhaps so she can go back to what she was doing.

I turn to look at the hut and wonder if Jacek is standing on one of the chairs inside to spy on me from the small windows at the top. Dirty glass eyes, too high to clean. We found that if we dragged one bed to rest on top of another and then stood on the headboard, we could just see the front gate.

A soldier steps off the truck. He holds a clipboard and a pen. I hear him say my name, and Frau nods. The girls stand on either side of me.

"It takes three of you?" jokes the driver. "This one must be a handful. Come on now! Bring it this way."

I am a thing, not a child. He doesn't even look at my eyes. Perhaps he doesn't recognize there is a human behind them.

CHAPTER
THIRTY-FIVE
WILLEM

The place where I am employed is under twenty-four-hour guard, its occupants considered a flight risk. It is a lower stage in the Germanization process, where the bad ones are weeded out and the good ones educated to Hitler's standards, using German propaganda.

The subjects I will be managing at the new center are mostly Polish orphans, husbandless mothers-to-be, and teenage girls. Several orphans require extra and specific instruction before they are adopted. The health levels—Father's code phrase for Aryan traits—of the orphans are to be checked by me, and as commander I am to decide who stays and who goes, who is admitted and who isn't.

I must enforce strict hygiene and health practices for all residents, and interview the families who apply to adopt the younger children. My father, it seems, has assigned me a very busy position, as I would expect; his aim is to prevent me from having time to reflect on anything but my role.

Admittedly, I am keen to start work. This job is a welcome diversion from other potential employment that Father originally intended for me.

Before commencing my new position, Father requested that I visit another center close by, a school for young, elite German women. My father believes it is a model for what all centers will become one day. Instead of security guards at the gate, robust girls greeted me at the door. The residents of these centers are part of the League of German Girls: an entitled group of members who keep active and domestically skilled and healthy and fertile for the future of the Fatherland. They are put through rigorous physical training, work the land, and stand ready to lend their support to war in any capacity that the Führer sees fit.

There is also a medical center installed just near the school not only for these girls but for the wives of the SS, and it is my father's wish that I call there once a week to operate this practice. I have visited the medical center and found it meticulous in its upkeep; sterile, white, and heavily supplied with medicine. However, I was keen to leave. Stark places often mean excessive control to me now, and rules that I suffer, rather than agree with. I yearn to be the one in control.

Elsi and I have spent several days settling into our home, several miles from the Center. Our new house sits between other houses, blending into the picturesque hillside. The town is colorful and quaint, with a school, restaurants, and churches now used as clothing and household donation centers for widows of war. Elsi has taken to the place straight away. She has mingled with the locals and, even with her strangely accented German, has been greeted well, perhaps because I stand just behind her. We have been employing furniture makers this past week, and Elsi insists on making the curtains and a quilt for our bedroom.

"Do you love me?" she asked me this morning as I was getting dressed for my first day of work. She was lying on her side, her legs bare, tangled in the sheets, her white back exposed.

"You need to sit up. I want to check your leg before I leave."

I pulled away the dressing and ran my hand across the shallow indentation. The wound is no longer sticky and raw, the skin now hardened and healing. There will always be a mark, a slight indent of the skin: a harsh reminder of our time in Berlin.

"You haven't answered me."

"What?"

"Love? Me?"

"Of course," I said.

Though the word is used too casually; is it not? Love is more than just a word. It is something you grow into with time. But I cannot explain that to Elsi. She may not understand, skeptical of my response at these moments. She has seen some cracks in my makeup that I am unable to explain.

It is only when she sometimes cries that she seems too young, and I wonder what I have done. It feels right, although in the eyes of some it is not. Not in the eyes of my countrymen, especially not my father, and perhaps not even Lena, now that our relationship has changed. It is not love I feel—perhaps that will come—but it is something more powerful. It is a sense of purpose.

I was deeply attracted to her, but it was not until the bombing in Berlin that I discovered just how important she was to me, that new thoughts arose: we could share a life together; we could build something out of the most tragic of circumstances. The thought of suddenly losing her was intolerable as I ran several blocks to our apartment. I believe that the feeling of potential loss was close enough to love, and enough for me to declare that I had feelings for her. After the bombing, we escaped to this house in the countryside.

As much as I hate to admit weakness, I believe that Elsi has saved me from self-pity.

"You only care about your work and my leg," she said.

"It is a good leg," I said playfully.

She laughed then, and it was a strange and wondrous sound, this new happiness that she is slowly unwrapping.

"Even when you joke it sounds serious," she said.

I turn into a dirt road toward a house surrounded by trees, acres of fields separating it from other farmhouses. Outside is a truck like many I have seen entering the ghetto and Auschwitz. Through the rear doors I spy several people sitting within the dark space. A guard stands at the back with a gun.

As I pull up to the gate, a girl is being led to the back of the truck. She does not wear any shoes, her hair is matted, and streaks of clean skin show where her tears have parted the grime down her cheeks to her chin.

I step out of the vehicle and stride toward the guard at the truck. The girl watches me carefully. She looks familiar.

"Soldier, where is this girl going?"

"The camps, Herr Captain."

"Why? I thought that the children here were marked for the adoption program, unless I decide otherwise. I am the new commander here."

"You can speak to Frau Haus. She has ordered it."

He lifts the girl onto the back of the truck. There are several other adults and children within the truck who view her with despondence.

"Leave her!" I say.

"I can't, Herr Captain," he says.

"You can, because I say you can. You have my permission."

I lift her featherweight frame from the truck, then hold out my hand toward her. She doesn't take it. She has fixed my eyes with her own: shining creek stones embedded in a muddied, soulless face.

I bend down to her, and she moves back a step.

"What is your name?"

She doesn't answer.

"If you tell me your name, I can tell the guard they have made a mistake and that you are not to get on this truck."

Her eyes veer fearfully toward the inside of the truck.

"Matilda."

Of course. I remember her now: a small voice from the dilapidated, dark-filled dormitory.

I turn to the guard. "I can vouch that she is not to go on the truck. Commencing today, no decisions are to be made without my approval."

He looks unsure.

"If you would like to phone my father, Major General Gerhardt, to check this, I will be happy to wait; however, I understand that you have a deadline and possibly many more people to collect."

"Yes, Herr Captain. Please excuse me."

The soldier walks over to speak with Miriam Haus, standing yards away in her smart-suited attire, alongside two stony-faced girls with skin like cream, safely distanced from the race-infected truck.

The soldier speaks in a tone too low to hear, and I see Haus view me, expressionless. She nods her head, and he returns to close the door, salutes, and disappears into the truck's cabin.

"Welcome, Herr Commander," she says, glancing briefly at Matilda. "I must tell you, Herr Gerhardt, that we had approval for the girl to go. She is a handful. I'm sure that after your own examinations you will agree."

"That is now for me to decide, and I can relieve you from making such distressful decisions," I say, perhaps too patronizing in tone. "I am most keen to go to the surgery, if you could lead the way. And bring this girl, also."

I follow Haus into the gloomy hallways, the smells of the kitchen again wafting toward me. The two older girls flank Matilda behind me.

Once in the surgery I tell everyone but Matilda to leave. I do not fail to notice the look on Haus's face that suggests she has bitten into something sour.

"It is a pleasure to have you here, Herr Commander," says Haus, unable to disguise a measure of resentment as she retreats from the room.

The surgery has been recently dusted, poorly, the streaks on cleaner furniture highlighting the lack of attention to the task. I wipe a finger across the top of the desk in disgust. Laziness will not be tolerated here. It is a dowdy room, painted a dull blue, and the desk is very small, the chairs old and uncomfortable.

Matilda stands in the center of the waiting area, her head down, arms behind her back, as if she is about to be punished. She is small, waiflike. I don't remember her being this thin; her cheeks hollow, the whites of her eyes too yellow.

"How old are you?"

"Ten."

She looks too small for her age. I push her gently in the center of the shoulder blades to lead her to the examination room behind the office. On the shelves inside an open cupboard I see that supplies of painkillers are low, and I write a note telling the nurse to order some more, and quickly. Bandages and other wound treatments are well stocked.

"Matilda, I am not only your commander but also a doctor, so today I will be examining you."

I see her eyes dart to the corners of the room suspiciously, as if there are things I haven't told her.

"I will need to take off your dress. I will need to listen to your heart and chest."

"Mama said no one should look under my clothes."

"I am not *no one*. I am a doctor who is keen to help you. Do you understand?"

Her little mouth pinches slightly, a frown above her nose. She is wary.

But I don't wait for her response. I unbutton her dress and pull it down to her knees. I raise the stethoscope, and she flinches slightly. Her heart sounds clear and strong, as do her lungs. But her ribs protrude, and there are sores across her arms and legs.

I am not prepared for what I see once I turn her around. There are pink welts on her buttocks and the tops of her legs where she has been lashed. I wonder what crime could deserve such punishment. There is none that comes to mind. This method of discipline is criminal and nothing short of barbaric. The state of her body tells me that little care has been given at all to this girl. Though several of the wounds have closed up, the affliction is recent, with some areas healing poorly and remaining inflamed. I can't imagine the pain she would have felt after such an injustice: both physically and mentally. It is inconceivable to think what else has been done to this child.

"What happened?"

She does not speak.

"Was this another child, an older girl perhaps?"

She shakes her head.

"Your secret is safe," I say, although I am not sure for how long. Someone must be held accountable, eventually.

She whispers something that I cannot hear. I turn her around to face me.

"Can you repeat that?" I say.

"Frau," she whispers again, and I see the streak of urine trickling down the inside of her leg, as if she fears she has done the unthinkable: that she will be held accountable for this release of information, also.

I close my eyes briefly to maintain my composure. Had I been here when the request for my employment first came through, I could have prevented this somehow. I indulged myself in activities of guilt and self-pity. I saved one but was not fast enough to save Matilda.

There is still time.

I pass her a washcloth with which to wipe her leg. "Matilda, I won't let this happen again."

She is still unsure of me, slow to take the cloth, her whole body rigid. I can sense her skepticism. She has perhaps been promised many things that weren't delivered.

"What brought her to do this?"

"I had not taught the other children to read *Mein Kampf*."

For the sake of the child, I suppress the anger that has lodged firmly in my chest until such time it is safe to release it, perhaps in the form of retribution.

"Well," I say, "the wounds have been repairing themselves, but after you have had a bath, I will put some more ointment on them so they will heal better."

"We don't have a bath at the hut."

"Where do you wash?"

"In the basins behind the laundry."

"In winter, also?"

"Yes."

Animals released for washing.

"Open your mouth. Let me check your gums."

They are red and angry.

I crouch down to face her so that we are the same height.

"Matilda, look at me."

She raises her chin.

"Why do they say you are a handful?"

She looks uncomfortable with the question.

"I have done bad things."

"Tell me. I will not punish you."

She stammers out the words. She tells me that she took a key so that the children could return to their parents, but one of them decided to go on her own and froze to death. It is clear that she blames herself for the death of the other.

These poor children whose parents have either died or given them up willingly, yet here they are fighting to return home again. The power of parental bonds is to me a fascinating case in conditioning. It takes years, as I have discovered, to break these bonds, though many of us try. Father has said that many of these children have been saved from far worse situations, where parents have pushed them out the door.

"Matilda, you can button your dress and follow me."

Nurse is waiting outside, perhaps concerned by what Matilda might say. She should be.

I head for the kitchen, Matilda in my shadow, Nurse Claudia behind her. Matilda has sensed that it is better to stand closer to me than to Claudia.

There are brief introductions to Hetty the cook, who shows me the quantities of food portions that are supplied to the orphans. I then ask her to double them in the short term. I also tell her that the children must have an orange every day, an egg and milk, and meat for the evening meal.

"Do you know if there is a bath or shower in this house?" I ask Matilda.

She nods, and I instruct her to go there now and meet me afterward in the surgery, where Claudia will bring fresh clothes.

Claudia is looking at Hetty. She is too afraid to meet my eyes.

"Claudia, who does the cleaning here?"

"The older girls do the dusting and polishing. The young ones the washing."

"Send the older girls to clean my office tomorrow."

"They have already cleaned it, Herr Commander."

"Then they will do it again. After that, I want you to hire a housekeeper."

I enter the dormitory and find several children ranging from three years to ten. Their faces are blank, their fear evident. It is the uniform, I believe, that frightens them. I tell them that they will all get warm baths today in the house. As I exit, I leave the door ajar and take the key, of which I will now assume control. There are enough guards and fencing and little to no chance of escape.

Claudia takes me on a tour of the house that was a guesthouse for the wealthy before it became a school. In the west wing I find three pregnant girls. Their room is comfortable, with its own bathroom. They have views of the woods.

The rooms where the other girls sleep, two each to a room, are on the second floor, above the dining and reception rooms. They are comfortable, well-furnished rooms. Only a handful of girls sit here reading and talking; several others are at the training fields nearby.

"How many are here altogether?"

"We have seven girls, ranging from fourteen to seventeen," says Claudia. "Most of them are currently doing athletics."

"When are they returning?"

"Some will be back soon. Others sometimes go into the town."

"And what time is their curfew?"

Claudia looks befuddled by the question. "They do not have one, Herr Commander."

"What do you mean by that?"

"They have certain privileges."

"Doesn't Miriam manage them?"

"Yes," says Claudia. She lowers her eyes, a sign to me that she is loyal to Haus.

"Then they must have a curfew. I'm sure their parents would hate to learn that they come and go as they want."

"Yes, Herr Commander. Though it is their parents who have paid to have their children trained at the Center," she ventures further. "The parents might be upset with any changes to the current circumstances."

"That is for me to deal with now. And what of the girls who are pregnant—do the fathers of the unborn visit?"

"No, Herr Commander. They already have wives."

I detect from the tone in Claudia's voice a slight disapproval in this particular practice of the Center, though she is a woman who would die before she admits this. Yet she failed to see that the portions for the young children were too small. She is as cowardly as Miriam Haus is cruel.

"I will examine these young women tomorrow."

"Yes, Herr Commander," she says, with more respect than Haus.

I force myself to visit Haus in her office, and it is there that I see the flaws that line the walls of this house. This woman, I believe, is incapable of management. She wears an expensive tailored suit and silk blouse, and she sits in her office doing very little to run the place, behind a desk that is twice the size of mine. She likes the control. It is clear from the look she gives me. She is not happy that I revoked her order to send Matilda to the camp.

I sit in front of her. I see on her face satisfaction that I am on the other side of her desk, as if *I* am the one who must report to *her*.

"So, Frau Haus . . ."

"Miriam."

"Of course. Tell me about the system of management here." My own tone is condescending. She is as detestable as Manz and Kohler.

"It appears, Herr Commander," she says, "that you are developing your own. But, Commander, you must know that some of those children barely passed the Aryan testing, which is why they are still here and not adopted by German parents. And we are expecting more. We are expecting quite a number now that our brave officers are bringing more children into Germany."

"Miriam." I speak calmly and pleasantly, though that is not how I am feeling. "As you are aware, I am in charge of the Aryan testing now. If you give me all the files, I will test the children one by one myself and check the results against yours. If, of course, I find that some are unsuitable, then I will send those children away."

I wait, and it is several moments before she moves to retrieve the files. I have passed empty rooms on my tour and ask why the younger children cannot live in the house. I also learn that the orphans are allowed out of the hut for only a few hours a day.

"The younger ones are at risk of fleeing," she says. "They must be locked away."

"Perhaps if they had more to eat and a warm bath, you would not have as much trouble keeping them here."

Haus looks at me as if she wants to swallow me whole. Her chin raises slightly, an act of defiance that could build to something more in time. I have caught all this before her manner changes to falsely demure, with a smile that is not really one at all.

"We all have our ways, Herr Commander. I believe mine are just as efficient as yours; however, I will respectfully and dutifully follow your orders."

I would like to tell her at this point that the rooms are filthy and the older girls have more freedom than they need. That the younger ones must never again be beaten, and, if they are, I will cane Miriam Haus myself as punishment. But I refrain. That will come. All good things will come. It is enough for the first day.

I wish her a good day, though it is far from my true wishes. Matilda sits in the waiting area in clean skin and fresh garments.

I apply some ointment to the welts on the back of her legs and the sores on her limbs. Once this is completed, I advise her to keep her head down, apply herself to her studies, and help guide the younger ones in their tasks once more. Of course, it is a lot to ask of these children, who are barely old enough to take care of themselves.

"You may leave now," I say, then proceed to write a note to add to her file. The pile of files sits on the edge of my desk—an undesirable, if not unnecessary, task to determine if they are Aryan. I have already made my decision.

Matilda looks at me through mountains of untamed curls. She has made no move to rise. I frown and smile at her at the same time and put down my pen curiously.

"You can leave."

"Nurse has to take me."

"No, you may go back to the hut with the others."

"But it will be locked by this time."

"Not anymore," I say, lifting my voice at the end in an attempt to calm any fear.

She hesitates before she leaves, opening the door with care, expecting an explosion on the other side.

"And Matilda . . . ," I say.

She turns to look at me squarely.

"Do not attempt to run away. It is not safe out there. Take it from someone who has seen much."

Her gaze lingers on me longer than before as she absorbs this. She is not only processing this information; she is studying me as well.

Claudia is standing in the hallway, waiting to lead Matilda back to her room. I call her in to advise that Matilda can find her own way back, that the place is not a maze.

Next Claudia sits in front of my desk, and I grill her on her role. It seems she is merely a supervisor who applies first aid occasionally. She says that the older orphans toilet-train the younger, and they have done a good job with that so far.

Her jaw drops when I advise her that nappies and toilet training are now her sole responsibility, along with the washing and sterilizing of cups and eating utensils for the children. I tell her that she must make up a chart to note the amount of sun they are receiving each day for their growing bones and to record their portions of food and how well they are eating. All medical treatment will be supervised and recorded by me. Any medicines are not to be removed from the surgery without my permission.

She is not one to argue. She, at least, knows that a person does not argue with a senior member of the party, and that it is perhaps unwise to follow orders from anyone but me.

"And, finally, Miriam's role will be to ensure that the housekeeping is done and the tutoring of students and orphans is completed. You will now report directly to me, and I require a file note on all incidents and accidents that occur in this place. Anything unusual must be reported directly to me to investigate and monitor."

I am not asking her; I am telling her. I do not require acknowledgment that she understands. She knows this, too, and thanks me for the new role. This one is easy to master. She has been led by Haus. She is led by whoever has the greatest power. Which in this case is me.

CHAPTER THIRTY-SIX

WILLEM

It is the end of the first week, and I have completed my examinations of the children.

In the main house, money from parents of the older German girls, the number of which has now risen to eight, supports their accommodations, and because of this they feel untouchable. After meeting these girls, it seems an opportunity for some parents to offload them. They are not quite in the league of Hitler's female youth—some whose wealth has not bought them loyalty and discipline—sent to this center to become accustomed once again to their German culture and expectations, and their parents' hope of a marriage to someone with rank. It appears that several are here purely for gratification, refusing to take their Germanization seriously, while the others desire to one day be upgraded to Hitler's League of Girls. The latter of some value, I believe, some moral fiber, while the former interested only in recreation or rebellion.

The second order of girls here, Volksdeutsche—ethnic Germans from abroad—have already been impregnated by Himmler's brutes and are then discarded to have their babies. During their pregnancy, they are not wanted by their parents, nor by the fathers of their unborn.

One Polish girl, Alice—who appears particularly sullen—says she will not return home after she delivers her baby, as her parents want nothing to do with her. They do not care that she is doing Germany an honor. I would, of course, be required to report them if I were anyone else. But I go on to learn that she did not like the man who fathered her baby, who had courted her purely for sex.

I have discussed the pregnancy with her, which is where she shows real fear. She is due in three months, and she does not wish good things for the baby. She has freely admitted that for the first weeks she starved herself in an attempt to lose the fetus. She does not drop her gaze when she tells me this, which leads me to believe that Alice does not care what else is done to her. She is unwanted, unadoptable, of an age that is neither young nor adult, without any clear future.

"What do you want to do then once you have had the baby?"

She hesitates. She is intelligent enough to realize that this is not an idle question, that I have asked it in earnest, and that if anyone might do something for her, it is likely me.

"I want to start again. I want to not have gone to meet the officer who is the father of this baby. I want to go back to my old school. I want my parents to want me back. And I don't want to have a baby."

"Alice, you know that you could be in trouble for saying such things."

She stares at the insignia on my collar and looks away.

"I'm sorry, Herr Commander."

"Do not say such things again."

"Yes, Herr Commander."

I cannot change the past, but I will do what I can, while I can.

Finally, "the orphans," as they are known here. We have five orphan girls and three boys. The hut is now filled to capacity. The stench from their toilet pots is ingrained in thin wooden walls barely sturdy enough to house barn animals. The building balances precariously on stilts that lean. It is uninhabitable. Haus and the others should never have allowed it to be used for housing.

Several of the recent recruits have passed Aryan testing, according to Haus, and will no doubt be taken to suitable homes. I check the youngest children. They are healthy and ready for adoption. On my desk is a list of candidates I have yet to evaluate. Haus has compiled a list of families she considers of German value, but whom I must approve. Interviews will commence next week. This is another job that I have taken from her.

When I arrive home at night, Elsi is keen to hear about the children. Each day it is like this. She is shocked that parents would give them up. She is not surprised they have been beaten. She finds Haus as detestable as I do. It feels good to tell her things. She is similar to Lena in that she is eager to learn. Her German is getting better, and she speaks no more Polish words.

It has been several weeks, and I see that the smaller children are beginning to fill out their skin. Matilda seems less cautious around me, more curious, her wide-set, catlike eyes always watching me. I have studied the children's academic examination sheets, and Matilda's results are astounding.

"Have you done your testing?" asks Haus.

"Yes," I say.

"You have not advised me of the results."

"The children have all passed."

Haus looks at me too long. I have briefly examined the previous reports and seen her comments about the children. I advise her that her results are incorrect, then conclude the conversation quickly. Anyone who beats a child deserves the very least amount of my time, if any.

Haus is interviewing for new full-time academic tutors for both the older and the younger ones, at my bequest. I have convinced my father to fund this teaching cost.

There is a knock on the door before Claudia enters.

"I'm afraid we are having a problem with two of the girls."

Claudia reveals that they are embroiled in a fight. Normally Haus would deal with it, but she has left the Center briefly. When I arrive upstairs, the grappling girls are tearing each other apart. I step between them.

"Stop!" I bellow, causing them to stop immediately and give me attention. "What is going on?"

They admit that they are fighting over a boy from town.

"And where do you meet this boy?" I ask.

"In the town center," says one.

"At night?"

"Sometimes."

"All right. I have a solution. Girls are not to leave the house from Monday to Saturday, unless there are circumstances that have been approved by me. On Sundays, your free day, you are welcome to go into the town, but provided only that you are chaperoned by Frau Haus. A book will be installed in the front room for you to sign in and sign out during these times."

"That is a stupid rule," says the girl.

"What did you say?" I ask.

She does not repeat it. She is now staring at her feet. Lena always said I was frightening sometimes, that like my father I could freeze water to ice with one look.

"Herr Commander," says the other girl, "I wish to write home to my parents and ask to leave here."

"Please do," I say. "I'm sure they would love to hear that their young daughter is meeting boys after dark. Boys who—since they, too, have much idle time—must themselves be ill equipped for military service."

The eyes of the girls are fixed to the ground in front of them.

"If there is any more fighting, I am afraid that I will have to write to your parents anyway." I am about to make a speech about their job and their service to Germany, but I am doubtful it will sound believable.

I turn to Claudia and nod before leaving the room, their eyes no doubt boring into my back with dislike. I have neither the patience nor the strength to deal with indulged teenagers.

"Why aren't the guards stopping the girls from leaving at night?" I say to Claudia as she follows me.

"The guards are not here for them. Only to stop the younger ones from running away."

This is a circus that has been run by clowns. Soon I will reduce the guards to one at the front gate only. In time, there will be none at all.

For days I have been cooped up inside the surgery, and I eagerly step outdoors for some fresh air and sun. I pass the dismal dormitory that sits in a pile of mud. The young children are near the swings. Before they have seen me, I take a moment to observe and listen. I don't normally find the sounds of children delightful, but there is something about these poor, miserable souls chattering that moves me.

"Matilda!" I call.

She comes over to stand before me, hands behind her back, imitating me.

"I have not yet had a tour of the grounds," I say. "Would you be so kind?"

Matilda leads me behind the dormitory and shows me the place where the girl died. I see that there are wildflowers that were picked from elsewhere on the property and left here on the ground. Matilda says that she and Jacek leave them there. When I question who is Jacek, she says that it is Ernest's real name.

"Who changed his name?"

"Frau."

She leads me to the fields, but there is barbed wire and a guard nearby. Then she takes me to the storeroom and the washrooms, before turning back toward the swings.

"What about the other side of the house?" I ask. There is a small wooden structure near the back fence, the building closest to the woods. "What is over there?"

She doesn't say anything but looks back over her shoulder toward the main house.

"Show me, please."

She looks down at her feet, and her legs are trembling. When I touch her shoulder, she shudders. I step back to view her curiously.

"Never mind. You can go back to the others." She is quick to disappear and does not look back.

The cabin she will not go near has a large steel bolt on the outside. When I open the door, something scurries to the corner of the room. The building is just a windowless room ten feet by ten feet. In the corner is a mattress, thin and covered with grease. I can see fleas bouncing off the fabric and remember the bites on Matilda's legs and arms. There is a cat-size door on one side, which is also opened and locked from the outside. A piece of wood is missing from this door where the rats are entering from. In winter, it would be cold and drafty; in summer, suffocating under the piece of tin that acts as a roof. Spindly bushes behind the building scrape the wood in the breeze.

This is a punishment room, the idea of which will no doubt haunt me for some time to come. The responsibility of nurturing children has been twisted and abused in the most barbarous of ways. I bolt the door from the outside and instruct one of the guards to affix a padlock and bring me the key. This door will not be reopened. I storm back to my office to sit, contemplate, and plan in silence. I have no heart to open the files but instead make a telephone call and then summon Claudia to my office. Haus is still out.

"Claudia, please assemble the older girls in the front reception—except those who are pregnant."

"Certainly," she says.

The girls line up, their hands clasped humbly behind their backs, heads down.

"I have some good news . . ."

After my earlier decision to have them grounded, they avoid eye contact with me, fearful that I might reduce their privileges further—to them, the worst kind of punishment.

"I have decided that you are all ready for the League of Girls. After speaking with each of you, I believe that your diligence and your commitment to your training and your country warrant reward. I would like you to pack your bags. Tomorrow a bus will collect you and take you to your new residence."

"Excuse me, Herr Commander," says one of the girls who was involved in the fight over a boy. "My parents would need to approve that first."

"I will be writing to your parents to let them know. It is what they had hoped for you, I am sure, and they will be extremely proud. I will personally sign certificates to hang on their walls, praising them for their commitment to this country, and will ensure that these certificates are countersigned by Herr Himmler."

I can see that several are pleased, and some wear expressions of contempt. But the mention of Himmler has halted any desire to complain.

Claudia follows me back to the surgery.

"But, Herr Commander, what about the extra tutor we have hired?"

"The tutor will be for the young orphans and the other girls who are expecting. As of tomorrow, the orphans from the dormitory will take over the rooms these girls vacate. You know as well as I that the dormitory is not fit to live in. We will not be taking in any more older girls until that building is knocked down and rebuilt to a habitable standard of living."

Claudia blinks away her shock.

"Yes, Herr Commander. But did you want to speak to Frau Haus first?"

I tilt my head in puzzlement. "Why?"

She bites her lip and looks away.

Miriam Haus has learned of the changes by the time she storms into my office.

"I'm not sure what you think you are doing, but a lot of money is invested here by the parents of those girls," says Haus.

"I have also ordered that their monetary donations will go to the League from now on. I'm surprised to hear you so upset. I thought you would enjoy having less responsibility."

Haus does not miss the slight, since her job here is almost redundant.

"Besides, we will not be short of funds," I say. "I can guarantee that."

"If you take the girls away, I'm not sure I can stay here."

"Is that a resignation then?" I say abruptly.

"No, of course not. It's just that I have grown attached to them."

She is lying. She is not attached to anyone but herself.

"Very well. You might best use your time to help the girls with their packing. I have already contacted the League. It is all arranged. The bus will be here this afternoon."

At the League, the girls will share larger dormitories. There will be less privacy than they had here. There are more rules.

Claudia checks the supplies of medicines and makes a list of things we are short of, while I write letters to the parents and sign certificates to send to my father. It is unlikely he will question this request since it will be seen by most as a positive step: eight more girls will join the war effort.

"Nurse, do you have the addresses of the children before they were sent here?"

"No, Herr Commander."

"How many of them were signed away by their parents?"

"I believe a few of them."

"And the others—where were they found?"

Claudia swallows before she speaks. "I believe they were rescued from the streets of Poland mostly."

"Help the orphans pack tomorrow morning and move them into their new rooms."

The dormitory will be demolished. I will see to it.

I enter Frau's office with its view across the lawn at the back of the house.

"You will need to advise the tutors of their new roles with the children."

"As you wish, Herr Commander."

"And perhaps we can arrange for some of these children to be returned to parents or relatives, or other people from their towns."

"If your testing is correct, then I hardly see the need, since they are all qualified for Aryan adoption. Are you suggesting now that they are not?"

Haus is sitting straight-backed on her throne.

"Not at all. It is just that some have been here too long, and we are expecting more very soon. I believe that the two eldest of the group are less likely to be adopted quickly, and we should be making room for new children, especially now that we have less space. I believe that the German skills we have given them are enough for now for them to take back to their homelands. Particularly for Matilda. I believe that she would benefit by being back with her family. I do agree with you that there are some issues with her personality that may compromise her candidacy for adoption."

"Of course," says Haus, "couples seeking to adopt are looking at very specific traits. And, Commander, while you might consider the children Aryan, others will not. Matilda is too impudent and unlikely to be adopted. She has hatred for Germany in her blood."

"Perhaps that has something to do with locking her in a room and punishing her in ways that are barely acceptable in some prisons."

She shifts in her seat uncomfortably.

"I see," she says. "You don't like my methods. But I can tell you, Commander, that they are not much different elsewhere."

"Then our new system will make us unique."

"I imagine, then, I will need to apply for other posts."

"On the contrary, I am more than happy for you to stay on to watch the improvements . . . in a temporary capacity."

She says nothing, though I can tell that she has weakened some-what. She has realized that she will not win here; she cannot. She will go, and I will make certain of it. A request for her transfer will be raised in coming weeks.

"What happened to Matilda's parents? There is nothing in the file, nothing on her background. Just her Aryan measurements and a brief comment on her health."

The records are poor. Some files show the children's parents having signed them away. Others have no details at all. Curiously, though, I have learned something through Alice recently. Her protest was, again, not to eat. Claudia warned her that she might be sent away, but that did little to encourage an appetite. During a consultation with me, Alice brought forward the subject of the orphans, and I commented that the Center gave an opportunity to provide a safe place for children. She scoffed at this.

"The orphan adoption is farcical. There is no such thing as adoption. I think the best word to describe it is *kidnap*."

I paused briefly to allow her to say more. People rarely like silence—a tactic I learned early—and will scramble to fill it.

"Their parents were forced at gunpoint," she says. "But you would know that already."

"As far as I am aware, they were given up willingly."

She smiles as if she has something over me.

"The children have been told lies," she says. "They are told their parents don't want them."

I then steered the questioning back to the topic of her eating, as her comments were disconcerting. The fact that I may have been kept in the dark, still, about certain matters here infuriates me. If some have been kidnapped, there is no one I can complain to, since the directive was likely to have come from Himmler. I realize that it is highly plausible, since I have now seen things that I would never have believed before.

Haus crosses her arms. "I believe that the officer who found her did not have any records. In any case, Matilda's whole family was killed in a bombing. She was the only survivor. Ernest's parents, however, signed him over."

"And there have been prospective parents here to see her and the boy, more than once? And they have not been interested?"

"No one is interested. Everyone wants the younger ones, and only those with Aryan characteristics. You know as well as I that she looks foreign. No one will take her, I can assure you. It was a mistake on my part to accept her, I'll admit. But she came recommended because of her German, and I felt I had little choice; we thought she would fill a need. I was wrong about that, too. Matilda should not have been brought here. She is not German enough, in either features or attitude. Regardless how long you wish to keep her here, the moment you are promoted, or ordered to take a posting elsewhere, even temporarily, someone else will see this and send her to the camps. You and I both know that. You are delaying the inevitable."

She says this with relish, and it is I who can no longer meet the gaze. She is right, of course. The non-Aryan children will stay here for as long as I do. But after that there are no guarantees they will remain. My plan to return Matilda home has failed. My admission that she is not suitable for adoption has put me in a corner and perhaps sent her to a fate her young mind could not imagine.

"And the boy?"

"He might be lucky enough to be chosen yet, but he is another whose characteristics appear less Aryan the more he grows, and in another year he will be too old for the orphanage." It goes without saying that, like Matilda, the boy will be sent to the camps if an adoption does not happen within the year.

I can see the children through the window. Matilda and Ernest play near the swings, discussing something they have found in the grass. They study it as if there is nothing else that matters in the world.

Children should not be affected by the infighting of adults, by large issues that take up much of their thoughts. They should have time to examine the small ones.

And then I find myself seeing into the future: something lost, something that I can find again.

"I will adopt her."

"I beg your pardon, Commander."

"I will adopt Matilda." I say this firmly, though I do not need to convince myself. I fight the urge to smile at the sight of Haus's churlish, hideous face. She is reasonably attractive if one views her from an aesthetic perspective only; however, I can only judge her on what I see inside.

"I'm sorry, Herr Gerhardt. National Socialist policy does not support the adoption of those who might diminish the German race, especially not by their officers. It is not what they want for German families. Your wife has not seen Matilda. The girls here will soon have newborns. Perhaps your wife would prefer one of those."

"I think I know my own wife and what she would want."

I have steered the argument to an area she knows little about: relationships. She looks down awkwardly and straightens some papers on the desk.

"I see."

But she doesn't. She walks for miles each day with her eyes closed.

"I just hope that your wife understands the issues. Matilda, as you know, is a willful child who came with many bad vices—"

"It is so wonderful that you have much concern." I stand up and turn away, dismissing what she has to say. "I would appreciate that you not say anything about this until the adoption is completed."

Her confidence is doubtful, though what she does with this information is unlikely to affect me.

I visit Matilda after leaving Haus's office to ask her about her day while examining her schooling work sheets. But I am not really looking at them. I am pondering her smallness and vulnerability, the way she suffered at the mercy of adults who let her down. I think of Lena and the baby I would be holding now had they lived.

As I leave, I touch Matilda on the shoulder, and she returns the gesture with a smile: one that comes without trying. Unexpectedly, tenderness feeds the sleeping emotional beast in my chest. I long to take this child in my arms, to tell her that she is now safe. It is the beginning. *It is possible, what I have begun.*

Walking through the halls, I am euphoric, immune to other petty concerns. I imagine Elsi's sweet face at the news of our adoption, and then I think of Haus's. I climb in the car and for several moments fight back laughter until my chest is weak. This is too much joy, an emotion rarely felt.

The guard steps up to the car window and asks if I'm all right, but I wave him away congenially. I perhaps appear deranged as I drive through the gates. Perhaps, deep down, I am.

There must be no going back.

JUNE–JULY

CHAPTER THIRTY-SEVEN
ELSI

I don't know when I first noticed it, the change in him. Willem rises each day, enthusiastic, effusive, as if there is nothing he can't achieve.

I have found plenty to keep me occupied: cooking, sewing, reading, learning. Willem has ordered so many books. My childhood dreams of becoming an actress are thinning memories: my previous life stripped bare, my new one rebuilt under Willem's careful eye.

He introduces me as his wife, something I am now accustomed to. Occasionally, we dine out in neighboring towns, blending in anonymously at crowded restaurants. My fear of people is lessening, yet there are times when I imagine running into someone from my past, someone who will remember me. Willem brushes these concerns aside.

"We are in a place where it is doubtful even I will run into someone we know. And besides," he says, half joking, "even if we ran into Hermann Manz, he would not recognize that you are the sheared waif from the ghetto."

Several times since arriving here we have had small disagreements. On one particular day, when I wore a heart filled with too many dark memories, and the rooms noticeably empty of my past, I questioned how much the purpose of my being here was to make *him* feel better, and not me. I instantly regret these things I say when he stands there undefended and confused, and I am then ashamed to have thrown such feelings in an untidy pile at his feet.

But these moments are quickly doused by his ability to dismiss my outbursts on his integrity as an expected reaction, in view of all I have been through and lost. There is a clinical distance in his words, and I feel that I know little about him. Yet he is always considerate and concerned about my welfare. We are like man and wife, just not in name, and with pasts that would not allow such a union.

He is passionate about the Center. After Willem sent away the older girls and moved the younger children into the house, the mood within changed for the better. At my suggestion, Willem had them create gardens at the front and back of the property, planting flowers and trees. He has told the two remaining guards they can stay on duty, but they must not carry their guns—to keep them out of sight of the children.

The old dormitory is now locked and no one must enter, and there are plans to demolish it. Willem says that even the nurse does not seem so nervous and confused. She has taken to her new position with vigor, though she is still wary of Miriam, who occasionally calls Nurse Claudia into her office. Willem thinks Claudia is grilled for information.

Willem is not a person who seeks attention, yet he is unwittingly charismatic. I've seen the eyes of people linger longer on Willem than on most. In a crowd, he is the first person you notice, even without the uniform. The reason for this cannot be explained by one notion. It is not just his height, the broadness of his shoulders, the magnetic color of his eyes that draws you in; it is all these things and the fact that he is completely unreadable and distant, as if he holds a secret that is worth knowing.

• • •

Willem will keep Miriam on a little longer. He has written to Berlin to request another posting for her, recommending something that involves the supervision of only older girls or women, and is still waiting to hear back. Meanwhile, she pretends to be busy overseeing the tutors who work with the younger children, though she has very little input about anything. Willem says the only authority she has at the Center is over the new casual housekeeper and Hetty the cook, and only because the latter allows it. He said that he likes Hetty, who quietly goes about her business and quietly despises Miriam. Matilda revealed to him that Hetty sometimes left the storeroom unlocked when the children were out at play. That sometimes Matilda would take several pieces of fruit, and Hetty knew about it. Willem thinks that leaving the door open was a deliberate act, though the cook would never admit it. She keeps her kindness hidden deep inside and thus is able to do these things without reproach from Miriam.

Willem has seen several documents in which parents have given up rights to the children. There are few details about the children whose parents were killed, including Matilda's. He said that in Ernest's files, curiously, the document signifying the transfer of rights is unsigned. Miriam's filing system and administrative practices are apparently very poor, and there is little information on any of the children. Education of the younger ones was almost nonexistent prior to Willem's arrival.

Willem talks often of Matilda. In the playground the other children look up to her and heed everything she says. Despite her mistreatment, she is tenacious and forthcoming—a born leader.

When Willem told me that the SS had been encouraged to impregnate Aryan women in Germany and all the occupied territories, to grow the Aryan race, I was appalled but not surprised. Nazi babies are being born across Germany, their births celebrated with ceremonies. When the babies are born at the Center, Willem is required to alert headquarters, and several officials will then arrive to swear them into the German fold. It is archaic and barbaric, I said, and Willem agreed. He said Lena would be appalled, also.

Sometimes when I look at Willem, I also see Lena, as if his eyes are mirrors that reflect the person he wishes me to be. Though I do not say anything about his dead wife, she is with us always, I feel. I am jealous of her ghost sometimes. Though he says her name casually, he is unaware of the effect it has on me. It is not that I dislike her. Quite the opposite. I admire the person she was: brave and honest. It is just that I so want him to love me as much as he loved her.

Willem is home early today, bringing flowers. He hands these to me, then lifts me off the ground and twirls us around, as if we are new lovers who have been parted for too long.

"What is it?" I ask, confused by the attention.

"I have been keeping something from you for two weeks. It has been difficult, but, as you will learn, I had to wait this long. I sought to first draw more trust from the children. Come!" he says, escorting me to the sofa. "Sit down with me."

He takes both my hands in his as we sit. I am somewhat fearful; perhaps I am still getting used to the new Willem. He watches me carefully and waits several moments before he speaks. It is like that with Willem. He is careful with his words.

Sometimes he is not always present with me, or only partially, as if he is saving some part of himself for someone or something else. Now I feel him here beside me. All of him.

"I have organized an adoption."

"For whom? Are they Germans? I didn't think you were allowing anyone to adopt until you were satisfied that the children were settled, until you had several more weeks to evaluate their health."

"This adoption is different. This one is ours."

The excitement that I had felt has turned to something less. I have an uneasy feeling that Willem has done something that will affect us: that will distract him from this relationship we are slowly building.

"Elsi, we are adopting Matilda!"

I touch my throat, the air around me thinning. We are not properly married, I am just short of twenty years, and yet he is talking about a girl who is ten, who comes damaged, like us both.

"This is absurd. We are three broken people. How can we possibly offer her some kind of normal life? I can't fix her. I don't know what to do. I don't know how to be a mother." I had imagined children with Willem, but not like this.

"We will be helping her," he says.

"Is this your plan? Save us all, one by one?"

"Do you wish I hadn't? Do you wish I had left you at the ghetto?"

I turn away. I am torn between the person Willem wants me to be and the person I was before. This is perhaps what I have known all along: my choices are not really mine.

"I'm sorry," he says immediately. "I should not have said that."

I run to the bedroom to hide my frustration.

"Elsi," he says, following me, "I'm sorry. You are perfectly within your rights to argue this. You are worth much more to me than you think, and I respect everything you say. I thought this would be good, even more for you than me. I believe, too, that Matilda would greatly benefit from a home with parents. She is very bright. Nurtured well, she can do anything."

"So it is all part of *Willem's* special project: to create the perfect wife . . . perhaps a perfect Aryan wife and mother."

"It is nothing like that. I promise. I like Matilda a lot, and I believe you will, too. If we don't take her and I am one day transferred, she could be sent to anyone, or possibly the camps. She does not pass the Aryan testing. Haus is right. Her features are changing as she grows. Her skin has become very dark after time in the sun. These things—things that matter not to you or I—will matter to someone else brought in to inspect the children. And if they do, Matilda will be gone. Already I have taken a chance in waiting this long. Why else do you think I've kept Haus, to be so slow with her dismissal? It is so I can keep a close eye on her, so that she does not talk to others. As soon as I adopt out the ones who failed the tests, I will be rid of her. Once she is out of the picture, I can do what I like, make up any lies to Berlin, move new children out quickly, without someone there to spy."

Of course he is right. I should have trusted him. Again I have feared the worst. I have thought his motivations perhaps selfish: thinking that adopting a child was filling in the space left by his child with Lena. Now I understand there is more to it. A child rejected by the very people who took her. Matilda's life at stake.

"Can you forgive me," I say, "for such an outburst?"

He stretches out his arms toward me, enticing me into an embrace.

"There is nothing to forgive. Now, would you like to come and meet her, meet all the children? They are inquisitive. They have asked questions about you. They are keen to meet the beautiful wife of the commander."

"I'll have to get changed," I say, pulling away from him. "My dress is covered in baking powder and sauce."

"Wear Lena's blue dress. The one with the white trim. And you will need a coat today. There is an icy breeze from the north."

Willem has bought me new dresses, but occasionally I still wear Lena's. I thought I had broken the connection with her when our possessions from the bombed apartment were unsalvageable, but shortly after we arrived, Willem organized for the remainder of Lena's belongings in Poland to be sent here. It is my intention that they all be given away eventually. Then there will be one less reminder that I am not perfect in his eyes.

At the front of the Center is a gate with a guard. The sight of him brings a chill to my spine, and my chest feels winded.

"Stay calm," says Willem. "You have nothing to fear. You are the commander's wife."

I lose myself briefly in his cool, pale eyes, and focus on his low, hypnotic voice. My breathing has evened out once more, and I nod formally to the guard as we pass. Freshly churned soil perfumes the air along a pathway to stairs at the front of the house. *One step at a time.*

Willem has told no one that I am coming.

He leads me along a hallway to the back of the house, first to the kitchen to introduce me to the cook. She is small and round, and shakes my hand with her floury warm one, gracious and genuine.

Miriam Haus has heard my stranger's voice and left her office to investigate. She is lank of figure, her facial features bland with pale, undefined brows, her coloring bleached and insipid. She is not nearly as frightening as Willem's description of her. Through a foxlike stare, she examines my clothes and the ring Willem has placed on my hand, perhaps comparing my worth with her own. Then she is quick to feign an excuse to leave us.

Claudia and I are introduced in the hallway. She appears efficient in the way she quickly responds to several instructions given, but also acts unassuming in Willem's presence. From this I gather she is somewhat in awe of him.

Upstairs, it is a shock to see such young girls with rounded stomachs. They are shy and awkward. Then we walk past the rooms full of young children, all sweet, all fair. Some smiling, some apprehensive, surrounded by books. I can smell fresh paint on their brightly colored walls. Another of Willem's improvements.

Then finally we come to the room at the end of the hall. This one slightly bigger for the older orphans, Jacek (his former name officially restored) and Matilda. They sit in the middle of the room between their beds. They are playing a memory game with words. They have to turn each card facedown and then try to remember where they first saw the card with the identical word.

The first thing I notice about Matilda is her thick, curling hair that circles her face like petals on a flower. Dark-brown brows sit above almond-shaped eyes filled with twists of blue and green. She sits still, her eyes resting first on my feet, then rising to look at my face, my dress, my face again. Her scrutiny is unforgiving, as if I am the one who must be chosen. She is beautiful, but she is certainly not what I have come to recognize as Aryan: her features too angular with high cheekbones and a pointed chin, nose too flat and broad. I understand what Willem means. Without him, she would not last here. Willem thinks that her facial features have developed and changed in the months since she arrived. That if the officer had found her the way she looks now, he would have left her on the streets of Poland.

There is an easy relationship between the two young children. I wonder if Willem has considered what the separation will do to them.

"Hello," I say.

"Hello," they respond in unison.

"Children," says Willem, "it is respectful to stand for visitors."

They jump up quickly, Matilda a little slower than Jacek.

"This is my wife, Elsi."

"It is wonderful to meet you," I say. "Commander Gerhardt has told me much about you. What is the game you are playing?"

"It is a word game," says Jacek, and he proceeds to explain the rules. "Matilda made it up."

"It sounds very good," I say.

"Matilda, would you come to my office?" says Willem. He has no time to waste on idle talk.

She does not hesitate to comply with his request, suddenly appearing at his side. He has won her heart, also, and as I follow them both down the narrow stairs I see the similarities between them. They have both been conditioned to give nothing away.

Willem has told me that Matilda does not like to talk about her parents when asked. He believes she is attempting to block out the memory of their violent deaths as a way of coping with it.

Once in the office, Willem turns to Matilda.

"You understand, Matilda, that the children from this center will all be adopted one day."

She nods.

"I have some good news. I have found a new home for you."

She pinches the tip of one thumb between the thumb and forefinger of her other hand.

"How do you feel about that?"

"I would prefer to stay here, Herr Commander."

"A few weeks ago you wanted to leave," he says. Willem does not wait for her response. "I know it is better here now, yes? The children are happier in the house?"

She nods.

"But unfortunately this house is not a permanent place for children. It is a temporary place to care for children who have nowhere else to go. Jacek will be gone soon, too, and the others. You will lead the charge. You will be the first from this group to find a family who is eager to take care of you."

There is no doubt she understands her role, and from Willem's description of her, I know she is capable of reasoning. Yet the line between her brow and the clenching of her jaw show that she is not happy about the news and would fight this if she could.

"Now, I have some even better news. My wife, Elsi, and I will be adopting you."

Matilda turns toward me, her eyes penetrating the surface of me, looking for my thoughts, searching for my secrets and weaknesses.

"Where are you from?" she says, her gaze lining me up as if I am at the other end of a pointed gun.

"Berlin."

"No, you are from elsewhere. Your accent is very strange."

I am surprised she has picked this up, being a foreigner herself, and I tell her the fabricated story of my parents living in Poland for much of my life.

"Do you have any other questions for us?" I say to take the focus away from me.

"Will I see Jacek again?"

"Perhaps," says Willem. I recognize the tone. It is falsely conciliatory.

"And I will call you Mutti?" she says to me.

Did I hear scorn? With this question she has revealed that she sees the idea as farcical, and that she is somehow ahead of me. She seems remote, devoid of the elements that might connect us: trust, background, history. I wonder if in time it is possible to fuse our differences.

"There is plenty of time to get used to names and terms," says Willem. "But first things first. You will move to your new home today."

This is news to me. I want to protest, but Willem is the commander and he will get his way. I am just his wife.

"Can I go and see Jacek?" She has not shown a shred of emotion, and this bothers me more than anything.

"Of course. We will come to collect you shortly."

"Willem," I say, once she is gone, "this soon? We have not prepared a bed for her yet. I am not even used to this new freedom, this town. I need more time . . ."

"You underestimate yourself," he says. "You are capable of so much more than you think. It is better to make a quick separation from the

Center now that she knows. Her opinion on the change might unsettle the others. She has lost her whole family, and now we are giving her a second chance, perhaps a better one."

I am suddenly thinking of my own mother, who could never be replaced. Each day I light a candle for her when Willem leaves, and I say a prayer for her. I do not light candles for Leah or Papa. I refuse to believe they are dead. Willem has said that after the war he will help search for my father. But right now it is too dangerous. If he asks questions, it will only draw attention to him and to me. He does not mention Leah. He still does not hold hope that she is alive.

He reaches out to take my hand. His hands are warm as they wrap around my cold ones. The touch of him always lessens my concerns.

"It will be fine. I promise. There will be an adjustment, but I would not have done this if I didn't think it was good for you. Good for all of us. You deserve a good life."

But a life that I choose.

Willem asks me to go to Matilda's room to collect her, but when I arrive, neither she nor Jacek is there. Their game lies abandoned between the beds.

CHAPTER THIRTY-EIGHT
MATILDA

"Shh!" I whisper to Jacek. "She will hear us."

"Who?"

I have dragged Jacek underneath the bed. Elsi has just opened the door to our room, then left again to search for me. I hear her entering the other rooms, asking the other children if they have seen me. She has gone to the end of the hall to the bathroom, then stops again at our doorway as she walks past.

"The woman with Commander . . . the wife and Commander," I say. "They are taking me away from here."

"What for?"

"To adopt me," I say.

"The commander?"

"Yes."

"But I don't want you to go."

"I know. That is why I am hiding."

Jacek is looking at me as if I am not telling the truth.

"But . . . ," he says.

"But what?"

He can't think of anything to say. I like Jacek a lot, but he thinks too hard about things before he speaks. I have to wait so long sometimes.

"It's true, Jacek. They want to take me home to their house today. We might never see each other again."

Jacek's thinking has turned to something sadder. I see in the darkness underneath the bed that he is blinking back tears, his mouth writhing like a worm.

"I do not want to leave you either," I say.

He has put his face in his hands so that I don't see him crying. I have told him what Catarina said of people who cry.

"That is why we must stay under the bed," I say.

Jacek wipes at his wet face and sniffs back the tears in his nose. I want him to stop because it could be heard if someone comes into the room, if it is the woman again with the strange accent.

"It is the first place they will look," says Jacek.

"No. They will not think us so stupid."

Elsi's feet are in the doorway once more, and I press a finger to my lips to warn him to stay quiet.

She wears shoes that are slightly too big for her. She has very thin ankles on long legs. She is taller than Mama, yet she looks almost as young as the older girls who were here. She does not walk proudly like a German woman.

The commander's wife walks around the bed, and Jacek's head turns to follow her steps. She walks to the window, stands a moment, then walks fast from the room. If she knew anything about children, she would look under the bed.

When she is gone down the stairs, I walk to the door and shut it quietly.

"Now what?" says Jacek.

"We have to leave together."

I can see that Jacek doesn't like the idea. He is not moving like me to grab some clothes. He is caught in the middle of the room like a rabbit in a trap.

"There is no way to get out. There are guards out there."

"I know this, but we have no choice. We will hide under the old building, then burrow under the fence in the night when the guards aren't looking."

Since we have come into the house, we have not discussed our future escape, though the thought is still there. Commander once asked me about my parents and to describe where I lived. The officer who stole me did not write down where I came from in the brown file that has my name on the front. I did not tell Commander anything in case one day I do escape, and the child thief, Herr Lehmann, has hopefully forgotten where he stole me from.

It seems that Frau has no control over us now, and Nurse has not said a bad word to us. Cook talks to us, even sings sometimes, and gives us large plates of food.

One day Commander took us for athletic training in the field. He made us race across the paddock toward the woods where there was no fence, then back again. There were no guards anywhere. We could have escaped into the woods, but he didn't seem to care. Commander and Nurse were both impressed by our fitness. Commander gave all the winners some chocolate.

We have been planting flowers and trees along the front fence. Sometimes the guard at the front waves at us, and we wave back. It is a different house since Commander came.

Though, still, when the trucks and other cars drive near the house, we wonder if they will stop, whether all the nice things are a trick to stop us from running away. Commander has told me that no truck will take us to the camp, but he did not tell me that I was to leave. We had almost forgotten about the adoptions.

Now the news that I am to go away. I do not want to be apart from Jacek.

"What was she like?" he asks.

She was nice, but I don't want to say that, so I shrug.

"She seemed very kind," says Jacek.

I am pulling the sheets from the bed to tie together. We will lower ourselves from the window, but Jacek isn't helping. He is still, transfixed on his feet as if he has never seen them before.

"Jacek . . ."

He looks at me, and some of the tears are still there.

"Maybe you should go and live with them. It could be worse. It could be like Juliane and the others who did not know the people who took them."

Juliane was taken by new parents while I was locked in the small house.

"I do not think escape is a good idea," says Jacek. "It will take too long to burrow. The guards will find us. We can never escape from here."

I am shocked. Perhaps he never liked me. Perhaps he wants me to go so he can have the room to himself.

I sit on the bed and cross my arms. Jacek has given up on me. He is no longer my friend.

He moves closer to me.

I cannot look at him.

"Please don't be angry," he says. "This was going to happen. It is better than the other worse places we have heard about. You are very lucky. I like the commander. He is always fair. If you live with him, life will always be fair. That doesn't mean I want you to go. It is just that it will be fine for you if you do."

He is right, but I still cannot look at him.

"It is very likely," says Jacek, "because the commander is so kind, he might let you go back to your real home when Germany has taken everyone's countries."

I hadn't thought of this. He is right about this, too. I want to shout at him that he is right about most things, but the door to the room opens and Commander and his wife are there. "Matilda," says Commander, "there you are!"

"They weren't there before," says Elsi. She looks around the room. She has realized that she is the one who is stupid for not looking under the bed.

"You were hiding under the bed, weren't you?" he says, but he is not angry. There is laughter between the words. I know at least that Jacek will not be punished, that I will not be either. If it had been Frau, we would be beaten or, worse, sent to the small house.

"Come on, now. Pack your bag and say your good-byes."

Jacek blinks several times fast. He wipes his eyes with the back of his hand, and I see that Elsi is watching this. She is looking slightly distraught, though she is attempting to cover it with a false smile. I have seen adults do this before.

I pack while Elsi talks to Jacek. She says that it is a comfortable room and that Commander will make sure he always has a comfortable room wherever he goes. When I sneak a look at him, I see that he believes this. I don't like the way he smiles a little when she talks to him.

I stand ready with my case, and when Jacek turns to me I still won't look at him.

"Very good," says Willem.

I have only one dress, a cardigan, underwear, a nightgown, and some sheets of paper where I have written my stories. I also have a picture that Jacek has painted of the two of us. I leave the word game in the middle of the floor. I have nothing else.

"Good-bye, Matilda," says Jacek formally.

I am led from the room, but my feet are so heavy I can barely lift them; my legs are stiff, and they can hardly bend. Once I am through the doorway, I may never see Jacek again.

I turn and rush back into the room. I throw my case on the floor, open it, and take out the sheets with my stories.

"Here, have all of them! I have plenty more inside my head," I say. Then I throw my arms around him. He is shocked by this, then puts his arms around me. I squeeze my eyes shut so that the sadness does not escape, though I hear Jacek whine. I know that his sadness is leaping from his face.

Then I turn quickly so I do not see him anymore. Elsi looks at me, and I am shocked that her eyes are watery, too.

"Everything will be fine, Matilda," she says. "You are going to a lovely house. Just wait and see."

Cook hugs me good-bye, crushing me with her large bosom; then Nurse shakes my hand and wishes me well. Frau does not come out of her office, and Commander does not knock on her door.

I follow Commander to his car. It is the same kind as the one that first stole me. I am being stolen again. Perhaps someone else will steal me again after this. Elsi follows me. She is frowning.

Then we drive along the roads. I look at the white houses with their pretty red roofs. Some children play on the side of the road with sticks. They wave as we drive by. They do not have a tall fence around their house. Then we drive toward the mountain, and I think that perhaps we will drive to the top, but we stop and turn down another road. The house we stop at is bigger than the others. It has a box at the front for mail, and there is a pathway to the door. There is no fence around this house either.

Inside the house it smells like flowers. Flowers are in a glass vase on the table. There is shiny wooden furniture.

I am taken to a room that has only a bed, nothing else.

"We will get you a desk and a mirror and a wardrobe, Matilda. Perhaps you would like to choose those yourself from the store."

I look around the room. It has wallpaper with stripes and carpet on the floor. There is a window at the back. Behind that I can see a very big garden.

I sit on the bed and look at my case.

Commander has left the room, and I am alone with the wife again.

"I know this is hard for you," she says. "I know what it's like to move to a new place."

I don't look at her. I see that there is mud around the edges of my shoes, and I have walked a trail into the house.

"Tomorrow," she says, "we will visit a store and buy you some new clothes. Would you like to do that?"

I don't answer her. I wonder if Jacek will be able to sleep tonight, if he will be frightened of the dark. He is always frightened of the dark, and I do not like to sleep alone. We should be together.

"I will prepare our dinner now and maybe even make some pastries. Would you like that?"

I miss Cook. She felt so soft when she hugged me good-bye. I have never felt her before. It reminded me of Mama.

The commander's wife leaves the room.

I stay sitting on the bed. I tell stories in my head. I imagine telling the children the story about the tree monster that stole children during the night. They love and hate that one. They cry and cover their faces, and then the next day they want to hear it again.

Commander comes into the room and switches on the light.

"What are you still doing sitting here in the dark? Dinner will soon be ready. Come with me."

He takes me to the bathroom, where a warm bath is ready. The soap smells like lavender, and I think of my real home. When I have taken too long, Commander knocks on the door. He says that dinner will get cold.

We sit around a table in the kitchen. There are four chairs and one is empty. I imagine Dragos sitting there. He is smiling and pointing at the woman. He thinks it is funny that I am in such a nice house, that Mama would be jealous because she hates her little house. She wants Tata to build them a big house like this one.

"Did your parents not teach you to smile?" asks the commander, teasing me, and Dragos is suddenly gone.

I want to tell them that I was taught to hate Germany, but I dare not say it because the commander is German.

The woman stretches out her hand to touch my shoulder, and I slide it slowly away so she can no longer reach me. Her smile shrinks a little.

The food is salty, with lots of meat and potatoes swimming in a thick, murky pond. Then there are pastries filled with peaches. I eat until I am full, and I see that Elsi likes this. She likes to watch me eat.

"Will I be going back to my real home after this adoption?"

"Real home?"

"When the war is over and Germany owns the world."

Elsi looks at Commander, and there is a look that people make when they can't think of words.

"Does she not know?" says the wife.

"Did they not tell you?" says Commander.

I don't know why the questions.

The woman turns my chair toward hers and bends down in front of me. She picks up my hand, which is all limp and heavy in hers. I do not want to hold her hand.

"I'm sorry, Matilda. Your home was bombed. Your family was killed. Were you not there when it happened? Were you somewhere else?"

"She has forgotten," says Commander. "Sometimes that can happen after trauma."

I pull my arm away and stand. I push the chair across the floor and run to the room. I lie on the bed and try and remember my home, but I can't. I am picturing piles of rubble. I am losing the pictures. I can no longer remember all the colors there. I cannot picture my tata. It is as if they have vanished into dust.

CHAPTER
THIRTY-NINE
ELSI

Willem is hesitant to find a tutor for Matilda until she is settled. It has been three weeks since she arrived here, and we are still strangers. Since the first day she was here, she rarely speaks to me except to answer a direct question. I believe that she does not want her mother replaced. With Willem, however, she is less guarded. She asks him questions when he is home from the Center.

Willem believes she has still not accepted the death of her family. To help Matilda deal with the awful truth, he has questioned Miriam to gain more information about the circumstances, but the woman has none. She believes that Matilda might be playing with us—that she is trying for sympathy. She also warned again that Matilda was difficult and would be impossible to tame. I do not believe much of what she says, though I am leaning toward her view concerning *difficult to tame.* Sometimes when Matilda finally meets my eyes, I see nothing but detachment. She does what I direct her to do, but that is all. She is a peculiar, unfathomable creature who does not respond to touch and is resistant to kind words.

One day when I raised my arm to reach for something above her, she flinched and then quickly recovered. She was clearly embarrassed and hoping that I hadn't seen this weakness. She has suffered at the hands of her vicious supervisor, at the hands of the German system. It is so very difficult to know what to do with her.

Today we went to a store to buy her some clothes. There was a rack with several dresses her size. The shopkeeper said something to me, and I misunderstood her words. Matilda responded to her on my behalf, but she did not tell me what was said. Her German is better than mine, and she appears to enjoy this power that she holds over me.

What has Willem done to me? I ask myself when Matilda and I sit across from each other at the table, no words passing between us.

When Willem comes home from the Center, he asks about our day. I do not say that it was terrible, and Matilda says that it was well enough. It is like this day after day. I long for Sundays when Willem is here all day, when we picnic in the thick, soft grass on the hills that surround the town.

Sometimes at night I see light coming from underneath Matilda's bedroom door. One night I found her writing a story. She is always writing stories. I asked her if she could read me one of them, and she told me a story of Gypsies who were set on fire in the forests and whose souls wandered the earth, looking for revenge. This is the only time she has spoken more than a few words to me. But she could see this story shook me. I do not want to be reminded of horrors. At times it feels as if she is tormenting me, punishing me for replacing her mother.

At lunch I serve her some soup, and she helps clean the kitchen afterward.

"Matilda, I do not want to replace your mother, but I believe that we can live as a family. You can call me Mutti, Mama, or Elsi, and you can call Willem by his name, Vati, or Papa, whatever you wish. You do not need to call him Commander anymore. He is no longer your commander. Do you understand?"

She does not respond.

Willem falls asleep before we can talk. He is so tired, and even when he is there beside me he feels absent. He has been spending his days visiting the homes of potential adoptive parents, as he prefers to meet them away from the Center first, so as not to frighten the children. And he regularly drives a distance to another practice where he has to examine the pregnant or infertile Nazi wives.

Matilda has locked herself inside her room and will not come out for lunch. It is as if she cannot hear me calling or knocking on the door. Only when Willem comes home does she come out to greet him. I am livid with anger.

Willem bends down to place his arms around her, and she puts hers around him. I am jealous that she hates me, jealous that Willem has her affection and she has his. The two are made for each other. I leave the room.

Willem comes to find me.

"What is wrong?"

"This isn't working," I say, not caring that I am emotional, that desperation has made my voice frail. "She hates me. We will never be a family, Willem." I explain what she is like during the day. I have avoided telling him. I have avoided telling him that I am failing. I am missing the times we had together before Matilda.

He takes me in his arms. "Elsi," he whispers, and I sink against his chest. "In time it will be easier. Poor, dear Elsi. You are still so young . . ."

I pull away. It is always that I am too young, too inexperienced!

"What is the matter now?"

"I just want you to understand that she is not easy."

"I do."

But he doesn't. I do not think he is intentionally avoiding the truth; I believe that he thinks that I must become strong enough to cope with her.

"I will talk to her."

Back in the sitting room, Matilda is waiting. She perhaps has heard my outburst. Willem is talking to her quietly, saying that she must respect me, the person who has dedicated time to her. She listens as she always does, soaking up the information without a response, without giving her thoughts away.

"And what of Jacek?" she asks, interrupting the conversation. Willem seems relieved that she has asked.

"Who?" he feigns forgetfulness, then continues playfully. "Oh yes. The boy formerly known as Ernest. Well, we have adopted him out."

Her body sags.

"What's the matter? Did he not want to be adopted?"

"None of us did," she says, her eyes briefly flickering toward me.

It hurts a little to hear this, yet part of me understands. We are each making do.

Willem says, "I suppose you would be happy to know that he is back with his parents now."

This is news to me, also. It is like this lately, learning information after everyone else. Willem forgets to tell me certain things, forgets that I want to hear everything. That his life is my life now.

"His real parents?" she says skeptically.

He puts his finger to his lips to signify that it is a secret. "Frau Haus would not be happy to know this," he says.

She nods. She is taking this very seriously.

"The story has come true," she says.

"What story?" asks Willem.

"It doesn't matter. Only that some stories end happily and others don't." Her eyes dart toward me before returning to Willem.

"Matilda," says Willem, "if the situation was different—if your parents were alive—I would have returned you as well. So we should just make the best of things, yes? Elsi, my wife, is a good woman, and she will make a good mother. She is very kind. I will not let anything happen to you. No one will take you away again. Do you understand?"

"Will I see Jacek again?"

"One day, when it is safer, when the war is behind us, I will take you to visit. Perhaps Elsi can bake one of her orange cakes for the trip. She has been pestering me to take you to visit Jacek, but even if he was still at the Center, it would not be a good time to be doing this. I am too busy at the moment and often away from there."

Matilda looks past Willem to me, and this time her gaze is more curious than critical.

I have asked Matilda about her memories before the Center, but I am met with silence every time. She stays in her room, drawing sometimes, but mostly creating pages and pages of stories written in German. I have had to ask Willem to bring home more paper. I have read some of them, and they are dark and detailed, though often there is a message in them about hope, about finding lost parents, animals, children. Of strange, fantastical cities where there is no war.

Today we are off to the market, and she is reluctant to leave the bed. I am determined that she will come. I have to use a forceful voice and threaten that there will be no dessert. Eventually she follows me, lagging behind, her eyes down—always eyes down when she doesn't get her way.

Matilda stands sullenly while I converse with the stall owners. We blend in here, as there are many other new arrivals who have left cities that were recently bombed.

I am purchasing the last of the goods when I notice that Matilda is no longer beside me. Willem warned me that she had tried to escape before and perhaps still thinks about it. I wander around the busy stalls. There are lots of children here today, but none of them are Matilda.

She is not at home, and I walk the streets, knock on several doors, then return to the markets. The thought of Willem's and my secret being exposed is something that never leaves my mind. First I felt fear for myself, but the possibility of losing this strange little girl is just as worrying. I walk the low hills until finally I see the billowing white of her skirt. Matilda sits in the place where we picnicked above the valley. She is there with her writing papers and pencil.

"Matilda," I say, "how dare you run away!" My voice is shrill and brittle, even to my ears. I am not used to this stranger's voice. She drives me to frustration and despair.

She pretends that she doesn't see or hear me, and I pull her forcibly to her feet.

Then she throws her pages into the breeze—paper scattering across the grass—as she commences to stomp back down the hill.

"Stop!" I say, but she ignores me and continues storming back to the house.

"Stop!" I yell.

"Shut up, you Polish slut," she yells back to me.

"What did you say?" I run toward her and grab her shoulder, turning her.

She says it again, and I do the unthinkable. I slap her across the face, then retract my arm in horror at what I've done. After all the beatings she has endured, I am no better than any of my predecessors. I am a monster, also.

Her mouth is open in shock, and she cradles her reddened cheek.

"Matilda, I'm sorry."

Her eyes are not hateful. Rather, they look melancholy, as if she expected this would come eventually. I watch her thin legs carry her away from me. I have lost her now and may never get her back.

"Wait!"

I fall to my knees in the thick grass.

"Matilda," I call out, "we are alike, you and I. We were both taken by Nazis to places we didn't ask to go. I, too, was imprisoned."

She is still walking but not as fast.

"They killed my mother! They shot her in the head in front of me. They took my sister to the camp. She was your age."

She turns to look at me from under heavy lids.

"Why did you hit me?"

"You wouldn't stop. What you said was very hurtful, and I'm tired of wanting you to like me."

She says nothing.

"Matilda, if you stay with me, I promise you that I will never hit you again. It was wrong to do that. I will make it up to you."

She bites her lip and walks back toward me, though not all the way. She does not want to be too close and stops to sit down several yards away.

I cross the narrow space between us and sit beside her. She looks wary at our closeness but doesn't move away.

I tell her that I am not whom I appear. I tell her about my past. I tell her about my life and family, about how it was before the ghetto. I tell her how Willem saved me. How I nearly went to the camps, that we have so much in common. I cry while I speak for some of it, until my mouth is too dry to talk. And then I look away. It is all that I can give. There is nothing more. If she goes, then I will accept that I have failed.

It is then I feel her tiny hand on my leg, her fingers pressing gently into my flesh. She is not looking at me but across the rolling hills. I put my hand over hers, and we sit there for some time like that, both of us prolonging the closeness and stirring only once the shadows have replaced the streaks of light.

Side by side, we walk down the hill.

AUGUST

CHAPTER FORTY
WILLEM

Father sent another message saying he wishes to have dinner with me. I travel to Berlin in the evening to meet him at an apartment that I have rented, the address now officially recorded as my permanent residence. I have made it appear that I am there much of the time when I am not at the Center: a coat on the back of the door, food in the refrigerator, cups and plates on the table. Some books and reports lie strewn across a reading table, along with opened mail. I have everything sent here. Father knows nothing of my other life, nor do I intend to tell him.

"You should move closer to the Center," he suggests over dinner. "It would be better if you didn't drive so far each day."

I would prefer it if Elsi were sitting in front of me instead of him. She has lost weight again, due to the stress of coping with Matilda. Matilda is willful, but I have seen deep within her, where many can't see. She feels vulnerable but is clever enough to hide it.

Father says that he has heard reports that the children at the Center are becoming quickly Germanized, that I have employed excellent tutors and improved the athletics program. He does not agree with the decision to have the older girls transferred, but he understands that the new building will ultimately hold more young women. I do not tell him I have not yet commenced any work on the project. He says that he is pleased to hear of my dedication to treating the SS wives at the clinic, and says he received a letter from an officer commending me. My father is sounding proud of me, without the full truth, of course.

"I will come and visit the Center soon and view the progress firsthand."

"Not yet," I say. "I would like all the changes to be in place before you come. After the renovations. This is something I would like to do completely on my own."

My father views me carefully. "Very well. I can wait."

This life is a pretense. I wonder how long I can carry it.

As long as it takes.

"And how is your work, Father?"

"We have made great progress. At the women's camp the chemists have developed a drug that aborts the fetus up to the third month of pregnancy."

"And if administered beyond that?"

"The baby also dies, but the situation is more serious for the mother. She will still have to deliver her baby, stillborn. It is not something we advise. Though we are currently testing that, too. Both genetics and the mother's health at the time factor into the success of her recovery."

"So much disposal work to ensure race preservation," I quip, but smile at the end of it to appear as if the lives of the test subjects mean little to me.

"All these achievements are important, as you know. Each success in the laboratories and surgeries is another step toward the preservation of our German people. *Your* people, Willem. But I believe you understand that. You seem . . . different."

He is perhaps thinking that without Lena I will now become more like him, and I despise him for that. I do not question him on the validity of such experiments or the success rate of the drug. These are things

I choose not to learn. Flashbacks of Auschwitz are rare now, but discussing the subject of testing with my father brings back thoughts I had cemented into the corners of my subconscious. One discussion with Father and the memories are seeping through cracks like poisonous gas.

"The drug has also been tested for use in sterilization, but we are still conducting those trials. Early results show that one tablet per day over a course of a fortnight causes irreversible infertility. Regrettably, some women have reacted badly to the drug, while others, perhaps those who are more robust, have experienced few side effects."

The word *regrettably* when used by father refers to the failure of the experiment, rather than the mortality of the Jewish test subject.

"At this point, it is not something that we would recommend in the short term, not for our German women," continues Father. "However, ultimately, those women who have previously had complicated births and whose health is compromised by pregnancy will benefit from this."

Father retrieves a stout brown bottle from his briefcase and passes it to me across the dinner table. I suspect that it contains the tablets he is referring to.

"What do you want me to do with them?"

"There may come a time."

The truth of my father's visit is surfacing. Always, my father has a motivation for seeing me, and regrettably it is not merely to check on my welfare.

"Can you explain, Father, when you think that time will be? I look after German women now."

Father takes a sip of wine before he answers. He has aged, his hair more gray, face more pale, and the lines in his face perhaps deepened by the stress of his role.

"Our boys in the field are not always as discreet or overly selective about the women they choose to lie with. You see firsthand the young women in need of obstetrics, and the Führer would hate to see centers like yours tarnished by . . . poor administration. I want you to make sure that there are no mistakes."

My father leans comfortably back into his chair. *Poor administration*: an interesting term meant to imply failure to carefully screen out foreigners. It is hard to believe what he is asking me to do, and it is hard to believe that we are of the same blood. Yet, at the same time I am thinking that my father is stripped of all things good, my mind turns to Lilli, and then to wonder if I might be the son he wanted after all.

"I am not sure there will come a time," I rush to say, to distract my train of thought. "Heinrich's boys in the field have been doing an excellent job."

I hold his gaze, daring him to question the sincerity of my false statement.

He looks at me down the center of his nose. He is a man I used to look up to, yet I do not feel anything for him. There is no shame to not love your own flesh and blood. As I have discovered, the people I value most in the world do not share mine.

"Father, were you aware that some of the children were taken by force from their homes before being delivered to the Center?"

I see the muscles around my father's jaw tighten as he clenches his teeth and arranges his mouth to speak.

"Willem, please don't preach your thoughts on false morals to me. Whatever is done is a necessary task, one that is often unpleasant for the men who undertake such work."

"On the contrary, Father," I say offhandedly. "I was merely curious if you knew."

My father blinks slowly, perhaps relieved. I am better at pretense now.

"Just remember that you are there to serve Germany and the interests of the German people, Willem. That is your job."

"And their best interests are exactly my intentions, Father. You have my word."

It is easier to deal with him if I lay a bone at his feet.

The next day I drive back early. Matilda has been talking to Elsi more, though there is still distance between them. It will take time, and Elsi has the patience for it. The beatings Matilda endured, the isolation and separation from her home, and the final revelation of her family's death: she is as resilient as a steel shield. It is something I admire in her. She will survive this period of time.

As for sweet Elsi, she will need more time to repair. She thinks I do not care, but she doesn't know what it is like for me to wake up beside her before she rises. To see her face against the pillow, one long arm stretched out above her head. She does not know the joy I feel when she greets me in the evening. I have put much responsibility on her, and in time she, too, will know how resilient she is.

I am falling for her, Lena. Please forgive me for that, too.

I have just called in home to check on Elsi and Matilda and to wish them good day. Matilda appears happy and settled and pleased to be with us. We have found normality within the chaos happening around us. It is quiet and peaceful in the house, but it is a different story as I arrive at the Center. The guard leaves his post to greet me. He says that I must hurry, that one of the girls is having some kind of fit. That she has lost all consciousness.

I enter the house and follow the sounds of commotion to the kitchen. Cook has Alice cradled in her lap, and Claudia is beside her. Haus is ordering the other children back to their rooms.

"Commander!" says Claudia. "Thank goodness. It's Alice. She is convulsing . . . has lost consciousness but still breathing."

I smell Alice's breath, check her pulse, then pick her up and carry her to the surgery to place her on the bed.

"The rubber tube," I say. Claudia greases the tube before handing it to me.

I gently thread the tube into Alice's throat until the tip has reached her stomach, then I carefully roll her on her side and commence to squeeze the suction pump near the end of the tube. It is not long before the foamy contents of her stomach trickle into a bowl. She is groggy and mumbling, and Claudia helps me sit her upright. I force her to swallow some charcoal tablets to dilute the last of the toxins. She vomits this up, and we repeat the process two more times before she can finally keep the tablets down.

After she is stable, I ask Claudia to check on the children upstairs.

"And, Claudia, not a word about this to anyone."

She nods and leaves the room.

Once Alice and I are alone: "What did you take?"

She looks at me through narrowed eyes, nauseous still.

"I don't know. I didn't read the labels closely. Painkillers, sleeping syrup. I'm not sure."

I pull my chair up near her head to look closely at her face.

"Why?"

"You know why."

"I am your doctor now. At this point I am not the commander. Everything you say is private. Tell me what you are thinking."

"I don't want to live. I don't want to birth a Schutzstaffel bastard!"

I know that she is frightened about the birth. That she wants to return to her family. I have written to them, invited them to visit, but have yet to receive an answer.

"In a very short time this will all be over. Once the baby is born you will pass the infant over to German parents to raise. You can move on with your life."

"And then where will I go? I will be considered too used. Do I wait here for another officer to plant his seed in me? My own parents despise me for the affair. They have denounced me. I have no family to return to. I do not see a life ahead that is of any value to me."

"You might find there are other options. I can help you."

"Unfortunately, Doctor," she says spitefully, "since this conversation is *private*, I can say that your words come cheaply. The Führer teaches you all to lie so that you get what you want. I wasn't successful this time, but I will try again. Next time I won't fail."

I do not doubt this. She is bitter and irrational. In previous conversations I learned that she once had plans to work close to the battle lines, to run errands for the soldiers, or at the very least to join the League of German Girls. But she is like so many who have had their dreams shattered.

When I open my medical bag to retrieve the stethoscope, my hand brushes past the bottle my father has given me. Coincidence, maybe?

No, it is a sign.

The image of the pills has taken control of my thoughts. Once again I find myself in a moral dilemma.

She is too close to giving birth.

I check the baby's heartbeat, which is strong.

"Healthy, I suppose you are going to say."

"Yes."

What if I can save one life instead of losing two?

"What if I could do something to help you?"

"What kind of help?" Her tone with less acid.

"What if you lost the baby?"

She assumes a less defensive position as she leans toward me to get closer to the information, her head only inches from mine. She knows that walls can sometimes hear.

"I can attempt to reverse the problem," I say, "though I can't guarantee the outcome."

"What are you saying?"

"I am saying that whatever I say to you here, whatever I do, must never leave this surgery." I know my tone has changed into that of my father. It is only a slight change, but I know it will have an effect. Her eyes widen slightly. She is suddenly not so full of bravado and strong words.

"Are you saying you can stop the pregnancy?"

There is no need to answer. I can tell she already understands.

"If I help you, do I have your promise that you will never breathe a word of this? That you will not try to end your life again? I will return you to your family, even if I have to threaten them to never abandon you again. And they will honor everything you do. They will do whatever it takes for their daughter to succeed, and never cut you off financially again."

There is hope in a face that has been submerged in gloom since I arrived.

"We will wait a couple of days until you are stronger," I say. "We will tie in the miscarriage with this event somehow. Do not talk of this to anyone in the meantime. If Haus visits your room, pretend you are sleeping or too sick to talk."

I lock the medicine cabinets just in case, though I can tell that she believes what I have told her. She has not seen me go back on my word since I began the command.

"I do not know how you will react to the tablets," I say. "I have never used them before. Are you certain you want to risk this?"

"I will die anyway if I don't risk it. So what does it matter?"

It is a long drive, and I am exhausted by the time I reach the clinic for SS wives. The fertility work has offered moments of reward, but the travel and the hours I must spend here are becoming too much. I will soon need a replacement for Haus, someone who is good at what they do, someone who can keep the children safe.

The wives I see have too much money and idle time, and it is less than enjoyable treating them. They talk of their husbands' bravery, not knowing that some of them practice debauchery, and only a short distance away are the results of their so-called labors of bravery upon young women, not the battlefield.

But I am nothing if not officious and courteous. I listen to their desires for children, their failures to conceive. I listen to the early heartbeats of their babies. I listen as they babble about the war, parroting comments they heard on their radios and from their husbands during discussions at their dinner parties. I commiserate about the recent Allied air raids, smile when required, am as gracious as I need to be. By the time they leave, they are confident that whatever their medical problems, or psychological ones, I am the one to cure them. The receptionist comments that the women are very smitten and I must be careful since I am still single. Of course, this is my other life, the one that belongs to my father. The life at the Center, the one I want to live, is the one I will build upon.

One day it occurs to me—while I am sitting, listening to one of these women, whose knowledge of warfare is even less than my knowledge of planning for a women's tea party—that perhaps here is another opportunity to stop what I believe is the most heinous crime of these times: promotion of one race at the annihilation of another. And in a small part only, I could help balance the score.

I have been going through the applications for adoption. Some families seem reasonable. I have visited their homes, examined the environments. I am not looking for German loyalty, though they all think otherwise. The Nazi flag flies everywhere, as if they will earn points by the flag. I am looking for signs from the other children in the family, from the smells and the food on the table, and in the gardens and animals they tend. I can tell whether they will beat the children or nurture them. I observe them closer than they know. I ask for two letters of recommendation from people who know them well. None of this is policy. If the young children can't have their real parents, then I must find the next best option.

Two days have passed since Alice attempted suicide. She is sitting up and strong but has spoken very little in the surgery. She is anxious. To ensure success, and given her late stage of gestation, I decide to give her two tablets from the bottle my father gave me, and I pass her these to swallow with a glass of water. She waits a moment, examines them, and then takes them both at the same time, greedily almost.

I then write a letter to her parents, telling them to meet with me or else face a visit by another official who may not show as much courtesy as I. The two other pregnant girls are only weeks from delivering their babies, one of them only days from now.

Since I did not ask my father anything about these tablets, presuming I would never have need of them, I have no idea how long it will take for them to work. It is almost time to close the surgery, but I am reluctant to leave. I tell Claudia that I have seen a change in Alice's color and temperature and will stay in the surgery for the evening. While I wait for a change in Alice's condition, I sift through the children's files again. I make notes and plans for each of them. It isn't long before my patient calls out in pain. She is cramping badly, and bleeding has commenced.

I give her an injection to dull the pain. It is a long and difficult birth. I call Claudia back in, and the infant I have murdered is taken quickly away before I have time to question what I have done. The remains will be cremated. I write the necessary report. It seems too simple.

My report does not mention Alice's hatred for her unborn child. It says that she had not felt the baby kick and believed it dead, then attempted suicide over her failure. She will back up this story if she is ever questioned. In the report, I conclude that the baby had been dead for several days prior to her fit. Otherwise, the attempt on the life of a live Nazi baby would have dire consequences for her.

Alice is sleeping now. I have saved one and destroyed another.

You had no choice.

After several days of rest, I feel somewhat buoyed by my progress, not just with children, but with the administration of the Center. Alice has recovered fully, and I have received a letter from her parents saying they will honor their promise to look after her financially. I have written a letter of commendation to the German League of Girls—at a location that is far away, where no other girls will know Alice—to say that she would be of excellent value to the war effort. Her parents will pick her up from here, take her home for a break, and then she will commence her new role in the autumn.

The first live baby was born, and I did not see the need to report it to Berlin, or the need for Nazi ceremony. I did, however, find suitable parents for this child. It has been my sole discretion whom I think suitable. The birth mother has now returned home. Another came in her place in the early stages of pregnancy, although sadly, after some initial consultations, she miscarried. I have sent her back to her family.

We have received several new orphan children. They have arrived without paperwork. Whereas once upon a time, some arrived with former addresses and forms signed by parents, these have none. All have passed my Aryan testing, though I have seen the way Haus looks at these children and meets my eyes. She suspects that I am not who I appear to be.

• • •

On my wall behind me is a painting that Matilda has drawn especially for me, of the flowers in the garden at the entrance to our house. She has given each flower a name. One is Willem, one is Elsi, and the third is Matilda. Each petal is meticulously drawn and shaded. She has even drawn their shadows. The smallest one is Matilda. The faces in the flowers are neither happy nor sad, but each one appears vibrant. It is a message, perhaps, that there is still some way yet for us to go, though I feel hope that we have become a family, that she has drawn us together through art.

Claudia arrives at my office to report that one of the children has developed a cough. As she is talking, I notice a folder on the corner of my desk. I draw it toward me and discover it contains several documents.

"What is this?" I ask.

Claudia leans forward to look at the first document in the open file.

"It appears to be one of the children's files."

"Do you know who put it here?"

She shakes her head. "As far as I know, you have all the files, Commander. Perhaps it has come from Frau Haus."

I wish to be alone. There is something about its odd arrival that disturbs me, and that I caught sight of a photo of Matilda when I briefly flicked through the contents.

"Claudia, please check the temperature of the sick child and report back."

"Certainly, Commander."

I open the folder to examine the documents. The first is a statement that is usually signed by the children pledging their loyalty to the Führer. This particular document is unsigned. Underneath this is a photograph of Matilda clipped to a sheet that contains her measurements and description. In a handwritten note at the bottom, Haus has stated that Matilda has only just qualified as an Aryan. This is simply a duplicate of a document I have already.

The third document is one that I haven't seen before in the file I have for Matilda. I turn the pages of this custody document slowly, fearful of what I will find. On the last page is the signature of someone who shares the same surname as Matilda: a shaky scrawl, perhaps made in haste or under duress. I have already learned from Jacek's parents that he was not parted with willingly. Underneath the signature is a title: *Mother*.

A tremor begins in my right hand as I close the file. The coldness that plagued me shortly after my arrival in Auschwitz is back. Finding Elsi had sent it away but only temporarily.

I call Claudia back to the room.

"Matilda was found orphaned, was she not? Her parents killed in a bombing?"

"No, Commander, you are thinking of one of the others."

She stays a moment, made curious by my sudden distractedness, until I wave her away and ask not to be disturbed.

I remember the smugness of Haus and her bestial thin-lipped mouth when she told me her fabricated story of Matilda's family, recounted to deter me from the thought of returning her to her parents. If Matilda wasn't to go to the camps, she also was not to be returned home. This outcome was a personal win for Haus in her vendetta against the child.

The dread I feel that I may lose Matilda is nothing compared with what it must be like for her parents not to know whether their child is alive or dead. My head begins to throb. I draw the shutters closed and switch off the light.

I whisper into the darkened room, telling myself that it is right what I have done, that it cannot be undone.

Yes, it can!

I picture Elsi and Matilda waiting at home for my arrival. I think of all that I have lost and all that I have again: a wife and a child, these soon again broken angels.

CHAPTER FORTY-ONE
ELSI

Building my relationship with Matilda is like slowly building a bridge one stone at a time. Any faster and the other stones might crumble beneath the weight. Sometimes she disappears from me. Not in person, it is just that she has gone to some other place in her head: somewhere she prefers to be.

I have let her speak in her own time, and in doing this, in staying quiet, I have learned much about her while we cook together. She has shown me some of her dishes from home, and we are sharers of stories now. I have learned of her brothers and parents, of her house. We have a secret of our own: she will not tell Willem that she knows about my past. I do not want to give him anything else to worry about.

It was shortly after our meeting on the hill that Matilda's writing became lighter, that she preferred to sit a short distance from wherever I was. When I open her door in the morning, I am no longer greeted with scorn. While Willem has been very busy, working late, we have had much time together.

One night, of her own accord, she called him Vati, and from that point she has thrived. We all have. On Sundays we spend as much time as we can on the hills before the cold that is soon to arrive.

The sun has settled for the night by the time Willem enters. His hair sits forward across his forehead. His uniform looks crushed.

"Hello, Vati," says Matilda. "Mutti and I have baked apples with raisins and honey."

"That is very good," he says, looking through her to something else in his mind. I know at these times not to say too much.

"Willem, why don't you go and rest," I say. "We will talk later."

It has been more than an hour and Willem has not returned from the bedroom. I find him sitting in the dark facing the window.

"Willem?"

He says nothing, his gaze fixed to a shapeless night.

"Willem, please tell me what's wrong."

"I have made a mistake. I hope you can forgive me, Elsi."

"What is it?"

He is frightening me. I am afraid to turn on the light, to see bad news in the strain lines beneath his eyes.

"I am not who you think I am. I have done some terrible things . . ."

"What things?"

He is silent.

I take his hand, but he is like a statue: unmoving, unreachable.

"Whatever it is, you can tell me. I believe that everything you have done, every decision, has been the right one, Willem. I know it in my heart. You have given both Matilda and me a chance at life. God knows what sort of life we would have had without you."

"Vati," says Matilda, interrupting from the doorway.

"Matilda," I say, "Vati will be there in a minute."

She is not deterred but steps into the room. When Willem turns to look at her, she climbs onto his lap, and he accepts this affection easily. She has the ability to reach the soft flesh beneath his shell.

"You should not work so long," says Matilda.

Willem puts his arm around her and kisses her on the forehead before sending her away again.

When Matilda is gone, I ask him what it is that I should forgive. He says that he doesn't remember what he said—he was distracted. He says that exhaustion can make him ramble, and to ignore him when he is like this.

I can tell he is lying, though I believe it is futile to question his words. He might close up even further.

"Elsi," he says, "I am thinking that after this position, we will take a trip far away from here, perhaps to Sweden. Berlin and the rest of Germany will not be safe for a long time. Please know that without you and Matilda, I am no longer whole."

These are words I have longed to hear, to rejoice and respond to. Yet the vulnerability in his tone leaves me feeling equal measures of uncertainty and reassurance.

SEPTEMBER

CHAPTER
FORTY-TWO

WILLEM

Today I learned that one of the SS officer's wives has died. I suspect that the course of tablets I gave her was too much. Authorities have taken the body away for an autopsy.

I have visited the home of the dead woman's husband to offer my condolences. He has questioned the drugs I gave her. I have explained that a course of "fertility" drugs is unlikely the cause, that it is my belief a previous operation after a miscarriage—not one performed by me—had not been carried out effectively.

He has accepted my false explanation. He has said that I am a good doctor and is grateful for all I have done. He is one rank below me.

I cannot explain why I have no feelings at this stage, why I share none of his grief. I have become like those doctors in the camp. I have become like my father.

Yet when I am home with Elsi and Matilda, I am someone else. I am who I want to be. If the three of us could disappear somewhere, then perhaps the change could become permanent. It is always on my mind, yet what about the children at the Center—what about my project there? What would become of them without me? These are the responsibilities that bind me. Not my enforced duty to Germany but my self-imposed duty to set these people free. And more of them, if I can.

On Sunday Matilda told me that she is forgetting the faces of her family in Romania. I felt mostly relief that she has moved on, accepted her circumstance. But just beneath this feeling, always lying in wait, is the fear of losing her, the feeling of placing myself in her real father's shoes.

Elsi no longer grieves for the family she has lost. She has accepted her new one, though she still lights a candle for her mother, and now Matilda does this, too, for her own family. Such ritual gives me a sense of annoyance, but a small one. No one will take them away from me. We are woven into the same piece of cloth now.

Doubt lingers over the death of the officer's wife. I am awaiting the release of the coroner's report.

Today I met with the parents of one of the purported orphans. I located his real parents and made arrangements for them to take the child home. I have told Haus and Claudia that I have been interviewing German families, not several of the real parents I have traced and met in secret. Claudia believes this. Haus is somewhat suspicious of everything I do. I believe she is still attempting to extract information from Claudia, which is why I must also keep her in the dark. It is why I keep the children's files locked away.

• • •

Haus has requested an audience with me.

Before she says what she has come to say, I tell her the good news: I have found a job for her as a women's supervisor at one of the camps. I have gone to great lengths to find her work that has nothing to do with children, where *she* will be told what to do. The camp is in Poland, as far away as I could send her.

Haus squeezes her hands into fists, perhaps attempting to gain back some control.

"I know what you are doing, Commander."

"And what is that, Miriam?"

"The children you are admitting are not Aryan. I have sent a letter to Berlin to someone more senior than your father, telling him of my suspicions. I also suspect that you have returned some children home again, and I have asked for an investigation. I expect we will receive a visit from an official shortly."

My throat feels thick, and I am unable to speak, yet strangely I feel calm. There is no obstacle that isn't surmountable.

"Well, Miriam, could I at least obtain a copy of your letter so that I know what charges I am answering to?"

"I have a copy here." She slides a carbon of the letter toward me across the desk, offering a smile that is smug, perhaps even triumphant. She appears pleased that I am reading this, that she might finally bring me to heel. My hatred for her has grown more than I thought possible.

Her letter does not mention Elsi, nor does it mention any names of the orphans in particular. I have hidden several files. But she also alludes to some other practices within the Center involving those girls who carry the future of Germany in their wombs. She states that there are a high number of miscarriages occurring. There is, however, even in her own words, no record of proof that I have anything to do with this.

"Thank you, Miriam. Whatever you think of me, there is a good explanation for everything."

"If you have nothing to be concerned about, then neither will the Berlin officials."

"I should warn you, though, that if you call these officials here and they find nothing, they will not take kindly to their time being wasted. I assure you that the next post they find you will be worse than the one I have recommended."

Some of the smugness has left her face.

She leaves my office, and I detect with some gratification that she now carries misgivings. Should she be proved wrong, she would be considered a troublemaker and her opportunities for future employment compromised. Though, should a thorough investigation be pursued, it will be the end for me. I must write my father to prepare him. He will not take kindly to another question mark above the issue of my dedication, much less to a further stain on our name.

I visit the orphans, who show me their German writings, and I encourage them to keep up their good work. The rooms for pregnant women are empty. Two more were recently admitted, but both suffered miscarriages before returning home.

I wish everyone a good day, put my hat on, wave to the guard, and commence the drive home. It is just another day.

I tell myself again that there is nothing I can't fix.

CHAPTER FORTY-THREE
ELSI

Something is happening to Willem. He tosses and turns, and the bedsheets are damp in the morning. I believe he has a fever, yet he ignores my concern.

He has recently been the most loving and attentive he has ever been, but in the night he changes, perhaps haunted by demons he cannot talk about. He says he will take something for the insomnia so he doesn't disturb me. He says that he is overworked, that he will lighten the load, and he will employ more people.

Germany has been hit with many bombs recently, one of them not far from here, and many more around Berlin. Willem says that he will not be returning to the city for any reason now.

One evening Willem doesn't come home until early in the morning and only has enough time to wash and return to the Center.

When I question him, he says he had to attend to an emergency call from a wife at the clinic who has been hemorrhaging.

And then it happens again several nights later.

Willem is missing. I have not seen him for two days. I cannot go to the Center for fear that something has gone wrong. He has seemed anxious this week and more distant than usual. I fear that he is involved in things he has no control over. I believe that he does other work, secretive, perhaps dangerous, that he cannot talk about with me.

It is shortly before midnight when I hear the front door open. I creep into the living room, where I find him sitting in the dark.

"Willem," I whisper.

But he doesn't respond.

When I switch the light on, he has his head in his hands. I feel a wave of panic and rush forward to kneel in front of him. I gently reach for his hands that cover his face and ease them away.

I gasp. One eye is swollen and circled with lacerations and bruises.

"What has happened?"

He shakes his head, grimaces from the movement, and touches underneath his ribs.

"Will you get me some water, please?"

When I return from the kitchen, he has removed his shirt, and I see that there are several cuts on his torso and more bruising across his chest, where he now lays his hand.

He sees my stricken face.

"It looks worse than it is. I will manage." He takes a sip of water. "I will take a shower," he says and leaves for the bathroom.

It is always with Willem that I feel so helpless, that I have no control. He does not tell me things, and I do not know how to help him. I know he is suffering internally, his mind distant, his thoughts dark. At first I believed the issue was personal, that I was somehow a mistake he must deal with, but now I know that there are far worse things in Willem's world, and I must find out what they are.

He fetches some ointment, and I help apply it to the cuts on his face and side.

"You are the doctor now, yes?" he says, though there is no joy in his tone.

I help him bandage his middle, where there are deep lacerations.

"You will need stitches."

"No," he says, brushing the comment aside. For some reason his dismissiveness causes my chest to tighten. I feel anger rising.

"Willem, if you don't tell me what is going on, I don't know if we can continue together."

"I do not want to get into an argument with you. Please just leave things to me."

I pull away from him.

"I have done everything you have said, and now you tell me to go away, as if I have no say whatsoever. Is that what you think of me? I am not sure that you care about us after all. You have become a stranger to me in these last weeks, Willem. You disappear for two days and then come back and don't want to talk. Even Matilda does not know you anymore. She is becoming uncertain. She worries about you as much as I do."

Willem sighs and sinks back into the couch.

"Haus has asked officials from headquarters to investigate my procedures at the Center," he says. "They will be arriving in the coming days, and if these officials test the children, I fear that several will be sent to the camps. I have been searching for safe places for those orphans who are at the greatest risk.

"Hetty gave me a name of her cousin who she said may know someone. She didn't say much more than that because she, like everyone, is paranoid, but she suggested these people do not follow the Nazi cause and do not see eye to eye with the Gestapo. I gathered from her responses to my questioning that they have helped others escape capture, and they are participants in an underground movement against oppression. Hetty said that I must not tell her cousin where I got the information." He pauses to take a breath.

"I went to the address she gave me, hoping to make inquiries, but the people there didn't believe I was looking to help the children. I believe they thought I was a spy. The person in charge, Leon, told me that they support Hitler and I must not say another bad word against him or they will report me. But I know they were lying. They were panicked by my sudden appearance, as you can understand. They thought I had made everything up. I did not wear my uniform, but I told them who I was and who my father was. That only made it worse.

"After that, they offered to take me to a secret meeting place. Thinking they finally believed me, I climbed into my car, and they gave me directions to meet other people, who then drove me farther into some woods. I was beaten and kicked until I lost consciousness. I woke sometime later and went searching for my car until I found it many hours later."

"That is insanity! But why did you do that? You are lucky they didn't kill you."

"I did not expect the distrust. I did not expect them to hate so much."

"Are you sure they are part of the underground?"

"Even more so, now they have reacted this badly. If they hadn't, they would have called the Gestapo to come and get me."

"So, what will you do now? Can you get help from somewhere else?"

"I doubt it. I, too, would find it hard to trust a senior member of the SS who tells me he is an ally. In hindsight, it was naive of me to think this."

"What about Hetty? Can you ask her to contact them?"

"No. As I said, she cannot afford to become involved. I think she told me more than she wanted to. The fact that she could be remotely implicated is dangerous enough. She has to play both sides carefully or risk getting herself killed."

"Can you just take the children yourself? Tell Haus that you have found them German families?"

Willem shakes his head.

"It is too much of a risk. There are several of them, and I am running out of time. Besides, Haus will tell the officials from Berlin that these children did not pass the Aryan tests, and the addresses of the placements will then be checked. These resistance workers can drive the truck to the Center, dressed in Nazi uniforms. It has to appear as though the children have been taken to the camps. I can tell the officials when they arrive from Berlin that I agreed with Haus's testing, and this might stall further investigation."

"Where will you get the truck to collect the children?"

"In Berlin I requisitioned a truck and had it driven here. It is safely hidden in a rented barn. The uniforms I can supply, also. I kept several from my service in the field."

There is always something new that I learn about Willem. But that does not concern me at this point in time. A plan is forming in my head.

"Then let me go and talk to these people."

"Absolutely not!" Willem stands now, his torso slightly bent, though his face shows no pain.

"I must!" I say. "If you really want to save these children, you will have to let me help you."

He does not agree. He is difficult to convince.

"They will not harm me. Not when they know about my past. I will tell them that I—"

"Elsi, they might give you up. What if I am wrong?"

"You just said you believed it. If you were willing to trust your instincts, then I trust them, too. They may have beaten you to test you. Otherwise, it does not make sense why they didn't just bury you in the woods."

Willem searches for further arguments against my proposal but fails to find them.

I put my hand on his arm. "Please . . ."

Two nights later we drive back to the house of Hetty's cousin and park some way down the street to hide the vehicle from view. I am to walk to the door and ask for Leon.

Willem is watching me. We have left Matilda alone, telling her that she must not open the door for anyone. We have told her that we are visiting a friend of Willem's who helps with adoptions. Willem is concerned, but I am not. These people are on my side, and I have been through worse.

I knock on the door, and a woman answers. She is not much older than I am.

"Is Leon here?"

"Who are you?"

"I need his help."

"I do not know why you would need that. Leon is just a farmer, and we don't invite in strangers."

"My husband was here two nights ago. I am here because you and I are on the same side."

She looks at me and twists her mouth.

"I have no idea what you are talking about, but if you must come in and see Leon, then so be it. Fabien," says the woman to a young boy, "get your father and go fetch Leon."

I imagine that Leon must be someone important. I sit across from the woman at the kitchen table. She does not move but watches me closely. It is some time before the boy returns with two men and another woman, who stand around me at the table. The men are dressed in clothes, their skin darkly tanned and with hands that are grazed and calloused. The smaller of the men has a deep frown at the bridge of his nose that appears to be permanent, but with forearms that are large and used to heavy work.

"What do you want?"

"Are you Leon?"

"Answer the question."

"I have come seeking your assistance. My husband wishes to smuggle some children who were kidnapped and brought to Germany. My husband is part of the Nazi Party, but he does not accept what Germany is doing, stealing children—"

"They are doing more than stealing children," says the speaker of the group: the man I believe to be Leon.

"I know," I say quickly. "I know a lot of what they are doing."

"You live in a nice house," says the man. "We followed your husband and know where he lives. We know that he is the commander at the center for Aryan children. We also know what goes on there. Why would a commander who steals children want to hand them back? You have no idea what Germans are doing. Now get out of here! Go back to your nice house."

"I am not who you think. I have come from the ghetto in Lodz. The man you know as my husband rescued me after my mother was shot for visiting me at the ghetto prison, shortly before I was to be deported . . . gassed for being sick. My mother is a Jew. That is why I was in the ghetto."

The woman who has come in with the men looks at the speaker of the group, then back at me.

I have caught their attention, but they still appear suspicious.

"Please help us take the children," I say. "My husband plans to bring them to our house. I understand that you help people escape Germany."

"You should be careful with what you say aloud. You could end up with a bullet like your mother."

I ignore the threat.

"My husband has access to a truck. He wants someone to pretend they are SS officers and have been ordered to collect some children from the Center."

"Why should we bother? These children are fed and housed. They will be adopted out to wealthy Germans. It could be worse. How many children does your husband intend on taking?"

"Three, perhaps four. Most have been stolen from Poland."

"There are more than that at the Center. Why are these ones so special?"

"My husband says that these did not pass the Aryan testing, and officials from Berlin will send them to the camps, where it is unlikely they will survive."

There is a look between them as if this is something they haven't heard before.

"And where do we hide these children?" asks one of the men.

"Willem wishes for you to bring them first to our house, where we will keep them until you can take them out of Germany."

"How do you know I won't return them to the Center again, to receive a reward from the Gestapo for my find?" says Leon.

I say nothing at first, and Leon shrugs as if there is no point to further conversation.

"I can tell you that if you report me, they will discover the truth about me," I say. "And once they do, they will return me to the ghetto. You have that over me if you wish, if that's what is needed for you to decide if I am truthful."

"Leon! It's all lies! It is all a bluff!" says the woman at the table.

"Tell me," says Leon. "What was it like at the ghetto? Describe it for me."

I give him every detail that I can remember. I tell him about my mother and my sister. I tell him about the cost of the bread and the rotting vegetables, and the meager rations barely enough to feed a cat. I tell him what it was like to stand almost frozen waiting for soup that was little more than dirty water. I tell him how my father vanished, how I joined a group there that also helped smuggle people. How I watched my friend being executed. I tell them that the orphans might die without their help, and that we are running out of time.

The others are no longer still. They shift and move around the table. They are silently communicating with one another. Leon and the woman he came in with leave the room. Again, I wait at the table with the woman who answered the door, who appears to trust me the least.

"You don't look Jewish," she says.

I say nothing.

The couple returns. "We will need money."

"My husband has money."

"I can tell you that we have connections. We will send word to others. If you are lying, we will kill you. We will be watching you."

You won't have to kill me, I want to say. But his words are too serious, and I am not sure that I will be able to say it with confidence, without my voice breaking in the middle. Now that our meeting is nearly over, I realize the danger and breathe a sigh of relief.

"Send your husband back tomorrow night, and tell him to make sure he isn't followed. We will settle the details then. Everything costs money."

I return to the car and tell Willem what was said. He takes my hand in his and kisses it with his bruised and swollen lips. He does not need to say the words. For the first time I can read how he is feeling about me.

CHAPTER
FORTY-FOUR
MATILDA

I hear the truck pull up outside the front of the house. The sound of these vehicles always forces my heart to stop. Mutti tells me that trucks are for so many things, not just to take people to camps. I have to hold her hand tightly whenever I see one, even delivery trucks headed to the stores in the town.

But tonight the truck stops right in front of our house, and Vati gets out of it. He opens the doors at the back, and lots of children climb out. I run to Mutti's room to tell her.

"Vati's home—hurry!"

Mutti puts on her wrap, and we rush out the front door toward Vati.

"You have taken all of them?" says Mutti with disbelief.

But Vati doesn't answer. He is busy ushering the children toward the front door and telling them to go quietly. There is sweat across his brow and at the hollow of his neck.

"Where are the other men?" says Mutti. "I thought they were driving the truck."

"I met them on the road. I took over . . . I did not want Matilda to see strangers arriving in Nazi uniforms."

Mutti nods.

"Take care of the children!" says Vati to Mutti and me. "Find some blankets for them."

Once we are inside the house, Vati turns to Mutti. "I have to return and hide the truck."

While he is gone, Mutti boils some milk, but she has to add some water so there is enough to warm all the children, who wear only their cotton nightclothes. And then she adds some chocolate. We don't have enough blankets, so Mutti finds Vati's dressing gown and some of his coats for the children, and some cardigans and coats of hers, too. She turns on the heaters and lights a wood fire in the sitting room where they will sleep.

Mutti talks to the children and asks them their names. Some cry and suck their thumbs, and others look tired or scared. I do not know any of these children. They are all new.

She tells them that they will all be safe here and tells me that I must sit with them, also. They are more likely to believe another child who lives here. So I tell them this, too. Mutti sings a song in Polish to calm them.

Vati comes back with eyes that are wild with fear and worry. I have never seen him like this. He wants to talk to Mutti alone and asks me to stay in the room with the children.

Mutti and Vati talk in the kitchen, and I stay close by to listen.

"The officials will be even more suspicious now," says Mutti. "How can you explain the transfer of all them?"

There is silence from Vati, and Mutti sighs loudly as if she has been holding her breath.

"Willem, what exactly have you done?"

"If I am temporarily suspended during the investigation, as is likely, I cannot be there to guarantee the fates of the children who remain. I could not risk leaving any of them in Haus's care again, or in the hands of Nazi officials. They would interrogate and torture children if they thought they might gain more information."

"How can you be certain that they won't discover our address and come looking for them here?" Mutti asks. "What then will happen to Matilda? How can you guarantee that Haus won't have her accusations verified by this one act?"

"I have spoken to Hetty," says Vati. "I have some things in place. I will not leave any trace of us. I will not give Haus any opportunity to win."

I leave my position by the kitchen door not because there is a child crying in the next room but because the mention of Haus has caused my chest to pound with the thought that I am not yet free of her.

In the next room, the children are crying and fearful, and I console them with my stories—the happy ones that I have been writing recently—until they fall asleep.

CHAPTER
FORTY-FIVE
ELSI

I watch for the light to appear on the horizon. We have been awake all night. It seems today things will change.

Willem has asked Hetty to help him. He has asked that when she arrives at the Center this morning—for she is always the first—she open his cabinet and take all the files of the children and to then bury or burn them. The resistance drivers who pretended to be Nazi officers reported that Claudia was at first reluctant and suspicious of such action taken at night, also knowing that such approval was out of character for Willem. She was only partially reassured by the sight of Willem's signature on the paperwork, but then seemed keen to get rid of the Nazi impostors once they became annoyed and impatient at her hesitation. I imagine the men must have been imposing with their guns, leaving Claudia no other option but to do what they said.

Willem says he has sent his father a letter, but he doesn't say what is in it, only that he has told him the truth. He says that Matilda must be cared for, that no one must know about her background. His mind switches between topics. He is nervous, displaying unusual behavior.

He says that two people will collect the children tomorrow night, and that if he is not back from the Center by then to not worry, to remain calm, and to help the couple and the children. But if they don't come tomorrow night, not to fear—they are just playing safe, perhaps testing us. They will come the next night or perhaps the one after. They will not forget about the children, he says. They, too, are willing to help them escape.

Today, though, Willem has to face questioning. Today, he says he must cover all his tracks so that nothing leads back to Matilda and me. I am fearful for us both, but I am fearful for him, also. I want this day to be over. I want him back in my arms. I want him to resign from the Center and for the three of us to go north, to disappear until the investigation is over.

I am sitting on the edge of the bed, and he kneels down in front of me to rest his head upon my lap. He says that he has done some things that he is not proud of, but they were actions he felt compelled to do. He does not think many will understand, but he hopes one day that I will, should I learn of them.

I stroke his fine hair and tell him that I love him and that I will support him no matter what. I say that he is not to talk like that. "We have the future," I say, but my voice becomes small and strained and insincere.

He says that he wishes he could be a better person, that he was not shaped the way he is. He says he would prefer to sometimes lose control, to be free of constraint. I have seen him with the children at the Center. I have seen him with Matilda. I believe he is capable of showing much more love. I see in him a man I want to share my life with. He is everything I want, and I tell him so, and he kisses me more tenderly than he has ever done.

"You are the most patient, brave girl I have ever known. You saved your mother by bringing her to my surgery that night. You have also risked your own safety to speak to resistance workers to help these children. And you gave me purpose, and for that I am grateful."

I am about to tell him that it is *I* who should be grateful, but his mood suddenly alters and he attends distractedly to his clothing, his thoughts elsewhere once more.

He says that I am not to wait up for him if he is late. That if he has to go away for a while to not worry: to stay hidden until everything blows over.

"What blows over?"

He doesn't answer me.

He passes me an envelope. He tells me that inside is the address of a house he has recently bought. He says to open the envelope only in an emergency, then hands me a gun.

"What is this for? Where did you get it?"

He has just told me he will be back; now he is telling me something else that might happen. *What exactly is he telling me?*

"Willem, I need to know the truth. What are you planning? There is more to this investigation—"

"Elsi, please trust me."

"I want to do more to help you."

His normal calm is returning, though his face has gone a pale yellow, and beads of sweat dot his brow.

He shows me the gun, explains how it works. Like with all his teaching, he is detailed and clear.

He puts on his suit.

"Can you wake Matilda for me?" he says.

She is asleep in the sitting room. A younger child is asleep across her lap. They lie among a mass of sleeping bodies, peaceful. I touch Matilda to wake her, and careful not to disturb the sleeping boy whom I gently peel away from her.

In the kitchen Willem sits waiting. His smile is warm, not forced. He suddenly looks so radiant and confident I want to cry and tell him not to go. Everything is changing again. We were so happy. Life was better.

"Come here," he says to Matilda, who is yawning and stretching, unaware yet of the changes. "I have to go and I wanted to say good-bye."

"Why are you going so early?"

"I have to greet some visitors who are coming to inspect the Center."

"Will you be home late?"

"Yes," he says. "I want you to know that I love you, Matilda, and I must ask you to look after the children today. They will probably be scared and have lots of questions. You must tell them lots of stories. You have always succeeded at keeping other children under control."

She gives a brief smile, but it disappears because she has sensed that the situation is serious, that Willem has other more important things to do.

He walks into the bedroom to put on his long coat while I wait for him at the door. Rain disturbs the bitumen outside, and a faint smell of petroleum wafts through the open doorway. The day is bleak, and clouds hang low above the hills.

"Willem," I say, "please don't try anything dangerous, or say something that will find you in trouble."

"Elsi, you have to know something. I love you with everything that I am, which wasn't always enough. I believe that God has sent you and Matilda both to me, and he has then turned me toward him. I am now in his hands."

He kisses me longer than usual. It is rare for him to kiss me good-bye. When he pulls away, there are tears on his cheeks. I reach out to touch them, but he turns away.

"Willem . . ."

He does not respond. He is walking to work today, without an umbrella. There is no sign of his car.

I watch him walk stiffly, his arms and back straight, his head high, until he turns a corner. I stare at the empty space that held him before retreating into the house, where the children are beginning to stir.

Matilda has begun to prepare food for the children's breakfast. We crack the eggs in a bowl, and I whisk them until they are ready to pour into the pan for omelets. I am still thinking about the car. There is something about it being gone that bothers me. Without the car, there is no trace of Willem here. The words he said do not sit right with me. Willem has never once mentioned God to me before today.

"Matilda, I forgot to tell Willem something," I say. "I will be back soon."

I retrieve the gun Willem has given me and put it in the pocket of my skirt. I then step through the small gate and pass through the tight clusters of houses until they become sparse and the landscape opens up into farmland.

After a quarter of an hour, I can see in the distance the large house where Matilda suffered, where others have, too. It is a beautiful white building with dozens of windows and several gables. It is a house that Willem made safe. It is a house, Willem told me, that was once owned by Jews.

As I get closer, I can see Willem outside the house. He steps toward a car parked just outside the gate that is no longer guarded. I stop to watch. Several people wait beside the car: two German officers and Frau Haus.

I look up toward the windows to search for faces, even though I know there will be none. Hetty is likely to be in the kitchen. Claudia, Willem told me, has been let go for releasing the children while German officials investigate the reason. There is no one else, just the four of them outside. The makeup of this group bothers me, along with the fact that they are talking outside the gate, and the men—clearly important figures—have not been ushered by Willem into the house and out of the rain.

Willem stands in front of them, his hands behind his back. He is slightly turned away from me in profile, his mouth moving as he speaks, but I cannot hear his voice, only the pattering of the rain. His hair is out of place, strands falling across his eyebrows. It is curious that he does not brush the hair from his face.

Unexpectedly, one of the officers turns Willem roughly around. The man appears to be speaking tersely. The other officer commences to restrain him in handcuffs behind his back. Willem is now turned in my direction, though he is looking back toward the house, at those rooms that are now empty of children. The consequences of his many good deeds are unfolding in front of me.

Miriam is standing with her hands together, as if in prayer. She has won, perhaps she is thinking. But Willem is capable of anything. He will get out of this. He will call his father.

I step forward. I am exposed if they look this far.

I have not brought my coat, and my skirt clings uncomfortably to my legs in the rain.

And then he is turning his head toward me. He does not appear to recognize me. His expression is passive and unreadable, with a dullness that disturbs me. It is as if he has switched the lights off inside him. As if the Willem that I kissed before is no longer there.

Then they turn him back around so that I can no longer see his face.

I continue walking toward him because I am afraid to lose sight of him. I am close enough now to see the guns at their hips and the detail on their jackets.

"Willem," I whisper, "please come back . . ."

One of the officers grips Willem by the shoulder, forcibly pulling him toward their vehicle, but he stops when Miriam shouts and points toward me. Both officers turn to look in my direction.

My eyes are drawn back to the handcuffs that have tightly fused Willem's wrists. I see the tip of something in Willem's sleeve, something wooden perhaps, a stick or baton, something the others can't see. The fingers of Willem's other hand tug at his sleeve, and I catch a flash of something silver, also.

Willem then twists his body away from his captor so that he is almost facing me.

"*Run!*" he screams.

This sudden, loud command shocks me briefly into stillness, as I absorb the enormity of what is about to happen. He screams again, and I turn to run in the opposite direction. The noise from the explosion is deafening. I feel the rush of hot air behind me. I fall forward, my ears buzzing. A small piece of car metal crashes several feet in front of me.

I lie there for several seconds before someone from the town lifts me halfway up by the shoulders and puts his face close to mine. It looks as though he is asking if I'm all right, perhaps shouting the question, though his voice is dulled in my ears, which feel stuffed with cloth. I nod and stand, and the man moves away. Sound returns partially, the volume slowly rising as if a dial has been turned on the radio, but not all the way. I am glad I cannot hear the crackle of the fire behind me or the utterances people will make when they discover the burning remains.

Several people rush past me toward the pyre. Engines sound in the distance. I do not turn around.

I walk forward, away from the carnage, forcing my legs to bend, to walk and then run, my tears merging with the rain, but my legs do not hold me for long. My knees buckle, and I collapse to the ground. Another man stops to speak to me, but I ignore him and he is quickly gone.

More people rush past. They do not stop. There are greater things to see than a woman crouching on the ground. I stand, disoriented at first, grasping the reality of it, searching for reasons to go back to the Center, then searching for reasons to hope.

There are none.

I force myself to walk in the direction of home, only turning to look back once I am far enough away not to see. It is better that I do not see.

I breathe his name. But I know he is no longer here to answer. He will not walk through the front door, take my hand, and tell me everything will be good for us.

Our time together is dispersing with the smoke now in the sky.

*It was a sunny day, I was carrying a child in a long
white dress to be christened. The path to the church led
up a steep slope, but I held the child in my arms firmly
and without faltering. Then suddenly my footing gave
way . . . I had enough time to put the child down before
plunging into the abyss. The child is our idea. In spite of
all obstacles it will prevail.*

—*Sophie Scholl (1921–1943), German student
executed for her involvement in the nonviolent
anti-Nazi resistance group the White Rose*

1948

CHAPTER FORTY-SIX

GILDA

The Agency vehicle taps noisily along the narrow street bordered by gabled brick homes painted white, starkly beautiful under a light-gray sky. Through my open window comes the smell of freshly cut grass and gardens filled with fragrant flowers that tilt their pretty heads toward me, suggesting that life here has continued curiously untouched. It is as if the people who migrated to this city toward the end of the war possessed a gifted foresight that led them to a place where they would not only survive but prevail as before. The circle of life perhaps was never really broken here. Yet I know that behind the pretty curtains, people like me wear the scars of guilt; that somehow, through all the destruction, we arrived on the other side of war unscarred, our beds still covered with fresh sheets and our cupboards never empty of food, harboring a knowledge—and at times wondering at the luck of it—that whether we won the war, our houses remain sacred, our lives blessed.

I check the street numbers and park on the side of the road several houses before my destination. The file on the seat beside me lies open, and I look inside it at the small, grainy black-and-white photo of a group of children playing on swings in the backyard of a large property. One of the faces in the photo is circled, though the features are unclear, the face in profile, the girl unaware perhaps that a photo was being taken five years ago. It is little to go on, for all the children in the image look similar, Aryan in appearance. I think about taking the file with me on this visit but know that insubstantial evidence will add little weight to the argument that might ensue. I leave the paperwork behind and exit the car.

I walk past several houses, over a thick, damp, grassy footpath, and step toward a front door. I knock and take a deep breath. A raven flies up to the roof above and peers down at me. This closeness unsettles me, perhaps because the bird is associated with bad omens. I look at the sharpness of its gaze and the shining blue-black feathers that are the color of our deepest fears, and wonder what the creature sees and how much it knows. Whether it carries stories and secrets that humans will never learn, whether it sees more than any of us.

Without any warning of movement from within, the front door opens, and the raven takes rapid flight. A woman—taller than I am, composed—fills the narrow gap of the open door, concealing any view to inside. A small crease between her brows and a rigid gaze suggest that she has already sensed I am not here for a friendly visit.

"Elsi Winthur?"

There is some hesitation on her face, as if the name is not something she has adjusted to hearing. She looks beyond me to the street to see if I am alone, then to my hands, hoping to learn something more from what I carry. Though she appears calm, I can tell that she is suddenly wary. When you have been doing this job for a while, suspicion is the first thing you notice when you confirm their name with them. It either means they have something to hide or something to fear.

"My name is Gilda Janz," I say. "I work for an international agency that finds missing children."

"Why are you here?"

"We believe that one of the children adopted from a Lebensborn center is here—Matilda." I am not allowed to say the surname.

"My daughter's name is Matilda Winthur, Fraulein Janz. I can assure you that she is my daughter. There is no need for further confirmation."

"Her mother and brothers have been searching for her. They applied to our agency for help."

"Fraulein Janz, I'm sorry that you have wasted your time coming here. Please leave now. I will have to call the police if you don't."

"Please do. An issue of stealing children should certainly involve them, and then at least we can quickly prove that the Agency claim is valid and my purpose here is authorized."

"Her biological parents are dead," says Elsi Winthur.

"I can assure you that our process is thorough, that the claim is valid."

"How can I be sure that it is not false? That you are who you say you are?"

I wear an agency card around my neck, which she has also already seen, but I suspect that having lived through this war, she knows too well that forgery and false identities are commonly used ruses.

"Frau Winthur, I can easily prove my identity, but I must ask the same of you. The child was adopted to a Willem and Elsi Gerhardt. If you can't prove that you are Elsi Gerhardt, and if indeed you have the child I am searching for, then that alone is cause for a separate investigation into why you have a child who does not belong to you by any legal measure, Nazi or otherwise. Unless of course you have a certificate to prove the child is yours in another name."

She meets my stare with her own steely gaze.

"If you are honest with me, then I can make this as painless as possible," I say directly. "I am from the Agency, as I said. We are not looking for criminals. We are not prosecutors. We are simply looking for missing children. And if I do not succeed today, I will be back tomorrow and every day after that. I believe you are Elsi Gerhardt. I do not want to make this a police matter."

She hesitates in the doorway, holding the door partway closed. She is weighing options. She is wondering if she should close the door and run. It is important that we are prepared for this. I have noted the address of the local police station should there be a need.

The woman bites her lip, and her eyes finally release their hold on mine. She takes a deep breath.

"Winthur was the only way we could remain safe from being taken by the Germans. As you can imagine, any reference to Gerhardt had to be destroyed. It was in the child's best interest."

There is a bigger story here, yet at least I am close now. She has given me something: an admission that there is a child who may not belong to her.

"Frau Winthur," I say, "this is not easy on anyone, but I must ask for cooperation. Herr Gerhardt"—I do not say 'husband' because I have found no record of the marriage—"took the child. This might have been acceptable in extremely oppressive situations, but today it is considered illegal. We are just as thorough in investigating those who apply to find missing persons as we are in finding those who have them. I can assure you that Matilda's biological mother is very much alive."

Her face gives away nothing at first, and then she puts a hand to her mouth, and sadness washes over her.

As an employee of the international agency to find missing children, I have investigated hundreds of cases. Thousands of pieces of information have passed across my desk, and those of my colleagues, and I have sifted through these one by one. Handwritten descriptions of missing children, letters, photos, sometimes locks of hair, sheets torn from ledgers, camp numbers—every traceable element I can find.

Like a jigsaw, we piece together families, first by timelines and Nazi trails of destruction: towns they conquered. Then come the names from orphanages and Lebensborn programs. Though it is at most times an unrewarding job. The names of many of the children admitted into the centers were either changed or misspelled, or possibly never even accepted, the children sent elsewhere. It is a difficult, laborious process—frustrating, fruitless sometimes.

Making connections does not always mean success. Many times I have reported back to a parent or relative or friend that the missing person has been recorded as dead. Many families I cannot connect at all, sometimes getting so close to the truth before the trail finally peters out to nothing.

And, finally, the ones I do find: the most difficult task of all. Retrieving children from parents they have bonded to and delivering them home to parents they can't remember.

In the two years I have done this job, I have connected but a handful of children to their parents, and each time I question whether I can do it again.

"How did you find me?" says Elsi.

"It was lengthy. Can I come in?"

She does not answer me but opens the door wider and steps aside to allow me through. As I walk inside, she turns her head away from me. This tells me she is resentful, but not hostile, which can be another hazard of this job at times.

The house is quaint and well furnished, with several rooms leading off from a hall. There are bay windows overlooking the side of the house where a bicycle stands against a fence. There is a smell of herbs and coffee. Embroidered miniatures line the walls, though there is an absence of photos: items that usually give something away. She has been expecting this, I think. Perhaps she has always stayed prepared.

Certificates line the walls, academic and music. A newspaper article on the wall details the winner of a writing prize at the local school, the photo perhaps cut from the top of the article. First ribbons are pinned for long-distance running and other events. A violin sits in the corner in an open case. From descriptions supplied of a spirited, imaginative child, there is little doubt I have the right Matilda.

Elsi follows my eyes.

"My daughter is always in a rush to make it to the next activity in time."

She leads me to the middle of the kitchen, to a table built on wide timber legs. Everything is put away carefully, the house clean, the kitchen filled with color and light, bright plates and tea sets. Elsi's kitchen is perhaps her center, the place where she feels she has some control.

"You kept her true name," I say.

"Everything else had been taken from her. She had that at least."

I do not have to see Matilda to know that this woman has taken good care of her.

"So you are here to take her!"

"Yes."

"I see," says Elsi Winthur, though she does not look at my eyes. She is fair with a long neck, slender physique, and striking blue eyes that are large and round. Her connection to Willem Gerhardt is the final piece of this puzzle. She has not denied the adoption.

"A missing person's application was placed on Matilda," I tell her. "As you can imagine, there are thousands. We tracked Matilda through the German centers first. Our records suggest that the officer who took her brought many children to Lebensborn houses in the north. But there was no record in Germany that matched her name and approximate birth date. We even went to the centers outside Germany.

"Then, oddly, while scrolling through news records, we came across evidence of another center that had been temporarily closed at the end of 1943 due to a fire and never reopened. This led us to documents showing that in 1943 orders had been sent from Berlin for the Center to stay closed, and not be rebuilt. This was ordered by Heinrich Himmler himself, and any records recovered were to be sent to Anton Gerhardt.

I found these records in the Berlin archives, records that held the names of all staff employed there.

"We tracked down and interviewed those we could find: mostly tutors, academic and physical educators who had little knowledge of the operations there beyond their own roles. Miriam Haus, of course, died in an explosion. The nurse, however, seems to have just vanished; perhaps she died during the Allied raids or changed her name. Fortunately, we located the cook, Hetty Gerva.

"And it was through Fraulein Gerva that we learnt something of the commander, and ultimately the trail that led here to you. She said that the Center was a different place from the first day Willem Gerhardt took over the commanding position. Not only was it more efficient; the children were happier. She admitted that the nurse was very afraid of Miriam Haus and, under threat, had reported to her the results of Gerhardt's Aryan tests, supporting Frau Haus's suspicion that half of them had been falsified by the commander. Fraulein Gerva suspected this, too, though she did not speak of this to anyone, especially to Miriam, whom she despised."

"I believe Hetty was a good woman," says Elsi. "I believe she lived in fear like the rest of us . . . she kept the children's files, didn't she?"

"Yes, she did. I don't believe she ever planned to do anything with them. She had simply put them in a box in her attic and had not looked at them again.

"She said that the last time she spoke with Commander Gerhardt—someone she admired despite the information that has since come to light about his crimes at Auschwitz concentration camp—he gave her the key to his cabinet so she could take the files. She said that when she heard the explosion, she knew instantly that something had happened to him, and she retrieved the files during the chaos. Fraulein Gerva also told of the beatings that children received prior to Commander Gerhardt's arrival. She resigned from the Center immediately after the incident. I, too, believe she was indeed a good woman, Frau Winthur.

"The discovery of these files was the break I was looking for. They contained the names and addresses of some parents whose children were taken and then, unbeknownst to Berlin, were returned again. Were you aware that Herr Gerhardt was giving the children back to their families?"

"I knew of one or two."

"He returned four, using fake adoption papers and the names and addresses of fake German candidates. We recovered a letter Frau Haus wrote to authorities citing her suspicions of Willem Gerhardt's anti-Nazi activities, in particular his acceptance of children who did not pass the Aryan testing.

"Using the information from these files, we visited the reunited families, mostly in Poland, until we came upon a boy, Jacek, who remembered Matilda very well."

Her expression doesn't change. She is as still as marble. *Venus de Milo*, I think to myself.

"He told us that Commander Gerhardt and his wife had adopted Matilda. He remembered your name, Elsi, even described your appearance. Though curiously, we have records showing that Gerhardt's wife died before he arrived to work at the Center, and they also show she had a different first name. So your role in all this is still a mystery here. I asked myself, why would he blow himself up with a grenade, along with Miriam Haus and the officers who had come to take him? I believe they had come to arrest him, and he died to protect someone—Matilda, perhaps, or even you. Would that be fair to say, Frau Winthur? And his death also meant that all the missing children were potentially safe from recapture, their whereabouts going with him."

I see a slight flinch, fine and unnoticeable to anyone who is not watching as closely as I am.

"Given the other information that came to light since his death, it has been difficult to understand exactly which side he was on. Had he lived, he would have been tried and likely executed like his father,

Anton Gerhardt, for war crimes—experimentation on human subjects. Did you know about his war crimes?"

"Not until after . . ." She does not need to finish. What she has to say is written on her face: *after Willem died.* I suspect she read about it in the newspaper for months, years, like all of us.

"But there is also a report that was filed, which we found in Anton Gerhardt's possessions, that suggested malpractice by his son. A report filed by a Nazi officer whose wife had died from poisoning. Anton Gerhardt had somehow retrieved this report and hidden it, perhaps to protect himself or his son.

"Furthermore, we checked the history of Willem Gerhardt's property ownership and found that his primary place of residence had been an apartment in Berlin, but Fraulein Gerva said that she thought he had taken residence nearby. We found no such property leased in his name. He was clearly a careful man.

"But our investigators were not ready to give up. As you can imagine, the name was still on everyone's lips. Gerhardt. Anton Gerhardt, tried and hanged. An important Nazi figure, a vicious experimentalist . . ."

"Willem was nothing like his father. You should know that when you file your report."

"He has done some wrongs, Frau Winthur . . ."

"He gave many children a chance, Fraulein Janz. He did not know that her parents were alive when we adopted her. He would not have made her suffer . . . not Matilda. By the time the truth was known, it was too late—"

"It is never too late. You should have brought her forward. You should have found out for certain if her parents had been killed. Her father, unfortunately, never returned from war."

Elsi is trembling now.

"Something Willem said to me toward the end, about a mistake, made me suspicious. But we loved her . . . she was ours. And she loved us. You have to believe that Willem died for her."

I look away. It is always difficult to watch someone begging for forgiveness, especially when it is not my place to grant it.

"We looked into other properties held under the name Gerhardt—and there were many that he and his father owned and leased, the documentation most likely restricted while Anton was alive—until we found a transfer of a property in Oldenburg to someone by the name of Elsi Winthur. And that, of course, brings me here."

"You need to know everything if you are going to judge me."

"It will be for others, not me, to judge you. My job is simply to find the child and return her to her mother."

"Will you at least hear what I have to say?"

Her eyes glisten like melting ice, and her hand shakes as she reaches for a glass of water. She is breaking. She is no longer looking at me, but through the window and out into the street.

"I will tell you everything, if you let me," she says.

"Where is she?" I ask.

"School finishes in an hour. She will be home shortly after that."

I nod.

She begins her story from the same age as Matilda is now: fifteen. She tells me everything: the ghetto, her mother, her sister sent to the camps, and the rescue by her lover, Willem Gerhardt. She talks simply, plainly, without exaggeration or drama. She was a young girl, with big dreams, before being stripped of everything she held dear. It is like so many other stories of horror, of being reduced to nothing. Though to hear her tell it, to hear what happened to her whole family, and then to Matilda at the hands of Frau Haus, causes an ache deep in my belly. And finally the witnessing of Willem's suicide. He died attempting to save the other children. And he died for her and Matilda.

By the time she is finished, I am slightly exhausted. I have trained myself to listen, to not become involved, but it is always a challenge. Always after I hear these stories, it is many nights before I can sleep again. Elsi tells me of Willem's quest to save as many children as he could, something that should not go unrecorded. His name is currently associated with misdeeds only.

But there is no doubt in my mind that Willem Gerhardt, like his father, would have been executed by the new government had he lived. He assisted with murders at Auschwitz. That much has been proven.

Elsi is suddenly distracted and turns her head. I have time to study the tiny lines in her young face, etched too early by years of torment, before I follow her gaze outside the window. A girl strides across the street toward the house. She wears a dress of green, and her golden hair is twisted into a tail that hangs over the front of her shoulder. Her head is held high. She is someone with confidence; I can tell immediately. She is less breakable than the woman in front of me.

I turn to look at Elsi and find her eyes then fixed on me.

"Please don't tell her that I knew . . . please . . ."

The words wrench at me, they tear part of my heart from where it was embedded. *She knew all along.* And part of me says, *What have I done?* Should this woman endure any more?

Matilda opens the door, and her smile, already half-formed, disappears quickly when she sees me.

"Who are you?" asks the girl accusingly. She has sensed that I am unwanted here.

"Matilda," Elsi jumps in quickly, "please . . . sit down."

"Mutti, what is wrong? What has happened?" The girl looks at me with narrow, accusing eyes.

The concern she shows for her mother is so genuine, I have to remind myself why I am here, that I don't enter into any feelings of sympathy toward this woman. Yet I do.

"Your family is alive, Matilda. Your mother . . ." Elsi's voice trails off.

"My brothers?"

"They are with your mother."

"And my father?"

"Unfortunately, he did not survive the battlefield."

The smile that had nearly formed at the mention of her brothers fades at the news of her father. She sits down and stares at the table in front of her.

"I remember that he did not want to fight."

I allow her a moment to remember him, to take in the news, to grieve. But there are no tears for him. Instead she looks up to examine her mother's troubled expression, and I see then that Matilda's sorrow extends elsewhere; she had already grieved for her father years earlier. She had already dealt with the loss.

"Perhaps they can come to visit?" she says.

Elsi shakes her head, and tears trickle from the corners of her eyes. She knows immediately the implication.

"Oh God!" she says, as she reaches across to Elsi.

I cannot share this moment. It is too intense, too personal.

"I will give you a moment," I say. "But I have been asked to take Matilda back as soon as possible."

"I am fifteen," she says. "No one takes me anywhere I don't want to go. Mutti, how do you know that I can trust her? That she won't take me somewhere far away . . . to still another house?"

Matilda's look is fierce, and she is breathing rapidly.

"Matilda," I say, "the war is over. The only thing you need to fear is the boredom of my company on the journey to your home. I can also tell you that your brother Theo, who looks just like you, had to hide your books during the war to keep your mother from burning them for fuel, and that your handsome brother Dragos wishes to see his little sun again."

Matilda lowers her gaze to her lap, where she pinches the tips of her thumb nervously.

The silence lasts for several seconds until Elsi leans forward to hold Matilda's hand.

"You can trust her," says Elsi, her voice low and soothing. "I believe she is who she says she is. I believe that she is here in your best interests only."

Her words have an instant effect on Matilda, who seems to transform into someone softer before my eyes. The fierce look of a lioness is replaced by the gentleness of a doe. She trusts this woman's every word. Whatever wounds have befallen the girl, this woman has been the instrument of her healing.

I stand to leave, to give them some space.

"I'll wait outside," I say.

I wonder how it will be with Matilda and her mother when we get to Romania. I have seen this before. I have seen children balk at the prospect of any other parent than the new mothers they have bonded with. And I can see Matilda's protective streak toward Elsi.

"And what about Nathanial? How are you going to tell him?"

And then from the corner of my eye, I see movement. A child has awakened. His fists in his eyes, he walks into the room and climbs onto Elsi's lap.

This child has large eyes like his mother's and a thick top of light-brown hair. He leans forward to take hold of his sister, and she lifts him onto her lap the same way she has probably done a hundred times before. And then I see that Matilda, too, has a breaking point. She hides her face in the boy's thick hair, her shoulders shaking uncontrollably.

I close the front door behind me and light a cigarette. The house sits on a quiet street. It is one of the better ones I have been to. It is modest, comfortable, a house bought to fit in with the rest, to hide and blend in, but perhaps also to normalize what began as an extraordinary situation.

I wonder if I should not walk to my car now and drive away, if I should file my report: case closed, child still missing. It crosses my mind. That is why we are taught to leave our emotions at home.

• • •

It is perhaps forty minutes gone when Elsi comes out. "Can I have one?" she says, looking at my cigarette. It is my third.

"Sure."

She lights the cigarette, breathes it in, savors it—her eyes closed. I know how she's feeling at that very moment. Some relief, too brief. We stand there quietly.

"Nathanial . . . is he yours and Willem's?"

"Yes," she says.

"He has your eyes," I say.

Some children walk past us. They wave, and Elsi waves back.

"What happened after Willem died?"

"We helped some children escape and then came straight here. I didn't have time to grieve. I had done enough. It was time to look forward. Willem taught me that, in the brief time we were together. He left money and instructions, and this house, and I did everything he wanted. He was meticulous in his planning. I trusted him, and Matilda and I are alive because of it. We were lucky to escape the Allied bombs, and we have carved out a life here. Matilda has been wonderful . . ."

She clears her throat and swallows.

"I suspected that her parents weren't dead, though selfishly I wanted to believe they were. Matilda told me, even before Willem died, how she was taken. It did not match the story told by Miriam Haus, but I wasn't sure of anything at that time. I trusted Willem, and I believe that it was only after Matilda was ours and settled that he learnt the truth. And then I convinced myself that her parents were probably dead anyway, perhaps killed in a bomb blast later in the war. Matilda also believed this in the end. She believed everything Willem said."

Nothing from those years surprises me anymore.

"Look after her," Elsi says before she goes inside. "She has gone through enough. She is very bright and can be anything she wants. She wants to study medicine. She wants to be a pediatrician. Tell her mother to encourage this. Matilda would be brilliant at caring for others."

She smiles at this thought, though the expression slips away quickly.

"I can see that."

"What is her mother like? What is the place like where she comes from?"

"Her mother is . . . concerned," I say. I cannot think of another word for it. The woman I met, Catarina, was clearly missing her daughter, but it was her brothers who had placed an application to find her. I visited her to be certain and was shown through Catarina's house. She showed me the fields where a timber yard sits, where lavender used to grow. Now it is a factory where both her sons work. That is her only source of income now. The boys give her money, though the oldest has a wife and son to take care of, also. They all live in the small house. Catarina desperately wants her daughter back. She wants to start a poultry farm.

"A daughter should be with her mother," is all I say, because it is a line I am told to say. I am not to tell them anything about the family, in case they attempt to make contact, or worse, attempt to take the child back.

"I need you to tell me at least that she will be loved, that she will be happy."

"Of course," I say.

She turns and enters the house.

I light another cigarette. My fourth. I finish half of it quickly, then reenter the house.

I drove Matilda across the first border, and we stayed in a hotel. She did not talk the whole way, ignoring my questions. That night in the hotel room, she did not sleep, and neither did I. I cannot allow myself to sleep, in case the children try to escape.

We have breakfast early and then set out once more. We will be there late afternoon tomorrow, I predict, if I can find the place again; it is so remote.

"Do you remember your family?"

She doesn't answer.

Always there is this danger: that she will not recognize them and will then scream, not wanting them to touch her, and feeling that she has been forcibly taken by people who are strangers. But usually only with the younger ones. Matilda does not strike me as someone who will run. She might tell her family she doesn't want to be there, but she won't run. She is strong, intelligent, and above all—I can tell—quite stubborn.

"I met your brother Dragos and his new baby. They seem like a nice family."

I don't tell her that the little house is crowded and in some kind of chaos, the older brother building more rooms to fit them all.

"What did they call the baby?"

I can't tell her. I didn't think to ask.

"But I can tell you that your brothers, Dragos and Theo, are tall and lean, and they work long hours in the factory. They are very much looking forward to seeing you."

She makes a scoffing laugh.

"Theo wanted to go to university," she says. "I do remember that. I remember we had lots of books."

This is good. She is thinking, remembering.

They are poor, this family. I do not think that the brothers have time for study; they barely make do for money.

It is like this the whole way: brief conversations only. Elsi has packed everything Matilda owned and more. There are two large suitcases in the boot of the car, another on the backseat, and several bags filled with books and writing paper.

Many things to remind her of her life with Elsi.

CHAPTER
FORTY-SEVEN
MATILDA

There was a point early in the journey that I thought of opening the door and jumping from the car and not returning to anyone. To determine for myself where I will live, not where others want me to be.

When Gilda spoke my brothers' names, they seemed like people I didn't know, foreigners, someone else's brothers. Yet there is a yearning to see Dragos and Theo again, a tenderness I feel toward them when memories of them enter my mind unannounced—triggered by a smell or the sight of other siblings sharing affections.

But any feelings that come to me as I sit in the car are overshadowed by the reality that I am no longer with Elsi. I am some sort of prize to be snatched from others.

"It is my job to try and locate other children from the Center, now that I have their files," says Gilda, interrupting my thoughts.

"You won't find them," I say.

"Why is that?"

"Because you won't. Trust me. They are far away now."

"Where? Who took them?"

"People." I have said enough.

"If you know things that will help—"

"I can tell you that for however long you search, you will not find a trace of them. Those children came from villages, and many of these were destroyed. I know that there are no names in the files, no places—the children too young to even know their own names."

"I would be grateful if you could tell me anything you know about some of the children there," says Gilda. "Where they might have been sent to."

"I have nothing to tell you."

She doesn't say anything more straight away, but I know it isn't over. Fraulein Janz spends her days searching for ghosts, tearing apart families in her endeavor to piece together others.

We stay at another hotel on the second night and order a meal in a restaurant. I eat across the table from her, but I do not want our eyes to meet.

"Matilda," she says, "I know you have been through a lot. No one deserves that—to be taken away from their home and shaped into someone else. What was done to you was cruel. My agency is trying to right the harm that was done. It does not make sense to me either, this job. There is rarely a day that I feel like I've accomplished anything. Are there things you can tell me about the other children who were there? Perhaps where they might have been sent?"

I am missing Elsi and Nathanial so much already, and suddenly missing everyone I ever lost. I try to remember the faces of the children at the Center, but there were too many. I want to burst into tears. I want to throw the food in Fraulein Janz's face, but Elsi would be ashamed of me if I did. I stand up and walk away from the table, tears escaping.

Fraulein has said in the car that for the sake of my family I should not encourage future interaction: that Catarina has requested there be no contact with Elsi. Catarina wants her daughter back, and she doesn't want to share.

"I don't want to go back," I say when Fraulein infiltrates the space beside me.

Before I left with Fraulein, Elsi put Nathanial to bed, and I kissed his forehead. When he wakes each morning, I will not be there. At school my friends will see an empty chair in the classroom.

Gilda stayed in the car while Elsi and I parted. Elsi was being strong, avoiding an emotional good-bye. She was doing what she had to. We made no promises to find each other, though she said that if she moved she would leave a forwarding address with the Agency. She asked that I not fight the return to my family. Said that if she was in my mother's shoes, she would do anything to have me back.

"You are my mother," I said. "You can have me if you want."

She said nothing as she placed her arms around me. I held her so tightly, afraid to be apart from her. We could have run through the back door. I could have finally attempted the escape I once planned at the Center. I suggested this tearfully to Elsi.

"No more running," she whispered, and I could feel her body trembling.

She cupped my face in her hands and told me that I could be anything I wanted, that she would never, ever forget me. She told me to love my mother and brothers, who must have suffered when they lost me. She said that we'd had good years, healing years.

"I will never forget you," I said.

"And I will always be with you," said Elsi.

• • •

When Gilda sees my tears in the restaurant, she places her hand on my shoulder, but I pull away. I do not want to become attached to anyone else. The next person I love will be someone I have chosen.

"I know for you that this doesn't feel right, but it is. Elsi knows it, too, which is why she has not put up a fight."

"Shut up!" I say. "Do not say anything about her. You know nothing!"

"Why are you so protective of her? I know she has been through a lot, and God knows how she survived it. She is a brave woman, but you were not her daughter. She could have contacted our agency, at least to learn of your family's fate. She must have known we existed."

"I would be dead if not for her."

Gilda shakes her head. She is testing me to see how I am coping, perhaps even trying to distance me from Elsi, to break the bond between us. I am used to such tactics by adults. They always think that children can't see through their ploys. They are transparent like glass. I always felt that my mother was alive, but I loved Elsi so much I couldn't imagine leaving her. I let fate decide. At one point, I half hoped Catarina had really been killed in a bombing to justify everything. I had found a life again. A good one. I lived with the brightest star in the night sky.

"I understand that you love her. She has been good to you—that is obvious. But I search for missing children. It is what I do. Please come back to the table and finish your food. We have a long drive ahead tomorrow."

I sit down, but I am no longer hungry.

"Things will turn out all right," says Fraulein Janz. "Those times were extraordinary. Things will get easier. Life will go on. But for Elsi's sake as well as for your own, you should not contact her. I will, of course, inform her that you have reached your destination safely."

"You are going back to see her?" I am suddenly alarmed.

"I have to go back and see if she can tell me anything about the other children from the Center."

"You must leave her alone. She doesn't deserve your prying. She can't lead you to the missing children."

"She is the only link I have now."

"I will tell you some things . . . as long as nothing happens to Elsi. As long as you promise you will never go back there."

"Things about the children?" she asks.

"You have to promise that you will not report her for keeping me. Don't look so surprised. I didn't care about my past. I wanted to stay with Elsi. If I didn't, I would have run away. So please, promise me that you will remove her name from the file and say I was living with someone else. Promise me that you will never visit her again."

"I don't know if I can do that. In any case, she will not be in trouble for taking care of you. There were difficult circumstances. It was war."

"If you promise to change the name in the report, I will help you. If you promise never to go back there, I will tell you things. You can then put the files from the Center to bed. You can close the cases."

She is watching me. I know that she would give anything to learn information.

"All right," says Gilda firmly. "You have my word. I will use another name in my report. I will remove any reference to Winthur. I will note that it was a false name. I will note that you were living freely with a family who believed you were an orphan. I will mark the file as closed with no further leads."

"If I learn that you have gone back on your word—"

"I won't."

I stare at her a moment. I can often tell whether people are honest or lying. I think I can trust her.

"Tell me something about yourself first," I say. "Do you have children?"

"No. I am not married either."

"Why do you do this job?"

"I asked to work at the Agency because it was something I felt I owed to others. I lived a reasonably good life during the war. I did not suffer as much as many others, and I did not care that others did. I only worried about myself. If I can give back the children who were stolen by my own countrymen, then in some way I can forgive myself for ignoring the evil that was happening right in front of me."

I was not expecting that answer. What she said is something that most would not admit to. At least I know that she has nothing to personally gain from any of this, no vendetta.

"So, Matilda," she says. "Will you tell me also what happened after Willem died? I am interested in knowing how you coped after this."

I was serving up breakfast to the orphans when Mutti—Elsi—came through the door. She had her hands over her ears, and she walked straight past us and into the bedroom. I watched the children eat their breakfast, then took them back to the sitting room. I told them that they could talk among themselves but not too loudly, in case the neighbors might hear them and investigate.

I went into my parents' bedroom, and Elsi was sitting on the bed, staring at the floor. Her face and dress were covered in dust, and she had scratches on her arms and knees.

"Are you unwell, Mutti?" I asked.

She said she had a headache, but that she would be out in a moment. A short time later, after she had washed and changed, she went to help the children and told them they were very brave. Some of them were upset and confused and wanted to return to the Center, which they believed was their home.

A man and woman from the underground resistance came and took the children as promised the next night. The children were scared because the couple appeared fierce and very formal. Elsi and I had to comfort them, and we gave them blankets and food for the journey. She said that the couple would take them back to their country. She did not say "to your parents" because she knew that would be unlikely. Willem had told her that the new children arrived with no information, not even the names of their towns. But at least they would go somewhere safe to live with resistance families who were keen to take them in, and not to the camps, and not to Germans who were loyal to Hitler.

After they left, Elsi told me what had happened to Willem. She did not cry when she told me. She had grieved too much already, she said. Too many people she loved had died. She was running out of grief. But I wept, and she held me, and I did not stop crying for days. And then I stopped because she told me that I would have a little brother. And then that was all I could think of. That somehow all the things that happened were going to happen anyway. Elsi told me that God has a plan for everyone.

We were too close to the scene of a crime, one that we were connected with, and the police were certain to come. Elsi had an address of a house that Willem had left to her. She had begun to work on a plan to get there. She did not feel comfortable knowing that Nurse Claudia knew of her existence and my adoption. Undoubtedly, Nurse had been questioned by the Gestapo. Elsi felt that sooner or later the authorities would come looking for us in the town when nothing turned up at Willem's apartment in Berlin. It was clear why Willem had put the ownership of our new house under a false name, so there was no connection to him.

Before we left, however, we got some news that floored us both. Leon, one of the men who had helped rescue the children, arrived at our house in the middle of the day. This was rare that they should call on us. The members of the resistance only ever traveled to places at night. Elsi saw him from the window, and straight away she knew that something bad had happened.

Leon came to tell us that the two resistance workers and the smuggled children had been stopped in Denmark as they were transferring to a fishing boat for Sweden. Leon got word that they were all shot on the spot. He said that the couple had made the trip successfully twice before. He did not seem surprised when he reported this news, just disappointed. He had been hardened by tragedy—by previous failures elsewhere. He said they would have to find another escape route to help others.

After Leon left, we both felt stunned. What had happened was tragic, and Elsi felt responsible. After that, she seemed to grow very sad and weary. I couldn't sleep that night because I was remembering all the faces of the children. It seemed so unfair that they had died and I had somehow been saved. I dreamed of killing Frau myself. I wished I had.

A couple of days later, once Elsi's nerves had begun to settle, we resumed our planning. Elsi was trying to negotiate with someone from the resistance to drive us northwest to Oldenburg. Even though my adoption papers listed Willem's Berlin apartment as our address, Elsi was very worried that the authorities would never give up finding us, and she was convinced they were clever enough to find Willem's secret house near the Center. And she did not feel comfortable with traveling by train, though she need not have worried. In hindsight, I know Willem had been thorough in creating our new identities—mine as Matilda Winthur.

I was curious as to what was happening back at the Center now that Willem wasn't there. One day when Elsi went to the markets, I decided to go to the woods nearby and spy. The house and the grounds were quiet. It did not look as menacing from the outside as it had from within, yet my legs still trembled as I neared the place, especially when the punishment house came into view. It was only then that I realized it was not a house at all but only one very small room, built poorly and exposed to the elements.

For over an hour I watched the place, but no one appeared. I thought that it had been abandoned and wondered if perhaps it was haunted by Willem's ghost and people no longer wanted to be there. Then I saw a lady I had never seen before go into the food store. She was wearing Hetty's apron. Next I saw Nurse Claudia unlock the door to the old dormitory that Willem had been planning to destroy. Out came two new children that she led to the swings. I went home and told Elsi that whoever was there now had put new children back into the hut. Elsi had not seen it, but she had heard from Willem how disgusting it was, how it was unfit to live in.

Later that night she went to Leon to find out if he knew anything about the Center. He told her that a new temporary commander had been urgently installed, because two teenage girls had recently been taken there from occupied territories, as well as two younger children.

She came home very angry. Elsi rarely got angry, but she was pacing and she hit the table with a plate, smashing it into hundreds of pieces.

"Willem died for nothing! They have just started from where they left off. New children to send this way, to send off to camps, to abuse."

I had never felt scared of Elsi, even when she slapped me that one time on the hill, but I was frightened for her and the baby. Her nerves were balancing on knives, and I was worried she would slip and I would lose her, too.

Elsi said she was relieved that Willem didn't have to know his efforts had amounted to nothing. I reminded her that we both were still alive and that he would have wanted that.

She hugged me, her anger passing a little, and said that I had an old head on young shoulders. She became calm then, and we ate dinner, though she was thinking the whole time and not talking. I did not want to disturb her because whatever she was planning was important. Then during our meal she put down her fork.

"Matilda, it is time to end it . . . to finish what Willem started."

She told me the plan. I was also angry, perhaps not as much as Elsi, but I, too, had been thinking during dinner. I was angry about the children being shot, and about Sarah and Luise as well. Then to find out there were more children who would be sent away! I liked her plan because it was something I had fantasized about in the punishment room. To help the children escape. She did not want me involved, but she knew that she might not be able to do this on her own, so she agreed to let me help. If she had said no, I would have followed anyway.

Elsi took the gun that Willem had given her, and we left for the Center late in the night. Willem had kept keys to every door there, and we hoped that the locks had not been changed. She said that I was to follow her, but to stay well back out of danger, and that if she told me to run, I had to do exactly that, and everything else she instructed.

We went not by the roads but through the woods and into the back area where there were no longer any guards. I knew that Nurse stayed in the main house some nights, but we couldn't be sure if she would be there that night. Cook had never stayed there, so I did not think her replacement would be there either.

I recognized the large old key from Vati's ring of keys to unlock the dormitory, and I crept in and woke the two children who were there. That was my job because Elsi thought I wouldn't frighten them like an adult would. I told the children I was there to rescue them, and that I had once been a prisoner, also. They didn't believe me at first. In the torchlight they looked terrified. I told them shocking stories of children being sent away to worse places, and how I had been rescued. I can be very convincing. It worked, and they followed me outside. Then Elsi poured gasoline across the floor and threw a match. The timber was alight immediately.

As we turned to leave the yard to run toward the woods, Elsi told me to keep going with the children and to stay out of sight until she came later. She had to go into the main house and see where the older girls were, the ones who had been taken solely for the amusement of SS officers. I did not know their purpose for being there at that time, however, and did not learn it until later, when I was old enough to fully understand that young women were taken and used this way, and that a secret directive was given to Nazi men to sire as many Aryan bastards as they wished.

Elsi had never mentioned this part of the plan to me, where she would enter the main building. She had only said that we would free the younger ones and set fire to the dormitory. I had thought at the time that the gun was only for protection. I stayed hidden in the woods with the other two children and watched for movement in the silent house that was lit up brightly by the burning hut beside it.

We waited for maybe five minutes, and then three gunshots sounded from within the house. I told the children to stay in the woods while I investigated. I had to use fear to keep them there. I told them that they would be shot by spies who surrounded the house if they attempted to leave, but that I would return soon to finish rescuing them.

Then I ran back to the house, passing the hut that was now collapsing under the weight of the flames, and in through the kitchen door, left open by Elsi. At the end of the upstairs hall was a bedroom with its lamp switched on. Elsi was standing near the bed. The new commander was dead with a bullet hole in his chest, blood splattered across the sheets. I later learned that the first bullet had missed him widely, as she fired upon entering. Elsi had never used a weapon before.

A girl, a few years older than I, was in the bed whimpering, the sheets drawn tightly around her naked body. Another one was standing close by. The new commander had been bedding the new girls himself.

"Matilda, do you ever do anything you are told?" asked Elsi. I was quite scared, more so because Elsi was eerily calm, and I thought someone might hear the gunshots and see the fire and catch us all. "The girls tell me that Nurse Claudia is here inside the house. Can you check her room?"

I left Elsi to settle the girls, who were both crying uncontrollably. At that point they didn't realize they were being rescued. Nurse's room was on the same floor. I checked her door, which was locked.

"Nurse!" I called softly through the door. "We need to speak with you."

"Go away!" Her voice was frail. She was terrified.

"Elsi wants to talk with you."

"She is going to kill me."

"We won't leave until you come out. She only wants to talk." I said this with no idea of what Elsi was planning next. I just knew Nurse had to come out, and we had to get back to the children waiting in the woods. The room stayed very silent.

"Please come out," I called. "This house might catch fire and you might burn down with it."

I waited several moments, and then the door opened and Nurse stepped into the hall, trembling, her eyes wide with fear. From where we were standing, we could view the inside of the commander's bedroom, and she hesitated several times before following me into the room.

Elsi didn't turn immediately. She was talking quietly to the two girls, who were now huddled together in the corner. Then she walked toward us, her gun arm hanging loosely at her side. With her other hand, Elsi turned me around and lifted up my skirt to reveal the scars on the backs of my legs.

"Do you see these marks, these strikes?" she asked Nurse.

Nurse nodded.

"Do you see why this commander had to die? Why this can't continue?"

"I'm so sorry, Matilda," said Nurse to me. "It was never my choice."

Elsi raised the pistol and held it with two hands. I had heard Leon tell her about firing. He said that a gun can bounce in your hands if you aren't prepared. She must have told him what she planned to do. Elsi aimed it at Nurse's head.

"I will say nothing about you both if you let me go," begged Nurse, her hands pressed together.

"I doubt that is true," said Elsi, who had taken a step closer.

"Wait," I said. I had some reservations about another execution. I knew what it was like to be in a position of fearing for my life, and some part of me did not want this to happen to anyone else.

"Did this woman ever beat you?" Elsi asked me.

"Once."

"Did you see her beating others?"

"Sometimes," I said. "But not like Frau."

"Did she ever watch you being beaten?"

I hesitated before answering.

"Yes."

Elsi cocked the gun.

"Stop!" said Nurse frantically, holding up her hands.

Elsi lowered the gun slightly.

"Do you think you would have done differently in my place?" said Nurse. "That you would have risked your life? That you would have somehow made a difference here?"

I could see that Elsi was thinking about this, her eyes no longer seeing Nurse but somewhere else. And then she raised her eyes.

"Yes."

She fired the pistol into Nurse's head. It was over quickly, the first and only bullet causing Nurse to slump on the floor. I was shocked, but I cannot say I felt anything like sympathy. It was more of a regret that the spirits of death had claimed another soul. Catarina had always frightened her children with stories about death: not just about the act of dying but about the punishments that we would suffer after we died. Though my brothers would tease me with her stories, I am certain that Dragos believed none of it, and Theo learned to ignore her. But I had believed and feared every word. With Elsi's help I have since made peace with the God I once feared.

One of the older girls then began to wail fearfully, and Elsi had to remind them that they were safe.

I don't believe Nurse Claudia was evil, but I do believe she would have killed me if Frau had instructed her to. Nurse had been neither kind nor brutal toward me, and in the days after she was shot, I was still shaken by images from the commander's room. But Nurse had turned a blind eye to children being abused, and would have continued to do so, and by association in Elsi's eyes, she was as guilty as Frau Haus. Had we left her alive, I believe that under questioning she would have reported our presence in the area, and we would have been found.

Recovering from the shock of the shootings, the older girls came to understand they were being saved, and they helped us drag the bodies outside. One of them kicked the commander in the head even though he was dead. Elsi told us to wait outside while she spread gasoline around the house, in the bedroom and on the landing and stairs—anywhere there was blood. She set fire to the bottom of the stairs, then came outside.

We wrapped the bodies of the nurse and commander in rugs, dragged them into the woods, and buried them. Elsi wanted no remains to be found in the house, to leave no trace of their existence. That seemed to her the worst possible punishment. The children had not moved from where I had left them.

When we returned home, Leon was waiting for us with another vehicle. He drove us north to our new house, and he then took the two children and older girls on to another location. He did not say where he was going, and we didn't ask. We just had to hope that they would be safe. We would never see any of them again. Elsi told me later than Leon was not his real name, and that he was planning to move his resistance operation to another town, fearing that he was close to being discovered by the German police.

When we arrived at our new house in the early hours of the morning, Elsi opened it with the key Willem had left for her in an envelope, and we stepped inside into our new lives. As her belly grew, Elsi and I lost much of our anger. Once the war was over, we discovered that we no longer had to fear life so much, and that we could move past much of what we'd been through if we just believed that the worst was behind us. Elsi said that we must dwell on the future. She said that Willem had taught her that.

Tall grass brushes our car as it follows a muddy track between watery trenches. We have passed many towns where buildings still sit broken by war, funds not yet raised to rebuild. It is barely recognizable as the place I once knew.

Fraulein Janz has to pull over to the side of the road in a gully to allow a truck carrying timber to pass. Mud streaks our windows as it passes. At the end of the track sits Catarina's house. Piles of wood and tin lie beside it untidily. The sound of grinding comes from the factory behind it.

The front door opens as I walk toward it. Catarina stands in the doorway, waving at me and barking something through the doorway to whoever is inside. Two tall young men appear beside her, their faces eager.

I hug Catarina, this stranger who looks very small to me now, although I recognize the sharp eyes and the bony hands that were strong and used to hard work. She hugs me quickly, just as she used to, as if it weakens us to hold for too long. Dragos takes me in his bear arms and does not want to let me go. He is as I vaguely remember, though there are lines of adult worry now in his face. And Theo is there, blubbering, nearly beside himself with sadness at my arrival, at our long separation. I do not shed tears, though it is good to see them. I love them still, of course. But they feel like relatives I might visit, not ones I am about to move in with permanently.

Inside, it all looks smaller now. There is a large hole in the far side of the house that leads into another room only partially built. Unfastened wooden frames lean against the walls of the construction as a temporary barrier against the elements until it is completed. Dragos introduces me to his wife and baby. I am told that I have to sleep on a mattress on the floor until they build the new room.

Catarina is talking about her plans to build a poultry farm. She does not ask about the missing years. She has always been about the here and now. Although I'm sure that Theo will ask me about this later, when we are alone. Already his eyes are searching mine, looking for clues as to why I appear so altered.

"Your clothes are so fine," says Catarina in her native tongue. "It must have been a nice place. Well, nice places are not for everyone, I suppose. I've gotten used to our little house now."

Fraulein Janz discusses some formalities with Catarina: documents that have everything to do with me but nothing I want any part of. And then I walk Gilda to the car, perhaps just to give me some air. It is crowded inside the house.

Fraulein Janz takes a sideways look at me. She is not so bad. She almost looks apologetic. There are so many ironies I don't know where to begin.

"They seem nice."

"Yes," I say.

"Your brothers are so happy to have you back, especially Theo."

"Yes, we were always close."

We stand near Gilda's car. She scans the hills, the road, the factory, before her eyes rest on me. She seems reluctant to go.

"Thank you for trusting me," she says. "Now that I know that the children died, and others are untraceable, I will not be spending years searching for them. I will mark the Center files closed. And I promise you—this will not go on record. Some stories are best not told."

I nod.

"And, Matilda," says Fraulein Janz, taking my hand and squeezing it gently, "you will be all right. You can do anything you like in a couple of years. You can go wherever you want."

"I know," I say.

And I will.

Somebody, after all, had to make a start. What we wrote and said is also believed by many others. They just don't dare express themselves as we did.

—Sophie Scholl

1996

CHAPTER
FORTY-EIGHT
NATHANIAL

I did not learn of Mum's story for years, about a father never spoken of, absent from everything in my life—mysterious, foreign, perhaps dangerous. I had never questioned why there was never any shortage of funds. Money held in my mother's name, Elsi Winthur, a gift from my father before he died. And with this she had done so much for others. When her children had grown, she had fostered others, had two houses built, safe houses for the homeless, and she had volunteered at various charities. There were many she had touched and influenced, and they came to her funeral from all over the country. Mum would have been shocked, embarrassed. It was perhaps good that she couldn't see the fuss, the grief she had left behind.

We left Germany for Australia in 1949. As I later discovered, she wanted to be as far from Germany as possible. Knocks on the door filled her with fear. Shortly after I turned nine, Mum married Malcolm, my Australian stepfather, who came to us undamaged and died without regret: a schoolteacher whose sole ambition it was to make a home feel like one. He'd had a family intact and no stories of war. He had made life feel normal, easy. He had given me a feeling of freedom, of not wanting so much control. He taught us both not to fear strangers.

Not that Mum hadn't tried hard to make a good home; it was just that she took life too seriously. Everything structured, as if we were fenced, the outside world too great to navigate. I think it was these years with my stepfather that influenced me the most. He had taken us on beach holidays, shown us large family Christmases with my ste-paunties and stepuncles. He had taught me how to fish and to surf, to whistle. And while this was going on, Mum still made everything happen: house cleaned, food on the table, children raised with manners and love. Our house was balanced. And with three younger siblings to add to our family, we became like everyone else. I liked that. I was no longer the strange foreign boy with the mother who preferred not to come to the school, avoiding teacher interviews. During those first years in Australia, Mum was suspicious of everyone.

Then Malcolm died suddenly, natural causes. It hit us all hard. I was about to turn sixteen. I was ready to learn to drive my first car. Mum and I were then left to raise the younger ones. And it was after his death that the nightmares came for Mum. A delayed reaction to everything that had happened in her life.

All decisions seemed to fall on me, as if I had suddenly morphed into an oracle overnight. I missed Malcolm more than anyone, but no one seemed to care about that. The needs of my young siblings were shared between us, and my mother had also begun to assist with charity work, which kept her fully occupied. She was manic during the day, and panic attacked her at night. Home became unbearable, and I resented the responsibilities that now fell on me.

At seventeen, when I thought she had been through the worst of her nightmares, I packed a bag and disappeared to join the league of drifters and misfits, finding odd jobs in various towns, picking fruit and cleaning motels. Then finding several months of solace in an outback commune, erasing brain cells with weed; sleeping in tents, sleeping with anyone; dressed most days in dust, dungarees, and a leather choker; and washing in ice-cold rock pools—all this in an attempt to "find myself."

It was not until I returned home a year later, disconnected from life, that I learned the whole story of my beginnings. My mother had seen that I was disillusioned, unable to find a peaceful place in my head. Unable to find the starting blocks for a successful life.

"Nathanial, you are a consequence of history and its turns." She had sat me down and told me the whole story. It was the first time she'd ever told it in full; other shortened versions had not included in detail my father's role in war. It seemed so unbelievable in the civilized world that I lived in. But one day after she was diagnosed with her illness, Mum asked me if I could brush and pin back her hair while she gazed, from her usual spot, across the soft bed of treetops that eventually reached the sea. The radiation therapy was making her sleepy as well, and some days she could not find the strength to lift her arms.

I ran the comb through the fine white hair, and much of her DNA came away with each stroke. Beneath the thinning strands I saw a scar across the top of her head and remembered the story of her in the ghetto prison. It wasn't so much that I never believed what she told me, but up until that point—until I saw the evidence of such unbridled violence— such a story seemed too extreme to be real.

In that small scar I saw my mother's early life play out before my eyes. I saw the terror, the pain, the loss. I saw a broken soul that had been forced to mend itself and bend into someone else for the sake of others. It was as if a doorway suddenly opened, and I could feel something of what she had been through. I felt *her*. Her blood, which carried her suffering, rushed through my veins, and her memories were suddenly alive in me, as if they were my own. I was overwhelmed with sadness.

She had felt me stop combing and turned her head slightly. Sensing that I had somehow broken, too, in that moment, she reached behind to hold my hand. A grown man then on his knees wept into her lap. I didn't have to say anything as she gently stroked my head. She had known—perhaps she had been waiting for the moment when I would truly understand.

She had wanted only a plaque. She did not need "a pompous headstone." I did not heed her request.

Her story is now left to us, her family, to share and discuss among ourselves. And one day for the grandchildren, also, when they are old enough to appreciate their beginnings. "We raised you well," said my mother before she died. And I have often wondered whom she meant by *we*. I believe it was Malcolm, although when the nightmares came, it was always Willem she would call to.

I tried to find Matilda even though my mother asked me not to. "To let sleeping dogs sleep," she said. (Her attempts at clichés were often hampered by a slight language barrier.) The description of Matilda's home, vague from my mother, and with a surname she never knew. My mother kept a grainy newspaper article about her, and a separate photograph of her taken at the same time. In the picture, Matilda holds a certificate for a writing competition at school: socks around her ankles, hair escaping her plaits, and appearing more interested in something else to the right of the camera than the black box in front of her. Her story about a child who runs an orphanage for abandoned animals, considered clever and inspiring, was later published in a magazine.

Matilda never tried to contact Mum either in the years that followed, though Mum told me she would check the letter box every day in hope. I believe that they were together for a reason, that it was not the separation that we should dwell on but the time they had together to build again, to gather strength from each other.

After the war Mum learned that her own father had died in a labor camp several months after he had left the ghetto, and my aunt Leah never made it to any camp, dying on one of the notorious gassing trucks after she left the ghetto. But by then, my mother said, she had accepted the fact and had already been grieving them for years.

I don't feel connected with Willem, my biological father, in the sense that I understand him, but sometimes I feel him in me. He is there, they both are, and I will carry on what he and my mother started. I will endeavor to find peace, which is what they had been searching for when they first met. Mum believes that my love of writing stories, factual and biographical, came from Matilda. She believes that everyone we meet influences us, that we need to hear *their* stories to learn more about ourselves.

It wasn't the smoking that killed Mum in the end, although Clara and Louisa nagged her persistently to quit and kept the grandchildren out of the smoke. I remember Mum quipping, "You want to see smoke? You should live with a war." Though the fact itself was serious, we had all burst into laughter at this comment, at the words she used, at her comical attempts to counter attacks. Even Mum saw the funny side that day. Mum had later agreed to smoke outside the house, though it was too late for me. It is when I go outside and sit on the wide veranda to light up a cigarette and observe the mountains and their various moods of blue that I feel closest to her. It is where we shared so many conversations, where she offered so much advice. And then the many times we sat there without words, comfortable with the silence.

And now it is my turn to be nagged by Clara as I drive her and the girls to the airport, the others gone quickly after the funeral and back to their lives. *Find a partner, stop smoking, get a real job, settle down. Stop being such a hermit.* Clara doesn't count writing novellas and magazine articles as a real job.

"Whatever you choose to do with your life" was one of Mum's favorite sayings. She never interfered with our career decisions. I am filled with gratitude for the life she gave us.

I hug each of the grandchildren, pull their noses, make their toys magically disappear behind my back. Then Clara says to me as she hugs me good-bye, "Aren't you lonely up there in the mountains?"

"Raise your children well," I say, cheekily deflecting the comment and using the term my mother always said to my siblings after the birth of each grandchild. A term they were at first annoyed by and then got used to. I punch Clara in the arm playfully, and she punches me back harder. She was always competitive.

I wave good-bye and look forward to the drive home, to watch the sinking sun flickering through the trees.

Are you lonely, darling boy?

The letter box protests when I open it, aging, like all of us, arthritic, guarding the entry for more than forty years. An envelope, with an air-mail stamp on the front, is addressed to me with the name "Lederberg" on the reverse, the handwriting decisive, letters tall and fearless. I unfold the typewritten letter inside and have finished the contents by the time I walk the long driveway back to the house and my bottom reaches its favorite chair on the veranda.

I dab at the tears welling even though I find myself smiling at nothing, perhaps because the last chapter has finally closed. I calculate the time in New York before dialing the number listed at the bottom.

No, Mum. I'm not lonely. There are too many people inside of me, too many from my past to ever feel lonely.

The sun still shines.

—*Sophie Scholl*

CHAPTER FORTY-NINE

Dear Mr. Morley,
I read your story about your mother published recently in
a Jewish newsletter that we subscribe to. It was a beau-
tiful story but even more beautiful to me because I be-
lieve that I knew her well. If Elsi Winthur is indeed your
mother's former name—and I am fairly certain I have
the right person, since the name and the story would be
miraculously coincidental—then I had the privilege of
knowing you also.

Firstly, let me tell you, Nathanial, that you were my
brother for five years, that from the day you were born, I
rarely let you out of my sight when I was at home. I spoilt
you, and Elsi, my mother (at the time), had to tear me
away from you many times. You were a bubbly, laughing
child with the uncanny ability to find chocolate and other
treats our mother went to great lengths to hide.

From your story, it is obvious that you know some of
my past, and I appreciate the fact that this piece, although

it refers to me, does not mention my name. My story is one that I have chosen only to share with family.

From the point in the story where you talk about my leaving, I can honestly say that my memories of the day I was led away from our little brick house—which always reminded me of the houses from fairy tales—have replayed in my mind many times. Elsi was a very strong person, and she and Willem Gerhardt, who you also mention (though not by his real name), undoubtedly saved my life.

I know all about the Anton Gerhardt trial and the subsequent rumors and information that came to light about his son. I have seen hateful things written about the both of them and just printing his name alongside your own would no doubt encourage plenty of hate mail. Though I hope that in time you will write more about Dr. Willem Gerhardt, that perhaps you might find and interview some of the people he saved. My memories of Dr. Gerhardt are muddy, though I remember distinctly that he was the first adult who was not afraid to show me kindness after I was taken from my home. Sometimes it takes years to appreciate the good traits, since the bad ones are unfortunately the ones that often define us. It is because of him that you, Elsi, and I are alive. I have never stopped being grateful. Many people suffered as a result of this war. Loss is not confined to one race or one ideal.

"He has taken everything with him," Elsi said to me one day in Oldenburg, during one of the rare times she spoke of Dr. Gerhardt. I can't remember what else was said then, but these words have somehow stayed with me, and only much later did I think I understood what she meant: that perhaps she never really knew him at all.

That perhaps many secrets have gone with him to the grave.

I hope your mother can forgive me for being so bold, but I believe that she had loved him deeply.

I was returned to my real family. My father had died in battle, on the side of the Germans in a war he saw no need for, and his body was never recovered from the field. We had little money, and my birth mother and I tried to run a poultry farm, but it failed, and we relied on the support of my brothers before I eventually found work in a factory an hour's walk from home.

Sadly, the years apart had impacted our relationship. My brothers and I were never as close as we should have been, though this did not mean I didn't love them (and we have remained in contact over the years), but I perhaps became someone else. My mother, Catarina, and I fought often. She had different ideas about raising me than I was used to. She had planned for me to marry a boy from the village whom I didn't love. When I told her that I loved someone else, a Jewish boy I had met at work, after the war had ended, she forbade me to see him. My mother was an anti-Semite unfortunately. Of course, by then, I'd had enough of people telling me what to do. I ran away with Josef.

It was Josef who had suggested we go first to Germany. He thought that Berlin, in particular, in its period of growth after the war, would offer more work and opportunities for new careers. The second reason he chose Germany was to find you. I had told him so much about you. Truth be told, I was not comfortable with the idea of Germany at first. I still had a grudge against the place and some of the people there. I admit also that

I was nervous about seeing Elsi again. I wondered, per-haps naively, if she might not want to see me, whether I would be a reminder of memories she wanted buried: memories that might somehow interfere with a new life that she had since created for herself. And we had both been through enough!

I was, by that stage, and despite our differences, feel-ing a measure of loyalty for Catarina and guilty that I had left her again. I can, today, with hindsight, appreci-ate the suffering she, too, endured because of the war. And the loss of her husband, my father, was felt greatly by us all.

From Berlin, Josef and I took a train to Oldenburg and located the house that you and I and your mother had shared, but by that time you and Elsi weren't living there, and the new occupants knew nothing about her or of any children who had lived there. The transfer of ownership had been done through a lawyer who resided in another city.

I wished so much that I had found her. I had expected her to answer the door, and walking away that day I grieved terribly, almost as much as when we had last parted. It was the first time that Josef had ever seen me cry. The house alone reminded me again of how much Elsi had taught me. How much I had healed.

Josef and I were too young and poor and inexperi-enced to attempt to trace you both any further. As well, I was a young woman then, impatient and with no more time to waste on the past. Josef and I then returned to Berlin.

We did not stay long in Germany. Josef had survived the war by hiding with friends, but he had lost most of his family, and speaking to other Jews who had returned to Germany, and hearing of their experiences, the country quickly lost its appeal. It did not take long to find people who would help us emigrate to America. And there, in a new country, the horrors and losses now in our wake, we began an exciting chapter in our lives.

The rest of my life has been fairly even, with a few more of life's bumps along the way that few people can avoid. But there have been so many happy times since we arrived here that would require many more letters to all be told.

Josef and I own and run several successful medical practices, which, if you respond, I can describe in more detail. We have been blessed with many angels—two wonderful children and three delightful grandchildren.

I can tell you that when my second daughter was grown, and curious of my past, she took a trip to the place where I had first met both Dr. Gerhardt and Elsi, to find that a beautiful hotel now stands in its place. I had told her about Elsi, and she was keen to reach out to her. She also wrote to the Tracing Agency to search for information on your mother. My record was eventually found, but there was no mention of Elsi Winthur or Elsi Gerhardt. I believe that Gilda Janz, the woman who returned me to Catarina, had been true to a promise she made me to protect Elsi's identity. She had removed any trace of her name and any address that Elsi might have forwarded.

Your mother had seemingly vanished, and I can't blame her for that. Even now I have moments where I can clearly remember the fear of being found when we lived in Oldenburg. How in those first years there, with war still going on, we would turn out the lights when we saw a stranger's vehicle parked in our street, and sit near a window to spy on the occupants. These feelings of fear at being found—and your life as you know it suddenly broken—might be pushed to the side, and mostly out of sight, but they never really go completely.

I am pleased to learn that Elsi, like me, found her own place on this amazing planet.

I have never forgotten her sincerity and selflessness, and how she raised me with love and faith and self-belief. I don't believe I would be the person I am today without her.

You also mention in your article that Elsi has been ill with ovarian cancer. As a doctor, this is a field I am very familiar with. I would very much like to talk to you and Elsi, if you both wish it. I think the time for buried memories has long passed, with too many good ones to replace them. Please find my telephone number at the bottom.

I hope you receive my letter favorably.

Yours sincerely,

Matilda Lederberg

ABOUT THE AUTHOR

Gemma Liviero holds an advanced diploma of arts in professional writing, and she has worked as a copywriter, a corporate writer, and a magazine feature writer and editor. Liviero is the author of two gothic fantasies, *Lilah* and *Marek*, and the historical novel *Pastel Orphans*. She now lives in Brisbane, Australia, with her husband and two children.